Other Books by Stephen Baxter

continued ...

"Action-filled." — *Midwest Book Review*

Stone Spring

"Engaging and evocative ... a memorable and by and large successful imagining of a prehistoric world.... There are few speculators in fiction with a greater reputation for boldness and breadth than Stephen Baxter." — *Strange Horizons*

"A learned, imaginative, bold, sweeping, wonderful evocation of life and the world ten thousand years ago." — *Daily Mail* (UK)

"Baxter proves to be not only a gifted storyteller but also a master of speculative fiction, bringing together ancient civilization with present ecological uncertainties to tell an epic tale not unlike Ken Follett's *The Pillars of the Earth*. His series debut should appeal to fans of Jean Auel's *The Clan of the Cave Bear*." — *Library Journal*

"Fans of Baxter and Jean Auel will find a lot to enjoy here.... Based on this first entrant, I look forward to the rest of the series." — SFRevu

"While a very different writer from Ms. Auel, Mr. Baxter's book is as vivid in its characterization, descriptiveness, and storytelling." — Night Owl Reviews

"Close to being a prehistoric companion piece to *Flood* ... gripping ... an impressive and relevant novel." — *SFX Magazine*

Ark

"Never has Baxter presented a more thrilling and moving glimpse of a possible future: *Ark* could well be his masterpiece." — *The Guardian* (UK)

Stephen Baxter

Iron Winter

THE NORTHLAND TRILOGY

A ROC BOOK

ROC
Published by the Penguin Group
Penguin Group (USA) LLC, 375 Hudson Street,
New York, New York 10014

USA | Canada | UK | Ireland | Australia | New Zealand | India | South Africa | China
penguin.com
A Penguin Random House Company

Published by Roc, an imprint of New American Library, a division of Penguin
Group (USA) LLC. Previously published in a Gollancz hardcover edition. For
information contact Gollancz, an imprint of the Orion Publishing Group, Orion
House, 5 Upper St. Martin's Lane, London WC2H 9EA. Also previously published in a Roc hardcover edition.

First Roc Mass Market Printing, November 2014.

ISBN 978-0-451-41919-4

Printed in the United States of America
10 9 8 7 6 5 4 3 2 1

One

1

Once the ice sheets had covered continents. The silence of the world had been profound.

At last the ancient ice receded, and life tentatively took back the exposed landscapes. Northland was a neck of land that connected the peninsula the people called Albia to the Continent. As the ice melted and sea levels rose steadily, from north and south the ocean probed continually at the dry land, seeking to sever that neck—only to be defied by the people who had come to live there.

A long warmth followed. Around the world populations rose, cities sparked, empires bloomed and died. But at last, unobserved by mankind, on islands in the far north of the western continents, the snow that fell in the winter began once more to linger through the summer. The ice waited in its fastnesses in the mountains, at the poles. Millennia had passed since its last retreat. Human lives were brief; in human minds, occupied with love and war, the ice was remembered only in myth.

But the ice remembered.

And now the long retreat was over.

2

The First Year of the Longwinter:
Spring Equinox

Pyxeas thrust his head and shoulders through the sealskin door flap and into the house. In the dawn light the Northlander's face was like a raw red moon, haloed by fur. "Avatak! Are you there? It's moving again, the glacier! Can't you hear it? Come on, come on."

Avatak, seventeen years old, was lying in a heap of skins and furs with his relatives: parents and siblings and aunts and uncles and cousins. As the cold pushed into the greasy, fart-smelling air of the winter house, his little sister Nona mewled and cried, and Uncle Suko grumbled, "Close the flap, man!"

But Pyxeas knew only a few words of the language of the People, and when he was excited even they fled from his mind like a frightened seal from its breathing hole. "Avatak! Where are you?"

Avatak knew he wasn't going to give up. And now he could hear the glacier for himself, a distant rumble deeper even than his uncles' snoring. So he fumbled under the heap of clothing until he had got his fur trousers on over his leggings, and his jacket with its heavy hood, and he crawled toward the door, pulling on his bearskin boots as he went.

Outside, the sky was a clear blue-black still dusted by stars, although the sun was already peeking above the flat white horizon. Avatak could feel the chill in his cheeks and nostrils, a dagger-cold that cut and probed, and he wished he'd had time to grease his face. He saw that there had been fresh snow during the night, just a hand's depth, but enough to cover yesterday's tracks and to lie on the fur of the huddled dogs. Not *much* snow—but any snow-fall at all at this time of year was an unusual event in Avatak's short life. Which was, it seemed, why Pyxeas had come here, to the island the Northlanders called Cold-land, and for which the People had no name, for it was all the world they knew. He'd come to observe the unusual.

"At last, sleepyhead! Come, come—it's on the move, and if we hurry we might witness tremendous events!" And Pyxeas was off, hurrying east toward the rising sun and the coast.

Avatak had no choice but to follow him. He would much rather have had a chance to check the man over, to see he had his boots on properly and his mittens and a slap of grease on his face, for the scholar had nearly lost a couple of fingers to the frost in his early days by making mistakes like that. But there was no time, no time.

As they hurried through a loose layer of fresh snow, again Avatak heard that tremendous groan coming from the coast, overlaid with cracks and bangs and grinds.

"Can you hear that? Can you *feel* it through the ground?"

Avatak thought he could. Pyxeas had taught him how the whole island was covered by an immense lid of ice, all one piece, of which the glaciers were mere extensions. And when the glaciers were on the move, the ice cap itself shuddered, shaking the ground on which it rested.

"Have you brought your pad? Your stylus, eh? No matter, no matter. Watch. Listen. Remember my commentary as I, Pyxeas, interpret what we see. And write it down as soon as you're home, and make more of those sketches of yours. As soon as you're home!"

"Yes, scholar."

Now they reached the glacier itself. It was a river of ice that poured down from the higher ground toward the sea, where open water lay dark beyond a tide-cracked fringe of pack ice. All this was dimly illuminated in grays and pinks by the dawn sunlight that smeared the eastern horizon. The scholar clambered up onto the glacier's slick surface, slipped, and would have fallen immediately if Avatak had not grabbed his arm. The man just wouldn't learn to walk on the ice the way the People did, one foot pressed down flat after the other, slow and steady and safe. After that they went ahead with more caution, pushing down the shallow slope of the glacier toward its termination at the sea. Soon they came to a place where a second glacier joined the first, a mighty tributary whose boundary could be seen in stripes of debris on the surface of the flowing ice.

"The ice cap is a dynamic thing," Pyxeas said, growing breathless as he scrambled. "Fresh snow falling on the center of the cap fails to melt, and compresses to ice, and thus the cap grows. And as it becomes heavier the ice must flow out and away from the center under its own weight — as a mass of mud will flow out in all directions from under the ass of a big fat man sitting on it. The ice reaches the sea via the glaciers it spawns. And when there is an *unusual* amount of snow, as there has been on your island the last few years, there is an *unusual* rate of glacial flow —"

"Scholar!" Avatak pulled him back.

They had come to a crevasse, a slice right through the surface of the ice. It was new; it hadn't been here a few days ago, and the bulk of it was hidden by a thin crust of fresh snow. But Avatak had spotted its extension to either side, thin black cracks. Cautiously he kicked through the snow crust, and they both leaned over to peer into the crevasse. The gathering sunlight caught hard old ice that shone green and blue, as if lit from within, and Avatak could hear a foamy rush of running water from far below.

"The great weight of the glacier melts its own base," Pyxeas breathed. "And thus, lubricated, the ice falls ever more readily to the sea. Come on, come on!" They stepped over the crevasse and hurried on, Pyxeas talking on, endlessly speculating.

It was this curiosity that had prompted Avatak to volunteer to help the scholar from Northland when he had come here three summers ago to make his "studies." The People knew the world changed. They could hardly not know; they depended on these vagaries for their very existence. They knew of the fluttering cycles of day and night, the seasons that swung between bright summers and dark winters, and they knew, thanks to memories stored in folklore and anecdote, of the grander evolutions that spanned generations. But when change came, they just adapted. Went out on the pack ice a little earlier in the summer, or later. Fixed up the winter houses a little later, or earlier. If you got such judgments wrong, you starved, and so did your children.

But what they didn't do, what they had never done, was try to *understand*. What *caused* these changes in the world? And what would be the consequence if these changes, such as the increased snowfall in the interior, were to continue, year after year?

It wasn't because they were in any way less intelligent than the scholar's Northlander folk, Avatak had come to see. In most ways that counted, his own father, say, was much brighter than Pyxeas, certainly when it came to the brutal business of staying alive. And the People's shared memory, stored in the epic songs they sang together through the winter, was detailed and accurate. No, it wasn't a question of intelligence. It was a question of how you thought about the world—not as a plaything of the gods to be accepted without question, but as a puzzle to be solved. And Avatak was drawn to the way Pyxeas' mind worked as he challenged this huge, baffling, complex, secretive puzzle, and to the sheer delight the man showed when some small piece of it was resolved, and the world made a little more sense.

So he had worked with the man. Pyxeas had taught Avatak to read and write the way the Northlanders did—how to *think*. And Avatak had shown Pyxeas how to keep from falling on his backside with every other step on the ice. They were a good team.

But Avatak had glimpsed something darker in Pyxeas. A kind of sadness, he thought. If Pyxeas had family, children, he never mentioned it, but sometimes he reminded Avatak of a grieving, bereft father. Pyxeas himself was a puzzle. And that was the reason Avatak had chosen to work with him.

At last they passed a pinnacle of frost-shattered rock, and their view of the ocean opened up fully. Here Pyxeas stopped, panting, and even he was awed to silence, if only briefly.

The two of them had come here only days ago, but everything about the panorama had changed. Then the glacier had terminated in a mass of dirty, blocky ice that had fanned out into the sea, merging at last with the salty pack ice that littered the ocean surface. Now that whole formation had gone, the grimy blocking mass had vanished, and the glacier as it reached the sea was much thicker, and was truncated by a veritable cliff of blue-green ice from which bergs splintered and sailed away into a chaotic, half-frozen ocean.

"I knew it," Pyxeas breathed. "I knew it! The glacier here was blocked in by its own deposited ice, a natural dam. But such was the pressure of the glacier, thicker and faster-flowing than it has been for centuries, that the dam must, at last, give. And when it did, the glacier bounded forward like an animal loosed from a cage—and the result is as you see, tremendous masses of ice dumped into the ocean." He was almost breathless with the sheer delight of being proven right. "Can you see what this means, boy? What are the implications?"

Avatak watched the icebergs sail away. "Trouble for the fishermen," he said.

"Well, yes," Pyxeas said testily. "But that's hardly the big picture." He made swirling gestures with his mittened hands. "Like the ice cap, the ocean and the air above are dynamic systems—huge bodies of air and water that swirl around the world, transporting heat and moisture. Now, what do you imagine is going to happen when all this ice-cold freshwater is injected into the salty currents of the sea?"

Avatak had learned the student's trick of turning the scholar's questions back on him. "What do you think?"

"Well, I'm not sure. Nobody is. But . . ." Abruptly the energy seemed to go out of him, and the pleasure, and he sat down. He fished a scrap of parchment out of a pocket. "Make a note of the date, boy. Listen now. One. Two. Three. One. Two. One. Two. One. One. Five. Five."

Avatak mumbled the numbers. "That is a date?"

"In our oldest calendar, the Long Count, yes. We Northlanders have been counting the days, *each day,* since the year of the Second Great Sea, which is more than seven thousand years ago. Ours is the oldest, and the most accurate, calendar in the world." He couldn't resist a chance to lecture. "In the old system we counted in powers of five. *And* we had no zero, so it's all a little clumsy. We count in eleven cycles, with the last being a cycle of five days, and the first being a grand cycle of five multiplied by itself ten times."

Avatak thought that over. "So we're still in the first of those big cycles."

"Yes."

"What will happen in the future? When you run out of those big cycles?"

Pyxeas stared at him, and laughed. "That won't happen for a hundred thousand years. But it's a good question. I daresay we'll agree on some extension to the system before then. Just remember the date, boy. Remember this day."

"Why?"

The scholar looked out at the sea, the glacier, the jumbled ice. "Because today is the day I have *proved,* at least to my own satisfaction, that the longwinter is on us."

That word was a new one for Avatak. "The longwinter, scholar? What does that mean?"

Pyxeas looked at him bleakly. "Why, that the world is changing. Death will cut across the continents. *Northland must die*, Avatak."

He said this bleakly, simply, and while Avatak still did not understand, he saw that Pyxeas told the truth as he believed it. And now he saw where the sadness within the scholar came from. A sadness for the whole world, which would suffer from a blight no other could yet see.

Avatak said, "Then what must we do?"

Pyxeas smiled. "Convince others of this. But that will take time. We have work to do, my boy—work, and lots of it! And in the summer we must take our conclusions to Northland, and the councils of Etxelur itself."

We, he had said. *We* must go to Northland. Pyxeas had spoken like this before. He seemed to just assume that Avatak would leave his home, his responsibilities to his family—Uuna, to whom he was betrothed—and follow him to an alien country to pursue this strange, lofty project.

Would Avatak go? Of course he would. How could he not? Thanks to Pyxeas, his head rattled with strange ideas and vivid dreams. But it would take some explaining to Uuna, and to her mother, who had never much liked Avatak anyhow.

And, he thought, if Northland was to die, what would become of Coldland?

The glacier shuddered anew under their feet. Avatak took the scholar's mittened hand and drew him away from the crumbling edge, and back to the security of the land.

3

The First Year of the Longwinter:
Midsummer Solstice

"The steam caravan is late." Thaxa watched the
sun, which had already passed its highest point
on this midsummer day. He squinted up at the
elaborate mechanical clock face built into the light tower
over his head, and looked along the gleaming track of the
Iron Way, bonded to the roof of the Wall on which he
stood with his wife. "If the envoys from Daidu don't arrive, the afternoon is going to be awkward to say the
least. *And* that wretched uncle of yours is late too. At this
rate we won't get the ceremonies done before they fire
the end-of-day eruptors."

Rina tried to hide her irritation at her husband's fretting. It didn't help that she was cold too. She tucked her
hands into the cuffs of her long-sleeved robe; it was the
peak of summer yet there was a chill in the air, and there
had been a ground frost when she rose this morning. "Try
to be calm. You don't want to alarm our guests." Who
stood to either side of Rina and Thaxa in a row on this
parapet atop the Wall, representatives of nations from
across much of the known world, more of them riding up

to the roof in the steam elevators all the time. Near Rina, for example, were three women of the Western Continents, strangers before they had traveled, Rina had learned, from different nations and dressed as differently as could be imagined, standing together now like exotic birds of variegated plumages. This was a typical scene in Etxelur on a midsummer day, the world brought together in Northland hospitality. "As for Uncle Pyxeas, I'm imagining Crimm is doing his best to bring him back across the ocean. But Pyxeas hardly matters."

"He's to address the Water Council about the weather changes he thinks are coming."

"For the foreigners the issue at this Giving is dried fish, not maunderings about the weather. Oh, stop fussing and fidgeting, Thaxa! There's nothing we can do about the Daidu caravan, or my uncle. When there is nothing to do but wait, then you wait."

"I do my best to support you, you know," he said with only the mildest exasperation at her ill temper.

This was the reality of their relationship, as, at the age of fifty years and nearly thirty years of marriage, they both understood very well. Rina knew she could not have functioned nearly so well as an Annid without her husband's patient, fussy, competent assistance, and his tolerance of her bossiness. She allowed herself a smile. "I do know. How are the twins getting on?"

Thaxa looked through the crowd atop the Wall. "Nelo is with the Hatti party, and he's doing a good job of not laughing at their incessant praying to Jesus. Alxa is still with the Carthaginians. Hmm. See the way that young princeling of theirs is looking at her? She's only fifteen."

Rina didn't worry about the twins—or rather, she didn't allow herself to. Rina and her husband were both from families of the House of the Owl, the Annids, the ancient guild of rulers and diplomats, which had long practice in inducting its children into the subtle arts of compromise, negotiation and flattery. Besides, fifteen was seen as a pretty mature age in most parts of the world; if she were Frankish or German, Alxa would probably already be married off, already worn down by childbirth and never-ending work in the fields. The twins could look after themselves — at least, Rina thought, they could in normal times. But at the back of her mind there was a niggling awareness that there was little normal about this particular solstice.

This was Northland's midsummer Giving, the heart of the year at the heart of the world, and a ceremony of great age — older than the pyramids of Egypt, far older than the upstart empires of Carthage and New Hattusa. In the great library of the Wall Archive, documentation existed to prove that antiquity. The world flocked here at midsummer as seabirds flocked to their nesting cliffs in the spring; it always had and always would, for this was Great Etxelur, Navel of the World, and the central and oldest of the Wall's many evenly spaced Districts.

And, in the midsummer light, the Wall itself swept from east to west, horizon to horizon, separating land from sea, order from chaos, as it had done for more centuries than anyone save the most learned scholars could count. It was a thing of layers, built on an ancient core of rubble and mortar and ultimately, it was said, compacted seashells. In this age the landward face had been built up into an elaborate vertical city, with walls of thin-cut stone and tremendous stained-glass windows, all supported by sturdy flying buttresses. Looking along the roof of the Wall now, Rina could see how the character subtly changed from District to District: to the east the Springs with its taverns and inns, then the Market and the Manufactories, and to the west the more formal Holies and Embassies and Archive, the whole carefully laid out according to harmonic principles set out by the great sage Pythagoras. The upper roof itself was marked by ancient, heavily eroded blocks that were said to represent the visages of Annids and hero-gods of Northland's past. Standing over these sculptures were modern light towers, ornately carved spires where lanterns burned to guide approaching shipping to the ports cut into the seaward face. And along the spine of the roof ran a new miracle, the Iron Way, a ribbon of rail, coal dumps and way stations that united all the Wall's far-flung Districts. This great structure loomed over Old Etxelur and its hinterland to the south, while to the north the sea growled, gray and flat to the horizon, excluded by the Wall as it had been since the day of Ana, the woman become little mother who had first built the Wall.

And today the Wall's roof was crowded with foreign dignitaries, here to welcome the party from Cathay, empire of the east. Aside from the women from the Western Continents, here were Hatti priest-warriors, their armor emblazoned with the crossed-palm-leaves motif of their god Jesus Sharruma, whose bones were interred deep within the Wall. And Islamic princes, Egyptians perhaps, laden with gold, legs bare despite the chill breeze of this cold northern midsummer. And Carthaginian merchants, a splash of purple in their long robes. The Albians, from their forested land, stood apart from the rest, their heavy furs and carefully unwashed hair tokens of their adherence to the oldest gods of all. Everything about this moment was stage-managed—even the ranks in which the guests stood, so that no one had mortal enemies on *both* sides at once. These powerful men and women were dwarfed by the sheer scale of the landscape in which they stood, their talk diminished by the steady churning of the great pumps buried inside the Wall's fabric. That, of course, was the whole point of bringing the dignitaries up here: to impress them with Northland's power.

But the mood was difficult this summer. After yet another year of drought and famine across the Continent, this Giving was no formality, however joyous, but a hard-nosed negotiation over vital food supplies. The weather was odd too, for all Rina dismissed Uncle Pyxeas and his foolishness about worldwide weather changes. There was ground frost in the summer mornings, and a strange drabness in the land: this spring and summer you rarely saw a flower in bloom, or a butterfly.

And now, on top of all that, the steam caravan was late. For months communications had been disrupted by drought, famine, and petty banditry. But this was yet another thread dangling loose, and Rina did not like dangling threads, and as time wore on she could sense the dignitaries' impatience slowly growing.

Now, at last, far to the east, Rina made out a white plume of steam, a caravan like a chain of glittering toys crawling along the track. But even before the caravan reached Etxelur, runners on horseback delivered the message that the Iron Way had brought nobody from Cathay this year.

"Then we must proceed with the Giving negotiations without them," Rina murmured to Thaxa. "The Mongol princes of Daidu were only a ceremonial presence anyhow."

"That's not what Pyxeas says," Thaxa pointed out. "Your uncle claims that the Cathay scholars have information which—"

"Information, information!" she snapped. "What good is that? Can you eat it? Dried fish, however, you can eat, and that's what matters. Let's get these people back inside the Wall before that breeze gets any sharper and they start complaining even more loudly." She pulled her tunic closer around her and made for the Carthaginian party, smiling fixedly as she prepared her apology.

4

Alxa was faintly surprised to find that one of the Carthaginian merchant princes, called Mago— the man-boy who had been staring at her chest the whole afternoon—knew one of the younger Hatti delegates, called Arnuwanda, a prince it seemed, or some relative of the current King in New Hattusa. And now, while her mother Rina led the other foreigners back into the warmth of the Wall, these princes, restless, bored, wanted some sport. They wanted to wrestle. Apparently they had come up against each other at a royal wedding party in Greece, where such sports were common among the guests, and fancied another crack.

Alxa spoke about this to her father, Thaxa.

"Go with them," he said. "Take your brother too. You can keep them out of trouble. And having Nelo around might keep that Carthaginian brute from giving *you* any trouble."

"I can handle the likes of him."

"I'm sure you can. But if you're to be an Annid, child,

you have to learn that the best way to deal with trouble is to avoid it in the first place . . ."

So Alxa and her brother took the princelings down the growstone staircases to one of the better gymnasiums, an airy room cut into the growstone, with neatly plastered walls and a large stained-glass window shedding splashes of color across the wooden floor. Alxa and Nelo sat on a bench as the princes stripped off their finery, showered, and coated their skin with powder. The Carthaginian, Mago, made absolutely sure Alxa could see everything there was to see about his nude body.

The princes stalked to the middle of the floor. They were both around twenty years old. They faced each other, bowed—and launched themselves at each other. The Hatti got the first break; with his head down, he got his shoulders under his foe's belly and flipped him so he landed hard on his back. But in an instant Mago was up and at his opponent again.

Alxa murmured, "They look so alike, especially without their clothes. Warrior boys, bred for a life of fighting."

"They're not quite mirror images," Nelo said. "Look, the Hatti has Jesus symbols tattooed on his back—the fish, the palm fronds. And the Carthaginian's the one that's been drooling over you."

"Hush. I think they're talking about us."

Between thrusts and throws the princes had started a conversation in Greek, evidently a common language, which they seemed to imagine the Northlanders would not understand. "So you like the little girl," said Arnuwanda, the Hatti.

"Not so little," said Mago. "Did you notice the udders? She was looking at my tupping tool, that's for sure."

Arnuwanda snorted.

Mago rolled on top of his opponent and got his arm across his throat. "I suppose the boy is more your sort."

"Yes. Sure. And I'd do to him what a Roman legionary would have done to your Carthaginian grandmother if we Hatti hadn't saved the day . . ." And he flexed, flipped, and managed to roll Mago over so he had him pinned facedown, if briefly.

Alxa murmured to her brother, "Romans?"

"Some trading post in Greater Greece, I think." Nelo shrugged. He produced a block of paper and began to sketch the wrestling princes, in brisk, confident strokes.

Mago pushed his opponent off, jumped to his feet, and the two closed again with a shuddering crash. "So," Mago grunted as he worked, "what do you think of these Northlanders?"

"What am I supposed to think? They have mountains of dried fish, culled from that ocean of theirs. We have famine. So here we are."

"They also have the bones of your god Jesus stuffed in their Wall. And His Mother."

"True," Arnuwanda said. They pretend to a moral authority which— Get your finger out of my ear, African!" The Hatti forced Mago's arm away from his head by brute force. "They pretend to impose peace between warring religions. In fact they draw pilgrims to the relics they have stolen, and milk them of their cash. They are hypocrites."

"I agree." Mago whirled, tried to get the Hatti in an armlock, but Arnuwanda spun away and Mago ended up facedown on the floor again. Spitting out dust, Mago twisted his head to speak. "And they claim to despise farmers. We're all 'cattle-folk' to them. Yet they hire soldiers from the farming lands, the Franks and the Germans and the others, to keep out the rest of the rabble."

"Hmm. Well, that might not help them much longer." Arnuwanda got one arm free, pinned Mago with the weight of his body, and slammed his forearm down on the Carthaginian's head. "Had enough?"

"Bugger yourself. What do you mean, not much longer?" Mago twisted with a mighty heave, throwing the Hatti off.

"The Germans and Franks have been hit by the droughts too." They came together again—*slam*, heads down, arms and legs straining, hands slapping for a hold on flesh greasy with sweat. "And some of them are coming here. The farmers, I mean, abandoning their dustbowl lands and wandering into Northland. Well, you've seen it, there's plenty of room."

"Yes." Mago snorted with laughter. "An empty country. A ghost of a place. The ghost that rules the Continent." He turned, dropped onto his back, flipped up his legs, locked them around the Hatti's neck, and sent him flying.

"Oof!"

Mago got to his feet, yelled, leapt cat-like into the air, and would have slammed down on the Hatti—had not Arnuwanda rolled out of the way at the crucial moment, so that Mago came down hard on the floor. "Oh, by the bones of Melqart . . ."

"Always a mistake to rely on mercenaries, I say," the Hatti said. He crawled over to the Carthaginian and drove his elbow into the small of Mago's back. "Had enough *now*?"

A horn sounded, distant, carrying.

Alxa glanced at her brother. "The eruptors?"

"Yes. That's the first call." Nelo tucked away his sketches. "Come on. Let's put these two back on their leashes."

They walked toward the princes, who broke and stood, panting, sweating, wiping dust and powder from their skins. Mago grinned at Alxa. He said in his own clipped Carthaginian tongue, "I saw you watching."

She replied in crisp Greek, "I saw you lose."

Arnuwanda frowned. "You understand Greek? You should have had the manners to tell us so."

Nelo said, "And you should have had the manners not to insult your hosts."

Arnuwanda faced Nelo, glaring. He wasn't as showy as the Carthaginian, Alxa saw, his musculature wasn't as impressive, or, come to that, his manhood, but the Hatti had a composure, an inner strength, his opponent evidently lacked. And here he was facing down her brother.

Alxa stepped between the two of them. "Let's be friends," she said calmly. It wasn't good for a student diplomat to get into fistfights with foreign guests.

Nelo was angry too, but he nodded and stepped back. With a sneer, the Hatti took a towel from his opponent and turned away.

"So you heard it all," said Mago. "Well, what of it? Anything ring uncomfortably true? The charges of hypocrisy, of greed—"

"Insults cast by the ignorant," Alxa said. "One thing you were wrong about, though."

"What's that?"

"We don't rely on mercenaries for our protection. Not entirely." That horn sounded again. "Get yourselves back up to the roof before the third sounding and you'll see."

She walked away, with Nelo, without looking back.

5

As the second horn sounded, and the evening of the long midsummer day approached, the three women from the Western Continents who had stood near Rina earlier met in a bar, set in the face of the Wall.

Walks In Mist had discovered this tavern. It was on the fringe of the Wall District called the Springs, a precise eight hundred paces from Etxelur, a place full of taverns, hostels and, Walks In Mist suspected, brothels. This place seemed respectable enough; built into a terrace in the face of the Wall, it gave onto a balcony overlooking Old Etxelur and the lowland.

Her friends joined her now, Sabela from the southern continent's High Country in her robe of llama wool, and Xipuhl from the Land of the Jaguar with her fine steel mirror at her breast. Walks In Mist herself, from the Land of the Sky Wolf, wore her eagle feathers in her hair. Each of them proclaimed who they were in this baffling, crowded place — the center of the world, if only for mid-summer.

"I know it isn't much to look at," Walks In Mist said as the others settled. And she was right; the floor was rough, the walls unfinished growstone. "But that's what I like about it. That and the view."

They turned to look out over Northland, a tremendous plain that stretched to the horizon. The sun was low now, the sky a rich deep blue. The marshes and canals shone like ribbons of sky, the old flood mounds cast long shadows, and fires sparked everywhere. At the foot of the Wall itself were tremendous warehouses where even in the gathering dark a steady stream of traffic came and went, and rows of brightly lit shops provided their customers with food, drink, pilgrimage tokens and Giving-day souvenirs.

Walks In Mist leaned from her chair and ran a hand over the lip of the growstone balcony. "Think how *old* this stuff must be. Think what it's seen, how much history. And now here we are."

"Cradled like an eagle chick in the palm of an old man's hand," said Sabela.

Xipuhl laughed, and the dancing mirror on her chest cast reflections from the candle. "You are always the poet of our little gang," she said to Sabela. Xipuhl was a little older than the others, and was prone to be the one who did the teasing.

But Sabela was right, Walks In Mist thought. She did feel cradled here. She always felt safe in Northland, with its antiquity and stability and the obvious physical strength of its great Wall. Why, here they were, three women from across the lands Northlanders called the Western Continents, all of them comfortably speaking in the only tongue they shared—the liquid language of Northland, a tongue that had nothing in common with their own native speech at all.

The three of them had found one another during the long sea crossing on a huge Northlander ship. Every three years the elders of Etxelur sent a flotilla across the Western Ocean to the Land of the Jaguar to pick up a selection of especially honored, or especially well-paying, guests from the Western Continents to come to the midsummer Giving. Walks In Mist herself was here for trade; she was one of a delegation from Sky Wolf seeking to expand cotton exports. Xipuhl was part of a formal diplomatic legation from the Land of the Jaguar, and much of her midsummer had been taken up with "stuffy meetings with old men in airless rooms," she had said.

Sabela was the only one without a job during the trip. It was her husband who was in the business of exporting llama and alpaca wool and other High Country textiles to Northland. Sabela's people were always honored in Northland because of historic links; the High Country had given Northlanders the potato, a precious crop which, they said, had enabled their unique culture to survive on the fringe of a continent full of farmers. Of the three of them Sabela was the junior partner, Walks In Mist supposed, and she was a rather vague young woman—her head in the clouds, Xipuhl said, just like the pretty country she came from—but on the ship, she had been the one who had brought them together.

"Well," Sabela said now, "I think what I'm going to like about this tavern is the drinks they serve. What a selection!"

The menu was inscribed into the oak surface of the table itself, in the loops and bars of the unique Northlander script. The three women chose drinks from across the eastern half of the planet: Albian ale for Xipuhl, a decent Gairan wine for Walks In Mist, and a fine potato spirit from Rus for Sabela. When the drinks arrived, the women knocked their cups together.

Xipuhl said briskly, "I imagine the next time we drink together we will be back on the ship, for it's going to take me the rest of my time to get packed up."

Sabela pulled a face. "Be grateful you don't have children. I'll swear my two support the economy of the local trinket makers single-handed." The breeze turned, an oddly chill wind blew in from the west, and they all reacted, shifting, pulling their wraps tighter. "It has been a cool summer," Sabela murmured. "My two have complained about that."

Walks In Mist frowned. "I've heard mutterings about great meetings of scholars, discussions of the turning of the weather. Do you think there's anything in it?"

"I've not much truck for scholars," Xipuhl said firmly. "Who can know what the future holds?"

"And we'll not let it govern our lives," Sabela said.

The horn blasted for a third time, announcing the noisy eruptor display that would end the long day of celebration. People started to drift out of the tavern.

"Let's make a pact," Walks In Mist said impulsively. "We'll keep in touch. Let's meet when the Northland fleet comes again to the West, in three years' time."

Sabela laughed girlishly. "Oh, yes—what a lovely idea."

Xipuhl grinned. "Well, as you are the only companions I've found on this trip who haven't wanted to get some kind of business out of me, I'm for it."

"And we'll come back to this very bar," Sabela said. "And order the same drinks, three years from now."

"Agreed," said Walks In Mist, and they raised their cups again and toasted the pact.

But the breeze gusted once more. The candles on the tables flickered, and around the bar people pulled cloaks over their shoulders. A few people laughed, and sent mock curses at the little mothers and other gods for their willfulness.

"That's if we're all still here in three years' time," Xipuhl said with morbid humor.

6

lxa stood with her brother on the roof of the Wall, surrounded by a crowd of Etxelur elite in their fancy ceremonial House robes, waiting for the wrestling princes to return to the parapet.

The sun was near the horizon now, and the day felt markedly colder, as if this were an autumn day, not midsummer. Lights sparked over the face of the Wall below, and in the curving reefs of the lower city. People had gathered on the plain beyond, filling the open spaces and lining the canals, waiting for the show. The crowds always came to the Giving at Etxelur, although this year, Alxa was sure, there were plenty of nestspills, that cruel Northland word, people displaced from their homes by flood or drought, by poverty or hunger or disease, here for handouts rather than celebration.

But, nestspills or not, the crowd all responded with gasps and cheers when the show started: the tremendous banners unrolling down the face of the Wall, the fireworks filling the sky with dancing light. And then came the fire-drug eruptors themselves, suddenly thrust from their portals in the Wall's upper face, a hundred of them shouting simultaneously. Smoke belched and shot flew, gleaming red-hot, to fall in empty spaces beyond the crowds.

While the Etxelur folk applauded and cheered, Nelo watched the princes, who were stunned by the display of the mighty weapons. Only Northland, of the western countries, had the secret of the fire drug from Cathay. "Look at them, those loudmouths, Mago and Arnuwanda. They won't be bragging about the might of their cattle-folk armies now."

Their mother came pushing through the crowd. "*There* you two are," Rina snapped. "Your great-uncle's back. Dock West One Four. Go and help him. And ask him how he managed to be eleven hours late after three *years* away . . ."

7

The next morning Alxa and Nelo were summoned to the Hall of Annids for the formal Giving Bounty meeting. As apprentice members of the House of the Owl, they had to wear their formal uniforms, a black shift topped by a cloak quilted and stitched to look like the wings of the emblematic bird.

The setting was spectacular. The Hall of Annids, relocated and rebuilt extensively over the ages, was contained within the body of the Wall, just under the roof, and its great stained-glass ceiling was one of the wonders of the Etxelur District. Though the sunlight gleamed through the glass it wasn't a particularly warm day—there hadn't been a *really* warm day all summer—but the steam-pipe heating was running, and Alxa knew she was going to get seriously hot in this rig.

"And it's going to be as dull as a Hatti funeral," she moaned to Nelo, as they filed into the Hall behind their parents and other Northland dignitaries.

Nelo just laughed.

The session was already coming to order, if slowly,

and Alxa and her twin sat with their parents behind their
distant aunt Ywa. Ywa was Annid of Annids and the
speaker of the Water Council, the semi-permanent body
that governed Etxelur and Northland. Crimm was here,
another uncle, the fisherman who had brought Uncle
Pyxeas home from Coldland. Other members of the
Council attended, along with senior members of other
Houses: the priest-scholars, the masons who maintained
the Wall, the water engineers who managed the drainage
of the countryside beyond. Dignitaries from the Wall's
many Districts had gathered too, their gowns emblazoned with the numbers and symbols of their homes:
Four East, Seventeen West. Only Great Etxelur itself
had no east or west designation, no number; Etxelur was
the center, the zero. Before the stage, below the Northlanders, sat the guests in their parties: Carthaginians and
Hatti and Muslims and Germans and Franks, even a few
Albians, stern and silent. In all there were perhaps fifty
people here in this great and ancient Hall. And as they
waited for the session to begin, the foreigners, dignitaries
in their own countries, showed signs of restlessness.

They were all waiting for Pyxeas.

At last Alxa's great-uncle came bustling into the Hall,
with slates and scrolls of paper under his arm. He wasn't
in the stylized wolf-fur cloak he should have been wearing to mark his membership of his own House of scholars
and priests; instead he wore smelly-looking furs that
seemed as if they were still crusted with seawater. And
he was accompanied by a young man, short, stocky,
plump-looking, with a flat, sketchy face and short dark
hair. He too was bundled up in a fur jacket and trousers,
and he looked uncomfortably hot. He was a Coldlander,
Alxa realized; he must have traveled back across the
ocean with Pyxeas. The scholar glanced around, squinting, shortsighted, comical with his ruddy face and shock
of snow-white hair sticking up around a bald pate. Alxa
hadn't seen him for three years; he seemed a lot older
than she remembered.

Everybody was staring. One of the foreigners laughed behind her hand.

"Oh," Pyxeas said at last. "Am I late? You should have started without me."

Ywa stood, her black owl cloak rustling, and indicated empty seats on the stage close to her. "Please sit, Uncle. And your, umm, companion."

"Where's the delegation from Cathay? My colleague Bolghai promised me his collated information on the changing mix of atmospheric gases which, which— Well, we won't achieve full understanding without *that*. But if he's not here, he's not here." He looked up at Ywa. "Carry on, child, carry on!"

Alxa admired Ywa's calm in the face of such provocation. She glanced around the room. "Welcome to the Distribution of the Giving Bounty. Who would like to approach the Council first?"

The visiting parties each sent up a delegate to speak before the Annids, one after another.

A Frank, from northern Gaira, was the first to speak. He wore a woolen tunic over thick leather leggings, his graying blond hair was worn long, and he had a carefully shaped and combed mustache. He was old for a farmer— more than forty, at least—and Alxa thought his face was oddly slack, like an empty sack, the face of a man once plump. "It began with the years of rain," he said. "Five years back for us, it was—I know it's been different for some of you, the detail of it anyhow. That first summer we got hailstones the size of your fist that just smashed down our crops . . ." As he spoke, translators from the House of the Jackdaws, the traders and negotiators, murmured into the ears of the Annids. "We tried harvesting the grain but it was wet and soft. Even the hay was too wet to be cured. Animals stuck in the mud or drowned, cattle, sheep. Come the next summer our reserves were exhausted, and it rained so hard we couldn't get the planting done. That was the year the rest of the animals were slaughtered." He was a proud man, Alxa could see that. He hated to be standing here begging for help. Yet here he was.

As the Frank spoke, Pyxeas made notes with pen and ink on his lush Cathay paper, muttering and murmuring. The Coldlander lad helped in small ways, handing him paper, fetching him water. Pyxeas was nervous, intent, but he seemed on the edge of exhaustion. Alxa saw his head nod over his papers, the scribbling stylus slowing, until he drifted to sleep—and then he would wake with a start, and an odd barked grunt, and he would turn his head like a shortsighted bird.

"I'll cut it short," said the Frank. "We had hopes for this year. But the winter was from the gates of hell—you know that. We had snow on the ground long after the spring equinox, and even when that melted back, the ground stayed hard frozen beneath and you couldn't get a hoe in it. We ran out of wood to burn! We have pleaded with our gods. We have sacrificed what we can—we have little left to give. My priests say it is only the little mothers of the Northland who listen. So I am here, Annid of Annids. In the past we have come to your aid in your hours of need."

"I hear you in friendship," Ywa said. "Even now we have troops of Frankish warriors patrolling our eastern flanks against incursion of German bandits."

Rina murmured to Alxa, "Just as in the south we have German soldiers kicking out Frankish nestspills, but don't tell this fellow that."

Before the man's dignity, Alxa was faintly repelled by her mother's cynicism.

Everybody seemed relieved when the old Gairan at last bowed and withdrew. But the next supplicants, more from Gaira, then from the German nations south of the great forest, had much the same story to tell: of years of rain, failed harvests and famine, and now the cold. The dismal accounts began to have a cumulative effect on Alxa. Was nowhere spared?

Now there came a Carthaginian, a worthy of some kind called Barmocar. He was a man of about forty with hair that looked suspiciously deep black to Alxa, and he wore a robe of heavy cloth dyed richly purple, a shade much envied in the fashion houses of the Wall but which remained a Carthaginian secret. Alxa had met Barmocar's wife, an elegant if arrogant woman called Anterastilis. She wondered what relation Mago was to Barmocar—a son perhaps, or a nephew. The Carthaginians were an empire of merchants who didn't have kings and princes like other farmer-nations, like the Hatti, say. But just as in Northland, in Carthage family ties were everything when it came to the distribution of power.

And Barmocar spoke, not of rain as in the northern lands, but of drought in the once-fertile plains of North Africa.

"Years of it. I doubt you can imagine the consequences. The earth itself cracks and dries, and the soil blows away on the wind. The cattle lie in the heat, too listless to brush away the flies swarming around them. And the children too, their bellies swollen, whole communities ravaged by diseases. Yet despite our own privations, we of Carthage ensure that our neighbors do not suffer, if we can aid them ..."

Rina whispered to Alxa, "I never liked Carthaginians. Arrogant, bullying and manipulative. I've been warned about the sophistry this one's to come out with. He'll make a case that Carthage is a great nation, a *giving* nation, all the while wheedling under his breath for fish and potatoes, so he has it both ways—oh, I can't listen to this." She stood and said loudly, "With your permission, Cousin Ywa. Good Prince Barmocar, I am confused." Her words were hastily translated into Barmocar's own thick tongue. "This tale of woe you recite—are you here to beg for bounty? Begging like these others, the Franks and Germans and the rest, these 'poor rudimentary farmers,' as I have heard you describe them? And a bounty from us, whom I have heard you describe as 'a thin godless smear of ignorance and incompetence on an undeveloped landscape'?"

Barmocar glared, his face suffused with red.

Ywa sighed. "Sit down, Cousin. The man is an ambassador."

Rina complied. But Alxa could see from the look on her face that she was satisfied with the work she had done.

Barmocar continued. "On the contrary, madam. If you had not interrupted me I would have explained that we are here solely to offer what succor we can to our neighbors and allies." He smiled, arms open in generosity, and spoke on about gifts and giving.

But Alxa, relatively innocent in this kind of dueling, saw that her mother had forestalled whatever subtle request for assistance he had intended. His humiliation was apparent, as was the barely concealed gloating on the faces of the Hatti, longtime rivals of the Carthaginians. Alxa wondered how many children in Carthage would go hungry because of this nasty little exchange.

Nelo whispered, "Good old Mother, she always has had a tongue like a poison dart."

Still the delegates came forward with their tales of agony, one after another. Pyxeas made endless scribbles, and his pile of notes grew to a heap of papers and slates under his seat.

Only the gruff Albians sat unmoving, massive men in furs of bear hide, neither pleading poverty nor boasting of riches. They were known across the Continent; their priest-warriors traveled the northern lands, through great belts of land that had once been farmland and were now given back to the forest, preaching of the return of the old northern gods. Everybody knew *they* were all right. These bulky, powerful men were here only to remind the representatives of the starving farmer folk that any attempt to share the bounty of their rich, ancient forest would be met by uncompromising force.

Alxa murmured to Nelo, "Remember what Giving days used to be like, when we were little? Races on the beach. Swimming. People coming from all over with exotic fruits and stuff, and all those spicy meat treats we weren't supposed to eat. Swordfighting and cavalry charges . . . Now this."

Nelo shrugged.

But it was true. The world's slow collapse into cold, flood and drought and famine, had coincided with Alxa's own growing up, her own journey into the complicated years of adolescence. Sometimes she wondered if she was just projecting her own mixed-up moods onto the world. But no, the world really had been getting worse, and it was just her bad luck to be growing up in the middle of it.

When the submissions were finished Ywa turned to Pyxeas, and waited.

It seemed to take him some time to notice that the Hall had fallen silent. He looked up at last, stylus in hand. "What? Eh? Are we done?"

"We are, Uncle. Have you not been paying attention?"

"Well, of course I have, my girl, and you were just as impatient when you were a child," he said, rebuking the Annid of Annids, oblivious of raised eyebrows around the room. "I take it you're ready to decide on the allocation of the Giving Bounty this year."

"That is why we're here," she said drily.

"Well, I, Pyxeas, have something to say." He glanced around at the banks of foreigners. "But not in front of these fellows. What I have to say is for your ears first. You and the other Annids—the Water Council. For the ears of Northlanders. Then you can decide what to say to your guests."

Ywa considered this for a long moment. Then she stood and turned to the delegates. "Forgive me. We must withdraw for a private session. We will resume in the morning. I assure you we have taken all you have said into our hearts. In the meantime please enjoy our hospitality. Thaxa, perhaps you could ensure that everything is organized?"

"Of course." Alxa's father got to his feet with a beaming, inclusive smile; this was what he was good at. "Please wait—you will be served refreshments, while I arrange for escorts and guides for all of you . . ." As he hurried from the room, the foreigners, scowling or shaking their heads, got up and began to mill around the Hall.

8

They gathered in an anteroom, much smaller than the formal Hall. Here the Annids and the House elders loosened their formal clothing and stripped off their stiff cloaks, sat informally on benches and chairs, and sipped water and tea brought to them by the servants Ywa summoned.

Only Pyxeas stood, at the center of the room, with his Coldlander companion at his side. Alxa remembered her great-uncle from the long-gone days of her childhood, a big, beaming, avuncular man who would play clumsy magic tricks, and later he had tried to coax a little scholarship into her head. But looking at the expression on his face now, and having heard so much dismal news already today, she feared what he had to say.

The scholar began speaking even before they were all seated. "You must understand how my conclusions remain contingent upon the information I was to have been supplied by the Cathay scholars. Without that—"

Out of hearing of the foreigners, Ywa gave way to her

irritation. "You went to Coldland with the financial support of the Water Council—"

"And my travels aren't done, by the way."

"You were given this support on the understanding that you would learn sufficient about the changing weather to enable us to understand what comes next, for us and the world."

"There can never be a definitive answer, that's not in the nature of philosophy—"

"Now you have interrupted the bounty ceremony and carted us all off in here, and the mothers only know what our guests will make of that!"

"You'll understand why when I tell you—"

"Tell us, then, man! What have you learned?"

He paused, and considered. "Only that we have the answers already. The cause of the dismal seasons we are suffering, as attested across the Continent too. Our ancestors knew it all along—or rather, they *remembered*.

"Avatak, give me that scroll—no, boy, that one." He took the yellowing scroll, rolled it out, and began to read. " 'In the beginning was the Gap. / The awful interval between being and not being. / The tension of emptiness caused the creation of an egg, out of nothing. Its shell was ice and its contents were slush and mud and rock. / For an unmeasured time the egg was alone, silent.' "

His gravelly voice, the familiar text, fixed the attention of everyone in the room. Alxa knew these words, as surely did everybody else. This was the mythos of Northland, the oldest, deepest part: the account of the earliest days, before history, before the Black Crime of Milaqa, before the heroism of Prokyid, who defied the Second Great Sea, even before the exploits of Ana herself, who had founded the Wall.

" 'Then the egg shattered. / The fragments of its shell became ice giants, who swarmed and fought and devoured each other as they grew.

" 'Meanwhile from the slush and mud grew the first

mother. She gave birth to the three little mothers, and to their brother the sun, and to the earth serpent and the sky thunderbird. The first mother tended the ice giants as lovingly as her own cubs.

"'All time might have ended there, with the first mother and her family. / But for the restlessness and envy of the giants.

"'They fought each other for the attention of the mother, and drove off her true children. / At last, sadly but with love, she allowed the giants to destroy her in their wars.

"'Enraged and saddened, they threw the sun in the sky, and cast the little mothers into the dark. / Then they made the world from the mother's body, the land from the bones of rock and the mud, the sea from her slush blood. / Their sculpting was violent and rough, which is why the world is such a jumble now, with shaved-off hills and valleys too big for the rivers that contain them . . .'" He skipped ahead. "'The three little mothers and the sun had stood by dismayed while the giants fought. / Now the mothers spoke to the sun, and together they woke the shell of ice, and asked her to lift the weight of death from the world. She did so, and the ice sailed into the sky to become the moon. / The three mothers touched the revealed world, and shaped the wreckage the ice giants had left behind into a living world . . .' I think that's enough." He rolled up the scroll. "You see? You see?" He slapped the scroll to emphasize his point. "It's all—in—here."

Rina scowled. "What is? By the mothers' bones, don't give us children's stories, man."

"Children's stories? Have you heard of Euhemerus?"

"Who?"

"Greek philosopher. Or perhaps Hatti. Died a long time ago. Anyhow *he* believed that our myths are our oldest account of ourselves. They're not just stories, you see, though that's what they teach you in school nowadays. *They describe events that really happened.* Important events, major, world-changing events. That's why they were remembered, and written down, and why they became the strange sort of mass memory we call a myth.

"And any of you could have confirmed the truth of those myths for yourselves, had you gone out in the world and *looked*, as have I, Pyxeas. *If* you had learned to read the great book of the world, as I and some others have learned. I have seen the shorelines of lakes long vanished. I have seen ridges of rubble strewn across the continents, left by the retreat of great ice sheets. I have seen valleys gouged by long-melted glaciers. And indeed you could have found the truth in our own Archive. We have records going back millennia—not even the Hatti, not even the Egyptians go back as far as we do—"

"Oh, Uncle!" Ywa cried. "Get to the point. *Why* did it start to rain five years ago, all across the Continent?"

"Because the air got cooler. You must know that the air, invisible all around us, is a jumble of gases. It contains vital air which sustains a flame, and fixed air which is *produced* by a flame, and other inert components. And water! In the form of vapor." He glared at them. "Come on, come on! I taught too many of you these basic principles; have you forgotten how to think while I've been away?"

Alxa said slowly, remembering her lessons as she spoke, "When the air cools, it must drop the moisture it holds."

He pointed at her. "Yes! You have it. The abnormal rainstorms themselves were a sign of the cooling of the air. Then as the rain washed out, the currents of the air were deflected—pushed away by the gathering cold in the north—and settled into a new pattern of persistent and dry winds from the west."

"Which," Ywa said, "eventually brought drought to the southern lands. Is that what you're saying?"

"Yes. But *why* is the air cooling, and indeed the world as a whole? The ultimate cause seems clear . . ." He dug out a bit of Albian chalk, and rapidly began to sketch on the plaster wall: a spinning sphere, its axis tilted, swooping on a curved path around a scribbled sun. "The earth! The world on which we stand, spinning and sailing through the void in a manner long ago determined by the Greek scholars brought to Northland by Pythagoras, and measured in detail by generations of astronomers. It's a very precise art, you see; you can measure a star's apparent position in the sky quite exactly . . ."

Crimm the fisherman was a tough-looking man in his thirties. He sat in loose shirt and trousers, arms folded, legs outstretched, and he watched Pyxeas' performance with a grin. "I got this stuff in my ear all the way back from Coldland. You wouldn't believe he's talking about sunshine, would you?"

Ywa seemed baffled. "Sunshine?"

"Yes!" Pyxeas cried. "The world's spin is not unchanging, you see. The axis wobbles and nods, like a child's top spinning on a table. *Why* the world behaves this way is not clear. The Greeks were always divided. Some said the whole cosmic apparatus is like an imperfect machine— rattling like a badly tuned steam engine. Others believe that consciousness suffuses the cosmos; perhaps the earth makes a deferential dance around the sun, nodding and bowing like a courtier of New Hattusa.

"But the why is not important. The question is, what difference does this make to us? And yes, fisherman, the difference is the sunshine. No two years are identical. Because of these features of the planet's orbit and spin, in this epoch year by year the world is getting *less* sunshine—or to be precise, the strength of the sunshine falling on a given spot on the world, say here at Etxelur, at a particular time, say yesterday, midsummer solstice—"

Ywa said, "So you claim the whole world is cooling."

"I could tell you that," Crimm said. "More bergs every year. And the ocean currents are changing too. Any fisherman will tell you. We have to go further and further south to find the warm water that the cod like. And as for the catch itself—" He went to his chair, pulled a canvas sack out from underneath it, and produced dried fish. He passed them around the group. "This is all we're bringing home."

Alxa got hold of one, a fish as hard as a wood carving. Sometimes still called by its traditional name of Kirike-fish, this was the main produce of the Northland's fishing fleets, cod caught in masses and quickly salted and dried. It would keep for a year or more, and, easy to transport, was the staple of Northland's provision of food to the rest of the Continent. But the fish seemed small to Alxa, who had seen fishermen return immense specimens before, some as long as the fishers were tall; this was less than the length of her forearm.

Crimm said, "The point is, we're having to sail twice as far to return half the yield. Before you Annids decide how much to dole out to our continental neighbors, you need to remember that."

Now the debate on the Giving Distribution started in earnest.

"We must keep what we have for our own people," said one man. "If the trends Pyxeas describes continue, if our water courses freeze, if our trees fail to produce fruit—"

Rina shook her head. "That's shortsighted. There are always more farmers than us—and some of them are already here. Nestspills from their failed farmlands in Gaira and the Continent, even from the fringes of Albia. Our guard and the mercenaries might keep some of them out. Far better to buy them off with a little cod than have them come here and consume everything."

There were many objections to that, and the discussion grew heated.

Pyxeas was growing agitated. "You're not thinking it through. Any of you. *You're not thinking it through.*" But for now, in a swirl of argument, nobody was listening.

The Coldlander boy was with him, silent and stolid. Pyxeas rested his hand on the boy's arm. The stranger seemed to sympathize with the scholar, over dilemmas he

could surely barely understand, and the little scene surprised and touched Alxa. Alxa suddenly felt very sorry for
this ancient great-uncle, tortured by the knowledge that
was evidently eating away inside him, knowledge he
seemed so poor at sharing. She got up and went to him.

Pyxeas looked at her warily, squinting. "The light is so
poor in here. You're not Rina, are you?"

"No. I am Alxa. Rina's daughter." She took his arm
and made him sit down, and knelt beside him, holding his
hand. "Just tell me, Uncle. What is it that we don't understand?"

He looked at her with a kind of bleak gratitude. "That
this isn't some anomaly. Some variation from the norm.
These recent seasons of cold and rain and drought. The
astronomical calculations prove it . . . *This is the future.* It
will get colder and colder. This is inevitable. Maybe you
can buy off some of the farmers this season. But next
summer, when they come again—what then?"

Still nobody else was listening.

Ywa clapped her hands to call for order. "Pyxeas,
your contribution has been—umm, invaluable. Crimm,
perhaps we can discuss the question of the fish stocks
before we must face our guests again, and decide on the
bounty we can afford . . ."

They began to file out of the room.

Pyxeas, abandoned, collected together the scrolls and
slates littering the floor with the Coldlander boy.

But Alxa stayed beside him. "Uncle," she said cautiously. "Are you saying you *understand*! You understand
why, how, the world is cooling down?"

"Yes. No! Not quite," Pyxeas admitted miserably.
"There was a divergence."

"A divergence?"

"According to the historical record there was a *warming,* when the world should have been cooling. Lasted up
to about two millennia ago. An anomaly. I don't know
what caused it—don't know why it ended—I don't have
the numbers to match the anecdotal evidence. Still less

do I understand what caused it. And until I know all that, I can't see the future with any definitiveness. And that's why I needed to speak to the scholars of Cathay."

Much of this went over Alxa's head. "But you quoted the lines about the ice giants. You're not saying the ice giants were real? And that—what? That they'll come again?"

He looked at her, as if seeing her clearly for the first time with his rheumy eyes. "No, child. The ice giants weren't real. People can only describe the things they see in terms they understand. But the ice—that was real."

Rina came to Pyxeas now, and stood over him, evidently disapproving. "Then what must we do, in your opinion, Uncle?"

"Leave here," he said simply.

"What?"

"*Northland cannot be saved.* Leave here—now, if you can, next year, if you must. No later."

For a heartbeat Rina seemed so shocked she could not speak. Then she asked, "Who?"

"All of you! All the family! And take the treasures—the lore of the ancients, the information in the archives. For that is how we will rebuild in the future, by remembering the past."

"Leave Etxelur? Leave the Wall? What are you saying? Where should we go?"

"Anywhere that will take you—as far south as you can."

"Gaira?"

"No—further, further!"

Rina seemed outraged. "Our ancient family should abandon Etxelur, after so long, all for a little cold weather?"

"Not just weather. This is the longwinter, child. And it is returning—"

"You quote myth at us, Uncle. Do you remember the words of the blessed Ana, when the sea first tried to take the land? *We will not run anymore.* Single-handed she built a mound to defy the sea. *We will not run. This is the future! This!* That is what she said, and she inspired those who followed her, and Northlanders have not run from that day to this."

Alxa stared at Pyxeas and her mother, barely comprehending, struggling to believe any of it. "And you, Uncle Pyxeas? What will you do?"

"That's obvious, isn't it? My understanding is still incomplete, my compilation of information imperfect. I have to get it all together while there is still time . . ."

"Where will you go?"

"Cathay, child. Cathay. Oh, do be careful with that slate, Avatak, you clumsy oaf!"

9

The First Year of the Longwinter:
Autumn Equinox

*I*n the end it was a poor summer, and a short one, with the heavy frosts coming even before the autumn equinox.

It had been a summer dominated by the aftereffects of the previous winters. Lingering ice masses in the northern lands and in the mountains, though still scattered and separate, reflected away the sun's heat. Meanwhile more ice tumbled into the northern ocean from growing, unstable glaciers, and bergs marched steadily south. The sudden injection of so much cold freshwater disrupted the great, warm ocean streams, cooling the land further. All this during the summer months, the warmest.

Now summer was over, for better or worse, and the world's relentless orbital dance took the northern lands through the autumn equinox. Even as humans around the planet gathered to celebrate this latest moment of astronomical symmetry, the cold closed its grip once more.

10

Kassu was woken by a kick in the ribs, in the dark, in his house.

"Henti?" It was cold for an Anatolian autumn night. Under a heap of furs, with his wife beside him, he had been sleeping deeply, and it was taking him time to surface. Had he slept late? Today was the day of the *nuntarriyashas*, New Hattusa's equinox festival, and his wife wouldn't want to be late for that ...

A kick in the ribs, though? Henti was asleep; she hadn't delivered that.

He rolled on his back. There was a mass in the dark, looming over him. "Palla?" But through the thin partition walls he could hear the priest, Henti's cousin, the house's only other inhabitant, snoring. Who, then?

A stranger in his house. His heart lurched. The land swarmed with raiders, bandits, the starving. This farm was within the circuit of the city's New Wall, but that was no safety at all, not if you let your guard down. He kept a steel dagger under his pillow. He reached for it. It was gone.

And he felt cold metal on his bare chest. "Looking for this?"

"Zida. You're a dog's asshole." He said this softly to avoid waking his wife.

Zida cackled, and he pricked Kassu's chest with the dagger's tip before he set it down, just to make the point. "You're getting slow, old man."

"I'm younger than you."

"Get your finger out of your wife's honeypot and put your boots on. We've got a job. A bit of scouting. Assignment from General Himuili himself."

Grumbling inwardly, longing for sleep, Kassu rolled out of bed and searched in the dark for the night-soil pot. Henti's breath was even, undisturbed. She hadn't noticed a thing. And in the next room the priest snored on, oblivious.

When he emerged from the house a little light had seeped into the sky, which was a lid of cloud. He glanced around at his farm, silent and dark, the main house, the meaner shacks of the slaves and itinerant workers, the pens that contained his few scrawny cattle. To the south he saw the great mass of the city within the ancient Old Wall, the central mound of the Pergamos on which the tremendous dome of the Church of the Holy Wisdom was picked out by lantern light. The carpet of suburbs outside the Wall glowed with night fires. This was New Hattusa to kings and administrators, but the city was still Troy to the bulk of its inhabitants, a thousand years after the Hatti kings had made it their new capital.

He could see Zida standing at the edge of one of Kassu's potato fields, stirring dry muck with his toe. Kassu walked that way, pulling his woolen cloak around him. A few flakes of snow swirled out of nowhere, heavy and moist, settling on his cloak and on the ground.

Zida looked him over. Kassu wore his scale armor over his tunic, greaves on his legs, helmet jammed on his head, and he carried his short stabbing spear, curved sword, dagger. Zida, similarly equipped, grinned. "Expecting trouble, are we?"

"I don't imagine the Chief of the Chariot Warriors of the Left got me out of bed to dance for Judas."

"Oh, yes, it's Judas Day, isn't it? Well, we've some scouting to do before we join in the hunt for the Missing God."

"All right. Which way?"

"North." Which was beyond the potato field, and away from the city. "I don't want to trample your precious crop of Northlander apples with my big feet. Which way to walk around?"

Kassu shrugged and set off across the field. "Doesn't make much difference." More snowflakes fell on the churned ground, where the potato crop was a mess, with furry growths on leaves that looked black in the low light. A couple of rows had been dug up from the dry earth to expose tubers that were nothing but a pulpy mush. "The blight got them," Kassu said simply.

Zida grunted. "I once met a Northlander who said you should plant different sorts of potato, because then one kind of blight can't get them all."

"Northlanders are full of shit."

"Well, they're full of something, for you rarely see them starve."

"I thought we'd get away with it this year. It hits overnight, you know. The blight. One day you think you're fine, the next your potatoes are rotting in the ground."

Zida laughed, striding out. "Your choice, my friend. You decided to become a Man of the Weapons. I prefer my pay in silver, not in dusty land."

"But somebody has to work the land. If nobody grows any food, what will there be to buy with your silver?"

"Whores," Zida cackled.

Kassu said no more, for he knew there was no more to say. Zida, a few years older than Kassu at thirty, was a solid man with a face left battered by years of warfare, of pitched battles against the enemies of the Hatti King, and in more recent years smaller-scale actions against packs of hungry wanderers and bandits. Zida really did think no further ahead than the next pay purse, the next whore. He was a soldier, he expected to die in battle sooner rather than later, so why worry about the future?

But Kassu had a wife, they had had a child who had died of an infant sickness despite all the ministrations of the surgeons and the priests, and they wanted to try again. And Kassu had come of age in the years when the great drought had clamped down, and the farmers had abandoned their land. He had seen the reasoning when King Hattusili had set up his scheme to have soldiers made Men of the Weapons, to be given farmland and tax breaks instead of a regular salary. *Somebody* had to work the land. It wasn't just the shortage of food; when the farmlands were abandoned, tax revenues imploded.

But Kassu was a city boy. He had not anticipated the impact of the drought, and now the cold that worsened year on year. In the spring the plants would not grow and the trees would not bud; in warmer, moister intervals later in the year you might get a surge of growth, but then the early frost would ruin your crops, and anything that did grow the rabbits would take. They even chewed the bark off your fruit trees. In the very worst months your soil would dry out and blow away, just dust.

And now snow: snow, on Judas Day! In New Hattusa! He had thought last winter was as bad as it could get. What was to come this year?

Zida watched the snowfall suspiciously. "Let's hope it doesn't lie. Don't want to leave tracks. They say Old Hattusa is cut off already. Snow in the passes."

Kassu shrugged. "It always snows on Old Hattusa, up on that plateau. No wonder the kings moved out."

"You'll be warm enough with that plump wife of yours."

"Not if you keep dragging me out of bed in the middle of the night."

Zida laughed. "Who's Palla, by the way?"

"How do you know about Palla?"

"You asked me if I was Palla before I had your dagger at your throat."

"A priest. Cousin of Henti. Quite high up; he works in the Church of Our Lady Mary of Arinna. Knows Angulli, I think, the Father of the Churches."

"So why's he sleeping in your hovel?"

"He's close to Henti. Has been since they were kids. He came out a while back to bless the potato fields, when we heard the blight was in the neighborhood. He's come out to stay a few times since."

Zida looked at Kassu. "That's good of him," he said neutrally. "Can't be much of a priest, though. Didn't save your potatoes, did he?"

Kassu shrugged. As Zida seemed to be guessing in his own crudely insightful way, Palla had actually caused a lot of arguments between Kassu and his wife. Kassu resented the priest's frequent visits, resented having to feed the man. "The will of Teshub Yahweh is not ours to question."

Zida laughed again. "That's for sure." But he spoke softly, for they were heading into empty country now, away from the city. He put his right hand on the hilt of his scabbarded sword, and Kassu found that he'd unconsciously done the same thing.

They moved without a light, but by now their eyes were fully open to the dark. The land, much of it disused farmland, was mostly empty. Once they saw an animal, like a big dog. It could have been a wolf; animals like deer and wolves had been spotted much closer to the city than they used to come. The abandoned countryside was reverting to the wild, some said, even so close to New Hattusa.

Kassu pictured the landscape. New Hattusa sat by the shore of a bay that opened up to the north; to the west a spit of land separated the bay from the Middle Sea. The city was protected by layers of defenses, some inherited from the deeper past, some planned by the Hatti kings when they first moved the capital of their empire here. There were rivers to north and south, and to the east a tremendous New Wall, a mass of Northlander growstone and hard facing stone, that ran from the valley of the Scaramander in the south all the way to the Simoeis in the north. To the west, along the coast, there were sea walls and heavily defended harbors. The bay itself, where dredgers worked constantly to clear away the silt of the rivers, could be closed by the raising of a great chain across its mouth. And at the heart of all these defensive layers sat New Hattusa, Troy, within the ancient walls that had once famously failed to expel the Greeks, but had long since been rebuilt and had not been breached for a thousand years. But there were always threats, especially in these times of hunger and rootlessness. And given the way they were heading, Kassu guessed that this night the threat was approaching from the north, from the line of the Simoeis.

As they neared the river, they sought out scraps of cover, staying away from the high ground, keeping to the shade of desiccated copses. Soon Kassu could smell the river itself, a stench of rot. The water was no more than a dribble through a bed of sour mud.

Then Kassu smelled woodsmoke.

He and Zida found a lying-up point in the ruins of a farmhouse, which they entered cautiously. This must once have been a favored location, a bit of high ground close to the river, even if it was near the boundary of the city's hinterland. Now the house was long looted, burned, looted again, and the interior was open to the sky. There was a huddle of bones lying in one corner, which Kassu didn't look at too closely. The snow, falling heavier now, was collecting on what had once been quite a fine floor of stone tiles.

Crouching behind a broken wall, the two of them peered out at the river valley. On the far side they saw a line of sparks, along the bank. Kassu tried to count the fires, but gave up when he got to thirty.

"There they are," Zida muttered.

"The river won't be hard to cross. Not with the water as low as it is. You could just ford it."

"They might have started already, before it's fully light. I would. Lucky for us a scout spotted them and came running back with the news. This is supposed to be part of the outer defense, along with the New Wall. If I were Himuili I'd build up this border. Walls and ramparts. The river isn't enough of a barrier anymore—you said it yourself."

Kassu shrugged. "But Himuili can only do what the King and the Hazannu and the rest tell him to do." The Hazannu was the city's top administrator, its mayor, a tough ex-soldier called Tiwatapara. "They haven't got the manpower to do everything, not anymore."

"So I'd buy some in. Rus. Scand even. Big hairy idiots the pack of them, but they can fight if you point them in the right direction."

"Who do you think *they* are? Turks? Franks, maybe?"

"Hard to tell yet. Listen. You go back, take the bad news. I'll wait until it's lighter, identify them, count them, maybe spot when they cross, if they haven't started already."

Kassu nodded. Splitting up had its obvious dangers, but the sense of it was obvious too. "All right. Jesus protect you."

Zida, no theologian, laughed at the childish prayer. "Oh, stop off at your farm and tell that priest the Turks are on the way. Watch how fast he runs back to his church so Jesus can protect *him.*"

11

By the time Kassu had got to the city, and had talked his way into the Lower Town through the Sphinx Gate in the Old Wall, the day was well advanced and the *nuntarriyashas* festival was already under way. The narrow alleyways and public places of the Lower Town were crowded with townsfolk, with farmers like himself who'd come in from the country, with traders and merchants hoping to make a quick profit on this day of autumn celebration—and, no doubt, with hungry folk from far and wide who had used the excuse to get into the city in the hope that King Hattusili would be generous in opening up the grain silos.

And, as he tried to get to General Himuili at his station at the King's Gate, Kassu got stuck behind the Procession of the Searching Jesus.

The march was a cacophony of noise, color, dance, working its way around the circuit of the walls in search of the penitent rogue Judas-Telipinu. At the head of the crowd rode Jesus Sharruma Himself, mounted on an ornate chariot. The statue, larger than life, brought out of its church in the citadel for this special day, shone with gold plate and was adorned with precious stones. Jesus wore a Hatti soldier's tunic with golden mail, but also the soft felt cap of a scribe; He carried a sword in one hand and a shepherd's crook in the other, and tremendous palm leaves cast in gold, crossed to make an arch over His head. And under all the grandeur, it was said, the statue's core was a simple wooden figure carved by Jesus Himself, son of a carpenter, in His old-age exile in Old Hattusa.

The chariot itself was a grand affair, driven by two soldiers along with burly guards to keep away any over-eager celebrants. The holy chariots were one responsibility of Kassu's own general Himuili, whose formal rank was Chief of the Chariot Warriors of the Left, an archaic title, with cavalry units having replaced the chariots centuries ago, but its ancient meaning lingered in ceremonials like this. The great chariot bearing the god was followed by a crowd—men, women, children—dancing, chanting prayers and singing hymns, and crying out supplications to Judas-Telipinu, the Missing God, to reveal himself. Jugglers, dancers and conjurers worked the fringes.

This ceremonial commemorated the culminating incident in the life of Jesus the Carpenter, a story familiar to every child of New Hattusa. After years of holy oratory that had infuriated the religious authority in the Hatti's vassal territory of Judea, Jesus had been betrayed by allegations of heresy by one of His own followers, Judas. He was turned over to the Hatti governor, the Lord of the Watchtower, at his palace in Jerusalem, with a recommendation of execution. This Lord, who represented a state with an open pantheon, was repelled by these demands. And meanwhile a rumor swept the city that the rogue apostle Judas had repented, and had confessed the falsity of his allegations. The Lord of the Watchtower decreed that Jesus would be spared if Judas could be found to repeat his recantation in the Lord's own presence. So, throughout the city Jesus' followers began a frantic search for the rogue apostle—and Jesus, some said to His own astonishment, was spared. Much later Jesus was brought to Old Hattusa in chains, but was raised up by priests and scholars, who recognized in the prophet's message an ethical foundation for their own relatively tolerant, compensation-based system of laws.

After His peaceful death Jesus was welcomed into the Hatti pantheon. Now even a king would prostrate himself before Jesus Sharruma, son of Teshub Yahweh, the Storm God, and Mary, His Mother, Goddess of Arinna. With time the incidents of Jesus' life were incorporated into the tapestry of the Hatti religious year—and so every autumn the citizens of New Hattusa went searching for Judas, who had been identified with an older deity called Telipinu, the Missing God, who had to be brought out of hiding to bring the rains.

Usually the *nuntarriyashas* was among the most popular of the many festivals of New Hattusa's religious calendar. But today Kassu, standing impatiently until the procession passed, could sense a tougher edge to the crowd's pleading with Telipinu. No wonder, he thought, for judging by the evidence of the years-long drought, the god had never done such a good job of hiding before. As soon as he could get by, Kassu pushed forward, making for the Pergamos, the old citadel with its temples and palaces. Even away from the procession route the city was crowded—it was always crowded these days. As the drought had worsened and banditry went on the increase, more people from the countryside had got into the habit of coming into the city's safekeeping at night. So the marketplaces had been built over, and even some of the great temple places were crowded with huts and shacks, with fires burning on the marble pavements and children chasing around the pillars.

When Kassu reached the King's Gate in the wall

around the Pergamos he was surprised to find the King himself was already out of his chambers, before the open gate. Shielded by a fine curtain and sitting under a huge parasol to keep off the snow, Hattusili the Sixteenth was a small man, portly despite the years of famine and drought that had plagued his empire—but then he was the King, and kings did not obey normal rules. He was muttering to a chamberlain, a flabby man in a purple robe who had the look of a eunuch to Kassu; the chamberlain was going through a scroll, densely printed.

The King was surrounded on three sides by guards in suits of mail so complete that even their faces were covered, but with ornate embroidered tunics, and elaborately painted almond-shaped shields. And before the King stood the supplicants, ordinary folk of the city in a long line, carefully shepherded by more guards with swords and stabbing spears. They all wore hooded cloaks so they could not look at the King, and he did not have to look at them; they were like mounds of grimy laundry, Kassu thought. At the head of the line they were addressed by more chamberlains with wax tablets for note-taking. On festival days like this you could approach the King in person, and in his presence you would speak to one of his close advisers—never to the King himself, who stayed back from the unwashed, discreetly shielded by a veil of near-transparent linen. The Hatti kings had always had a deep fear of contamination, of filth and dirt and corruption.

To one side of this small piece of theater stood a group of men, some in mail, some in elaborately embroidered courtiers' robes. Earnest, evidently powerful, they spoke gravely and quietly. Kassu recognized Himuili, his own commander, as well as the Hazannu, the mayor, and Angulli Father of the Churches, the empire's high priest—and Prince Arnuwanda, nephew of the King and cousin to Uhhaziti, the *tukhanti*, the crown prince. Behind this group, as Kassu could see through the open gate, the Pergamos itself rose up, the wide avenues lined with grand buildings, the summit of the ancient hill crowned by the royal palace and the Church of the Holy Wisdom. All this Kassu glimpsed in a few heartbeats.

Then a rough hand shoved him in the back and he fell heavily to the cobbled ground.

With a scrape of armor, heavy steel plates stitched into leather, Himuili, Chief of the Chariot Warriors of the Left, came and stood over Kassu and kicked him in the ribs, as it happened just where Zida had got him that morning. "Get up, idiot."

"Yes, sir." Kassu scrambled to his feet.

Himuili was half a head taller than Kassu, maybe forty years old, with a face like a clenched fist. "Kassu, is it?"

"Yes, sir. Of the Fourth Infantry—"

"Shut up."

"Yes, sir."

"I told that idiot Zida to take somebody and go scout out whatever's going on at the Simoeis. He said he'd take you, Kassu. He said you're an idiot."

"Yes, sir."

"But he didn't say you're an idiot that deserves to get his head stuck on a pike for failing to prostate himself before My Sun," and they both nodded their heads at the King's title. "A dozen lashes. Report to the wall barracks later."

"Thank you, sir."

"Shut up." Himuili beckoned, and led Kassu back to the group of high-ups.

Father of the Churches Angulli regarded Kassu with curiosity, Prince Arnuwanda with a kind of grim readiness despite his youth, and the Hazannu stared with contempt. They were all tall, well-fed men, like great trees standing around Kassu, and he prayed that his tongue wouldn't tie itself up.

"Well?" Himuili snapped. "Good news from the Simoeis, or not?"

Kassu briskly described what he had seen on the far

bank of the river, the fires he had counted, his own rough estimate of the force that was approaching the city.

Arnuwanda spoke now. "The question is who they are. The Franks rarely come so close to the city and we can usually buy them off anyhow . . ." The prince was no more than twenty years old. He wore his hair long but loose, his upper lip was clean-shaven, his beard carefully shaped, and his young skin shone with expensive oils. He had a new tattoo on his cheek, a circles-and-bar design that looked like a souvenir of his long summer visit to Northland. His accent was smooth, Kassu thought, but oddly spiced, probably thanks to the Greek and Northlander tutors who had been imported to educate him. But he held himself like a warrior, having been educated in those arts by men like Himuili, and having ridden out in battle at the age of fifteen, or, some said, even younger. The Hatti had always needed their princes to be generals. "If it's nomads," the prince went on, "we might have more trouble. Difficult wretches who don't know when they're defeated. They just scatter on their ponies hoping to lure you into traps—"

"If they haven't eaten their ponies already," Angulli said, and he giggled. This was the Father of the Churches, Brother of Jesus; he sounded slightly drunk to Kassu.

Himuili rolled his eyes. "We've ways of dealing with nomads, sir. The Turks are more persistent nuisances, especially now they've captured so much territory in eastern Anatolia. Gives them a base to fight from, you see."

Arnuwanda nodded. "But at least, again, we know what we're dealing with. The problem will be, as always, raising the manpower. And feeding the men." Another swirl of snow came down, thicker than before. Arnuwanda pulled his expensive-looking purple cloak tight around him.

"Not the Turks," came a booming voice, immediately recognized by Kassu. "And not the Franks either."

There was a commotion among the outer layers of the guard. Zida, for it was he, strode boldly toward the group of dignitaries. He had taken off his cloak and had wrapped it around some kind of trophy that dripped deep red blood as he walked.

"Let him through," Himuili snapped. "Let him through, I say!"

Zida, standing before his general, panted hard. Even the King, Kassu noticed, peered out of his linen tent to see what the fuss was about.

"You've been running," Kassu murmured.

"Faster than you, farm boy."

"A dozen lashes for your failure to prostrate," Himuili snapped.

"Of course, sir."

"Tell me what you have."

"The identity of our attackers." Zida held up his bloody bundle and pulled away the cloak—to reveal a human head, roughly severed at a neck from which blood still dripped, a pale face with a heavy mustache. Zida held it up by a hank of red hair. There was a collective gasp, a wave of shock that spread out through the crowd of onlookers. Even the hooded supplicants were distracted, even the King. Reflexively the guards clustered closer around their master.

Kassu spotted his wife, Henti, on the edge of the crowd, dressed in her *nuntarriyashas* finery, the robe shabby, faded, old, as everything was in New Hattusa these days, but still she looked radiant in his eyes. But she had come with her cousin Palla, the priest, who probably had business with Angulli. Side by side, the cousins looked very alike. Kassu saw that Henti held the priest's arm firmly as she stared at the head.

Himuili stepped forward. With his thumb, he opened one of the relic's closed eyelids, to reveal an eye as blue as the sea in summer. *"Rus,"* he growled.

"In fact he found me before I found him," Zida admitted. "He crept up behind me. Lucky I got him first. Otherwise—"

"Otherwise you would have died uselessly," Himuili murmured, gazing at the head. "And all that expensive training wasted. Careless, that. Make that two dozen lashes."

"Thank you, sir."

"But he *is* Rus. You established that?"

"Yes, sir. He lived long enough to convince me. But they aren't just Rus out there."

"Who, then?"

"Scand."

Another gasp of dismay.

"While he was begging for his life, he said it wasn't his fault."

"What isn't?" Himuili snapped.

"Their emigration."

"You mean their invasion. The assault they're mounting."

"No, sir. *Emigration* is the word he used. His Hatti was quite good. Well, it's no surprise. He said he's served in the armies of My Sun, a mercenary regiment. He said, *emigration*," Zida repeated. "And he said they've been driven to it by the drought and now the ice in their own lands, and by the wave of Scand that came down from their distant lands further north yet. The Scand sacked Kiev, it seems, before they all came to an arrangement."

Himuili grunted. "That's nice. An arrangement to attack us."

"Yes, sir."

Arnuwanda paced, fists clenched, the muscles in his bare arms bulging. "The Rus! Do you know any history, good Himuili?"

"Not as much as I should, sir," the general said drily.

"Throughout its existence the empire of the Hatti has been besieged by enemies, within and without. Well, we fought off the Kaskans and the Arzawans, and the Greeks and the Persians and the Carthaginians and the Arabs and the Mongols, and we're holding off the Turks—but now this! The Rus have been our allies. We gave them our god, they rejected Thor and Odin for Jesus! And now they turn on us."

Zida, eyes cast down respectfully, said, "But they're starving, sir. And freezing. This fellow told me about his own family, before he died."

Angulli laughed. "He must have taken a long time dying, soldier!" said the Brother of Jesus.

"That he did, sir. This isn't an army; it's a people on the move. They have made up their minds to come south—to come *here*, for there's nowhere else for them to go. So they came down their rivers where their traders have sailed for centuries, and crossed the Asian Sea to our shores. Their Khagan is with them, and just now he is preparing to lay siege to our port of Byzantos."

Arnuwanda grunted. "Which will cut our trade routes to the Asian Sea and the continent beyond, not that they aren't withered already."

"Sir, I think—"

And at that moment the assassins struck.

Two ordinary-looking supplicants broke from the head of the line, pushed past guards who had been watching Zida rather than attending their duty, threw back their hoods to reveal shocks of red hair, and opened their cloaks to reveal single-bladed battleaxes. And they fell on the King.

Kassu saw it. Saw the first strike lay open the King's chest, splaying ribs wide. Saw Hattusili the Sixteenth, still alive, looking down shocked at his own beating heart, his spilling organs, which looked like any other man's, Kassu thought, battlefield memories flooding back.

Then the guards were on them, led by Himuili himself, then Zida, and there was a brutal struggle. Arnuwanda went to the aid of his uncle. Kassu would have followed, but an officer snapped an order for him to stay back and help round up the other supplicants, in case there were any more Rus assassins among them.

So it was that Kassu saw his wife in the churning crowd. Saw her, terrified, folded in the arms of the young priest beside her. And saw Palla lift her face and kiss her full on the lips, before wrapping his arms around her and leading her away.

12

I t took until the equinox for Pyxeas to make the arrangements for his epic journey to far Cathay—and, Avatak suspected, to allow his old body to recover from the sea journey from Coldland only months before.

The family, led by Pyxeas' niece Rina, were opposed to him going at all, and they pressured a doctor, a family friend called Ontin, to tell him he wasn't strong enough. But Ontin was about as old as Pyxeas, and Avatak thought he secretly envied Pyxeas' boldness, and he would not stand in the way. After that, Rina, with very bad grace, insisted on accompanying Pyxeas on the first leg of the journey, as far as an eastern city called Hantilios, where, maybe, the old man would see sense and come back home again.

So they got packed up, and there was a day of farewells. Alxa, Rina's daughter, seemed particularly upset to see him go, as if she feared she wouldn't see him again.

And then they were gone.

They headed south down the Etxelur Way, and the Wall slowly receded behind them. Then, by canal boat and on foot, they traveled the length of Northland, following tremendous avenues and crossing bridges over wide canals, and Avatak tried to absorb the scale of this tremendous, orderly, sparsely populated country. It was a long, slow journey in itself, and occasionally Rina muttered about alternative ways to cross Northland, such as by steam caravan. But it seemed that the scholar wanted to see his country, to cross it on foot as his ancestors had for uncounted generations, one more time before his so-called "longwinter" closed in. After a few days, however, he did relent a little, and allowed Rina to hire for him a horse-drawn carriage, though to use horses was thoroughly *not* the Northland way.

On the southern coast of Northland they came to a port on the estuary called the Cut, a great wound that ran between the southern shores of Northland and Albia and the northern beaches of Gaira, giving ultimately to the open seas of the Western Ocean. Here they boarded a small boat, booked ahead by Rina, and as part of a small flotilla crossed the estuary and made their way eastward along the Gairan coast to a wide river mouth. Waves broke on a nondescript beach, and marsh and wooded hills could be seen beyond. From here they would sail upriver toward the great city of Parisa.

Inland, the countryside was quite similar to southern Northland and Albia, rolling and green, though even this far south they still saw the odd white splash of remnant winter ice. Gaira was a quilt of ancient nations, mostly Frankish, immigrants a thousand years before, but some older stock. The empires of the Middle Sea with their cities of stone had never come this far north, and so the Gairans' various cultures had been shaped by local influences, the Northlanders, the farmers to the south—even the otherworldly Albians of their great forest to the west. So Avatak saw a mix of neat farms surrounded by stretches of woodland, and then a swathe of lowland worked and managed as the Northlanders did, and then a town of stone where the natives sold lumber or minerals to merchants from the Middle Sea. But an older history survived; some of these communities were still centered on the circles of mighty stones bequeathed by distant ancestors.

At last they approached Parisa. A Frankish settlement, this was the westernmost city on the Continent, Pyxeas said, a trading conduit for Northland. Here they would board a steam caravan that would take them onward east in comparative comfort. They had a couple of days and nights before they were to leave. While Pyxeas locked himself away in a rented room with his books and scrolls and calculations, and Rina organized the final details of their onward journey, Avatak wandered around Parisa.

He had never been to a city before, and he was overwhelmed by the size of it, the buildings of smartly cut stone or shabby wattle and daub crammed in side by side on both banks of a languid river, and jammed in even more tightly on a central island. He walked through alleyways walled by shops and stalls and taverns, stepped over open drains running through the cobbles, and climbed rickety bridges to the central island, which was dominated by sprawling temples dedicated to the gods of the peoples who traded here, from the ancient forest gods of the Albians to the enigmatic Jesus Sharruma of the east. People rushed everywhere, or labored in open-to-the-street manufactories, or noisily sold wares in the many marketplaces. Pyxeas said the name of this place came from what the people who had founded it called themselves, in their own tribal tongue; they were "The People Who Worked" or "The Busy People," and looking around their city Avatak could well believe it. The place was nothing like the orderly, rigidly laid out, sparsely populated communities of lower Northland, or indeed like the tiny fishing villages of Avatak's homeland. His only comparison was with the crowded communities of the Wall itself. It was as if a District had been cut from that great structure and emptied out, a heap of stone and wriggling people. But the Wall, of course, would have utterly overwhelmed this cramped, smoky, shabby place.

And even here, far to the south of Northland, Avatak saw the mark of winter and the long drought: frosts every clear morning, the late potato crops struggling in the parched fields outside the city.

But Parisa, for all its detail and curiosities and wonders, was only the start of their true journey. Pyxeas warned him not to be too impressed. "You'll forget this ant-hill when you see the mighty cities of Cathay."

Rina, coldly disapproving of the whole enterprise, said nothing.

The day before their departure they walked down to the line terminus on the city's eastern side, with hastily hired servants bringing their luggage after them.

Avatak had ridden steam caravans before. In Northland their gleaming iron trails crisscrossed the countryside, north to south, east to west. And then there was the famous Iron Way, the line that ran along the crest of the Wall itself, uniting the far-flung Districts of the Wall and their peoples.

But the great caravan to Hantilios was a different beast. Of course it was like a Northland steam caravan in its fundamentals; much of it was built and maintained by Northland engineers. But it was so much *bigger* than any caravan Avatak had ever seen. Not one but two engines would haul passenger carriages studded in a chain of rusty trucks full of Albian coal for fuel, and freight carriages, and specialized coaches that looked like engineering shops on wheels. Pyxeas said that though the southern Continent was a crowded and civilized place ("Somewhat civilized," Rina corrected him), and though the Parisa-Hantilios line was a marvel of Northlander engineering, the technical support in these southern lands was sparse, and on the road the engineers would have to rely on their own resources.

The point of the caravan line was of course trade. The Parisa-Hantilios line, the longest in the world to date, had been laid at huge expense to connect two great trading centers: Parisa, a hub for goods passing to and from Northland, Albia, Gaira, and even far Scand; and Hantilios, central to the Continent, which lay on trading routes connecting north and south, west and east. So the bulk of the caravan was freight carriages laden with lumber and coal and tin and gold from Albia, furs and amber from Scand, and barrels of Kirike-fish from Northland itself, all bound for the needy markets of the east.

It was the passenger carriages, though, that caught Avatak's eye. In Northland such carriages were plain but functional boxes of steel and wood with sturdy windowpanes. They were even heated in winter (and increasingly in the summer too) by pipes through which steam was bled from the engine. The carriages here in Parisa, though, were topped by what looked like dome-shaped tents, covered for now by sooty leathers which boys were cleaning of grime as the passengers arrived. Avatak found the carriage they had been assigned, and clambered through a doorway, pushing aside a heavy flap. The tent was a frame of bent wooden slats heaped with vividly colored velvet. The floor was covered with a thick carpet, and there were couches to lie on, and trunks to store your luggage and food and drink. The windows were holes in the wall covered with leather panels scraped so thin you could see through them.

Pyxeas smiled at the boy's marveling reaction. "We will be transported by Northlander ingenuity," he said, "but on the way we will live in a yurt that the Great Khan in Daidu might not be ashamed of." For that, it seemed, was the basis of the design of the shelter, the portable houses of the nomadic tribesmen of the plains of Asia. "There was a scheme to build a new caravan line east into the heart of Asia itself, perhaps all the way to Daidu.

The representatives of the Khans traveled west to try out the technology."

"And so to snag their attention," Rina said cynically, "the engineers built these fake yurts on the back of caravan carriages, just to make the Khan's people feel at home. A blatant bit of salesmanship, Uncle."

Pyxeas was grumpy. "One must take the world as it is," he snapped back. "And anyway it worked. The pan-Asia line would have been built by now if not for the weather, and you and I, Avatak, would be traveling to Daidu in heated comfort all the way."

Rina snorted.

Avatak, his imagination snagged by the idea of crossing an unknown country in a tent as if he were a Mongol warrior himself, could barely wait for the journey to begin.

It took a full day and night to load up the caravan. Pyxeas' party spent the final night in their carriage, the three of them bundled up on their couches, separated by partitions of embroidered cloth. The yurt was comfortable, though not yet heated, as the engine was idle. They lit their lanterns, and they had a water tank topped up by servants, even a small stove and a food store; it was a home away from home, and Avatak enjoyed exploring more of its little gadgets. He slept badly that night, however, such was the racket of the loading.

Not long after dawn the caravan was ready to go. As the great engine built up its head of steam the protective leather shells were stripped off and the yurts were revealed as vividly colored pods, scarlet and green and purple, studded between the huge gray freight cars. The passengers stuck heads out of doors to see what was going on as servants loaded final bits of luggage into the carts, and engineers checked the strapping of the cargo bundles and the coupling between the carriages, and priests of a dozen faiths blessed the great caravan and those who would ride in it.

The Parisans turned out too, men and women and

many grubby-looking children, and vendors selling drink and food and little wooden toy caravans. The departure of such a great caravan was rare enough that it was an event for the folk of the city. Pyxeas told Avatak that more people could travel on a single one of these huge continental caravans than lived in all of Coldland, and Avatak, who didn't believe everything the sage told him, believed that.

At last there was a mighty shriek of a steam whistle that made the children clap their hands to their ears, and a growl like some huge beast, and the engine clawed its way along the track, the carriages bumping after it. Steam and smoke billowed from the engine stack, and Rina and Pyxeas retreated inside. But Avatak hung out of the yurt as the city receded, and he looked back at the shining curve of the caravan as it followed a great arc of rail across flat, chalky countryside, and the smoke streamed back in the bright air.

Once in motion the yurt was even more comfortable, steam-warmed now they were under way. The first stop came at about midday, beside a small service building in the middle of dried-up farmland. Servants hurried off the caravan and set up a kind of yurt, much larger than the rest. This was a kitchen, an eating hall, and soon the passengers were served a healthy meal of fish from Parisa, wine from Greater Greece and pickled eel from Northland. The country around the stop seemed empty enough, but there were guards, a troop of soldiers from Parisa, others from Hantilios. Their officers set up a perimeter and kept careful watch until the caravan was loaded and on the move again.

The caravan moved at a brisk and steady speed. Before the first day was done the nature of the country was already changing, with the chalky densely farmed plain giving way to higher ground grazed by cattle and sheep. Overnight they traveled south down a long river valley. By midday the next day they had reached another town, whose name Avatak never learned—another trading center, smaller than Parisa and subtly different in character. Here they offloaded some goods, loaded up more, took on coal and water, and pulled away again.

They reached a sea coast and followed the shore eastward, passing through more cities and towns. Looking out to the south, to the caravan's right-hand side, Avatak saw the ocean, glistening blue rather than a cold gray like the northern seas, and without ice as far as he could see. Fishing boats sailed from neat harbors, a variety of designs strange to his eyes, with billowing sails or rows of oars like insects' legs. This was the Middle Sea, Pyxeas told Avatak, itself a great and ancient transport highway. And to the caravan's left, when the route cut north away from the coast, tremendous mountains loomed on the horizon, capped with white, their flanks streaked with tongues of ice. To Avatak this was a wistful and unexpected reminder of home.

While the mountains were in view Pyxeas peered from the yurt, his rheumy eyes squinting in the chill of the breeze, sketching, making notes, muttering, frustrated at how little he could see. "The glaciers are growing," he told Avatak. "Harbingers of the coming of the longwinter. Any record of their growth is useful."

"It is like home," Avatak ventured. "We have such mountains. The ice, the white."

"Of course you do. I saw them. But here the cold mantles the mountain because of altitude rather than latitude. By which I mean . . ."

But Avatak wasn't listening. He had been trying to express his mild homesickness, rather than ask for a lesson on the nature of ice and cold.

"Oh, do shut that flap," Rina complained. "You're letting all the heat out. I don't know why in the mothers' mercy you're carting that Coldland boy along with you. You're going east, not north. You could hardly choose a less suitable companion. I mean, *listen* to him. That dreadful guttural language—those words as long as a book! Everybody's been staring since Parisa."

"None less suitable? On the contrary." Pyxeas pulled back into the yurt. "He is entirely suitable for the role. It's precisely because this boy is so far from his home environment that he fascinates me so—he demonstrates the suppleness of the human mind. *And* he is my reserve. Like the second walking stick I have packed in my luggage."

"Walking stick? What on earth are you talking about, Uncle?"

But Pyxeas wouldn't say, and Avatak didn't know what he meant, and the talk petered out.

The journey had been untroubled save for one mechanical failure, a half-day lost while a split boiler had been welded. But now a new problem arose, with the iron road itself. The caravan was halted and scouts ran ahead.

Rails were missing; even some of the rows of wooden slats pressed into the ground to support the rails had been removed. The workers and engineers gossiped in a dozen tongues. Avatak learned that the theft of rails was becoming more common. These were turbulent times, the country full of raiders and nestspills. Though a rail took some organization to lift and carry away, its iron could be sold on, or turned into weapons, or put to a hundred other uses. And as the weather turned colder the wood from the support beds was valued as fuel. Alternatively, sometimes bandits would lift a rail or two in order to stop a caravan and raid it.

But the problem could be fixed. Avatak was astonished to discover that one of the caravan's massive freight wagons was loaded with spare rails, and another with wooden slats for the base. The engineers called for volunteers from the passengers to help with the reconstruction, and Avatak, feeling restless after his immobility in the yurt, stepped forward readily. The work, quickly organized, was heavy but easy: lug the rails and supports from the carriages, push the supports into the soft ground, lay the rails down with careful leveling by the engineers with their plumb lines and water gauges, and hammer home massive rivets. The guards kept up diligent patrols.

Soon the track was fixed, the caravan reloaded, and they were off again. They reached a broad, rich valley that they followed east. Pyxeas, earnestly sketching maps, told Avatak that this was the north of a large peninsula called Greater Greece. They reached another sea coast, and at last they were a mere few hours from their destination, where they would spend much of the winter.

Hantilios! The name seemed to be on everybody's lips, up and down the caravan, and people poked their heads out of the felt-laden carriages to look around and swap bits of gossip. Even old Pyxeas stirred with interest, putting aside his obsessive note-taking. Avatak, who barely understood where he was, felt excitement build.

But Rina merely sighed. "Hantilios! I can smell it already." She retreated to the back of the yurt.

13

Hantilios was not like Northland, not like Parisa. It was something new again, to Avatak's wide-open mind.

It was a city built on islands scattered over a lagoon, crowded, cramped, untidy and nowhere level. The only clear area in the whole city surrounded the palace of the Watchman, an ancient title for the city's ruler. The islands were joined by bridges of wood and stone, some more sound than others. Alleyways ran between the houses and shops, connecting marketplace to temple to granary to dock, but only foot traffic and the occasional horse used the alleyways, for they were too narrow for anything else—and besides the true roads of Hantilios were the waterways, the natural streams between the islands supplemented by the bold straight lines of artificial canals. Just as the alleys were crowded day and night with people and goods, so the waterways were constantly packed with vessels, some no larger than the simple kayaks used by Avatak's people, some elegant shallow-draft barges that were driven by poles pushed into the murky water, and a few larger ships that looked as if they could brave the open ocean, so close to one another in the lanes that their hulls rubbed.

Rina warned Avatak not to fall into the water, or to drink it unboiled, for the common belief in Northland was that the Hantilians used their waterways not just as roads but as sewers too, and the place was one big fetid swamp. Well, it wasn't without its aromas, and the water didn't look too clean, but it was not as bad as Rina seemed to believe, Avatak quickly learned. Hantilios had once been a Hatti city, endowed as a trading center by the Hatti King who had allowed the city to be named after himself—"Watchman" was a relic of a Hatti title for a local governor—and even now, though it was fiercely independent, the city had retained more than a trace of the Hatti's famous obsession with cleanliness.

And in this age, clean or not, the city was busier than it had ever been. Hantilios was "the hub of the world's trade," as Pyxeas called it, connected to all points by good routes on the water and overland. Now the long drought and the cold winters were stirring people up all across the Continent and beyond, and they all seemed to be flowing through Hantilios. There were parties of Germans from the north seeking passage to Greater Greece or Africa, and Carthaginians from the west trying to secure grain imports from Islamic Egypt, and Hatti and Muslim traders from the east looking for new western trading links as those to the east were increasingly disrupted, and so on. The city was a mosaic of skin tones and costume styles and languages, and in the teeming markets Avatak glimpsed goods from all over the world: spices, drugs, fabrics, weapons, gems, minerals from iron to gold and silver, ivory and wool and ostrich feathers—and slaves, many, many slaves, desolate-looking folk, some whole families together, brought from who knew where.

In this swarming city Pyxeas was looking for one man, a Northlander merchant called Xavu, who was to be the guide for the next stage of the journey. They had no address for Xavu; all they could do was put out contacts through traders and various officials and wait for the man to get in touch. As the waiting wore on, Rina grew increasingly impatient. The caravan back to Parisa wasn't going to wait for long, and when it left Rina intended to be on it, Xavu or no Xavu.

On the third day a messenger, a barefoot boy, brought them a note, inviting them to a meeting. It was not from Xavu. It was from a Hatti, a woman called Uzzia.

Both Pyxeas and Rina were frustrated. But they could see no alternative but to go and meet the stranger, and Avatak accompanied them.

Uzzia's home, on the outskirts of the city, turned out to be not large but quite grand, a walled compound with a spacious house and garden within. "In the Hatti style," Pyxeas mused, as a servant showed the three of them in. "Just like New Hattusa."

"Hmm," said Rina, but under her breath as their host entered. "And I suppose *she* is dressed in the Hatti style too, is she?"

"Welcome!" The word was in clipped Northlander. Uzzia was dressed like a man, Avatak thought at first, with a tunic belted at the waist, breeches, scuffed knee-high boots, hair tied back in a queue like a Hatti warrior. But this was a woman, aged perhaps forty, with a sturdy frame and a pleasant, weathered face. There was a whiff of the road about her, of dust, of horses. She glanced over her visitors. "You are the Northlanders. Welcome, Pyxeas, Rina, and . . ."

"Avatak. The boy's name is Avatak."

"You were not mentioned in the note to Xavu. What are you—a Coldlander?"

"Yes, lady."

"Well, you may be from a cold country but I hope you like hot mulled wine, for that's what I'm drinking today. Please, please."

She led them across a courtyard to the house, and into a lounge. The servant who had been at the door briskly brought them drinks, the mulled wine they had been promised, and water, fruit juice. Avatak took a cup of water and sat cautiously on a couch he shared with Pyxeas. Rina took her own chair opposite Uzzia, who sat relaxed on a three-legged stool. Avatak glanced cautiously around. This was a living room, it had a hearth, unlit today, and a rug of woven wool on the floor and a tapestry on the wall. But there was traveling gear heaped in one corner—a leather cloak, bridle gear, a whip—and a desk piled with scrolls and parchments. A working room, then. A quilted coat hung on the back of the door, heavy-looking, practical.

Rina got down to business. "We were expecting our countryman Xavu, who was to arrange passage for my uncle and his companion to Cathay."

"Of course you were. And I intercepted your note to him. Well, he picks up my mail when I'm away. Unfortunately Xavu is out of town, and has been gone for months. Too long."

Pyxeas frowned. "Is he in trouble?"

"Possibly. Or exploring some new opportunity. These are turbulent times, my friend; things change constantly, and communications are terrible. Either way, he's not here. And besides he couldn't have helped you—not old Xavu."

Rina snorted. "You're sure of that, are you?"

Uzzia smiled at her. "You want to get all the way to Daidu, don't you? The writ of the Khans isn't as strong as it used to be, what with the drought and the bandits. It would have been too much for dear old Xavu. But you're in luck."

Rina's eyes narrowed. "In Xavu's place—you? Is that what you're offering?"

"I've made many journeys east. I've even been as far as Daidu, once. Yes, I believe I could get you there, even in these troubled times."

"For a price!"

"That goes without saying."

"You are a woman," Rina said coldly.

Pyxeas stiffened. "Many of our great Northlanders were women, niece. From the great Ana onward."

Uzzia smiled. "I'm stronger than some men, and smarter than most of them. The secret of my success. Trust me."

And, looking at her, Avatak realized he did trust her, completely, after just this brief meeting. He really believed she could do what she claimed.

Pyxeas leaned forward. "But why, madam? Why would you do this? There must be easier ways to make a profit. Why would a Hatti wish to guide two Northlanders to Daidu?"

She seemed impressed by the fact that he'd asked the question. "You go beyond haggling over fees to ask me why. I hope you'll do me the courtesy of letting me ask you the same."

He nodded curtly.

"I do this because I sense opportunity here. In you. I want to achieve more with my life than scraping a bit of petty profit in a place like Hantilios. I am Hatti, yes, but more than that. I am of the royal line."

Rina snorted laughter. "Everybody in New Hattusa says they're of the royal line."

"Perhaps they are," Uzzia said evenly. "Our dynasty, my family, is thousands of years old, the only dynasty ever to have ruled the Hatti empire. After so long, yes, perhaps every Hatti save the slaves has royal blood. But in my case, the divergence from the root stock is only a few generations back. My grandmother was Tawananna, which is a word that means senior queen. She was pushed aside by enemies at court. We remember, my family."

"And you would have your place back," Rina said, sneering.

Uzzia kept her gaze on Pyxeas. "You say you are a man of learning. I have read history, and I have learned the story of a previous Tawananna, called Kilushepa, who more than two thousand years ago was pivotal in a stratagem that saved the Hatti, and indeed Northland."

Rina frowned. "You speak of the Trojan Invasion. Yes, Northland was saved. Yes, otherwise my ancestors would have been enslaved, Northland ploughed up for crops. But we were saved through a terrible act we call the Black Crime. It is a history that shames us."

"Then you should be glad your ancestors were stronger-minded than you are, madam, or you would not be here to indulge in that shame. As for the Hatti, we venerate Kilushepa. She is remembered as a hero; she made the Hatti great again, where we might have been forgotten. Erased. And at her side was a warrior princess called Mi, said to have been a Northlander. Imagine that!"

"And you want to be a new Kilushepa—is that it?"

"Not that. But the Hatti kings have little contact with Cathay. Who knows what might come of such a venture, especially at times like this? Ambition is easily mocked, but times of crisis are also times of opportunity. What one must do is to seize that opportunity when it comes along. And I sense," she said, turning to Pyxeas, "that in you that opportunity might have come knocking on my door."

Pyxeas smiled. "On Xavu's door, strictly speaking."

"Now your turn," she said bluntly. "You are an old man, yet you want to make a journey halfway around this hazardous world of ours. You must want to achieve something very badly."

"I do."

"Tell me what that is."

And he began to speak of the weather.

Avatak recognized Uzzia's expression; she was like a student struggling to keep up in one of Pyxeas' classes. "And why must you go to Daidu to pursue this?"

"Because the scholars in Cathay—and they have managed to continue their work under the Mongol dynasty—have been making complementary studies to mine. Measurements of other aspects of the world, the atmosphere—oh, it is too much to explain without my scrolls! Suffice it to say that I believe that putting together my studies with the science of Cathay, specifically of a scholar called Bolghai with whom I have corresponded—"

Uzzia held up a hand. "Tell it more simply. Tell me why you want to go to Daidu. The real reason, the core of it."

He thought for a moment, baffled by the question.

Avatak said, "He wants to save the world."

They were all staring at him, Rina openmouthed, Pyxeas oddly moist-eyed.

And Uzzia—Uzzia was excited. The Hatti woman leaned forward. "When can you leave?"

"Mad," Rina said. "You're all mad. Do you have any more of that mulled wine? The sooner I'm back home in Etxelur the better, though the mothers only know what the weather must be like there . . ."

14

For Crimm, as for most people, the day of the Autumn Blizzard started normally, like any other day. With no warning of what was to come.

That morning, when Crimm got to the dock on the Wall's ocean face, Ayto, his navigator, was already waiting, with, Crimm counted, only two missing of the *Sabet*'s ten-man crew, their gear at their feet, a heap of provisions on the growstone ledge beside them. Not a bad turnout for a blustery, blowy autumn morning. At least there hadn't been any frost, for once, and up here the growstone footing was always sound.

The *Sabet* herself looked solid enough, but she had had to be tied up outside the shelter of her berth, a deep notch cut into the Wall growstone, for the level of the sea had now dropped so much that she would have grounded at low tide if they'd tried to take her in. The engineers were talking about hacking into the growstone to deepen the berths, but that was only worth doing if the sea level wasn't going to rise again—or indeed if it didn't fall further. Well, *Sabet* had brought Crimm and the crew, and

Uncle Pyxeas, safely back across a berg-strewn sea from Coldland, and had been out almost daily in the months since then. Crimm would have been happier if she could have had a spell in dry dock, but it had been a tough summer, and Northland needed as much cod as could be hauled in, so here they were. This morning, in fact, most of the fleet was already out on the deep ocean.

Ayto, bundled up in a heavy fur, was glaring out to sea. He was over forty years old, about five years older than Crimm, and his face, weathered, scarred by his years on the ocean as well as his boisterous life on land, was crumpled with suspicion. Crimm, respecting Ayto's experience, stood by him, inspecting sea and sky. The ocean was the color of steel, flecked with white where it churned under the wind. Waves broke against the impassive Wall, throwing up spumes of spray over the fishermen. The wind itself, coming straight from the north, was not exactly warm, though not as cold as it had been. But the northern horizon was obscured by mist and a bank of thick gray-black cloud that seemed to churn as Crimm watched.

Ayto moistened a finger and lifted it to the wind. "Northerly. Wet."

"Yes." Crimm looked up. There was an odd, translucent quality to the air, something silver about the light. "That's a snow sky, I think. Early for snow. Not even a month after the equinox!"

Ayto shrugged. "Not unheard of. It's been a funny year from start to finish, thanks to your uncle's famous longwinter, no doubt."

"We're not going out in that."

Ayto nodded curtly. "Let's make her secure and get into the warm. At least that's what I'll be doing. While you'll be getting into your famous Annid of Annids."

"You're just coarse. Jealous, and coarse."

Ayto laughed.

So they called the crew together, those who had turned up, and they got to work on the boat, taking down the two big sails and the main mast, lashing her tight to her berth. They worked fast and efficiently, a competent team. Much of this drill was what they'd go through if a storm approached at sea.

And then, quite suddenly, the first snowflakes came billowing out of the northern sky, big, moist, sticky. The snow clung to the men's furs and their beards, falling so thick and fast that it quickly started building up on the decking and the berth. The wind picked up, becoming colder, and ice coalesced on the rigging. Crimm worked on, the snow blasting in his face, hands rubbing raw as he hauled at the thick rope, debating whether to dig his heavy mittens out of his coat.

It was universally agreed that the single most spectacular location on the Iron Way east of Northland, if you discounted the run along the parapet of the Wall itself, was the viaduct that spanned the great estuary of the World River. On this viaduct now, heading back west toward Northland, Alxa could peer out of the thick glass windows of her cabin and look north over the ocean, or south over the mighty river itself, its broad body studded with shipping, its banks clustered with docks and towns, the country beyond incised with fields and drainage ditches. But this morning Alxa couldn't appreciate the view at all.

For one thing, the caravan had been stuck here for an hour, right in the middle of the viaduct. The officer who had come to check on her steam-fueled heating box had told her that the engineers had decided to stop and fit snowblades. Snowblades, this early in the season! What a waste of time—so she'd thought. And yet she had to admit the engineers had been right, for even while the caravan had been waiting the clouds had bubbled up from the north, and the first big fat flakes had come swirling in to slap against the small panes of her windows.

On top of that, her head was still full of the arguments she'd had with her mother about Great-Uncle Pyxeas. As she'd grown to know the old man who had come back into her life at the midsummer Giving, she'd come to admire him hugely. Alxa was fifteen years old. She wasn't sure what she wanted to do with her life, not yet, and as far as she could see, as the weather closed in on the world, her options were diminishing. But she had felt she wanted to help Pyxeas, if she could. She didn't understand his developing theories, and she didn't quite believe his doom-laden warnings of a frozen world—or maybe, a small voice nagged, she didn't *want* to believe them. But at least this increasingly frail old man was trying to understand, as he had been for all his life, including the three years he had spent shivering his ass off in Coldland, trying to scry the mechanisms that drove the changing world, with his peculiar muddle of astronomical wobbles and a dance of sea and air.

Then, as a horrible summer ended and a worse winter started to close in, he had shot off to Cathay! She had wanted to go with him, to help him on his journey, but her mother wouldn't allow it. That had caused a huge row, and in the compromise that emerged her *mother* had ended up disappearing to Hantilios with Pyxeas, while Alxa had been given the consolation prize of a trip to the World River, as part of an Annid mission that Rina had been supposed to support. It had been a marvelous journey, but it didn't resolve anything.

And now, trying to get back, here she was, stuck, alone, far from home.

The wind picked up. A new volley of snow slammed against the north-facing side of her cabin, so solid and dense that from her windows she could see nothing but driving flakes coming at her from gray infinity, like one of Nelo's look-deep drawings. The cabin shuddered and creaked, rocking slightly. She clutched the rim of the padded wooden bench on which she sat, and wondered when the engineers would get the caravan moving again.

When the snow started to come down Mago was taking a walk along the Wall Way, the broad track that followed the foot of the Wall. There was some flooding here—had been for days, it seemed, maybe the big mechanical pumps the Northlanders boasted about weren't working so well—and you had to watch where you walked.

But the Wall itself loomed above him, busy as ever, crowded, complicated, a vertical city that stretched to left and right as far as he could see. Today was some kind of market day, and stalls had been set up before the row of shops, manufactories and warehouses along the Wall's lowest run, just wooden posts fixed into slots in the grow-stone walls and then draped with big awnings of cloth or leather, a simple way to increase selling space. And now, even though the whole area was stuffed with nestspills— pathetic little groups of them, whole families sitting in the dirt, empty hands held out in the cold—the grand folk of Etxelur were out shopping for jewelery and shoes, and dishes and cutlery and pots and pans, and knick-knacks brought here by traders from across the known world.

Mago had been in Northland for four months now, and since his uncle Barmocar had taken so long to close his negotiations over supplies to Carthage of Etxelur's disgusting salted fish, it looked as if the weather was going to close in and they would be stuck in this dismal lightless hellhole for the winter. Well, Mago wasn't going to be intimidated by the mighty Wall, even though he knew intellectually that you could take all of Carthage and its environs, wad it up and stuff it inside the Wall's great carcass, and it would be utterly lost. For, he had learned, the Wall wasn't quite the symbol of smug unity some Northlanders would have you believe. The Wall was so vast that you had to think of it as being many communities, several cities with separate traditions, even separate customs and dialects, all joined in this one giant structure. And at least once, he had heard it murmured, there had been an intramural war when one of these culturally distinct blocks had defied the will of the rest—a War of the Districts—but you wouldn't find any reference to that in Northland's official histories.

The snow fell suddenly, just dropping as if somebody had emptied a tremendous bucket over his head.

Shielding his eyes and looking up, he saw that it was coming from the north, the ocean side, big fat flakes swirling over the Wall's parapet and billowing down in sheets to the ground below. Already it was gathering on the ledges and protrusions and buttresses of the Wall's upper surfaces, and on the roofs of the structures below. And Mago had come out without a hat.

He ducked into the nearest shelter, a wide, heavy awning over one of the market stalls. It was no warmer, but it was a relief to have the snow stop falling on his head and trickling down his neck. The awning was wide enough to shelter quite a number of people, and the traders under here were selling some kind of art, he saw, paintings set on stands. He recognized one of them, the kid Nelo, gawky brother of a cuter sister who had, briefly, been assigned to provide Mago with some company during the summer.

Mago wasn't alone in seeking shelter. Some of those hapless nestspills were filtering in now, old and young, a skinny mother carrying a scrawny baby, people with faces and clothes the color of the dirt they had been sitting in. One trader, a fat Northlander in a rich fur cloak, tried to block their way. Nelo, the kid, stepped forward, had a quiet word and the man stood aside. A couple of the traders pulled a sheet across the open stall front to keep out the snow. Somebody lit a lamp. The nestspills started to settle to the muddy ground, squatting in little groups. They seemed to be used to squatting, waiting on events, on somebody noticing them and helping them.

The awning above all their heads bulged and creaked softly. A mass of snow was evidently gathering there already.

Mago walked up to Nelo. "Please don't turn me out

in the snow," he said in a mock whine, using his limited Northlander.

Nelo looked at him, and walked back to his paintings. "You're funny," he said in toneless Greek.

"I'm just teasing you. You did a good turn back there. Of course if that sister of yours—Alxa?—ever fancies doing a Carthaginian a good turn—"

"Shut up."

"All right, all right." Mago, trying not to shiver despite the cold that probed at his bare arms and scalp, inspected the paintings. They were just a jumble to him, figures and shapes of all sizes and positions. He squinted at the nearest canvas. "Ouch."

"What?"

"You're the artist, are you?"

"Of some of them," said Nelo, withdrawn, defensive.

"Let me guess which. This one, with the great big pig and the little tiny horse?"

"You've no idea what you're looking at, have you? What do you know about art?"

Mago shrugged. "I like a nice drinking cup. Do you do drinking cups? With a few warriors going at it, and maidens fiddling with each other's titties. That's real art. Chuck in a few swords and lutes and laurels and so forth—"

Nelo snorted. "*This* is art, you Carthaginian ox. A new kind of art, neither the abstraction of our own tradition nor the simple representation of you easterners. Look again. That's not a 'little horse.' It's further away—further from you, the viewer, than the animals in the foreground. And see the lines of the barn—the edges of the road, the way they converge . . . It's a new technique called look-deep. Pioneered by Pythagorean scholars here."

Mago tried to see what he meant, and for a heartbeat he thought he got it—it wasn't so much a painting as a window into another world, with depth beyond the surface—yes, he saw it. But then the illusion faded, as quickly as it came. "Well, it's not for me. But I daresay there will be people who'll buy this stuff."

"Not enough of them. But I'm hopeful about the future. This is what I want to do with my life."

"Paint horses?"

"Not just horses . . . But if Uncle Pyxeas is right it's not a paintbrush I'll be wielding in the future, but a snow shovel."

"Hmm. Mind you, all I was ever good at was fighting and screwing, and the world will always need those skills." The awning creaked again. "Speaking of the snow . . ."

He went to the front of the stall and tried to pull the curtain back. It was heavy, stiff with frost, and weighed down by the depth of snow outside. He dragged it aside, using his strength. Outside the snow lay deep, already halfway up his shins. He kicked his way out into it. Once more the flakes fell heavily on his bare head, his neck. It was soft, light stuff, oddly not too cold, but it was hard work wading through the settled snow. The world had been transformed, the sudden layer of white softening every shape, from the great earthworks of Old Etxelur to the detailed texture of the ground. Through it people struggled, slim dark shadows, dimly seen. And the snow still fell heavily from a silver-gray sky.

He turned and looked back at the stall. The snow heaped up on top of the awning was just as deep as on the ground, and the heavy cloth sagged, pregnant. He called, "Hey, artist. I'm from Africa. What does snow weigh?"

Nelo came to the front of the stall and reluctantly stuck his head out. "How much?"

"That much, say." Mago pointed up at the loaded awning.

At that moment a support beam gave way, a tree trunk snapping like a twig. Mago grabbed Nelo's jacket and pulled him out into the open. The awning collapsed, the snow falling with a rush. It was sudden, shocking, normality gone in an instant.

"My paintings!"

"Never mind that," Mago growled in Greek, "what about the people?"

They strode forward together and began to drag at the fallen awning. It was frozen and heavy with ice, and the snow slid awkwardly around their legs as they tried to work. But people started pushing their way out from under it, the vendors and the sheltering nestspills, struggling and sprawling in the cascading snow. There were injuries, and blood splashed the snow, brilliant red on white.

Then the screaming started, from under the very center of the awning. The woman with the baby, Mago remembered. She had gone right for the center of the stall, where it had been warmest. He began hauling harder at the awning. "Help me." He repeated, louder and in Northlander, "Help me!"

The others gathered around, Nelo, the vendors, the bewildered nestspills, pawing at the wrecked stall with their bare hands, trying to reach the woman and her child.

15

When Crimm had come back to Ywa's house that morning, after he'd given up on the idea of taking the *Sabet* out, they had considered making love. It was a kind of unspoken negotiation. They knew each other too well to need words.

But it was *cold* in Ywa's house, this snowy morning, cold in the home of the Annid of Annids, and it was likely to get colder yet. The house was of an old design, one of seven roundhouses on its flood-defying mound, a structure of oak beams and thatch and wattle of the kind Ana herself might once have lived in eight or nine thousand years before. The house was an honorarium for the Annid of Annids and a living memory of Northland's heritage, but it was not *warm*. Meanwhile, Crimm might have had a day off, but Ywa had a lot of paperwork to get through, after the latest meeting of the Water Council, which had seen yet more arguments about ration allowances and the guard draft. So they just draped blankets over their shoulders and huddled together over the central hearth, where the smoke seeped up to the thatched roof, and drank bitter coffee, a gift of the Jaguar folk from across the ocean, and talked softly.

"I should probably go back to the Wall," Ywa sighed. She glanced over the mounds of scrolls on the carpeted floor, the slates and books open on her desk. "It's just that I get so much more *done* if I squirrel away in here."

Crimm grunted. "Maybe you ought to get back before that snow gets much deeper."

"Surely it will stop soon . . ."

The wind picked up, and the house creaked, a deep wooden groan.

"When you go I'll walk with you. Can't have the Annid of Annids stuck in a snowdrift with her ass in the air."

"I'm sure I can feel a draft," she said, and pulled her blanket closer.

"The snow will pass," he said, trying to reassure.

"But a blizzard like this, so soon in the year. How will we cope?"

Crimm thought he knew how she felt. Ywa felt she bore the burden of all the Northlanders' fates on her slim shoulders, just as he felt responsibility for his crew on the *Sabet*, in the middle of storms, or when becalmed. Mind you, in his opinion her fellow Annids should have been doing more to help, his cousin Rina especially—Rina, just back from a pointless jaunt to Hantilios with old Pyxeas; Rina, who seemed more concerned with politicking and feathering her own nest than with the welfare of others. He shuffled up and put his arm around Ywa. "You'll get through this."

Briefly she relaxed, and let her head drop to his shoulder. "I'm lucky to have you. *Lucky*—funny word. It took the loss of your wife and baby to bring us together. What kind of luck is that?"

"Lucky for me, in the end," he murmured. Lucky that he had found something drily comforting in the strength of this woman, a distant cousin older than him, widowed a decade ago, her only son long grown and left. Even though they both felt it was best to keep the relationship as private as possible. He kissed the top of her head, the graying unbrushed hair. "We'll still be here in the spring—"

The house groaned again, and there was a snap, of wood splitting. They both sat up. From beyond the walls came a crackling crunch, like a tree trunk breaking, then a softer collapse. Cries of anger and pain.

They looked at each other. "We need to get out of here," Crimm said.

It took only moments to pull on their cloaks, hoods, boots, mittens. Crimm kicked dirt over the hearth, damping down the fire. Ywa glanced once at her papers, but she didn't need Crimm to tell her there was no time to pack them up.

They pushed their way through the door flap and out into the open. The snow was nearly up to their knees, Crimm saw with shock. How could so much have fallen so quickly? And so *early*? And still it came down. When they stepped out of the lee of the house, the snow, blasting on a wind straight from the north, came at them horizontally, thick and hard, heavy flakes stinging as they slapped Crimm's face. He staggered, and reached for Ywa's mittened hand.

A few steps away from the house, they looked around. Ywa pointed. "There. It was Canda's house."

The house, or the wreck of it, was barely visible. Crimm saw supporting beams, some broken, sticking out of the heaped snow like snapped bones. But already fresh snow was covering over the wreckage.

"We should help them."

"No." He pointed to figures plodding through the rush of snowflakes. "They're already heading for the Wall. They must be all right."

She hesitated, then nodded, and they set off.

There was a shortcut to the Wall, a diagonal path, but they were walking through a uniform whiteness. Wary of getting lost, Crimm led Ywa to the Etxelur Way, the main road that ran south to north directly to the heart of the

Wall. The Way was cambered and lined with poles where banners flew on festival days; following the poles they couldn't get lost. He put his arm around Ywa's waist, and they pulled their furs up over their mouths, and pushed their way through snow and wind.

When Kia wanted to be nice to Thux, she would tell him she had two sons, him and Engine Seventy-Four. But on a day like today, with her engine struggling, there was no hiding the fact that there was only one true priority in her life. Still, in a corner of her heart she thanked the little mothers for giving her a son like Thux: smart, strong, flexible, and even handy with a wrench. He was young yet, but already one of the true *mechanikoi*, like herself; it must be in the blood.

Now the two of them stood in the engine room, watching the laboring of their steel beast with some anxiety.

This chamber, with its rough plastered-over grow-stone walls, was entirely embedded within the body of the Wall, not far below its parapet. Shelves were cluttered with the paraphernalia of their profession: precision screws, gears, transmission chains, camshafts, pistons, valves. The engine itself was a massive cylinder that filled the room. Its big rocking arm converted the heat of good Albian coal to motive force, the force that helped keep the ground by the face of the Wall pumped dry, and worked elevators within the Wall, and lifted cargo cranes on the sea-facing side. The whole apparatus was surrounded by condenser pipes and feeds that kept the engine working to its best theoretical ability, and bled steam and hot water off into the body of the Wall to keep its inhabitants in the warmth and comfort to which they had been accustomed for centuries, even in the hardest winter. Engine Seventy-Four was dumb, but it was big and strong and reliable—just as Kia liked to say of her son, not inaccurately. But today it was in trouble. You didn't need to read the liquid-level gauges showing pressure and temperature and steam output and all the rest to know that; you could feel it, standing in this growstone pen before the laboring beast.

As Kia and Thux stood there bewildered, a few flakes of snow came drifting down the ventilation shafts from the outside world, quickly melting in the heat of the engine room.

"It's overheating," Kia said.

"I don't understand," Thux replied. "I know it's snowing—"

"I've never known it to snow so hard before, I have to say. Certainly not this early in the winter."

"But the loops should be too hot to be affected by the frost." Big radiator loops were embedded in the Wall's outer surface, to enable the engines, buried in the body of the Wall, to lose heat. "In fact," Thux said, "the colder it is outside, the better the heat loss. Right? What then, Mother? Ow!" A mass of snow came tumbling down a shaft, straight onto his head and shoulders. Splashing onto the floor, it quickly melted, leaving a shallow puddle. As Kia tried not to laugh, Thux brushed the residue off his hair and shoulders. "How could *that* happen? It's impossible."

Kia peered up the shaft. "Not if the snow's falling fast enough. Maybe ice is forming on the protective grilles . . ." She snapped her fingers. "That's it. The exhaust shafts must be blocked by ice and snow. Our baby's choking. One of us will have to go up and clear it. I'll go," she said immediately.

"No," he snapped.

"You've never seen conditions like this before."

"Well, nor have you. My job, Mother. I'm younger than you. And it wouldn't cost as much to replace me." He went to a locker and began to pull out his kit.

"All right. With weight like mine I'd probably break the ladders anyhow. But make sure you suit up properly. Scarf, peaked hat, mask, heavy gloves."

"I know." Struggling, he pulled a tight coverall lined with gull feathers over his regular work clothes.

Kia went back to her gauges. She wasn't about to say it, in fact she didn't really trust herself to say anything, but today, at forty-three years old, she felt unreasonably proud of her only son. And of herself, she admitted, not to mention Engine Seventy-Four. People had always looked down on the House of the Beavers, Northland's engineers, even though it was as old as any of the nation's ancient guilds—and their nickname of the *mechanikoi* showed they had absorbed as much of the tradition of the learned Greeks who had once flocked to Northland as any of the more academic Houses. After all, without the Beavers' work on the Wall and the various other sea-defense measures in the very beginning, Northland would not even exist; it would all have been lost under the sea before Ana was cold in her stony tomb in the Wall, probably. And these days the Beavers, equipped with new skills, worked harder than ever. The sages, nodding in deference to their inspirational founder Pythagoras, might lecture the world about the principles of heat flow and mechanical advantage, but it took a Beaver, one of the humble *mechanikoi*, crawling about in the dark and smoke and steam and sweat, to make it all work.

Except today it was only just working. All the Wall's engines were laboring to cope with the flooding at the Wall's base, caused by a brief warm spell. But that wasn't the only stress on her engine. On such a day as this people must be flocking into the Wall for shelter, those who lived in smaller properties out on the plain—even those with homes in the chambered cloisters of Old Etxelur, which wasn't as well equipped as the Wall. As they arrived, settling in the apartments and inns and taverns, they were all turning up the heat, and running deep steaming baths to soak away the cold of the day. She could see it all reflected in the bubbling levels of the gauges, hear it in the deep mechanical groans of the engine.

And now the engine itself was being choked by the snow.

What if Engine Seventy-Four failed? Then Seventy-Three and Seventy-Five would be quick to pack up too, as they strove too hard in an effort to compensate, and the whole system could come crashing down. Without heating—why, without even running cold water, for that had to be pumped up from the ground too, a fact not many citizens of the Wall were even aware of—what would become of the Wall and the citizens snug inside, like bees in their honeycombed hive? Seventy-Four must not fail—that was all. And on this shift it was Kia's job, and Thux's, to make sure of that.

Thux was ready. Swaddled in his protective suit and peaked hat, he was barely recognizable. But his eyes creased when he smiled at her behind his mask.

She took his head and kissed the top of his hat. "Be careful," she said. "One mistake out there—that's all it will take."

"I'll be fine."

"Just make sure you are, or you'll have me to answer to. Now go." She turned him around and pushed him toward the elevator to the roof.

16

When she made it to the Wall, Ywa toured the ground-level doorways, and the main staircases and elevator shafts. There were injured folk pouring into the Wall's Etxelur District from all over the adjacent part of Northland, even from Old Etxelur. They came with broken bones from falls, crush injuries from collapsed houses, frostbite—or they came just looking for shelter, the already ill, the very old and very young, nestspills weakened by hunger, and some in what the doctors described as a state of deep cold, the very cores of their bodies losing essential heat.

It was soon obvious that the Wall's hospitals couldn't cope.

Ywa made some fast decisions. First she sent for Ontin, a distant cousin, not the most senior or learned medical professional in Northland but the family doctor she had always trusted herself. Then she went to the Hall of Annids, the largest single chamber in the District. Maybe this place could be used to house the influx.

She found her way barred by a pompous official. To

her astonishment she learned that a poetry competition was proceeding in the Hall, a handful of elderly men of the House of the Wolf declaiming bad verse to one another in archaic tongues. Ywa pushed the doorman aside and strode in. The big room was colder than usual—and darker too. When she glanced up she could see snow gathering on the big glass panes of the roof. She broke up the competition, and co-opted the poets to help get the chamber set up as an emergency receiving hospital. To their credit, as soon as they realized how urgent the situation was they ran to help. "Why," said one well-spoken gentleman, "I hadn't even noticed it was snowing." Others came as word spread, with pallets, chairs, boxes of medical supplies such as bandages, splints, medicines, surgical instruments.

And soon the wounded, ill and displaced began to trickle in.

Ontin showed up, carrying his own bag of instruments. A small, potbellied, balding man of about sixty, he looked taken aback when he saw the number of cases already here.

More volunteers started to arrive. Rina's son Nelo came stumbling in, with that cocky young Carthaginian—what was his name?—Mago. Between them they were carrying an injured woman, filthy and in rags, her leg obviously broken; she cried out with every step. But she held a baby against her chest, swathed in dirty cloth. The boys laid the woman down on a pallet, and the well-dressed daughter of an Annid came hurrying over to help her.

Nelo and Mago approached Ywa. They were both panting, soaked from melted snow, their tunics stained with blood. Nelo asked, "What can we do to help, Annid?"

She smiled at them. "It looks to me as if you've been helping already." She pointed to Ontin. "Do whatever he tells you."

Nelo nodded. But Mago looked up at the glass roof, uneasily, distracted.

Ontin had been thinking. "We need to set up a system. Sort the injured into categories: those who need urgent care, those who can wait, those who don't need help at all and those we can't help. You boys can do something straightaway for those who've been caught by the deep cold, like her." He pointed to one young girl, limp on a pallet, pale as the snow itself. Her parents were hovering over her, gently shaking her, trying to get her to wake. "Get her parents to cuddle her—body warmth, that's the thing, until we can get more organized. Run around and do that wherever you see somebody in that condition."

The young men hurried away. But Ywa heard the Carthaginian muttering, "Look up, my friend. That ceiling."

"A lot of snow."

"Yes."

"Never seen it like that before. Covered over. We don't normally get much snow in Etxelur."

"Hmm. Have you ever had the feeling that you've lived the same experience twice?"

Ywa said to Ontin, "Whatever you need, tell me, and I'll find it for you."

"Thank you. Do you think it's getting cold in here?" He walked over to a wall hot-water tap, opened the valve, let it run, and dipped his fingers into the flow. It was obvious it was running cold.

It felt as if the steam caravan had been stuck here for hours. Since the crew had fixed the snowblades, the cabin had lurched forward for a while, and, under way once more, Alxa had started to relax. Then the caravan stopped again, for no apparent reason, and she had nothing to do but sit in the gathering dark. And then off again, and another stop, and off again, and a lurched halt that felt somehow final. Not knowing was the worst part, in a way, that and having no control over her own fate.

It had been a long time since the heating pipes had gone cold. In the end she had swallowed her pride and opened her luggage; she pulled on dirty clothes for extra layers to keep warm, piled a spare coat over her legs, and jammed two hats on her head, a Frankish woolen cap under a big fur bonnet. But still her breath steamed in the air.

And now it was growing darker and darker, and a more intense cold was closing in. She felt as if she were being swallowed. She had a box of small candles in her luggage, and a flint. She set one candle up in a bowl on the seat beside her. The little circle of light showed the heavy flakes that still fell beyond the window, and her own pale face reflected in the small panes of glass. Perhaps the caravan would never move again, she thought. Perhaps the snow would simply bury the rail line, and the caravan, and her, and when the thaw came in the summer the engineers would find her frozen corpse . . .

The tugging on the cabin door startled her. Perhaps she had nodded off.

The door seemed to have stuck in place and took some force to shift. It opened with a crack of splintering ice, letting in chill air and a swirl of snowflakes. A burly man carrying an oil lantern clambered up a ladder to the doorway. Aged maybe forty, he wore the uniform of the Iron Way guild, a subdivision of the ancient House of the Beavers, the Wall engineers. He held up his lantern. "Are you all right, madam?"

She forced a smile. "Not exactly. Cold. Bored. Hungry! But alive, as you can see, and keeping myself warm. What's going on, officer?"

He rolled his eyes. "You name it. We've got drifting snow in some places. It fell too thick for the blade, and we had to change that for the midwinter design, and in places we've had to send the lads out ahead with shovels to clear the line. Then there's trouble with the boiler, external lines freezing up and splitting. Sorry for the delay."

"Don't apologize. You're stuck as well. As long as we get there in the end." She glanced through the window. "Where are we, by the way?"

"On the Wall. But still well to the east of Etxelur. We'll get there, miss, you'll see."

She frowned. The Wall was inhabited from end to end. "But it's still snowing. What District is this? There must be places we can shelter for the night. Maybe we should disembark and—"

"We'll get there," he said with some determination. "The engines of the Iron Way always get through. That's what we live by, miss." He passed up a glass bottle of water, and, apologetically, a wooden bucket. The latrine system's seized up," he said.

She took the bucket. "Keep safe, officer."

He was already closing the door. Listening hard, she heard his heavy tread through the snow, and then his rap on the next cabin in the line. But if he got a response, she couldn't hear through the rushing of the wind. After that there was only the cold, and her candle.

She felt a draft. Since the officer had forced the door it wouldn't fit back in its frame.

Up on the Wall parapet above Engine Seventy-Four, Thux was struggling.

It felt like he'd been out here for hours, and maybe he had been, for it was getting darker and darker. He had a lantern fixed into a prepared socket on the growstone surface, but all he saw by its light was a bubble of snowflakes, flying horizontally. The wind was coming from the north, flat and hard and muscular, and it sucked every bit of warmth out of any exposed skin, out of his cheeks, out of his hands when he flipped back the clever little lids on his mittens to expose his fingers for the finer work. And though the snow wasn't settling up here, except in the engine's vents and chimneys, the wind was depositing ice on every surface, on the growstone under his feet, on the pipework and handholds and rungs he had to use to clamber about.

He'd been up here without a break since the engine had first started to struggle. But there was no choice. The vents were the problem, the vents that fed the great engine with the air it needed to burn its fuel, and expelled its excess heat and steam and smoke. The swirling snow was forever clogging them up. Even on the hot chimneys the snow fell and froze in place faster than it could be melted away. So Thux was following a dismal circuit, clambering around the growstone with his pack of tools at his waist, clearing snow and ice from the vents with hammer and chisel and, sometimes, when he couldn't find any other way, with his mittened hands. He was exhausted, cold to the bone, wet through from snow that had got under his hood and down his collar and melted against his skin. And, when he thought about it, also hungry. He wondered how much longer he could keep this up. He was pretty sure there'd be no relief shift tonight. Every one of the *mechanikoi* available would be at work somewhere in the Wall's battered infrastructure. If he gave up and went down, he knew that his mother would insist on coming up here to take his place, and he couldn't have that.

And Engine Seventy-Four couldn't be allowed to fail, nor any of the hundreds of engines implanted along the mighty length of the Wall. Not on a night like this. Up to now they had been winning; he couldn't hear the engine, such was the howl of the wind and the muffling of his ears by his big fur cap, but he could feel its steady vibration through the growstone, like a beating heart buried within the Wall.

But now he heard an ominous groan from the Wall's sea-facing surface. A sharp crack. A hiss of escaping steam. Something new, then.

He scrambled across the growstone, crouching in the

wind. Facing north, he lay on his belly, holding his hood to protect his face from the blasting wind, and looked down by the light of his lantern. The Wall face itself was caked with ice. And there was a broken pipe venting steam, just beneath the edge of the roof. The pipes here, stitching in and out of the growstone surface, were part of the radiator system; the steam would pass through these exposed sections and lose a little heat in the open air before being drawn back into the closed cycles of the engine. Now, Thux could see, even though the radiator pipes were usually blistering hot, the cold had won. The pipes had become coated with thick masses of ice, flowing forms that must have melted and refrozen as the heat battled the snow, and the fluid in one section of the pipe must have frozen and, expanding, split the pipe wide open. The engine was bleeding steam pressure, and, worse, if the radiator wasn't working, the engine would soon be overheating too.

It wasn't an impossible job. The system, already centuries old, had evolved with time for ease of repair. Lying flat, he could reach down to the broken section. He checked that his rope harness was fixed securely to a stout rung, and then dug out a wrench and a short length of brass sleeve that he would use to join the broken ends of pipe to make a temporary fix. The welders could come up here and make the joint good when the weather relented. He flipped back his mittens' lids to expose his fingers, taking care not to touch the still-hot pipes, and grabbed the broken section with his right hand.

As his hand closed around the freezing metal he knew immediately he'd made a horrible mistake.

The agonizing cold sank into his fingers and palm. When he tried to loosen his fingers, he found the flesh was glued firmly to the metal surface. He tried harder, and he could feel the flesh tear, and blood oozed out onto the metal, where it froze immediately, a glistening crimson. He was stuck. Lying here facedown on the growstone, his right arm outstretched down the Wall, he couldn't even reach the locked right hand with his left. *Be careful,* his mother had always said. *One mistake out there—that's all it will take.* And she'd been right. This had been that one mistake, for him.

He could feel the cold penetrating through his hand, up his arm. The wind picked up again and blew back his hood from his head, so his face and scalp were exposed to the driving snow. The flakes were heavier now, harder, and they stung as they slapped at his skin. He could feel ice on his face, below his eyes. He couldn't tell if he was crying or not. He was going to die out here, he realized. It wasn't just that he'd messed up the job. He would freeze to death, trapped like an idiot up on this Wall. He tried again to force open his fingers, but again he felt flesh rip, and what felt like a web of muscles beneath the skin tearing. The pain was astounding. He slumped back, exhausted, defeated, agonized. He yelled into the wind: "How could I be so stupid?"

"Good question!" It was his mother's voice. Kia was lying facedown by his right-hand side, bundled up in her own furs.

"You shouldn't be up here." His teeth were chattering.

"No, I shouldn't. And I shouldn't have given birth to an idiot like you. But one thing follows the other, doesn't it?" She pulled his hood back over his head, and kissed him on an exposed bit of forehead. "Now hold still or you'll pull that hand to bits." She dug her own bare fingers into a pot of oil and reached down and began to massage the fingers and palm of his locked hand.

"What is that?"

"Sperm-whale oil. Had it in the store for years. Old Coldlander trick, although they say seal oil is the best. It'll take a little time but we'll get you free. Leave it to Mother."

Thux rested his face on the fur of his hood, with the cold growstone beneath. He seemed to be falling asleep, his thoughts receding into the warmth of his own skull.

It was almost comforting to lie here, in the care of his mother as she worked at his damaged hand. He couldn't even feel the cold anymore.

But there was something missing.

He forced his head up. "Mother. Can you hear that?"

"What?"

"The engine."

She lay there for a moment, silent and still as the wind howled around them.

The pumping heartbeat of the engine had stopped, and the growstone beneath them was as inert as a corpse.

17

I t was Mago who spotted the first cracked pane in the roof.

By now it was the dead of night. Nelo had been working flat out, like everybody else, since he'd first come here to the Hall of Annids, and he had no precise idea of the time. Doctor Ontin had gotten his emergency hospital running pretty quickly. Mago and Nelo had been used as spare muscle in Ontin's scheme to sort out the continuing trickle of injured and ill as they kept arriving through the night. Ontin himself, with other surgeons and nurses, was working hard on the more serious injuries, the broken limbs and crushing wounds, the frostbite, the cases of exhaustion, even a couple of heart attacks.

Things had gotten steadily worse. The heating had been off for hours, and the running hot water. Then even the cold water supply had failed, then the gas supply that fed the lanterns. Ontin, bossy, exasperated, had coped with all this as it had unfolded, barking out commands to anybody who would listen, including Ywa, Annid of Annids, who made sure that what he wanted got done. Soon the Hall was studded with candles, and open fires blazed in antique hearths unused for a century. Clogged chimneys trapped smoke and the ash, and there wasn't much to burn save smashed-up furniture—it was very expensive firewood—but the fires gave out enough heat to keep them all from freezing altogether.

But all through the night Nelo and Mago, remembering their adventure with the awning, had kept an eye on that roof, a great glass lid over them all, that had been covered with snow thick enough to block out the daylight even before the sun had set. In the dark it was easy to forget about, you couldn't even see it in the flickering light of the candles. Nelo had tried a couple of times to warn Ywa about the problem, but she hadn't really listened, and he understood; you couldn't deal with everything at once. But the two of them had kept watching, and listening.

It was Mago who heard the first pane crack, even over the noise of the hospital, the cries of the injured, the squalls of babies, the general susurrus of conversation. He grabbed Nelo's arm, almost making the Northlander drop the bundle of blankets he'd been carrying. "Look," he snapped in Greek. "Up there . . . near the center . . ."

The roof was barely visible in the candlelight. But Nelo, squinting, made out the latticework of iron strips that held the panes in place, and the panes themselves, gray with snow. And there, yes, in the center, he saw a spiderweb of cracks.

"I don't know what's holding it up," Mago said. "If one pane fails—"

"The rest will follow."

"It's just like that accursed awning again." He shook Nelo's shoulder. "Come on, Northlander. These are your people. Make them listen!"

And then another pane cracked, more loudly. All around them people looked up.

Nelo dropped his blankets and ran to Ywa. His urgency finally got through. She barked out commands, and with impressive speed the evacuation of the makeshift hospital began. All the doors were flung open, including the big ceremonial entrance through which the Annids would process into the room for the Water Council meetings and other great occasions of state. Soon folk were streaming out into the corridors outside, tunnels dug through the ancient growstone of the Wall.

Then that first pane collapsed. A column of snow fell vertically, with a tinkle of glass from the window fragments that came with it. Around the Hall people stopped what they were doing and peered up at the roof. More panes cracked and failed, dumping more snow. Then the iron structure as a whole started to sag like a bulging, overloaded net. As the frames holding them distorted out of shape, more panes shattered with brief pops, and glass and snow showered. As Mago had suggested, Nelo saw, once one pane failed, the integrity of the roof as a whole was lost. People, wary, backed off toward the walls.

The roof gave way completely. Amid a hail of glass and bits of iron, the snow roared down in a single massive load, falling all at once. People screamed, and ran if they could, but many were overwhelmed by the snowfall as it covered the pallets and operating tables and heaps of blankets and medicine chests. It even washed into the fires in the old hearths, dousing them immediately, Nelo saw.

It was over in a moment. Then came the first groans, the first cries for help. Nelo hurled himself into the drift, digging with his bare hands.

Fresh snow fell, the flakes gliding down from the sky and through the smashed roof, visible in the dim light of the surviving lanterns, fresh snow still falling thick after all these hours and settling on the heaped masses on the floor.

Too fast, Alxa thought. After spending half the night not moving at all, now we're going too fast.

Anxious, bundled up, she peered out of the window

of her cabin. She could see nothing but flakes of snow, still falling, in the light of her candle. The door was admitting a chill draft, even though she'd tried to stop up the cracks with bits of her own clothing. She had no idea where they were. On the Wall, of course, but the Wall spanned the whole northern coast of Northland. She had no idea how close to Etxelur itself she was, how close to home.

But she did feel that the caravan was rattling along too fast—too fast! After all the trouble the crew had had, all the stops, the times they had to stop to knock ice off the snowblade or to dig out drifts, you would think they would have had more sense than to go plummeting into the dark now. But then, she supposed, the crew themselves were exhausted. They too must be longing to get this nightmare journey over with.

The caravan leaned sideways, to her right, as if taking a bend in the track. For a horrible moment it hovered, as if it might tip over. Then the cabin settled back on its rail with a jolt.

She breathed again. The caravan rattled on.

But the cabin tipped again, once more to the right. This time it was a sickening lean that went on and on, with a squeal of metal on metal. Still holding the candle, she hung on to her seat, or she would have fallen against the wall. *This is it . . . This is it.* The cabin was tipping over the seaward face of the Wall. She wondered what would kill her first—the crash itself, the fall into the water, or the ocean's chill? And what had the final accident been—a frozen point, a rail bent from contracting in the cold? She supposed she would never know—

A fresh jolt knocked her out of her seat, spilling her to the tilted floor. She lost her candle at last, which flickered out. The ride became much rougher, the squeal of metal deafening. Had the cabin jumped the track?

She had to get out.

She scrambled up the sloping roof to the door, and grabbed for its handle. The door, damaged by the officer, fell inward easily, and the bits of clothing she'd used to stop the gaps fell around her. She grabbed the door frame. *One big effort, Alxa. One heave. Don't think about it . . .*

She pulled her head and upper body out into the lashing snow. The night was wild, the wind blasting, the noise of the caravan on the track insanely loud. By the few working carriage lights she could see the caravan ahead, scraping along the track with a spark of metal on metal. And the cabins were peeling off the track, one by one, falling into the ocean almost gracefully. Soon it would be her cabin's turn.

Don't think about it.

She jumped into the dark.

Fell through the air.

Landed in snow, a deep, soft drift, powdery and uncompacted, but still she hit hard, and the cold stuff filled her mouth and eyes and ears with a rush.

But she was not yet dead.

18

The storm blew itself out overnight.

The next morning the Annids' priority was to organize teams to dig their way out of the Wall, through snow that lay thick on the roof and was heaped up in deep drifts on the landward side. It took until midday to secure safe access to the roof.

In the early afternoon Ywa and Rina, dressed for the sake of morale in their formal Annid robes, walked up to the parapet. They used a staircase, for the elevators were still out, and would be, along with the heating and running water and other systems, until the *mechanikoi* could make their repairs to the engines. They emerged into brilliant sunshine, under a clear blue sky. Just here, over Etxelur, the Wall roof had been scraped clean of snow from one face to the other. Further out, Rina could see, only the central track of the Iron Way had so far been cleared; the snow lay heaped up in great banks to either side of the rail. There were no caravans running this morning. Rina saw people plodding through the cleared spaces, dark, slumped shapes in the brilliant light.

"That sun is actually warm," she said now, and she lifted her face to its light. "But then it is only early autumn. That will cheer everybody up."

"Not the dead or the grieving, it won't," Ywa said tightly. She was drawn, tense, her eyes hollow with exhaustion, and she had a smear of blood on her cheek.

Rina had spent the night huddled in her own apartment in the Wall, simply enduring. Ywa had been out working, trying to stabilize an ever-changing situation, and to save lives. Rina, faintly guilty, realized she had gotten off lightly. But Alxa had not yet come home, and a worm of worry burrowed in her stomach.

They walked to the rim of the parapet and looked out over Etxelur, and Northland. The snow blanketed the land, smoothing out some details but oddly enhancing others, Rina noticed, walls and ridges and gullies picked out by sharp blue shadows. The great waterways, the canals, were plated with ice, shining silver in the sunlight. All over the landscape people were moving, dark huddles trying to force their way through the snow. The snow had drifted in great mounds against the face of the Wall itself, and lay thick on its ledges and walkways and buttresses. From up here the dreadful collapse of the Hall of Annids was clearly visible. People still worked down there, still dug into the bloodied snow.

Ywa said now, "What are we to do, Rina? How are we to cope?"

"We will recover," Rina said firmly. "The *mechanikoi* will get the engines started again. We will rebuild. The Coldlanders ought to be a model for us. If they can survive their harsh winters, so can we."

"Come, Rina, don't try to fill me with false hope, that's not what I need you for. We are *not* like Coldlanders. We depend on a network of systems, of flows of goods and people. Now all that is disrupted, from the food supply to the drains. Even before the blizzard we were already stretched to the limit. And *winter has barely begun*, Rina. What if Uncle Pyxeas is right that next winter is going to be just as bad, and the next after that?"

Rina said nothing. But now she recalled the advice Pyxeas had given his family. That they must go, flee to the south before the crowd, before it was too late to travel at all. She pushed that thought firmly to the back of her mind, but she knew it would not be forgotten.

"Mother?"

It was Alxa's voice, cutting through her thoughts like a knife through soft fat. Rina whirled. A group of battered people, swathed in soaked, filthy clothing, some of them blood-smeared, came limping along the Iron Way track from the east. One separated from the rest and hurried forward, trembling and wide-eyed with exhaustion.

Rina ran to her daughter, who fell into her arms.

19

The First Year of the Longwinter: Midwinter Solstice

Kassu tried to get out of the farmhouse without waking his wife.

It should have been possible. They no longer slept together. Henti had the marital bed, and Kassu a heap of blankets and furs by the big hearth in the main room. He particularly didn't want to wake her this morning, for today was the day he had asked to see Himuili, his commanding officer, in New Hattusa, for advice on the legal aspects of his divorce.

But of course she woke when he did. Maybe it was the soft rattle of his armor as he buckled it on.

She came storming out of the bedroom. "Ha! Off to see the boss, are you? Off to ask him how to fix your marriage?"

He kept silent as he shook out his heavy cloak and pulled it around his shoulders. It was no use being dragged into an argument. She always won arguments. She always had been cleverer than he was, he admitted that—even though, he felt, he had a better sense of what was right, of what was true.

But Henti was not herself this morning. Her hair was tangled, she was wearing a robe she hadn't changed for too long, her fingernails were still caked with mud from yesterday's work with the animals. She was distressed and frightened, he thought, behind the blustering anger. As well she might be, for under Hatti law a possible penalty for her adultery was death, for her and her priest.

He couldn't help responding. "Yes, I'm seeing Himuili, if you want to know. He agreed to meet me at the Lion Gate. I'm going to ask him to sponsor me if I decide to go to the courts."

"This is you all over. Always asking somebody smarter than you to tell you what to do. Palla is twice the man you are, in every way."

Kassu sighed. "Maybe he is. But he's not your man. *I'm* yours."

"But I don't want you." She looked at him for a heartbeat, trembling. "Not anymore. Why did you ever take up the offer to be a Man of the Weapons? My father was a church scribe! I never wanted to be a farmer's wife. I don't want *this*, a farm that's dust in the summer and frozen in the winter, and we have to give half whatever we do grow in taxes, and I spend my life queuing at the city granaries for the bread dole, and the cattle are scrawny and they kick and try to chew your clothes when you squeeze a drop of milk out of them . . ."

"Nobody wants the drought," he said more gently. "Nobody wants the winter. At least we're playing our part. I fight for the King, for New Hattusa, *and* we produce more food than we eat, and there's not many can say that these days."

"Oh, how noble you are," she said blackly. "*Playing our part.* You are a lump of the dirt you love so much."

"The whole world is suffering. The story isn't all about you."

She lifted her head, her cheeks stained by tears. "Oh, of course it is. Of course it's about me, and you, and *him.* What else is it about? You useless lump. You understand nothing. Palla understands ... Go." She picked up bits of his clothing, scattered on the floor where he'd been sleeping, and started throwing them at him, breeches, socks, tunics, woolen caps. "Go! Go to your precious general!"

He left with as much dignity as he could muster. Burning with humiliation. Burning with thwarted passion, for he still loved her.

The morning was still early. No fresh snow had fallen overnight but nor had yesterday's fall melted, and it lay in the furrows and ridges of the churned-up mud. Everybody was getting used to the snow now, but Kassu remembered childhood winters when snow in New Hattusa had been a rare event.

But he forgot about the snow when he met Himuili at the gate in the city's Old Wall. For, beneath the gaping mouths of weathered stone lions, Palla, the adulterous priest, was here too.

The gate itself was firmly locked, a great barrier of wood and bronze. These were times of insecurity, and had been even before thousands of Rus and Scand had shown up in the autumn to make camp on the far bank of the Simoeis river. But Himuili's party, plus Kassu, was evidently going out into the country, not into the city. It was an impressive force. Kassu counted fifty men, all heavily armed—plus himself, though he hadn't known about the nature of the assignment before now. He thought he recognized a couple of them, Men of the Golden Spear probably, an elite unit close to the King and second only to the Bodyguard. There were no mercenaries among their number, as far as he could tell from their armor and equipment, which was unusual for a Hatti force.

These formidable-looking men stood by a dozen carts, which were covered with leather sheets and harnessed to depressed-looking donkeys, with shivering boys standing by with switches. Kassu wasn't so surprised by the strength of the force when he glimpsed what the carts were carrying, as one of the wagon covers was shifted to make it more secure. Bread! Loaves, hard-baked, heaped up. They were still warm from the oven and Kassu, never far from hunger himself, could smell their delicious crisp heat. There was no greater treasure in all of New Hattusa just now, he knew that. Kassu had no idea where these supplies were to be taken—some suffering town deeper in the Troad, perhaps.

As for Himuili himself, he knew that Kassu wanted to speak to him, but not for now. Himuili was in deep conversation with his senior officers, a huddle of men in heavy cloaks and expensive plumed helmets. General Himuili looked as if he had been made for days like this, Kassu thought, days of bleakness and cold and tough duty; he was a pillar of a man, and his battered face, scarred and asymmetrical, was a mask of defiant strength.

But here was Palla, the priest, wrapped in a military cloak, even wearing a steel helmet. Standing with Himuili himself in the huddle! When he saw Kassu, the recognition jolted Palla; there was no mistaking that. Evidently he'd not expected his lover's husband to show up, not to-day. Palla was a slim, tall man, a few years younger than Kassu—closer to Henti in age, in fact, and that was prob-ably part of the problem. His hair was dark, but his eyes were a pale blue, blue as a Scand's. He wasn't particularly handsome, Kassu thought. But his face bore no scars, his nose hadn't been broken even once—his face was that of a soft city dweller's, and so what Henti was used to, that and his evident learning. When Kassu looked at him now there seemed no harm in him. He was not the kind Kassu would ever seek out as a friend, but he was the kind Kassu had sworn to Jesus Sharruma to protect, the kind that made New Hattusa what it was: literate, intellectual, civi-lized. He seemed *likable*. But Kassu had seen this *likable* young man kiss his wife.

Inwardly he cursed his fate. Why must life be so com-plicated? Why couldn't whatever malicious angel was toying with him have sent him a rival he could cheerfully hate? Because, he realized, thinking about it, such a man would never have been good enough for Henti, as, perhaps, *he* had never been good enough. And that was a true measure of the angel's spite. All they had to do was to turn your own weaknesses against you, and your heart was smashed.

The priest looked away and visibly tried to concentrate on the conversation around Himuili. But then the group broke up, for a newcomer approached, walking around the curve of the city walls, and Kassu immediately understood who this shipment of bread was for, why it needed to be so closely guarded.

The newcomer was a Rus.

With his aides, Himuili walked forward to meet him. All the Hatti save Himuili himself had their cloaks pulled back so their weapons were free, though for now their swords stayed in their scabbards. The Rus was, after all, a representative of a force that had sent assassins into the heart of the capital to murder the King.

The Rus, though, came alone. He was a big man, with the blue eyes and red hair every Hatti associated with his people. He wore a loose cloak over a long tunic and baggy trousers, and linen wraps around his legs over long leather boots. He wore a cap rather than a helmet, and had one weapon, a single-bladed axe a Scand might carry, slung over his shoulder by a leather strap. His hands were empty.

Himuili grunted to his men. "Ugly enough to be a Rus. That rust-colored hair."

To Kassu's blank astonishment it was Palla who replied first. "Careful, lord—he may understand more Nesili than you think. See how carefully he has been selected."

"Selected?"

"The red hair, the blue eyes—not all the Rus share that coloring. This man looks like a Rus, *to us.* Notice the brooch that clasps the cloak, quite expensive. A warrior and a prince of the Rus—that is who they have sent to accept our gift. This is a game of symbols, you see."

Kassu had perceived none of this.

Himuili grunted. "You should know, priest, you've spent enough time among them. Well, I hope he can read the symbolism of the crowd of big murderous bastards I've brought out to meet him."

"I'm sure he can, sir."

The Rus approached Himuili, recognizing his authority, and began to speak in his own heavy tongue.

Palla translated smoothly. "His name is Jaroslav . . ."

"I come from Kiev originally. I moved south with my family and my men, for we were starving. After the famine there was little left of our country, and what was left was ravaged by the Pechenegs and other scum, and we suffered badly, and so we moved. But in the new place the Scand came, and we fought them, but soon we were all starving again, and we moved on. And so we have come here, to Miklagard."

"Which is the Rus name for New Hattusa, sir," Palla added. " 'The great city.' "

"And he's still starving, is that the game? Well, tell him we've got a load of good Hatti bread to fend off the pangs for him and his whores and his squalling Rus brats, and we'll transport it to the riverbank for him, and we'll be back again with more, and come the spring we'll see what's what." He glanced at Palla. "You could probably leave out the bit about the whores."

"I'm very discreet, lord." He repeated the general's message to the Rus, who chattered volubly in return.

This response, that New Hattusa would feed the enemy horde, astounded Kassu. But the decision wasn't his to make.

Himuili's officers quickly formed up their troops to escort the bread wagons to the river. There would be a tight escort walking with the wagons themselves, and scouts on horseback riding further out. Kassu himself took a place beside one of the wagons, but barely had the party started to trundle away from the city walls before Himuili beckoned to Kassu and brought him forward, to where the priest was walking with the Rus near the head of the little caravan.

"You are Kassu."

"Yes, sir."

"And this priest is the man you're thinking of prosecuting, is it not?"

"Yes, sir, I—"

"Shut up. Walk with each other now. Talk. See if you can't sort this out without bothering the courts. Or me." And he stalked off back to his position at the head of the caravan.

So Kassu walked with Palla, resentfully. Palla's nervousness had evidently returned, as well it might, being within striking distance of a heavily armed cuckold. But he had composure, Kassu saw, you had to give him that.

They both walked behind the broad back of the Rus.

"I can't believe we're dealing with these people," Kassu said. "Taking bread from the mouths of our own children and giving it to these northern brutes, who killed our King. And are we really going to keep feeding them until the spring?"

Palla dared to smile. "That's what the opponents of the policy ask, even in the presence of the Tawananna herself."

Kassu gaped. The Tawananna was Queen Hastayar, widow of the murdered Hattusili. It was the Hatti way that she retained power and influence after her husband's death. "You're saying this is her idea?"

"Her and her advisers."

"But the Rus struck down her own husband!"

"What choice is there? Look at the reality of it, Kassu. The Rus and their Scand allies are *here*. They aren't going anywhere, certainly not until the spring. And even then they won't be going back north. This party is just a vanguard. The whole of their people are on the move. Those trading cities they have on the rivers stretching back north are all abandoned now, everybody fleeing south, young and old, healthy or not. Because winter has got their northern lands in its grip and it doesn't look like it's going to let go.

"So here they are on the northern bank of the Simoeis, less than a day's march from New Hattusa. Yes, it feels unacceptable to deal with an enemy that has tried to decapitate us. But what if we didn't feed them? Surely even you can imagine the consequences."

"Your condescension, priest, is going to get you killed."

"I apologize."

"How come you know so much anyway? Why was it you who talked to the Rus? How do you know his dog's bark of a tongue?"

"Well, it has been the priests who have always dealt with the Rus, ever since they first brought their dragon boats down the rivers to the Asian Sea, and began to plunder our coastal cities. My predecessors brought the word of Jesus Sharruma to them. We sought a syncretism between Teshub Yahweh and their own great god Odin."

"A what?"

"Never mind—a philosopher's term. The point is that followers of Jesus are less likely to go to war with each other. We began to trade with them rather than fight. And we taught them to read and write. Did you know that? We actually devised a written language to represent their tongue and taught it to them. And all this against a drumbeat of war. That is how I know them, Kassu. Some would say that civilizing the Rus is a great achievement of the Church."

"You brag a lot for a priest, don't you? What would Jesus think of that?"

Palla actually blushed. "I don't mean to be immodest."

"And what would Jesus think of what you've done to my wife?"

Now there was a dash of anger in Palla's look as he

turned on Kassu, though he kept his voice down. "I didn't do anything *to* her. It was her choice too. We'd met when we were younger, at the Church of the Holy Wisdom, where she trained as a scribe like her father, before . . ."

Before she gave up the city to become the wife of a farmer-soldier, with Kassu.

"Then I bumped into her again at a festival. We remembered each other. We talked—we'd always talked. She was full of questions about the court, the Church."

"Discussions she could never have with me."

"No," the priest said bluntly.

"I was a good husband. I left the soldiering at the door, every night. I never bragged of the killing, as some men do. On campaign I never raped, or took whores—"

"You never gave her a child."

"That was her choice! We discussed it. We'd lost one child already. We wanted to wait until the bad weather is over; this is no world to bring a child into."

Palla said, almost gently, "Look around you, soldier. How many others go childless? Even though we're all in this world-winter. She was keeping you at a distance, Kassu. She knew she had made a mistake, with you. She loved you—the strong solid core of you. She still does, in a way, I think. She still speaks of you when—"

"Don't tell me."

"All right. But it wasn't enough."

"And then you showed up."

Palla took a breath. "We love each other," he said defiantly. "Perhaps we always did when we were younger, and never knew it. We knew we could not have each other. But we could not stay apart, we are not strong enough for that. If you had not spotted us, if not for the extraordinary circumstances of the day the King died—"

"You'd be carrying on now."

"Our lives are yours to dispose of," Palla said, calm now. "That is literally true. You must make your decision."

They said no more, walking on in silence into the deeper snow.

Long before they reached the river and the Rus camp, a runner on a fast horse came dashing out from New Hattusa. Himuili was summoned back, urgently, to a council with the Tawananna. The mission to the Rus would have to be handled by his juniors.

The general picked men to accompany him back, and he glanced at Palla and Kassu. "You two. With me. Let's go. Now."

20

ack at the city they were met by palace guards and court functionaries, hurried through gates and guard stations to the Pergamos, and, to Kassu's blank astonishment, brought straight to the House of the Kings.

This squat stone building was not the grandest of the great buildings here on old Troy's famous peak, and it was exceptionally cold, even on a good day, for it rested permanently in the shadows of its greater cousins, the Church of the Holy Wisdom and the great modern palace. But the House of the Kings was the oldest, the very first of the keystone buildings to be erected here at the heart of Troy when Hattusili's ancestors had moved their capital from Old Hattusa on its central Anatolian upland. Now more than a thousand years old, the House remained lodged in the heart of the dynasty and the minds of the people, for it was here that the bones of Hatti kings were interred, more than fifty of them so far.

And here, in a chilly pavilion just before the main entrance to the House, Kassu found himself in a scene that astonished him even more. The great of New Hattusa had gathered under a single canvas awning, heavy with snow: he recognized Uhhaziti, the crown prince; and Arnuwanda, his cousin; the mayor, Tiwatapara; the high priest Angulli, all sitting on wooden chairs in a shallow arc. At their center, on an elevated platform and seated on a chair slightly grander than the rest, was Hastayar, the Tawananna, widow of the King.

This arc of seats faced another chair, solitary, heaped with burned bones. These, Kassu knew immediately, were the cremated remains of King Hattusili the Sixteenth. But, according to Hatti belief, the King, though dead, had not left the mortal world. On a small table before the King's chair was set out his final meal, a selection of loaves, a cup of wine. Servants were discreetly circling with trays, bringing the King's final guests food and drink at this, his last banquet.

Behind the King two doors were open, leading into the recesses of the tomb. One way was lit, which led to the mausoleum of the kings, and here, soon, Hattusili would be laid to rest at last, with provisions for the journey, food and wine, and tools and a scrap of turf so that he could build himself a farm in the endless sun of the afterlife. The other way was dark, and Kassu knew it led to a symbolically empty tomb, the Tomb of Jesus and His Mother Mary—empty of their sacred bones, which had been purchased and taken away from Old Hattusa by unscrupulous, far-seeing Northlanders not long after the death of the carpenter-prophet. Some, however, remembered older gods than Jesus, and spoke of that gloomy way as a route to the Dark Earth, a bleaker afterlife than Jesus', a plain of bones and rags and ash where you forgot who you were, forgot even the names of those who loved you.

All this Kassu saw in an instant, before he threw himself to the ground before the King's chair. Not fast enough for Himuili, who, on the ground already, murmured, "A dozen lashes."

"Yes, sir."

When they were ordered to rise, Hastayar faced Himuili. "Welcome, General. You may sit with us." She was a formidable woman, Kassu saw immediately, with a square face, flaring nostrils, and direct gaze—a soldier's face, he would have said. She wore the gray clothes of mourning, with a cloak to match. So Himuili sat in the arc before the King, and accepted a cup of wine. Palla touched Kassu's sleeve, and the two of them retreated to the back of the pavilion. Nobody served them food or wine.

Hastayar began, "I apologize for summoning you with such little notice, Himuili. Call it an impulse. We face a grave decision—and I would rather make that decision in the presence of the King, before Jesus embraces him. Are you comfortable, General? This custom of ours, of sitting out with the King, evolved in the days when the summers were warmer and the winters milder than today. Yet custom must be respected, especially at such times as these. If you need a heavier cloak—"

"I'm fine, madam, thank you," Himuili said. "For one thing I'm a lot warmer than those Rus were before they left home."

"Yes, the great winter that seems to threaten us all. My husband wasn't terribly impressed by it, you know. The winter, I mean." She eyed the bones critically. "'It will pass, my dear. Weather always does.' That's what he said, even the day he died. But that's not what the Rus think, is it? Otherwise they wouldn't have worn themselves out coming here—and more on the way, I hear."

Angulli snorted and waved his cup for more of the King's wine. "What do the Rus know?"

Himuili glanced back at Palla, who stepped forward and spoke. "Sir, with respect—they know rather a lot about winter. There is their direct experience of course. And as the weather has changed they have consulted sages, from Northland and elsewhere."

Hastayar asked him, "And would they have agreed with my husband?"

Palla could not contradict the King. Instead he cast down his eyes.

Hastayar turned now to the Hazannu, the city mayor. "What of our city, Tiwatapara?"

He shrugged. "Madam, you know it as well as I do. You've seen the figures on the bread ration—we're only just at midwinter, and we'll be lucky if we don't have starvation before the spring. *If* it ever comes. That's even before we started doling out to the Rus horde."

"And the population reduction measures? Are they working?"

The man grimaced. "With difficulty. Of course we're keeping refuge seekers out of the city; that's not too hard, unless one of them has a relative inside. As for active reduction, we're finding the most effective way is to target groups. Specific peoples. The Kaskans, for instance, and the Arzawans, and you'd be surprised how many there are here."

"Many of several generations' descent," Arnuwanda put in now, anger in his voice. "I know some of them, or did. They think of themselves as Hatti, not Kaskans or whatever. They think of themselves as belonging to the city, and many of their families have been here since the time of their grandfathers' grandfathers."

Kassu was shocked to hear this. He had witnessed the expulsion of Kaskans. He had even taken part in some of it. He had had no idea it had all been an officially sanctioned, officially *planned* exercise in population reduction.

Arnuwanda went on. "I've fought alongside them, for the King. And now we've kicked them out."

The Tawananna eyed him. "Nephew, it is better to pick on a group the rest can identify and despise, rather than have us fight among ourselves."

"Though we're doing that too," said the Hazannu reluctantly. "Well, people always do. There are religious tensions, followers of the older creeds and the banished gods—I mean the divine ancestors of Teshub Yahweh, who have been declared apocryphal by the Church—

their adherents are coming out and denouncing the Jesus followers, who in turn are calling for their opponents' executions as heretics, and so on. And as soon as you get a rumor that somebody is hoarding so much as a crust of bread, a whole District collapses into a riot. Well, we just have to contain it all."

Angulli mused, "And what of liberty? What of rights under our law?"

"Liberty is for the summer," Hastayar said bleakly. She turned to Himuili. "General, what of the grain supplies?"

He nodded. "I have checked. Our only reliable source of grain the last few years has been Egypt, ever since the Turks occupied so much of Anatolia. But the route is precarious. If I had a map—"

"Just tell us, man," Arnuwanda said.

"Once the grain was brought across the sea to Ura, which is a port on the south coast of Anatolia, and then overland to New Hattusa and elsewhere. The pirates' activities and the Turks' raids made that too hazardous. Even the Carthaginians have been roaming our waters. So now it is brought overland to Ugarit, which is to the north of Judea, and then by sea, the short crossing to Ura. It is a tenuous chain—"

"And too easily broken," Hastayar said.

"Yes, majesty. Also—the Carthaginians, again. They're outbidding us for the Egyptian grain. Of course it's safer for the Egyptian merchants to ship it overland through Africa to Carthage, than over the sea to us."

"The Carthaginians!" Arnuwanda snapped. "To think it's not long since we fought alongside those scum and the Muslims to keep the Mongols out of Egypt. Curse them to the Dark Earth!"

Himuili said frankly, "My feeling is that they seek to use the opportunity of these bleak winters to bring us down."

"Starving us out!" Arnuwanda made an involuntary crossed-wrists sign, the sign of Jesus' palm leaves. "What a foul way to wage war."

The Tawananna said coldly, "The point is, gentlemen, we must look beyond these emergency measures and decide what to do next. By *we* I mean the Hatti as a people. And by *next* I mean in the coming year, or two years or five years. The Father of the Churches is begging Judas-Telipinu to be more forgiving with the sun and the rain," and Angulli suppressed a belch in response, "but with all due respect we cannot rely on that happening. Must we sit here and freeze and starve, while fending off the Rus and the Scand and the Pechenegs and whoever next comes walking down from the north?" She counted the points on her hand. "Rationing wasn't enough. Kicking people out wasn't enough. We can't rely on the Egyptian grain, our last staple. What then?"

Arnuwanda studied her warily. "I know you, Aunt. When I was a boy you played tougher games with me than my father did, and he was a seasoned soldier. I still have the scars . . . You have a plan, don't you? Something bold, something outrageous—"

"Something you would never have thought of, that's for sure. Or my much-lamented husband. But it's actually a plan brought to me by another. General?"

Himuili looked embarrassed for once, as the eyes of the elevated company turned to him, and Kassu understood for the first time why he had been summoned back from the Simoeis. "It's my plan, of sorts. It's this. New Hattusa is becoming increasingly unviable."

"Yes, yes," Arnuwanda said. "So?"

"So we move."

"We?"

"All of us. Like the Rus. The whole population."

That made jaws drop, including Kassu's.

"I'm the city's Hazannu," said Tiwatapara. "And I can tell you now that the population won't stand for it. To wander around the countryside like booty people? No, sir—not Hatti!"

But now Palla discreetly stepped forward. "If I may . . ."

"Go on, priest," Himuili said, before anybody could shut him up.

"There may be a way to persuade them." He glanced at Angulli, his superior. "Of course, there is the historical precedent; the Hatti capital has moved before, a thousand years ago. And under the wise guidance of the Father of the Churches, I have been considering theological precursors also. Remember that Jesus Himself was once booty; He was transported across Anatolia to Old Hattusa, after the Judean uprising."

"Ah," Hastayar said. "And it did Him no harm in the end, did it? Now He can lead us all on a new journey, into the sunlight. The people may not follow me, but they will certainly follow Jesus." She nodded at Himuili. "You've found a smart young man in that one, General."

Arnuwanda demanded, "And, if we move—where, in the name of Teshub?"

Hastayar regarded her nephew slyly. "Where would *you* suggest, Prince?"

"We have a whole empire, much of which is south of New Hattusa. I suppose anywhere to the south would be preferable."

"And if we went beyond the empire?"

Arnuwanda goggled, clearly out of his depth. "Beyond?"

"Egypt," Angulli said. "What about Egypt? We could go to the grain, rather than have the grain come to us. We could live in the sun on the banks of their great river, whose waters, as you know, never fail, even in the worst drought."

Himuili nodded. "Egypt is the key, I agree with you there. But even if we succeeded in taking it from the Muslims, we would be vulnerable to attack from the rest of their domains, which are pretty extensive, as you know, sir. *And* there would be the Carthaginians to deal with, who want the grain for themselves. We would step off the boat and immediately be under attack on two fronts, east and west, which is a poor deal militarily. Sir."

"Then where, man? Don't drag it out. Where?"

Himuili deferred to Hastayar.

And she said: "*Carthage*. We go to Carthage. All of us, every Hatti who can walk or ride or swim. We fight a monumental war, and we drive those pagan camel-traders out of their own city, and we establish a new kingdom in the name of Jesus Sharruma. And then we take Egypt at our leisure."

Arnuwanda said, "And the empire?"

"The whole of the empire," Hastayar said coldly, "will serve as a buffer between the new capital and whatever savagery comes out of the freezing north, while we make our escape."

There was a stunned silence.

"It's insane," blurted Tiwatapara.

"It's magnificent!" cried Angulli, and he half stood and raised his cup. "More wine, boy. I say, more wine! For tomorrow we will be warming our feet in the smoking ruins of Carthage itself." And, overcome, he fell back, tipping over his chair. Guards rushed to his aid, and the gathering broke up in confusion.

21

While the chaos inside the pavilion was sorted out, Kassu waited outside, in snow that was gathering despite the efforts of frantically sweeping slaves.

At last Himuili came striding out, blowing on his hands. "Shut up," he said, before Kassu could say a word. "Listen to me, soldier. You asked for my advice. Far be it for me to lecture you on the state of your marriage. My two previous wives will assure you I'm no expert on *that*. I'll tell you this, though. Our laws on marriage here in Hattusa, and our customs too, are pretty civilized, at least compared to some shitholes I've fought in. The Germans, for instance—well, never mind. *Civilized*—you know what that means, man? Liberal. Practical. Fair to all parties.

"Having said that, and I consulted a lawyer friend, I can tell you this. You do have a right to prosecute your wife and her lover for their adultery. If you can gather the evidence, and since they both seem to be admitting it that won't be a problem, you'll secure a conviction.

And then you'll be able to request the sentence." He said this last heavily, emphasizing every word. "For that is the way we Hatti do things. And you know what the maximum is, don't you? Tell me, man."

"Death. For either of them—"

"Shut up. No. Not for either. *For both.* Both or neither, and that's the law. If you want to punish your wife for spreading her legs for this Jesus-chaser—well, that's up to you, but he goes with her. If you want to take revenge on him—fine, that's your choice. But you can't keep her, you lose her too. Understood? Good. Shut up.

"Now here's the next thing." He moved subtly closer to Kassu; he smelled of leather, woodsmoke, the expensive wine he'd been drinking with the queen. "Here's why I'm bothering to speak to the likes of you on such a day as this. No matter what you may think of Palla, and I tend to agree with you that he's a horny little bastard who needs his ass kicking, I dragged your sorry weight along with us today because I wanted you to see what he can do. Do you understand?

"First of all there was the Rus. I can tell you this, it's Palla who's been the leader among the priests in our dealings with them. He's worth ten of that flabby drunken fool Angulli. And then this business of the great walk. As soon as I floated the idea, he was immediately able to come up with the analogy with Jesus. He's a sharp man, for all his mild looks—a man who knows how to use his religion for the good. I think he could be priceless in the months, the years to come. *But* you have his life in your hands, and he knows it.

"I understand how you feel. Well, I don't, it's never happened to me. You want him dead. And you know what—*I* want him dead, in a way. Cheating on a serving soldier is despicable. But look, Kassu, you've done your duty in the past. I've seen it with my own eyes. Not just in the lines, but taking on your farm too. If we had a thousand like you maybe we wouldn't have to move at all. Now I'm asking you to think about your duty again, before you decide what to do about the priest." He stepped back. "All right? Good man." He clapped Kassu on the shoulder, and turned to walk back to the pavilion.

Kassu had to ask one question. "Sir—will the walk happen? Will we leave Hattusa? Has it been decided?"

Himuili looked back at him. "Ah. If we don't have to walk you'll be free to get the priest topped. Is that what you're thinking? We resolved to wait until the spring. If it looks like a good season, we'll stay and make the best of it. If it's bad . . ." He grinned. "I suppose Palla will be praying to Jesus for the snow. Now get on with it."

"Thank you, sir—"

"Shut up."

Two

22

The Second Year of the Longwinter:
Spring Equinox

All across the northern lands people watched for the end of a terrible winter. The scholars examined their almanacs, the farmers eked out the last of their stores, the hunters prepared for the migration of the animals they preyed on, and the warriors sharpened their blades in advance of the new campaign season.

But this year was to be like none that had gone before, not for ten thousand years. This year the growing masses of ice on land and sea, cloaked with cold air, would significantly divert the currents of air and moisture that flowed over them. This year the spring winds would not come from the balmy southwest, but from the chill north. There was a spring equinox. The planet's orbital geometry mandated it. But there was no spring.

As the cold endured, all across the northern hemisphere, people began to look to the warm, to the south. Only to find, usually, that there was already somebody there.

23

The river rose, and rose. Walks In Mist, standing by the warehouse, drenched by the rain that had lashed down for days, watched in astonishment as the cargo ship lifted on the rising water until it stood high over its jetty.

This was the busiest inland port on the greatest river in the continent of the Sky Wolf. She had goods on that boat, cotton, a load of copper brought up from the south. She was supposed to be signing for them. The unloading hadn't even begun. And still the ship rose up, as the river swelled with runoff. People stood around laughing at the sight. Even on the ship itself the crew were laughing, standing by the rail, watching the world descend beneath them. One man mockingly clambered on the rail, arms spread wide in the rain. Every one of them was soaked to the skin, dark hair plastered flat, clothing heavy with the wet; she couldn't hear their voices over the hiss of the rain in the standing water.

Walks In Mist had never seen such a sight. She had an odd, sharp memory, of sitting in a bar in the Northland

Wall with her friends, with Xipuhl and Sabela, both of them far away now. A midsummer evening when the wind had turned chill, and people had laughed at that too.

Now, with a great creak of strained wood, the ship *tipped*. The laughter grew uncertain.

The man who had been clowning on the rail fell. Tumbled in the air, arms waving as if he were trying to swim. Hit the jetty with a sound like a sack of meat dropped onto growstone. Didn't move.

For a heartbeat people stood there, shocked to silence. Then some of the bystanders ran forward.

And behind them the ship tilted further, rolling out of its basin toward the dock. The strain on the hull was increasing: wood groaned, and ropes parted with a crack. The people who had gone to help the fallen man moved back, uncertain. A main mast snapped like a toothpick.

Walks In Mist saw what was to come, with terrible clarity.

She ran from the river, through the rain. She jumped back on her cart and ordered the driver to take her home, fast. The llamas trotted away, bleating in complaint at the rain that lashed into their eyes.

Behind her, wood cracked noisily, and there was a groan like a falling giant, and screams. Walks In Mist did not look back.

Her family home was just outside the great wall that contained the heart of the River City, a ceremonial district studded with holy mounds. The house was small and neat with a steep thatched roof, and plastered walls painted red and white. Walks In Mist had always liked its modesty; it was far more expensive, far more well built than its deceptively simple design would suggest. But this spring the small fenced garden was coated with the dust that had blown in during the long summers of drought. The solitary chestnut tree was withered. The plasterwork was faded by the relentless sun of the drought years, and stained by windblown dust.

And now, the rain had come. Walks In Mist had lived in this place all her life. She knew the weather. Every summer it rained; every summer the rivers rose—every normal summer anyhow. But the summers had been dry for years. Now, at last, the rain came, but this was spring, not summer, and never had she known such rain.

The River City was close to the confluence of several great rivers, including the mighty Trunk that ran all the way to the ocean in the south. The city's wealth came from the rivers and the trade goods they brought through this place, copper and mother-of-pearl from the south, buffalo and elk hide from the north, more exotic goods from over the oceans. But anybody who had grown up here knew that the rivers were also a danger, when the rain came heavily. And the rain had never been as heavy as this.

She approached the house at last. Through a curtain of rain she could see the Mountain of the Gods looming beyond—not a mountain at all, of course, but man-made, the greatest of more than a hundred mounds in the ceremonial district, an artificial mountain built on a flood plain to celebrate the divine generosity that had produced such a rich country as this. The view of the Mountain of the Gods inside its walled compound was one of the house's best features. But today water was pouring down the mound's stepped slopes and, as she watched, a chunk of one face broke away, disintegrating. Floodplain clay was not an ideal material for building mounds, she had once learned from a visiting Northlander engineer; now he was proven right.

The cart pulled up by the house. She told the driver to wait, and ran to the door. Her children were both inside, she found to her relief, Bear Claw and Yellow Moon, fifteen and ten. They were playing chess on the cotton carpet, with the expensive set she had brought back from Northland last year. The rain hammered on the thatch roof.

"Where's your father?"

Yellow Moon glanced up, her pretty face pulled into its usual pout. They had named the child for the color of the moon in the dry, dust-storm spring in which she had been born. "Out," the girl said. "Mother, you're dripping on the carpet."

"Where did he go? Did he say?"

"He might have gone to the fields." The family owned stretches of the maize fields around the central city.

She heard a noise now, beyond the hiss of the rain. A dull roar, like the breaking of a wave on an ocean shore. It was a sound she had grown used to in Northland, but in River City, in the heart of the continent the Northlanders called the Land of the Sky Wolf, she could not be farther from the ocean.

"Up," she snapped. "On your feet."

"What?"

"We're leaving, now."

"After the game," said Yellow Moon.

"Now!" Walks In Mist grabbed her hand and hauled her to her feet. "For once will you do as you're told?"

The girl started to cry.

Bear Claw got to his feet, eyes wide. He was tall for his age, with a fine black stripe painted down the center of his face. "You're frightening her."

"Good. Come on."

Bear Claw followed slowly. "What about our stuff? I'll get our cloaks—"

"No!" And she took his hand too, and dragged them both out through the door.

Outside the rain still fell hard and vertical, and that roaring noise was louder, coming from the north. People were emerging from their houses to see, curious, some in hooded cloaks, most with bare heads, all peering to the north, shouting questions to one another.

Walks In Mist thanked the gods of sky and earth that the cart was still there, that the miserable-looking driver hadn't driven away, or run off. She shoved her children aboard, and clambered up herself. "Go," she snapped at the driver.

"Where to?"

"That way!" She pointed. "South! Just drive south, as fast as you can."

The cart rolled off, the wheels sticking in the muddy ground. They made faster progress once they were on the hardtop main track. They hurried south, heading for the open fields away from the ceremonial district, clattering past more neat houses, mounds bearing shrines and gifts for the deities. People were leaving now, grabbing bundles of possessions, dragging children, pulling cloaks over their shoulders, loading carts. Soon, Walks In Mist feared, all fifteen thousand people in the town, said to be the largest city in the Continent, would be fleeing, or trying to. Probably most would leave it too late. She wished she knew where her husband was.

And now Bear Claw pointed back, the rain running down his face. "Look!"

Water was breaking over the city's northern wall. It spilled across the flat countryside, pink and muddy, washing around the holy mounds. Walks In Mist saw people fleeing, crying out, falling before its advance. Swarming like ants, before the water that rushed over them.

Walks In Mist clung to her daughter, who had been crying since being taken away from her chess game. "Go," she yelled at the driver. "Go, go!"

24

t was still snowing on the morning of Rina's appointment with the Carthaginian noble Barmocar, in his apartment in Old Etxelur. She walked alone to the old town, with a hood over her head. She'd tried to keep this assignation secret. She was, after all, intending to betray her fellow Annids, cousin Ywa, and most of her family.

As she walked, the snow fell steadily, as it had for days, not like the Autumn Blizzard and the storms that had followed, but a slow, unending, dispiriting fall that gathered relentlessly on the ground. Her cloak wrapped close, she passed workers laboriously clearing away yet another night's fall from the paths. You could see where the new snow was piled up on top of the old, some of which, dirty and layered with muck, hadn't melted since the early autumn.

When she reached Old Etxelur she looked back at the Wall, where people were working steadily to repair the damage the winter had done. The Hall of Annids was a huge wreck on its rows of supporting pillars, open to the air. All across the Wall, vast sections had been abandoned as people retreated to core areas and revived older, more robust systems, digging out chimneys, repairing ancient rainfall-trap water supply systems. This was spring! They had all waited for the equinox, and marked the end of winter with lavish celebrations—well, as lavish as possible. And all it had brought was yet more snow, yet more cold, as if the world itself had lost its way.

She turned, pulled her cloak tighter, and walked on.

In the anteroom to his lavish rented apartment in Old Etxelur, Barmocar received her graciously enough. His wife, Anterastilis, was at his side, the two of them resplendent in purple cloaks. The household was in turmoil, however, as the merchant prince's servants packed everything up in preparation for the long trip back to Carthage, postponed for half a year since Barmocar had been caught by the early snow, like so many others.

He was clearly surprised when she asked him to dismiss his servants, and more surprised when she made her blunt request.

He actually laughed. "You're serious. You want me to take you to Carthage. You, and who else?"

"Just my children—the twins, Nelo and Alxa, you know them." This of course meant the abandonment of the rest of her extended family. Ywa herself was a distant cousin. But to take more would have been like pulling a thread; the whole tapestry would unravel. No, just herself and her children, for now. Not even Thaxa, her husband, would come, not this time; he would follow later, they had agreed. And if things changed—well, the future would have to take care of itself.

"And when we get to Carthage, we will take you into our home." Anterastilis was a heavy, expensively coiffed woman. Her Northlander was stilted, but her tone was sharp as an icicle. "Is that what you're saying?"

Rina squirmed; the woman was clearly enjoying this, and was going to make her suffer. "Perhaps initially. Give us somewhere we can live, at least at first. A start in your society. Work for my children, a place for me."

Anterastilis actually laughed at her now. "'A place.' You could join the Tribunal of One Hundred and Four, perhaps!"

"I can pay my way—"

"Perhaps you can. Perhaps not." Barmocar turned to his wife. "My dear, you made a note of what this lady of Northland said to me at the Giving last year. Would you mind reading it back? You know the part I mean."

Anterastilis took a piece of paper from a desk and unrolled it carefully. "'Good Prince Barmocar, I am confused. This tale of woe you recite—are you here to beg for bounty? Begging like these others, the Franks and Germans and the rest, these 'poor rudimentary farmers,' as I have heard you describe them? And a bounty from us, whom I have heard you describe as 'a thin godless smear of ignorance and incompetence on an undeveloped landscape'?"

"I recall what was said," Rina said precisely.

"Then you recall mocking me. In front of the Giving gathering—in front of the whole world." He did not sound angry, merely analytical.

She didn't bother to deny it.

"And now you sit before me, begging me for shelter."

"I do not beg. I can pay you for your trouble. It will be worth your while."

"Are we to haggle, as if over a box of your disgusting salted fish? Tell me, then. Tell me what you have that I could possibly covet."

"My family owns extensive lands in Northland. Also properties in New Etxelur, and in the Wall. Many of these are in my own name. I could transfer—"

Again he laughed, cutting her off. "Madam, I am not the fool you take me for. You are abandoning Northland yourself! What value do you imagine your property has?"

"Other forms of wealth, then. Gold. Silver." In fact

she hadn't expected him to take property, and had already been converting some of her holdings into portable wealth—at ruinous prices, for she wasn't the only one with the same idea.

Now he nodded. "Well, that's a start. You can discuss precise quantities with my clerk later." He leaned forward. "But the world is full of gold and silver, madam. What else can you offer me? Something special. Something unique." And, even though his wife sat right beside him, he allowed his gaze to wander over her body.

He was treating her like a whore. She was an Annid of Northland, and this Carthaginian animal was treating her like a whore. She would not allow her humiliation to show. *She would not.*

"Knowledge, then," she said now.

"Knowledge?"

"It is our knowledge above all that has enabled Northland to prosper across the centuries, since the days of Pythagoras, and for millennia even before that. I could put this at your disposal—endow a library perhaps, to the greater glory of Carthage. A library of world renown in your own distinguished name . . ."

"A bank of dusty old scrolls? I don't think so. I'll tell you what I want. I'll tell you what you can bring to me, what will make it worth my while hauling your skinny backside to Carthage. You and your equally worthless children."

She had never before been spoken to this way. "Tell me."

"The bones of the Virgin."

"Who?"

"The Mother of the Hatti god-man. What's His name? Jesus, that's it."

She frowned. "Why would you want that? Carthage does not follow Jesus."

"But our enemies do. The Hatti. And if I have what they want, that gives me power over them. Do you see? Just as now I have power over you."

She shook her head. "The reliquary of the Virgin—I have no access. And the bones aren't mine to give."

"Find a way. Bring me the relics. Or, and you know it as well as I do, by this time next year your own bones will be lying in that Wall. Probably having been gnawed by your own starving children."

Anterastilis laughed prettily, as if he had made a polite witticism.

Rina took a breath, and looked from one to the other. "We have an arrangement, then."

"Not quite. One more thing." Again he leaned closer, and she could smell fish sauce on his breath. "You aren't the only craven Northlander trying to escape. You're not the only one selling off the treasures of millennia, in a desperate attempt to save her children from the ice."

She had no idea if that was true. But if she was keeping such a secret, why not others?

"This is the end of Northland's long and manipulative history—the end of your smugness and arrogance. And it ends like this. You have come here to beg, for all you deny it. I want to hear you say it."

She hesitated for one heartbeat, composing herself, ensuring her voice would be strong. "Then I beg. I beg you to save me and my children, Barmocar."

He laughed, slapped his thigh, and sat back. "*Very* good. If you have the relics before we leave, you come with us. If not, you stay. You can show yourself out." He turned away from her, and began to speak to his wife in his own thick tongue.

She stood and left the apartment, unescorted. She thought of Pyxeas. She had taken his advice in the end, she was fleeing to the south, just as he had recommended. But now she wished with all her heart she had taken her children with her when she had escorted him last year to Hantilios—and wished she had never been foolish enough to come back.

25

It had seemed a long winter, so far from home. But at last the morning came when Pyxeas' party was to leave Akka, and resume the journey east to Cathay.

Akka was a spacious, handsome town of wide straight streets and stout sandstone buildings, on the easternmost shore of the Middle Sea. Uzzia had brought them here across the ocean from Hantilios when the winter relented, and she had spent the months since scouring the city's tiny, crowded harbor for berths on a ship going east. The ocean had its own hazards, Uzzia told them, but a journey by sea was a much more feasible way for Pyxeas to travel to far Cathay, rather than to jolt his bones overland. But there were no berths to be had; the whole world was going through a tremendous convulsion, and there were too many precious cargoes to be shipped from one place to another to make room for an old man. So overland it would be, they had reluctantly decided in the end.

Even Pyxeas had agreed that the journey could not be attempted before the winter was done, but he had spent the whole season fretting with impatience, even while he buried himself in his studies. Avatak suspected he had seen nothing of this place—this beautiful town with the rich Arab-Muslim culture of its latest owners, laid over a deep history, all of it utterly unlike anything Avatak had encountered before. Avatak, though, had immersed himself. Now, this early morning, Avatak stood beside the clean stone wall of one of the many mosques that dominated the city. The sun was still low, barely risen over the eastern horizon, but already he could feel its heat on his face and bare arms, a promise of noon.

And here was Uzzia, walking up to him, wearing her quilted coat, a heavy pack on her back, her whip in her hand. There was a strength, a stillness about her, Avatak had thought since he'd got to know her, stillness and solidity. Which was reassuring, since he was going to have to rely on her to get him and Pyxeas safely through the unknowable days to come.

She fell in beside him as they walked up the street toward the mustering point, where Pyxeas and their guide Jamil would be waiting for them. They passed a few folk in the street, a bent old woman who sprinkled water to lay the dust, a boy sweeping dirt from a gutter, a couple of young men who might have been Carthaginians staggering home from a long evening. Mostly, the city still slept.

"You're going to be sorry to leave, aren't you?" In the course of the winter her Northlander had grown more fluent, though Avatak could tell she was picking up Pyxeas' own slightly clipped Etxelur intonation.

"It's not my place to be sorry. It's my place to look after the scholar. To go where he needs to go, to keep him safe."

"Yes." Uzzia laughed. "As Rina made plain before she left us at Hantilios. My ears are still ringing, and I was in the next room. That's a formidable woman, and I would not wish to cross her. But still—you have feelings, you're a human being, not a pack mule or a camel."

"What's a *camel*?"

"You'll find out."

They were passing the wall of a grand private residence, with an open doorway decorated with an intricately carved arch. Looking within, Avatak saw a courtyard centered on a pond, above which a fountain bubbled. More archways, supported by delicate columns, led invitingly to shady rooms.

"Beautiful," Uzzia said.

"My home is a place of hard ice and the dark. It can be beautiful." He thought of the colors in the big sky at this time of year, the shades of the ice on the ocean, every tint of blue you could imagine. "But this, this is beauty of light and water."

"The Arabs are people of the desert. They cherish water. They have turned that sensibility into high art."

"Cathay will have its own wonders. So Pyxeas says. But—"

"But you're going to miss this," she said gently. "Who wouldn't? And *her*. You're going to miss her too."

He felt the heat in his face. "You saw."

She laughed. "You're a man from the northern wastes, Avatak. In a city like this, you stand out. Yes, I saw. So did most of Akka, I think. What's her name?"

"It's got nothing to do with you," he snapped.

"I don't mean to pry. She's very beautiful."

"Nothing can come of it."

"Is she betrothed to another? She looks as if she belongs to a rich family."

"No. It is me. I am betrothed. There is a woman, at home. Her name is Uuna."

"Ah." She thought that over. "I never knew that."

"No, and you never imagined it, and nor did Pyxeas when he insisted I come away with him to study, for you both think me a boy."

"I don't think that. In some cultures a man may take many wives. Or one may take lovers."

"Not in my village."

"Well, that's that. You mustn't blame old Pyxeas. It's just that in you he's only looking for one thing, a certain kind of intelligence, or an openness to new ideas, new experiences—no, not even that. My Northlander is still poor; I don't have the words to express it. A capacity for wonder, perhaps. That's what he sees in you. Although he was unable to see the young betrothed man, with a life and responsibilities of his own. Well—what's done is done, and here we are, leaving it all behind, for better or worse." She took his hand as they walked; her skin was warm, leathery, a worker's hand. "You may see her again, if we come this way when we return."

"Is that likely?"

She sighed. "The future is even more unknowable than usual these days. I do know how you feel."

"How can you?"

"I am in the same position."

He thought that over. "You have a lover in Akka?"

"And others elsewhere. My life consists of long stays in places separated by tremendous journeys, and I seem to give away my heart at each stop. Each of my loves knows about the rest."

"And in Akka—who is he?"

"She," Uzzia said with a smile. "In my case, it's a she. But that's our secret. Ah, we arrive, and there is Pyxeas looking irritable, and Jamil looking greedy, and his horses looking like lazy overpriced nags. Thus it always was. Jamil!" She strode forward boldly toward the men. "Years of famine and you're still as plump as ever . . ."

Avatak watched her, bewildered, comforted.

Jamil wasn't all that plump, Avatak thought, although he had the slack face of a man who had once been plumper. He was perhaps forty, about Uzzia's age, and he wore a loose white jacket, trousers whose legs billowed as he walked, and a small round hat. He had bright merry eyes, as if he was used to laughing at the world.

He was arguing with Pyxeas about the luggage. As Uzzia approached he held his hands out, comically imploring. "You explain it to the wise gentleman, please, fair Hatti princess. How these great boxes and bundles will break my beasts' poor backs!" He spoke passable Northlander.

Pyxeas stood by a cart laden with his goods, with a protective hand on the heaviest trunk. "And you can tell this fellow that I won't leave a shred behind, not a page, not a bottle of ink. I spent months in Etxelur rendering this down, the wisdom of centuries crammed into a box. If I'm forced to leave any of it behind then you may as well leave me too, leave me to desiccate in the desert like a dead mouse!"

Uzzia sighed. "Gentlemen, gentlemen. Can't we come to some compromise?" She spoke softly, in Greek to Pyxeas, and Arabic to Jamil. It did not take long for her to bring about peace. Avatak marveled at her skill.

Meanwhile Avatak cautiously approached the beasts. The Arab had four horses—two were being harnessed to his cart and two were loose—and a single mule, already laden with a towering load wrapped in bundles of cloth.

His dispute settled, Jamil walked up, gaze lively, curious. "You're the ice boy, yes? I heard about you."

"Yes. I'm from—"

"If you're not busy, give me a hand with this trunk. It needs to go in the cart."

They soon formed up for the journey. Pyxeas was to ride on the cart, which was driven by Jamil. For now, Uzzia would walk, leading the spare horses.

"And me? What must I do?" Avatak asked.

Jamil grinned. "You, boy, can bring the mule." And he cracked a short whip and drove the cart away.

The mule, though small in stature, was a slab of muscle, with a sour smell and a blank, contemptuous stare. Dwarfed by its load, it simply looked back at Avatak when he tried to coax it forward, and was immovable as a rock when he tried to drag it. It was only when the cart and horses were almost out of sight that the animal deigned to follow, and even then at its own pace, stopping where it would, to piss or shit or nibble the sparse grass.

In the days that followed, Jamil and Uzzia took turns with the mule. Uzzia bribed it with bits of fruit, while Jamil noisily beat it with his crop. Avatak was the worst at getting anything out of the beast, and they laughed at his efforts. But he developed a grudging respect for the mule's unshakable sense of independence, even as it plodded along under its unreasonable load. Maybe in this company, he and the mule had a lot in common.

And he buried his resentment of their laughter. After all, he came from a country where only dogs obeyed man, where every other beast of air, sea or land was utterly beyond human control, and was maybe the better for it. He dreamed of being able to handle a dog team on the ice, at some point in this expedition. Then they would see what the mastery of an animal, a unity of human will with beast strength, really meant.

26

From Akka they turned away from the coast and headed roughly east, crossing higher ground.

At first the country was quite arid, and they followed dusty trails between water courses. They rarely saw other people, once they'd left the city and the crowded coastal strip. They did come across a few abandoned settlements, collapsed houses of mud brick and straw, the boundaries of fields given up to the dust. The days were hot, the sun high. Uzzia gave Avatak a thick oil to rub into his skin to protect it from the sun's heat.

When they stopped, they made camp in a kind of yurt carried folded up on the back of the mule. The yurt was cramped, uncomfortable. Some nights they preferred to sleep outdoors by the fire, all save Pyxeas. Jamil and Uzzia complained of the cold at night, and woke up in wonder, staring at the heavy dew or even ground frost. They had never known such cold, they said, not here. Avatak, though, slept deeply and well, enjoying the kiss of ice on his cheek.

After some days they descended to lower ground,

and the nature of the country changed, becoming moister, grassier. This was a country that had evidently been spared the worst of the drought, and they followed trails and a few better-maintained roads through small communities of wary but more or less friendly farmer folk, who grew fruit trees and raised herds of sheep and cattle. At this time of year new lambs clustered around their mothers, cautious of the visitors. Avatak watched them curiously. There were no sheep at all in Northland, and the cattle here were fat, sullen beasts with snow-white hides, nothing like the tall, splendid aurochs, the wild cattle of Northland.

Pyxeas spoke vaguely of great civilizations which had been nurtured in this clement country, watered by tremendous rivers flowing from the northeast. In an arid valley he pointed to the tumbled ruins of what must once have been a mighty stone city, and pale scratches in the dirt that might have been irrigation channels, now dry and dust-choked. The state of the roads showed that civilization still prospered here, Pyxeas said; the roads were for tax collectors and armies, but nowadays the great centers were far from here. Avatak thought that these old eastern cultures could never have matched the grandeur and antiquity of Northland.

Every few nights Pyxeas had Avatak help him maintain his records. They had a journal where Avatak kept a basic record of the date, the nature of the country, the number of days traveled, and the distance, which Pyxeas estimated, remarkably, by counting the steps of the horses' hooves. With sun sightings Pyxeas kept track of their direction of travel too.

And whenever they took a rest day Pyxeas brought out his "world position oracle." This was a gadget of bronze and steel the size and weight of a hefty brick, which he kept wrapped in soft leather when they traveled. The front and back were covered with dials, little windows that opened and closed, and images of the sun and moon made of gold and ivory. There were wheels to turn, levers to pull and switches to throw that would make the sun and moon dance against a brass sky. Avatak had seen this thing opened up. Inside was a bewildering mass of brass gears on spindles. Pyxeas expected Avatak to keep it cleaned and lubricated, though effecting any repairs would be far beyond either of them. To use this device Pyxeas took careful sightings of the elevation of the polestar at night, and if possible of the noon sun, made by tracking the shadow of a vertical stick. And wherever they traveled he had Avatak measure the hours of daylight, from sunrise to sunset, using an hourglass filled with fine sand; he wrote down the result every day, alongside similar numbers from the oracle.

Jamil and Uzzia were fascinated by the oracle. Avatak could see how they longed to turn the little ribbed wheels and make the little sun and moon rise and fall, to play with it just like every child who'd ever seen the thing.

On the third rest day, Jamil broke. "All right, I give in. What is that gadget, sage? What are you doing with it? And how much do you want for it?"

Pyxeas, irritated at being interrupted as ever, glanced up. "You could not afford the fees charged by the Wall *mechanikoi.*"

"The who? That's a Greek word."

"True. And their workshop District is often called 'the Greek quarter.' But few *mechanikoi* these days have more than a trace of Greek blood in them! The word is a reference to the deeper history of philosophy in Etxelur, for it was there that the sage Pythagoras fled with his followers some two thousand years ago, fleeing the reign of a tyrant in his native Samos. Pythagoras' essential legacy, you see, is his insight that the universe is based on order; that the cosmic order can be expressed in numbers; and that those numbers can be grasped by the human mind. It all follows, it is said, from Pythagoras' observations of the notes of a plucked lute string."

Avatak was used to discursions like this, and had

learned not to listen until the scholar got to the important stuff.

Uzzia, however, boldly laid a hand on the old man's arm. "Pyxeas. We get the point. It took hundreds of generations of string-plucking before some bald-pated genius was able to make this thing. But *what does it do*?"

"Why, it enables me to calculate where I am, as I cross the turning globe of the earth. And, in a sense, *when* I am." He eyed her, and Jamil. "You understand that the world is a sphere."

"Actually a somewhat flattened sphere, according to Hatti astronomers," Uzzia snapped back. "Who in turn have built on studies by the Babylonians and others going back millennia. Please don't condescend, old man."

"Very well. Then you'll understand that as we travel north and south, the apparent position of the polestar in the sky will change. It would be directly overhead if we were at the north pole, whereas if we travel south—"

"Yes, yes."

"So if I measure the star's position—"

"Or you get me to do it," murmured Avatak.

"What's that? Then I can determine the north-south arc of my position on the world's spherical surface. Now, knowing the date and that *single number*, the northern arc, I can use my oracle to predict for me"—he spun wheels and pressed levers, making the face of the oracle sparkle and shift—"the length of the day at this place, and the greatest height achieved by the sun in the sky. I have the boy check these independently with his sightings and his hourglass. The numbers are never identical, but the differences teach us about flaws in our methodology, and indeed the small digressions of the earth from its spherical state, to which you have alluded."

Jamil studied the oracle longingly. "Must be useful at sea, that. And in some deserts I've crossed. So you have your position north to south. But what about east-west?"

"Ah," Pyxeas said, enthused. "Excellent question,

considering it's you asking it. The oracle also contains, encoded into its dials and gears, a knowledge of eclipses of the sun and moon, both past and future." He tapped the face. "The little ivory moon slides across the golden sun ... It's really quite pretty to watch. And by matching the prediction with the reality of an eclipse, I can determine my distance from Northland, west to east. The procedure is a little tricky."

Uzzia said, "Just tell me this one thing. You dream of saving the world. Is it through such means as this, the numbers of the sky?"

"Yes! Yes, precisely. You see—"

But she held her forefinger to his lips. "Another time," she said gently. "For now, I understand enough. It is late. You two must finish your work, and come closer to the fire, and we will eat and sleep."

Pyxeas seemed oddly charmed by her motherliness. "Another time, then," he agreed.

Heading ever east, following the vagaries of roads and passes, they moved out of the fertile plain into a land that was higher, drier, much more forbidding. Avatak glimpsed mountains, streaked with ice.

They came to a small town fortified by a stout wall of mud brick. Beyond, the land was more arid still: the town marked the edge of desert. To enter the town the travelers had to pass through a wide gate, horses, cart and all—even the mule. There was stabling for the animals inside, and Jamil immediately did some business, selling off his horses in order to buy—what? Avatak glimpsed a new sort of beast in the shadows of the stables, taller than a horse, stately, foul-smelling. Jamil did keep the mule. Avatak wasn't sure if he was pleased or disappointed.

They spent a few nights here. The city was full of people of diverse hues, costumes and tongues. Jamil said this was a major meeting point for traders, who routinely traveled half the world for the sake of the profit to be made through the trade between Cathay and other eastern empires and the Continent and Northland to the west. Jamil said he'd half expected the town to be quieter than usual, because of flood, drought, plague, banditry and the coldness of the year; such things were bad for trade. On the other hand there were more migrants than usual on the trail, coming both ways—people coming from the west in the hope of finding a better life in the east, only to meet people from the east heading west with much the same ambition. These were times of turbulence. Ominously, Pyxeas pointed to heavy shipments of weapons and armor.

Jamil was waiting on a number of other traders to get ready to leave. They would travel together as a *caravan*—not steam-driven, but a train of beasts and people laden with goods. Avatak had never known that the word for the Northlanders' dazzling transport system was borrowed from a much older meaning.

The morning came when Jamil's caravan was ready—and Avatak was introduced to his camel. The beast was extraordinary. It had two fleshy humps on a back covered with dirty brown hair, and a small head mounted on a long neck, and massive teeth, and an oddly disdainful expression. When it walked on its long legs it seemed to stagger, and at first, after climbing clumsily on its back, it was all Avatak could do to hang on. More laughter from his companions.

But after a few days he saw the beast's advantages. It had broad hoofs that would not sink into the softest sand, and could travel for *days* without water. And all this with the weight of a man on its back. The stink, though—the stink was high! There were times when Avatak looked back at his mule, plodding through the sand, with almost nostalgic affection.

The caravan worked its way steadily west, a party of thirty people and twice as many camels, a few horses, one mule. The desert was flat, arid, featureless, but on the horizon mountains loomed, capped with ice, a grand setting.

Some days later they came upon their first desert town, at what Jamil called an oasis, a place entirely sustained by a single water spring. There were even trees here, their leaves bright and green against the background of the desert. Jamil had boasted of the melon you could buy that was a specialty of the region, which was sold dried out and cut into strips. But the weather was playing havoc here too; it had been a bad spring so far, too *wet* remarkably, and the melon crop was poor.

After a two-day stop and a change of animals, Jamil's caravan moved on.

The deeper they got into the desert, the clearer the air seemed, and the dryer, so that it sucked any moisture straight out of Avatak's skin. But the nights, though: the nights were spectacular, with a dome of star-filled sky framed by the shadows of the mountains on the horizon.

"Oh," said Pyxeas one night, wrapped in his sleeping roll beside the fire, "I would give a great deal to have the eyes of my younger self back again, just for one night. A sky like that is the little mothers' jewel box!"

Uzzia grunted. "Your understanding—all that business of the arc of the world, and the numbers, and your little bronze box—does that not diminish your sense of wonder, old man?"

"Not at all. The deeper the understanding, the more the universe *connects* with one's deeper self, the more one is enriched. That was the essence of the teaching of Pythagoras, I think. And our destiny is written in the stars, to those who have eyes to read it."

"You're talking about saving the world again."

"I'm talking about numbers."

Jamil shook his head, a shadow against the starlit dark. "All this sophistry and philosophizing. No man can know the past, scholar. Let alone the future."

"Can I not?" Pyxeas replied sharply. "The numbers know the future, and they speak to me—or they will, when I have completed my studies."

Jamil grunted. "Any god would punish such arrogance." He walked off to see to the animals.

Uzzia turned away and rolled herself up in her blanket.

Avatak lay silently, with the old man and the stars.

Pyxeas coughed painfully. "Oh, this dust."

The next day, not long after they had set off, a sandstorm hit them. It battered their faces and scraped their eyes, and made seeing and hearing impossible. They had to stop and make a rough camp. They were unable to move further for two days, until the storm blew itself out, by which time they were starting to worry about running out of water.

The camels, however, seemed unperturbed. And the mule expressed no opinion.

27

The first Pimpira knew about the March of the Hatti was when the escaped slave came running out of New Hattusa. But then Pimpira himself was a slave, born of slaves. Slaves were never told anything.

Even of the day they were to die.

It was a spring morning, though it was so cold you'd have thought it was winter. Old snow still lay on the silent fields, and on the ramparts of New Hattusa on the horizon, and in ugly soot-stained heaps in the yard of the master, Kassu the soldier, where it had been scraped up by the slaves. But the problem in the last few days had been not the snow, but the rain. By night Pimpira and his family had been forced to huddle in corners to avoid the freezing-cold water leaking into their shabby hut, and outside the rain pooled on ground that was still frozen just under the surface if you pushed your finger into it, and froze hard in great sheets. Pimpira's father said it was an extraordinary sight, something he'd never seen in all his years. Every year, every month, every day, brought a new sight, something that no-body had ever experienced before in the history of the world, he said. Pimpira's father was thirty-one years old.

Despite the freeze, this morning, as every other morning at this time of year, the slaves were sent out into the fields for another day of struggling to plough the hard earth, goading the surviving oxen. As the morning wore on they would be joined by more workers, paid free folk coming out from the city, desperate for work and food. Pimpira, fourteen years old, knew little about crops, about wheat and rye and barley—with his deformed foot he was rarely sent out into the fields—but he couldn't see how the seeds were going to take in ground frozen hard as rock. But they all went through the routines of the season anyhow, and the master seemed to see that they didn't need whipping to do it. For what choice was there, if they were to have any chance of food later in the year?

As usual, Pimpira was sent away from the rest. The boss told him to dig out an old storage pit under the floor of a demolished barn. It was the kind of job that suited him; he was strong in his upper body, but he wasn't too mobile because of his foot. It was tough labor, smashing the frozen earth into chunks that he could pitch out of the hole, but as he hacked away with his rusted iron shovel, he soon started to warm up.

He didn't know why he was digging this hole. It wasn't as if they were likely to need more storage pits anytime soon. He had a sneaking feeling that what the pit might end up storing was not grain but bones. People were dying, his own brother had been taken during the winter, leaving his mother clinging to his little sister, Mira. But it didn't matter. It wasn't his decision. To Pimpira life was simple; a hole was a hole was a hole. He got on with his digging, and he watched the pale sun climb in the sky. Like every other day the hours would stretch long and empty until the evening, when the slaves would huddle in their shabby huts, and speak of better times, and pray to their gods and prophets, Jesus or Mohammed or the little mothers of Northland or the sun god of Egypt, and Pimpira's father would relate the calm sayings of the teacher Zalmoxis from the old country. They would talk endlessly of food. People would describe the very texture of the meat as it was cut, the way the juices pooled on the hard bread that served as your plate, the feeling as your teeth cut into it, the spurting of blood and fat, and Pimpira's empty stomach would gurgle and twist.

And they would seek news of the future from the oracles—not the way the sages did it in the city, studying the writhing of snakes in boxes or the way sheep entrails fell from an opened bowel. The slaves had no snakes, and any entrails went straight into the pot. But they had their own ancient ways, studying the flight of the birds in the sky—not that there were many birds this spring save crows and buzzards—and dropping oil or blood in bowls of water, to see how the fluids flowed and spread. They argued endlessly about the meaning of each sign, and it seemed to Pimpira that they never agreed, but it comforted everybody.

This dull routine was the whole of Pimpira's life.

And it ended, cut off as if by the fall of a blade, when the slave boy came running from New Hattusa.

When he heard the boy coming, Pimpira climbed out of his hole to watch, and the other slaves and workers paused in their tasks, curious. The boy ran like a whipped dog, right through the farmyard, legs and arms pumping, his eyes wide, his mouth gaping. He was young, not much older than Pimpira, perhaps, though it was hard to tell anybody's age these days as everybody was so skinny. You could tell he was a slave, though. He was barefoot, for one thing. And his tunic and trousers were *old* in the way only slaves' clothes were old, patched and handed down, the color of mud, generations-old clothes so worn they were more like memories of clothing than the real thing. A slave, running away from the city.

Then there was a thunder of hooves. On panting horses, two soldiers in light mail and shining steel helmets came charging after the boy. One man carried a net, the other wielded a sword. Cavalrymen! Pimpira was thrilled at the sight. He had only seen soldiers on parade in the city, on occasional feast days when he had been allowed to accompany the master and his family. He pitied the boy, for he clearly had no chance of outrunning the horses; he must have had a good start to get so far. As the cavalrymen passed through, some of the men on the farm called out greetings and good-natured abuse. "I'll give you five to one the fat one falls off his horse!" The soldiers did not respond. Soon they were disappearing into the east.

After that Pimpira heard a rumble of noise, coming from the west, as had the running slave and the cavalrymen, and again he turned to look. More soldiers, he saw from a glint of distant armor, a small squad of them this time, walking before wagons.

The mistress, Henti, emerged from the big house, with the young priest Palla who so often seemed to hang around here, evoking much ribald speculation from the slaves. Henti walked to the fields and passed among the workers, speaking to them softly. It seemed to be the end of work for now. The slaves were told to gather in the courtyard, a square of beaten earth before the big house, while the hired hands laid down their tools and began to drift off toward the city. They muttered, looking confused, distressed; none of them could afford to be without a day's pay.

The squad of soldiers drew nearer. Pimpira, in his hole, stood on tiptoe, balancing on his good leg, squinting to see them better.

The punch in the back caught him completely by surprise. He was knocked forward into his pit, banging his head on the hard-frozen wall. Winded, he lay there, submissive. He had been born and raised a slave; you just accepted whatever was done to you.

"Don't move." It was his father's voice.

Dirt rained on his back, and heavier lumps. He turned, squinting up. "Father?"

His father had taken Pimpira's shovel and was frantically scooping the pile of lumpy, still-frozen earth back in the hole. "Shut up," he said, panting, glancing up. "Don't move."

"What are you doing? Must I hide here?"

"Yes, you must hide."

"How long?"

"You'll know. Then dig your way out." His father kept shoveling. The rubble was building up on his chest, his legs. Soon he would be buried. Pimpira, shocked, saw tears stream down his father's face. "Remember us. Now put your hands over your face."

The next shovel-load came raining down on Pimpira's head. He huddled in the hole, curling around big blocks of frosty earth. Soon the rubble had shut out the light, and he was covered. But the weight was not great; he would be able to climb out. He heard frantic scuffing. He imagined his father kicking dirt over the storage pit, to conceal it. Then running footsteps, receding.

And then the soldiers arrived, with a tramp of marching boots, a clink of scabbards knocking against greaves, wagons trundling to a halt. Pimpira longed to see them! But, as his father had ordered, he lay curled in the hole.

More footsteps. His mistress's voice. "Zida. I hoped it would be you."

"I told you I'd do it for old Kassu. I take it he's not here."

"Working on the roundup in the city. He knows in his head what must be done here, but his heart would explode out of his chest if he were forced to dispose of his own slaves."

Dispose of?

"That heart of Kassu's is his big trouble, for all he's a stickler for his duty. And if not for the generosity of his heart, lady, you might not be alive to see this day. Or that streak of piss standing beside you."

"The blessing of the Carpenter be on you too, Zida." That was the voice of the priest, Palla. He sounded good-humored.

"I asked Palla to be here," Henti snapped. "He's good with the slaves. I've seen him comfort them. They're not animals; they deserve consolation when it comes to the end."

Zida said sourly, "You're a big bucket of consolation, priest, while the rest of us bloody our hands with the killing."

Palla said evenly, "I think Jesus will understand what's to be done today, and He'll see the grain of goodness in you even as you slaughter, officer. You're here to commit a terrible act—and yet you have come to spare your friend the pain of doing it himself."

Zida snorted. "We'll have time to discuss it when we're all down in the Dark Earth. Let's get on with it. I've a dozen more farms to visit before this day is done. I see you've got them separated. Good. We find it's best to get the able-bodied out of hearing range before we start with the rest, because—"

"I think we know why, Sergeant," said the priest.

"You're sure you sorted them properly? There are to be no nursing mothers on the March, no child under five, nobody over forty, no invalids, no lame."

"I read the instructions," Henti said. "I did what's been asked of me."

"There aren't many, are there? What, a dozen able-bodied?"

"It's not a big farm."

"What did you tell them?"

"The lie I was told to repeat. That the able-bodied are being taken off for a few days to build new grain stores in the city. They believed it, I think."

"Umm. Well, the disposal has been going on for a few

days already. We started in the city. We wanted to get as many of the able-bodied out and the rest finished off before the news started to leak out. The last thing we need is a revolt."

"There was a runner," Palla said. "Came through the farm, not long before you."

"I sent a couple of lads after him. Won't get far. Look, it will take a bit of time before the walkers are shackled and taken out of earshot."

Palla said, "I will talk to the rest."

"Good. Distract them. Just don't get them stirred up before we're ready to process them."

Process?

Henti said, "You may as well come to the house, Zida. Bring your officers. I've some food and drink we won't be able to carry that needs using up . . ."

The voices receded.

Pimpira stayed in his hole, hungry, thirsty, cold, listening to the rattle of shackles being attached to ankles and wrists. He did not know what was going to happen, but he understood the meaning of the basic separation of the slaves into healthy and not healthy, lame and not lame. He knew which group he would be in. This was why his father had hidden him, so he could not be put with the lame and ill and old and very young. He stayed in his hole, and waited, and thought about his father.

After a time he heard singing, a wistful hymn to Jesus Sharruma, led by the priest's clear voice. Pimpira mouthed the words.

Then he heard a rumble of many voices, barked commands from the soldiers, and a shuffling tramp, a clink of iron that settled into a steady, slower rhythm. Shackled slaves being marched away. The line passed by his pit, and he cowered, fearful of discovery. There was a lot of weeping. He strained to hear his father's voice, his mother, but the weeping drowned them out. The shuffled steps, the rattle of the shackles, the occasional crack of a whip, receded.

Now there was only the soft murmur of voices from the group that was left. A child crying. The priest's steady voice. Pimpira imagined him walking from one to the next. Maybe Pimpira's grandmother would be cradling Mira, his baby sister. But the voices were sparse sounds against a greater silence. It was a spring of silence, no frogs croaking in the ponds, no songbirds calling for mates.

Then it began. He heard the sigh of steel, swords being withdrawn from scabbards.

The priest's voice again. "Kneel. That's it. Gather in a circle. Hold hands if it helps. No, Nala, it doesn't matter that Mira's crying. Just hold her. You'll see, soon she'll be smiling for you in the afterlife, in the eternal light of Jesus Sharruma, and bathed in the tears of the Holy Mother Mary. No—don't struggle. It helps if you just kneel up and keep still. The soldiers know what they are doing . . ." The little children were crying, afraid. "Now, I would suggest, Sergeant."

And there was a noise like a pig being gutted, like meat being sliced. Harsher scrapes, like a butcher's cleaver on bone. People tried to cry out, to pray, but their voices were drowned by a kind of gurgling, as if they were drowning. Somebody screamed, and Pimpira heard running footsteps. "Oh, no, you don't—" Heavier footsteps, a tumble, a brief struggle, a hiss of steel.

Soon it was done, it seemed, and he heard swords wiped on cloth and slid back into scabbards. Low soldiers' voices—a rumble of laughter.

Henti stormed, "How can you laugh? *How can you laugh?* The bodies at your feet—the children—"

"Hush, hush," said the priest. "They did it so you didn't have to. It's the Emergency Laws, remember. Think of it as a kindness. It's not these soldiers' fault, Henti. It's not anybody's, save the winter's. Now they will burn the bodies for you, and tidy up."

"But they laughed."

"Let it go, Henti. Without humor how could any man's mind survive such acts?"

"So what now?"

"The March begins in the morning, from the Lion Gate," Zida, the soldier, said. "Not that I'm expecting a prompt start. It will take a long time before thirty or forty thousand people are formed up and ready to go, no matter how willing they are. Believe me, I know; I've been on booty-people marches."

"Zida. I . . . Thank you. You've spared Kassu a lot of pain."

"You were brave to face it yourself, lady. Braver than most. One does become attached to these creatures, doesn't one? Their little lives—their babies, their mourning of their dead. Not that attached, mind you. People have been complaining more about getting their pet dogs put down."

"But is it all worth it, Palla? All this blood spilled before we even begin the March?"

"Wait until you see it tomorrow," the priest said. "It will be a magnificent sight—a whole city, the greatest city in the world, emptying out on the Troad. And the armies marching to either side, the cavalry too. Even the fleets will be setting sail out of the bay. The March of the Hatti is an event unprecedented in history, an event that will be marked for all time. It will be like a festival day! Jesus Sharruma will be brought from His church to lead. Then will follow the crown prince and the royal family. And then will come the priests led by Angulli Father of the Churches, who will proclaim the March and its meaning—"

Zida guffawed. "Ha! If *he* can be separated from his bottle."

Palla said in a lower tone, "Well, we have a plan for that. We priests, I mean. We've a copy of the words he is to say. Words to be repeated daily throughout the journey, until we reach the plains of Libya."

"What words?"

"About how Jesus was a booty-person once."

"Was He? My theology is a bit vague, priest."

"Then shame on you, Zida. It dates from the time

after the Lord of the Watchtower in Jerusalem saved His life from the Judean authorities. Jesus spread His message further, but He stirred up trouble too. There were radical Jews who rejected His divergence from their traditions, others who saw Him as the one who would lead the final holy war, and the usual malcontents who looked for any excuse to rise up against Hatti rule. Well, Jesus gave them all an excuse. He was an old man by then, sixty or seventy. The rebellion was put down with some effort, and the Jews had to be quelled."

"In the traditional way, I suppose."

"Yes. Jerusalem and their other cities were emptied and burned, their temples smashed. The population of Judea was rounded up and marched to the Land of the Hatti, to be put to the usual uses. Jesus Himself was recognized as innocent of trouble-making and would have been allowed to flee with others of the elite, but He insisted He stay with the people. He was lost in the march."

Pimpira, in his hole, found himself getting lost in the story. He had always liked the priest's stories.

"A few years after that a scholar called Hapati-urmah, of a school that was developing an interest in Jesus' teaching, heard a rumor He was still alive, and in Hattusa of all places, I mean Old Hattusa. So he hunted around and there was Jesus, bent and old, working as an assistant in a carpenter's shop. All around Him loved Him, it's said. Well, the scholars wanted to take Him up into the temple, but He refused to leave the shop, His life would end where it began, He said. So *they* came to *Him*, sitting in the sawdust as they listened to His words. So you see, there is the example we wish to promulgate to the people: for Jesus Himself, a booty-people march ended in redemption."

"Hmm. Until His bones were pinched by the Northlanders."

"There is that, yes."

"I'll tell you why the Hatti kings liked Jesus. Because the faith He preached was a submissive creed. A slave's creed. Makes people easier to handle, see, if they think you're enslaving them for their own good."

"That's a cynical point of view."

"All soldiers are cynics."

"Oh, no, they're not, Zida, believe me. Your friend Kassu for one. Look, I'm getting cold, Henti. Shall we go to the house?"

"All right."

Zida called, "You two! Keep an eye out for stragglers. And you lot get on with the pyre . . ."

Footsteps.

And there was Pimpira, alone in the dark. Soon he could smell burning meat.

28

He waited and waited.

He was growing very cold, because he had been lying still so long. He tried not to think of what had happened above, where his mother and father might be now. What he might see when he came out.

But when to come out? He had no way of telling the time; he couldn't see any daylight. He waited a long time. It might have been hours. It might have been heartbeats! It *seemed* long.

When he tried to move he found he had stiffened up; he had been lying curled up, like a baby. He moved as slowly and deliberately as he could, pushing the chunks of frozen earth away as noiselessly as possible. His father's hasty shoveling had left the earth loosely packed, and it wasn't difficult.

Soon he was standing, his head and shoulders thrust out of the pit. It was still daylight, but the light was fading under a gray lid of sky. The big house was dark. A fire burned in a corner of the farmyard—he didn't look at that too closely. There was no wind, and the smoke from the pyre rose straight up to a blank sky. He hoisted himself up, kicking away the last of the debris, and stood, a bit shakily, on the lip of the pit.

"Told you."

A hand grabbed the ragged queue of hair at the back of his head. With a cry, he fell to his knees. He felt cold sharpness at his throat, a blade.

Two figures stepped into his sight. It was the priest Palla, his face expressionless, and a soldier, wearing mail and a heavy, dusty cloak. The soldier said, "Always a few stragglers. Wily lot, these slaves. Well, let's get this done."

Pimpira felt the blade at his neck press harder. He stiffened, determined not to cry out, in case his father should ever hear how he died.

"No, Zida." The priest stayed the man's arm with his hand. "Not like this."

"Look at him, he's lame. He can't join the March. It's the law. You know that, priest."

"Yes, but have some humanity, man. Look at his face! There was hope there, even if he knows he's lost his family. Hope now replaced by a despair, so cruelly. What's your name, boy?"

"Priest, this is not a good idea—"

"Your name."

"Pimpira," the boy said, his voice a croak after so long in the earth. "My name is Pimpira."

"A Hatti name," said the soldier.

"Given him by his parents' owners on his birth, no doubt. And where do you come from?"

"Wilusia district." Which was where the farm was, where they stood.

The soldier laughed out loud.

"Well, if he was born here it's a correct answer," the priest said. "I mean your people. Where did they come from, originally?"

Pimpira couldn't remember the name, of a place neither he nor his parents had ever seen.

"Which prophet comforts you? Jesus, Mohammed?"

"The wise Zalmoxis."

Zida asked, "Who?"

"He's a Dacian." It was the voice of the master. Kassu himself walked up to stand before Pimpira, in mail and cloak and dusty boots. Pimpira tried to drop his head in submission, but the blade at his throat, the hand holding his hair, would not allow it. "His people are Dacian." Kassu glanced around, at the blood-splashed ground, the pyre of corpses. He glared at Palla. "You did this while I was away. To my slaves, on my farm. Your idea, I suppose, priest. Must you meddle in every aspect of my life?"

Palla said firmly, "It was Henti. Your wife wanted to spare you the chore."

"As I did," Zida growled, still holding Pimpira tight. "We're here to help you, Kassu. Anyway, you're back early."

"We've been setting up the March. There's a baggage caravan you wouldn't believe . . . We're being released in shifts so we can prepare our own families."

"Then go to Henti. I'll finish up here." Again Zida tensed for the strike.

But Kassu grabbed the man's arm, pushed him away. Pimpira, released, slumped to the ground. "No. Not this one."

Palla said warningly, "Henti said you would be like this. Sentimental. Not able to do your duty by the Emergency Laws."

"Not this one."

Zida said, "Look at his foot. He can't walk, man. He can't join the March."

"He's with me. He's—my nephew."

Zida stared at him, then laughed. "You can't be serious."

"My nephew, Zida. That's what I'm telling you."

Zida held up his hands. "Well, it's up to you, priest! It's your lot who announced the Emergency Laws. If you lie, if you help him hide a slave, it's your crime."

Kassu faced Palla. "You owe me your life. Now you owe me this."

"Is it worth it, Kassu?" Palla asked evenly. "For one lame slave boy?"

"You tell me. You're the priest."

Palla stared at Pimpira, and shrugged. "Fine. It's your crime. I will say nothing. Are we even now?"

"Oh, no," Kassu snapped. "Never that."

Palla turned and walked away toward the house.

Zida turned on Kassu. "You fool. You idiot. You walnut-brained sack of—"

"Enough."

Zida pointed after the priest. "That man is your worst enemy. He tried to take your wife. And you spared his life! Whoever forgave a man for doing *that*? And now you've given him a weapon to hold over you. And for what?" He swung a kick at Pimpira's good leg, and the boy twisted on the cold ground. "A slave boy who's neither use nor decoration. What's wrong with you, Kassu?"

Kassu had no more to say. He walked after the priest.

Zida stared at him, muttering under his breath. "And *you*." He turned on Pimpira, who cowered. "Get back in that pit, *nephew*, and stay there until I'm gone."

On hands and knees Pimpira scrambled over the broken earth.

29

The Second Year of the Longwinter:
Midsummer Solstice

Barmocar insisted on leaving Etxelur before the midsummer Giving.

Rina knew the Carthaginian hadn't done this just out of spite for her. He and his colleagues and agents had spent much of the winter planning the trek to Carthage; the earlier in the year they started out on this long journey, the better chance they had of completing it before the weather closed in again. In fact, Barmocar told Rina, he would have left even earlier if Northland's dismal non-spring had allowed it.

But the midsummer Giving was the high point of the year for all of Northland, when the people came together before the Wall, under the guidance of their Annids and the priest-philosophers of the House of Wolves. It seemed a dreadful betrayal for Rina to prepare for such an event with the other Annids, while all the time she intended to abandon Northland herself—and while she quietly planned to steal the bones of the Mother of Jesus from their thousand-year-old sarcophagus deep in the fabric of the Wall. She felt the pricking of what a priest of Jesus would, she knew, call her conscience. But it had to be done.

No, Barmocar wouldn't plan the timing of his journey just to spite her. She wasn't important enough even for that, she suspected.

A day after Barmocar and his party had left Etxelur with great pomp, Rina made her own furtive departure.

She collected her bewildered children, took them to the Embassies District of the Wall, and told them she had booked passage on an early morning freight caravan running south from here to the shore of the Moon Sea, where they would join Barmocar's group. Thaxa was here too, to say his own tearful good-byes. She'd given the twins no advance warning, so they had no chance of breaking the secret—or of escaping her clutches on the day.

Naturally Alxa and Nelo didn't want to go. Now sixteen, the twins had their own friends, their own ambitions, their own nascent place in Etxelur society. It had been Alxa who had pressed her mother to take Pyxeas' dire warnings seriously in the first place, but she was unhappy at abandoning her home, her family. As for Nelo, he had his art, his friends in the school of look-deep experimental artists, the scraps of money he was making from selling his work in the markets. It took all that was left of Rina's authority as a mother to force him to come away. "Carthage is one of the world's greatest cities, though it may not be Etxelur. There will be lovers of art. There will be Carthaginians who will buy your work!" Even then she had to compromise by allowing him to bring a stack of his sketchbooks and canvases. The arguments were heated, distressing, predictable. But she would not give way, and Thaxa backed her up. At last she got them both on the steam caravan, with a mound of luggage.

As the caravan made its cautious way south and west, locked together in a tiny passenger cabin, they took out their tensions and unhappiness on one another. The twins worked their way through their resentment, and were soon nagged by guilt at abandoning their friends, the rest of their family—even Thaxa, their father. It didn't get any better when the caravan wound its way through the bank of low hills called the First Mother's Ribs, and they lost sight at last of the tremendous world-spanning face of the Wall.

They were all in a poor state when they arrived at Alloc at the end of a long day's travel, to be met by Barmocar and his party.

Alloc was a major port on the eastern shore of the Moon Sea. It was a hub for trading links with Albia; from here timber and furs brought down the peninsula's great rivers were transported across Northland by roads and canals, and on a shiny new steam-caravan link to the south. Rina had been here many times on Water Council business before. But it had never been so cold, not at this time of year, so close to midsummer, with a nip in the air that felt like it promised a frost.

As hungry-looking porters unloaded their goods and heaped them up beside the track, Rina got her first look at the caravan Barmocar had spent the winter organizing. It was a lot more impressive than the caravan they'd taken from the Wall, with a string of expansive and luxurious passenger cabins, and goods wagons with fuel for the engine and provisions for the long journey. Rina felt a stab of envy, remembering how she had crossed Northland on foot and horse-drawn carriages with Pyxeas last year—but that had been his choice.

As they gathered by the track Rina recognized some of Barmocar's party from meetings and social gatherings at the Wall. There were more Carthaginians, nobles from the many small nations of Gaira and Ibera, even a party of Muslim Arabs who must be intending to continue their journey onward from Carthage across North Africa, or perhaps by boat the length of the Middle Sea. All these dignitaries and their families and entourages had been trapped by the winter weather in Northland, like Barmocar himself. There was a group of soldiers too, tough-looking Carthaginian veterans in their long cloaks and boots and with their weapons strapped to their backs, here for the protection of the travelers, Rina assumed. As soldiers always did, they eyed the women in the group with a kind of lazy calculation.

Amid this churning polyglot crowd, with the caravan's engine already venting steam, Rina and the twins stood uncertainly beside their heap of luggage. At last Barmocar himself approached them, trailed by Mago, his slab-of-muscle nephew, who leered at Alxa.

Rina bowed her head formally. "It is a pleasure to see you again."

Barmocar was wrapped in an expensive-looking cloak, confident, plump—*he* hadn't gone hungry during Northland's bleak winter—and he had an air of total command. He barely glanced at Rina. "You're late."

"We had no control over—"

"We'd have left without you. Maybe we still will." He strode over to the heap of luggage. "Is *all* this yours?"

"Only the essentials."

Mago pushed into the heap. "Look, Uncle. There's *furniture* in here!" He shoved boxes off an exquisitely polished table. "Nice stuff."

Rina winced. "That is an heirloom, in my family for generations."

Now Mago found Nelo's stack of artwork. He lifted a canvas, ripped off its packaging of thick paper, and theatrically flinched back. "Oh, good, Nelo brought his pictures!"

Nelo stepped forward, fists bunched. Alxa grabbed his arm.

Barmocar said, "Well, you're going to have a job fitting all this into your cabin. Which is that." And he pointed at the rear of the caravan, to a single battered-looking passenger cart.

Rina felt her own temper rise. "Is this all that the bones of the Virgin Herself bought me?"

Barmocar shrugged. "It was a buyer's market, wasn't it? We Carthaginians have always been traders. It's business—that's all. Nothing personal." And he eyed her, waiting for her response.

This was only the beginning, she realized. She dug deep inside herself, seeking patience. She was not without resources. Once she got through this bottleneck of the journey to Carthage, she would build a new life, a new position, and then she would wipe the grin off the face of this plump, foolish, cruel man. For now, she smiled. "What would you suggest we do with the rest of our luggage?"

He glanced at the heap of goods. "Sell it to the porters, if you can. Dump it. I don't care."

Nelo stepped forward, still fizzing with anger. "I won't leave my paintings."

Mago laughed. "Then stay here and eat them, Northlander."

"I won't leave my work, Mother."

"Silence. You're not a child. You can see how things are. If you aren't going to be any use just shut up. Alxa." She hauled a leather trunk from the heap of luggage and opened the buckles on the straps. "Help me. Whatever we can fit in here, we take. Nothing else. Clothes, a few sets of everything for each of us. And anything small and valuable. Jewelry—the money bags—"

"Yes, Mother." Alxa at least seemed to understand; she started opening boxes and cases, hastily pulling out clothes and other goods.

There were far more clothes than could possibly fit in the trunk. Well, they could wear some, Rina thought, a few layers each. They might need that during the cold nights of traveling to come.

Nelo stared at his work, his face ashen.

Rina relented. "Take some of it. One canvas, your

best. Your most recent sketchbook, and your earliest. That will go in the trunk. And take a blank book."

"What?"

"And your styluses and crayons. I suspect we'll be seeing some remarkable sights before this journey is through. Raw material—that's what you artists are always looking for, isn't it?"

The steam caravan departed not long after dusk, and traveled through the night.

Rina woke at dawn. She had slept in her seat, huddled under her cloak. She felt stiff, sore, and cold, despite her layers of clothes. The caravan was still moving. Alxa slept, lying on the opposite bench with her head on her brother's lap and her feet on their single trunk. Nelo had his sketchbook open, and was staring out of the window. When he saw his mother was awake he drew his finger down one of the window's small panes, and showed her a thin rime of frost under his fingernail.

The caravan rattled through one halt after another as it passed down the track, heading steadily south. The tremendous plain of Northland rolled past, rich, intensively managed, studded by flood mounds and crisscrossed by roads and dikes and canals. It was all but impossible to believe that all this would long have been drowned under the chill salt water of a rising ocean if not for the genius of long-dead Ana and her heroic generation, and the ingenuity and dedication of all those who had followed. And, Rina wondered idly, how would the story of the wider world have differed if not for the saving of Northland?

But had it all been for nothing? For the signs of Pyxeas' longwinter were visible all across the landscape. Banks of snow in the shaded hollows, even at midsummer. The telltale gray of ice on the wetlands where last year's reeds, brown and dead, were still frozen in place, and wading birds struggled to feed. Even the leaves on the trees, the oak and alder and ash, were pale and shrunken. In the communities around the caravan's halts she could see the damage done by the winter, houses of wood and stone smashed in by snow, the stumps of ancient trees hacked down for long-burned firewood.

The eeriest thing was the absence of people. Rina saw houses untended and unrepaired, and no threads of smoke rising from the fires. In one place she saw deer wandering through the big communal hearth space, nibbling at the thatch of collapsed houses, undisturbed. The deer themselves looked gaunt, their ribs showing. Where were all the people? Gone—south, probably, in flight from the cold, just as she was leaving Northland herself.

Still the caravan rattled on, rarely stopping, such was Barmocar's haste to get this long journey done. The cabin did have a privy with a vent to release waste through the floor, and running water from a tap, and a food box with dried meat, scrawny bits of fruit, bread, Northlander dried cod. Rina forced herself to eat every scrap, even the bread, the signature product of the farmers, disgusting, tasteless stuff that every Northlander knew would wear away your teeth.

They were all weary and feeling none too clean by the time the caravan reached its final halt, at a small port on the southern shore of Northland, at the Cut. Just as last year when Rina had traveled with Pyxeas, here the polyglot party were to embark on a flotilla of riverboats and make for Parisa. Boats were waiting, but not enough of them, and the transfer was messy and hurried. Now it was the turn of others to shed prized possessions for the lack of room on board, and to fume at Barmocar for his terrible service after extracting such high fees for the privilege of the journey.

Parisa itself, as they approached along its great river, was much as Rina remembered from last year, but even more crowded. Smoke rose everywhere, and people camped in shacks of rubbish on the quayside. The party was supposed to disembark here and proceed south

overland across Gaira to Massalia, a port on the Middle
Sea and a Carthaginian dependency. But when the lead
ships tried to put into dock they were blocked by a small
boat rowed by a team of oarsmen, to Barmocar's fury.

A uniformed official stood up in the boat. He wore a
thick mask over his mouth, as did the oarsmen. In the
argument that ensued, shouted across the river water, it
emerged that the Carthaginian flotilla had to make for
the island at the center of the river. There the passengers
could disembark, but the ships would have to turn
around and leave immediately. None of them would be
allowed into the city proper.

The reason for all this caution was the subject of rumor that swirled around the ships in half a dozen tongues:
"*Plague*. It is in the city." "No, not yet, but they fear it . . ."

Barmocar and his companions argued about how difficult this was going to make life, but it was clear the official wasn't going to back down. The oarsmen in the boat
were armed, and Rina saw troops drawn up on the quayside, all wearing face masks, clearly ready to repel anybody who tried to land.

So they disembarked on the island. Rina, with her
children and their single trunk, had to spend the night in
a dusty, empty, cold warehouse, sharing the bare floor
with perhaps fifty others, surrounded by snores and farts
and the sheer animal stink of people who had been traveling too long.

In the morning Rina woke early, as she usually did.

She walked outside, breathing air that was fresh and
crisp, with a tang of frost—not an unpleasant mix, but it
felt autumnal, even though the summer solstice was
barely gone. The travelers had been ordered to keep
within a perimeter around the dock marked by a crude
chalk line scrawled on the cobblestones. Rina walked up
to the line now, looking to the south bank of the river.
Raised up on an artificial mound very like the flood
mounds that studded Northland, she could see a sky temple, rings of massive stones polished until they shone. In

the low light of the morning sun, priests in white robes walked and bowed and prayed to ancient gods. But other deities were being addressed too. Banners had been set up within the innermost stone ring, showing the crossed palm leaves of Jesus, the star of Islam, even the crescent moon and outstretched finger of Baal Hammon and his consort Tanit, gods of Carthage. A temple of many faiths for this city of traders, and all the gods, she imagined, would be subject to ardent prayers for summer.

A soldier, patrolling in his face mask and bearing an ugly-looking spear, waved her back, and called something in his own guttural tongue. He looked ill himself; he coughed into his mask, his forehead was slick with sweat despite the cold. She hurried away, back to the warehouse and her children.

30

Pyxeas and his party, heading steadily east, were in a more varied country now, of arid plains, green valleys, towering snowcapped peaks. Water was more readily had, there was grass for the camels to graze on, and the caravanserai were more frequent, often no more than an easy day's ride apart. Here the way stations were called *robots*, in the local tongue, which came from an old word for a rope to tie up your horse. But just as further west, they were like small walled towns where you drove your animals into the shelter of the walls for the duration of your stay.

In the evenings, as Pyxeas studied or slept, Avatak sat shyly in bars with Jamil and Uzzia. Uzzia drank beer and wine and a particularly disgusting concoction that turned out to be fermented mare's milk, a specialty of the Mongols. Jamil preferred hot tea, and when he wasn't happy with the local offering he asked for boiling water and used dried leaves he carried with him. As for Avatak, who got drunk too easily, he stuck to watered beer. He listened to conversations in a hundred tongues, about the wealth that flowed through these little communities, from gleaming gems called rubies to the medicines and narcotics made from the produce of the poppy fields that spread wide to either side of the trails across much of this country. There were plenty of blood-chilling tales of bandits too.

In the mornings on they went, part of an ever-evolving caravan, heading always into the morning sun. At each stop the caravans fissured and split, and new trains formed up for the onward journey. Soon they traded away their camels for horses that would be more suited to the high, mountainous country to come, so Avatak was told. The mule plodded on, apparently unimpressed.

The land became more difficult, steeper, arid for long stretches, and their progress seemed painfully slow. Petty problems slowed them further: illness, scorpion bites, brackish water from fouled springs, lamed horses. Much of the summer still stretched ahead, but old Pyxeas was already fretting about the need to reach far Cathay before the autumn closed in.

One morning, crossing a highland at the foot of a mountain, they heard a deep groaning from beyond the eastern horizon, like the bellow of some tremendous animal, punctuated by sharp cracks. They all knew what this was, the locals and traders from experience, and Avatak and Pyxeas from memories of Coldland. Pyxeas was excited by the sound and insisted they hurry ahead.

They came to a glacier, a river of ice pouring down the mountain's flank. The back of the great ice beast was littered with rubble, smashed-up rock and timber, and relics of human living: wood panels, posts, what looked like a section of fencing. A river of meltwater gushed from the glacier's snout, littered with ice blocks, washing across the plain below. There were tremendous cracks and groans as the vast weight of ice pushed and jostled, seeking an elusive equilibrium.

Jamil, Uzzia and the other traders labored to get the horses and their single mule across the meltwater stream.

The sun was high, the air clear, the ice gleamed brilliant white, and the frothy water spreading across the plain below was the color of the sky. Close to the glacier, the stream, with its ice blocks, was impossible for the animals to cross, and the beasts had to be walked downstream to calmer water. There the travelers cast ropes across, clambered through the chill flow themselves, and then began to lead the laden animals one by one.

Avatak felt guilty not to be down there helping them. But Pyxeas had no regard for these petty human struggles; he had eyes only for the grand, cold drama of the glacier itself.

"Look, boy, can you see how the glacier is born up in that hollow in the mountainside? It flows down this valley," and Pyxeas mimed the movement with great sweeps of his arms, "grinding and smashing as it goes, ripping away any surface soil, any trees, any living thing, cutting down right to the bedrock and then cutting into *that*— and then it flows down onto the plain below. And I can see, Avatak, that this glacier's advance from its mountain root has been fast, and recent. Old glaciers, having retreated, leave behind ridges of rubble, fragments of rock they have smashed up and pushed down their valleys. Where is this glacier's rubble wall? Gone! A relic of past longwinters, overwhelmed by this fresh advance. And this glacial drama is only the start of it, only the start of the reign of the ice."

"Scholar, the people speak of all this. In the *robots*. You should listen to them sometimes. They live in the valleys, beneath the glaciers. They keep animals, farm. Then comes the ice, and avalanches, and sometimes great floods where the ice makes dams that trap water for a while, and then break. They have to flee. You can see the remains of their homes on the ice itself."

Pyxeas, faintly surprised, nodded. "Yes, yes. Good. But such accounts are merely anecdotal, of course. Well. Let us rejoin our companions." He took Avatak's arm and stood stiffly.

31

There were no steam-caravan links from Parisa south to the Middle Sea coast. So the next stage of Rina's journey was overland, on wagons, carts and carriages. The vehicles had been drawn up a short walk outside town, and as the morning wore on porters with masks over their mouths hauled the travelers' luggage to the meeting point.

Now the next problems arose, because there weren't nearly as many carriages as Barmocar had ordered, and even fewer horses. Once again Barmocar raged, but there was nothing he could do. After all, they had no choice but to go on; they were not welcome in Parisa. The locals just shrugged. Most carriages had been broken up for firewood, and the rest were being used to ferry the dead out of the city to huge mass graves in the country. As for the horses, skin and bone themselves, these were the few that had so far been spared the cooking pot.

So began another spasm of dumping and repacking. Rina and her children were forced to give up their one and only trunk, and packed up their remaining belongings in bundles improvised from cloaks and sheets.

With much ill humor, the journey continued. The country was eerily quiet, a landscape of small farms abandoned to the weeds and the crows. All this Nelo sketched assiduously. The road itself, following the bank of a canal heading roughly southeast, showed signs of the winter cold, frost cracks and potholes in the cobbled surface, left unrepaired for lack of workers.

Toward the evening they came to a substantial town, a mixture of wooden and stone architecture, a local market center. Again they were not allowed inside the walls, despite Barmocar's protests. They had to sleep in rough felt tents loaned by the town and erected by Barmocar's soldiers, and were shown where to find freshwater, and were sold shriveled fruit at astounding prices. The soldiers, who seemed competently led by a grizzled officer, set up a perimeter and organized a watch rota, helped out by some of the travelers.

At least Rina and her children had a tent to themselves. But the night was uncomfortable, the ground hard despite the layers of clothing heaped up on the ground under them—and *cold*, as if under the surface it had never thawed since the winter. In the morning Alxa helped out with brushing and feeding the horses. It was a novelty for her; horses were rare in Northland.

It took three days of jolting travel in the carts before they came to the valley of a broad river, leading roughly south. They were supposed to sail down this all the way to the great port of Massalia. But there were no boats. Barmocar, ill-tempered, betrayed again by his contacts, had to form up the party to continue the journey south by foot and carriage.

Worry nagged at Rina at the thought that the further they traveled, the more Barmocar's elaborate arrangements were breaking down, as if the world itself was steadily failing around them. Rina, fifty-one years old, had traveled extensively before, across Northland, and in

Gaira and Ibera, and, last year, as far as Hantilios with Pyxeas. But she had imagined, deep in her heart, that on this journey she would travel as she had before, in comfort, in well-equipped cabins in caravans and canal boats and ships, with servants and every luxury. Now here she was with no more luggage than she and her children could manage on their backs, rattling in rough carts and carriages over foreign tracks, sleeping under a felt tent on cold, hard earth, and not having had a decent wash for so many days that she probably smelled worse than the horses.

But she held her tongue for the sake of her children. Nelo was sometimes disturbingly quiet, but he was absorbed in what he saw around him—sights such as none had seen in generations—and he recorded with brisk strokes of his crayons. And Alxa was discovering a practical side that was, for the first time, Rina supposed, being given a chance to flourish. For their sake Rina did not complain, did not question.

Pressing south, they passed village after village in a landscape dense with farms, most abandoned. The towns here were built of stone, the streets set out to rigid grid patterns. This far south they were entering territory that had once come under the sway of Carthage itself, whose imperial holdings had waxed and waned with the centuries, but whose influence lingered in the older building stock.

Then, one morning, they woke to a smell of smoke.

Emerging from her tent, Rina saw an orange-gray smudge across the southern sky: a forest fire, and a big one, right across the horizon. They had no road to follow save the track that followed the river, no choice but to go on and challenge the fire, to walk right through it.

In the worst of it, it seemed as if the whole land around them was ablaze. The terrified horses had to be led by hand, and the people wore moistened cloths over their faces. There were firebreaks around some of the villages, but others had been abandoned to the flames.

Nestspills cluttered the road, people walking alone, families—everybody heading south, ever south. There was no sign that anybody was seriously trying to challenge the fire.

"They've had drought here," Alxa said to her mother, shouting through her mask and the noisy crackle of the flames. "That's what Pyxeas told me. Worse than in the north. He said we had to expect this. The trees dry out until the slightest spark hits, a lightning strike, and the whole landscape goes up in flames."

"Trees grow back," said Rina.

"Pyxeas said it may never be the same. The trees that grew here before may not prosper in the conditions to come—colder, dryer, windier. Maybe pine trees will grow here next, not oaks and ash."

"This far south? Surely not."

"That's what Pyxeas says."

It must, Rina thought, be terrifying to live inside Pyxeas' head. To predict such an appalling sight as this world on fire, and to *understand*.

It took two days to walk through the tremendous fires, and several further days' travel along increasingly crowded roads, before they came to Massalia.

The city was a sprawling port with a fine natural harbor and a broad estuary. Here, Barmocar boasted, in this Carthaginian dependency, after a long trek through countries of savages, he was sure of a civilized welcome.

Rina could see there was trouble here even before they came into the city itself. Beyond the harbor, on the broad face of the Middle Sea, she saw ships standing out to sea, apparently motionless. Had they been refused permission to come into the harbor? And on land, as they neared the city, the road was packed with nestspills, the fleeing folk evidently so fearful of plague they kept their distance from their neighbors and wore masks over their faces. It was a whole countryside, Rina saw, draining south toward Massalia.

But the city was closed. The landward side was surrounded by a stout wall, the gates were firmly barred. The wave of nestspills broke against this wall, and the result was a kind of ghost town of misery, with no provision for food or water, and sewage flowed down improvised gutters. The Carthaginian party cautiously passed through. Barmocar, weary, frustrated, angry, said loudly that it would be better if the plague came and swept these purposeless wretches off the face of the earth, just so long as they got out of his way.

Just like the nestspills, however, Barmocar and his party were excluded from Massalia. It was fear of the plague, yes, that and a shortage of food. But his party was allowed to pass around the city to the harbor — and here, to everybody's relief, the ships he had ordered were waiting, at least some of them. Again there was a weary flurry of packing and repacking, a shedding of still more goods, by now endured in grim silence.

Nelo was fascinated by the ships. They were quite unlike the wide-bodied sailing ships of the Northland fishing fleet. These vessels of the Middle Sea were sleek, driven by sails supplemented by banks of rowers, and they had mighty spikes fixed to their prows. They were ships designed to fight on an enclosed ocean that had been an arena for warfare for millennia.

As the ships were loaded, on this summer afternoon in Massalia, on the shore of the Middle Sea, the sky clouded over, and the air grew cold, and Rina watched snowflakes, just a few, fall from the sky.

They left the harbor the next day, at dawn. The wind was low, and they had to take to the oars; the professional seamen Barmocar had hired were supplemented by volunteers from among the passengers.

Cautiously they sailed down the eastern coast of Ibera. On the open sea Barmocar's soldiers kept an eye out for pirates. At night they put into land at small harbors away from the main population centers. Nobody knew what condition the communities on land were in after years of drought, after the plague. Some slept on the land; Rina, who found the movement of the creaking ship on the slow swell of the sea quite soothing, preferred to remain on board.

One night Rina was woken by a wind off the land that made the ship heave and roll, and the air moaned in the rigging.

When the morning came she found the ship transformed, heaped with red-yellow dust, in the hatches, over the decks, drifting in every corner. The crew, ill-tempered, were shoveling this load into the sea. The dust was due to a storm blowing from the coast, Rina learned. Desiccated farmland, topsoil turned to dust by years of drought and just blown away. The dust had gotten everywhere, wherever a window or hatch hadn't been sealed—into your clothes, your hair, in the fabric of the ships' sails. It took a full day for the little fleet to be dug out.

The journey resumed. After two more days the fleet turned south, away from the mainland of southern Ibera, with the crew nervously watching the horizon for pirates. Soon, the word ran around the ships, they would at last come to Carthage. Rina knew her troubles were far from over, but at least this journey with all its trials would end, and she would never have to make such a trek again. She felt an enormous relief, like a physical weight lifted from her shoulders. And she wondered how close her uncle was to his goal.

32

Day by day Pyxeas' party climbed. The air grew clearer and colder, the sky more blue. The sun felt stronger than ever to Avatak, and he kept his exposed skin covered with Uzzia's greasy unguents. The ground was bare and hard and rocky, and ice-bound mountains stood around, gleaming a brilliant white in the clear sunlight. In places they followed ridges, from which they looked *down* upon ice-coated slopes, and they could see glaciers pouring into valleys below, every detail clear, the merging ice flows and meltwater streams like models made by some sculptor of plaster and paint.

There were no people up here, no more caravanserai. Yet there was life. Sometimes Avatak glimpsed wild sheep, their coats gray-white, clambering up impossible-looking slopes to get at the sparse tufts of bright green grass. Jamil said there were wolves up here too, feeding on the sheep. And there were rumors of humans, ragged hunters in skins who preyed on the flocks with small bows, but who were timid and secretive and rarely seen. Those locals who had come this way before had their own names for this place. Jamil called it "the roof of the world."

And still they climbed, and climbed. Avatak found his lungs dragging at the thinning air, and the horses labored. When they stopped, the fires they built seemed to burn only fitfully, and Jamil grumbled that when water boiled it was no more than lukewarm, and spoiled his evening tea. Some of the locals, especially the hard-working bearers, were afflicted with headaches, nausea, giddiness, episodes of passing out.

Uzzia tended to these victims. "I've seen such symptoms before. Mountain sickness. If you're used to the high ground it's not so bad, and best of all is to have been born up here. But if you're born a lowlander you can suffer. Some of these fellows have probably never come up here before, never dreamed they'd have to, before the advance of one of your master's glaciers forced them out of their farms, to come labor for us like your mule."

"He's not my mule. He's his own, I think."

She laughed. "And if he's a lowlander, he's not showing it."

Pyxeas had an explanation for everything. He said the sickness was caused by the thinness of the air at altitude, and a lack of a particular part of the air he called "the vital air," necessary for life, and indeed for the sustenance of fires, as experiments had shown. As for Pyxeas himself, he actually seemed to thrive in the thin air. He even took to walking a spell each day, rather than riding. "Do you know," he said, as he trotted alongside his companions one morning, "the worst blight of old age is the constant *pain*. In your head, in your back, your joints, your bowels—*somewhere*. Constant, nagging, continual pain. Nobody talks about it, or if they do nobody younger ever listens, but it's there all the same. Up here, though, my own various aches, my faithful companions for years, are lessened—some of them gone altogether. Make a note, Avatak."

"Yes, scholar."

———

Still they climbed.

It grew colder. They woke to morning ground frost, and patches of old ice in the shadows of rocks and ridges. Pyxeas was fascinated by this, but fretted. "When we try to return, in a year, two years, we might not be able to come this way again."

Uzzia growled, "If we make it to Cathay, we'll find another way back. But in the meantime, sage—watch your step!"

And there was the silence. Avatak was increasingly aware of it, behind the small noises of the people, their morning coughs, their soft voices, the clink of pots hanging from the mule's back—a huge silence that stretched to the mountains all around them. It wasn't just the absence of people. It was the absence of any sound at all. Not even the sound of birds, he realized, not even their caws and cries and songs. Maybe the birds could not fly in this thin air. Pyxeas might be interested in the observation, but he would only make Avatak dig out his journal and write it down, so he kept the thought to himself.

Then they came to a meadow in the sky. It was a high, broad plain, suspended between two looming mountains. A meadow, complete with thick grass and dancing wildflowers. There were sheep up here, fat-looking beasts who fled at the party's approach. All of this lay under a brilliant blue sky, the green of the grass and the sheep's vivid pale wool. It was like a dream, Avatak thought; it seemed impossible this could be real, could be here. The horses tore eagerly at the rich grass. Even the mule could barely conceal its pleasure at the lush pasture.

Jamil and Uzzia both knew this place. "Here we will stop," Jamil said firmly. "For two nights, three, while the horses feed, and we rest."

Avatak could see the wisdom of it. By now the party was much reduced: just the four travelers of Pyxeas' party, and two other traders, Arabs who had kept to themselves from the beginning of the trek, and six local bearers and guides. They were all exhausted; they all needed time to get used to the air.

Still, Avatak was surprised that Pyxeas agreed to the stop readily. "But the timing is good," the scholar said. "Tonight the eclipse is due. Make sure you have the oracle ready, boy."

Uzzia, unpacking her own bundles, glanced over. "What eclipse?"

Jamil grunted. "What *is* an 'eclipse'?"

"An eclipse is a shadow play. When the world falls into the shadow of the moon, and the sun's light is blocked out . . . or, as tonight, when the moon enters the shadow of the earth, and turns the color of blood." Pyxeas had been in good spirits for days, buoyed up by the thin air. Now it was almost as if he was drunk. "A world of shadow, a moon of blood!" He repeated the words in other, fragmentary languages: Uzzia's Hatti, Jamil's Arabic, even in broken phrases in the harsh local argot.

The men working at the horses glanced across at him, and then up at the sunlit sky, uneasy. Jamil, watching, shook his head, muttering about folk who had so much cleverness it drove the wisdom out of their heads, and went back to unpacking his own tent.

The sun set and the moon rose, full and handsome. Sitting cross-legged with a blanket over his shoulders, Pyxeas set the oracle on the ground before him, working its dials, muttering to himself. Meanwhile he had Avatak set up the hourglass and record the hours since sunset.

The party had broken into groups: Pyxeas' party, the two Arab travelers, and the local men, who seemed particularly furtive tonight to Avatak, suspicious, watchful of the others. One of them giggled frequently, a man who had never got over the effects of the high land. Uzzia, too, seemed more reserved than usual, watchful. As did Jamil, his eyes glittering as he glanced at the others. Only the horses seemed unperturbed—and the mule, who cropped at the lush grass with an air of bored indifference.

Pyxeas, typically, showed no awareness of any of this tension. "Oh, I wish I had more light!" he said, squinting at the oracle's dials in the firelight. "But that of course would ruin the seeing. Still, not long to go now, before the moon is snuffed out!"

Jamil glanced at the locals. "Play with that toy if you must. But keep it down, will you?"

"Toy?"

Uzzia touched Pyxeas' arm. "Hush, those men are alarmed about something, and we don't want to scare them any further."

"Let them wallow in their superstitious fear. They are nothing. The eclipse is too significant, and I, Pyxeas, will capture it, and use it to determine my position on the curving belly of the earth."

Avatak could see that Uzzia was intrigued despite herself. "What are you talking about, scholar?"

"Know that eclipses occur on particular days at precise hours, which can be calculated in advance—years in advance, at that. And that knowledge is encoded into the gears of my oracle. You see? So I know an eclipse is due tonight—I know the exact time it will occur, by Northland's clocks. Now, to determine my east-west position, all I have had to do is observe the eclipse.

"Here I have Avatak measuring the local time—the hour at this precise point. Suppose I see, from Avatak's glass, that the eclipse happens at midnight for me, I mean some particular aspect of it, the moon's first entry into shadow, or the last exit. But the oracle tells me that the eclipse is scheduled for sunset at Etxelur, for example. Knowing the difference between those two times, I can calculate my arc east-west around the world—do you see? As if I am using the world itself as a gigantic common clock."

Jamil thought that over, frowned, and spat. "Lot of fuss to work out one tiny number."

The scholar, predictably, grew angry. "But with such 'tiny numbers' I, Pyxeas, map the heavens! Thus I know that eclipses happen, at full moon or new moon, just as the moon crosses the sun's path in the sky—"

"Enough!" Jamil clamped his hands to his ears. "You make my brain boil, old man."

Uzzia glanced across at the bearers. "Our companions are looking fretful again. I think it is the scholar's claim that he can predict the eclipse. As if he *controls* the moment the moon is to be devoured by the wolf god, according to the local beliefs."

"But it is only a question of simple numbers—"

"These men know nothing of your numbers, scholar. All they know is that their gods are angry with them. They must be, or else why would they send down drought and floods and rock falls and tongues of ice? Now, perhaps they believe you are challenging the gods, angering them further. I think it would be better if you kept silent."

"Ah, but I'm not one for silence," the scholar said. He lifted his gaze from the oracle dials to the sky. "And as for the prediction—" He pointed dramatically to the sky. "There! It begins!"

Looking up, Avatak saw that a sliver had been cut out of the moon's round dish, just a fingernail, sharp and distinct in the clear sky of this place. Avatak had been drilled for this moment. He grabbed a stylus and began making a precise measurement of the time as recorded in the hourglass.

Pyxeas stood with a single lithe motion that belied his years, lifted his arms to the disappearing moon, laughed, and did a kind of jig of celebration—or desperation, Avatak thought, for even now he thought he could see the bleakness hidden inside the old man's bluff character.

But his antics were disturbing the rest of the party.

"Sit down, you fool," hissed Uzzia.

Jamil muttered, "This isn't good, this isn't good."

The other men were moving around them, dimly seen

in the moonlight. Avatak put down his journal and stood up—

There was a tremendous slam, and the world fell away.

He was awake.

He was *alive.*

He was lying on his back. He opened his eyes cautiously. He saw blue sky, the deep blue of morning. There was the moon, still full, still high though it was daylight. The eclipse must be over. He had missed the moment of last shadow. Pyxeas would be furious. He tried to rise— but pain burst in his head, and he cried out. He managed to reach a sitting position, though the world spun around him.

"Take it easy." Somebody before him, a low, gentle voice. Uzzia. "Drink this."

His vision seemed to pulse, as if his blood was pressing at his eyes. But he saw the mug before him, the glistening water. He took it, managed to lift it to his lips, drank. "What happened?"

"Well, you missed all the fun. Some protector you are. You didn't even see the rock that knocked you down, did you? Good shot, actually."

"One of the men?"

"No. A trader. That fellow Ogul. Never did trust him. At the moment of eclipse the locals went crazy. Ogul and his buddy took the chance to get rid of us, I think, and get their hands on our stuff. Once you were down they rushed us, the traders and the bearers."

He considered that. "Yet I'm alive."

"True enough."

"The scholar?"

"Jamil saved him. Fought like a lion—Jamil, that is. Killed two of them before they overwhelmed him."

Avatak had to work through this news step by step. "He's dead. Jamil is dead."

"Yes. But he saved Pyxeas. Once Jamil was down they

turned on me. I got rid of one—Ogul, actually, and good riddance—and I scared off the rest."

"How?"

"I threw the oracle at them. It bounced off a fellow's hard head and smashed to pieces."

Avatak winced. "Pyxeas won't like that."

"I'll let you take the blame. The local men thought the god was broken, or something, and ran off for the horses. Pausing only to grab most of our goods."

"Are you all right?"

"More or less."

"So we've lost Jamil. And the luggage?"

"They took the blankets, clothing, trade goods, food, water, medicines. We still have the paper bundles, Pyxeas' learning. So, we lost nothing important."

Avatak actually laughed, but the pain in his head burst anew. "And no horses."

"No. But . . ."

Avatak heard a soft ripping sound. He turned and saw the mule cropping patiently, as if unaware of the devastation of the night.

"They tried to take that mule. Kicked one of them so hard I'll swear I heard a bone snap."

Avatak laughed again. "So what now?"

"Now we fix you up. We'll put poor Jamil under a cairn."

"It will have to be a big cairn."

"He would have smiled to hear you say that. Then we'll gather up what we've got left."

"And then what?"

"And then on to Cathay," Pyxeas said. The scholar was sitting up, rubbing his head. "After all, there's still a world to save. Well, don't just sit there, boy, help me up!"

33

Barmocar's flotilla at last approached Carthage.

The passengers crowded on deck. The Carthaginians chattered excitedly, understandably glad to be coming home at last. The rest were more apprehensive, Rina observed, wondering what kind of welcome waited for them in this formidable city.

From the ocean Rina could see little more than the blank face of a tremendous wall rising to seal off the shore, brilliant white in the watery sun. Behind the wall were low hills encrusted with stone buildings. From one tall mound rose a slim pillar bearing the statue of a man, or a god, evidently a huge monument to be visible from so far away. The sea before this walled shore was crowded with shipping; this close to land most of the ships had their sails trimmed, and she could see oars working along the length of their hulls.

The day was warm, though the sky was veiled by thin, misty clouds that softened the sunlight. This was the coast of Africa, she reminded herself. She had no idea what a "normal" summer day here should feel like.

Pushing her windblown hair out of her face, Alxa pointed. "I think that pillar is at the top of the Byrsa, the old citadel. And the hero on the top is Hannibal, son of Hamilcar, conqueror of Latium and savior of Carthage."

Nelo was silent, withdrawn, adding cramped little drawings to the corners of his overfull sketchbook. Alxa was more alive, Rina thought. Interested, engaged. "How do you know so much, child?"

"Because while you spent the journey sulking in our cabin, and my brother here has been scribbling, scribbling, I've been talking to people. Especially the Carthaginians. Finding out stuff. Learning the language. Don't you think it's a good idea, if we're going to spend the rest of our lives here?"

Of course it was. The problem for Rina was that she had lived all her life in a stratum of Northland society where people had been expected to learn *her* language, not the other way around.

Nelo just stared at the city blankly. "It is a great stone tomb," he said. "Dead, where Northland was alive. It will swallow us up like a sarcophagus."

Rina said, "We will find a way. You'll see." On impulse she took his hand.

He looked at her, surprised. She wasn't the kind of mother to make such gestures. He withdrew, gently, and there was an awkward silence.

Alxa just laughed and turned away. The boat sailed on.

They came to the entrance of the harbor. This close, the white facade of the sea walls was dazzling, but Rina noticed a few blackened scars, the relics of the war and banditry that blighted the age. The walls' smooth surface looked like growstone: Northland engineering, probably, Etxelur growstone laid over an older core; everybody knew that Northlanders mixed the best growstone in the world, and much revenue had been earned for the country by hiring out its expertise for such projects. The harbor mouth, a break in the walls, was guarded by a gigantic chain of which only a few links showed above the surface, ready to be pulled up to block the way. The chain was fixed to elaborate structures on which stood lighthouses, tremendously tall, with polished mirrors like staring eyes.

The harbor, once they entered it, was huge, overwhelming, like an inland sea lined by wharfs and jetties and warehouses and enclosed by the towering walls. The ships on the water were dwarfed, toys in a pond. At the far end, a gap in the walls led to yet another harbor, perhaps even greater than this one, lined by a kind of circular terrace, two or three stories tall, topped by shining red tiles.

"That one beyond is the military harbor," Alxa murmured. "One of the wonders of the world. So the Carthaginians say."

Barmocar's flotilla pulled up at jetties on the left-hand side of the outer commercial harbor. Rina saw elements of design in the utilitarian architecture, a touch of style, a portico supported by slim columns that ran the entire length of the waterfront. As Barmocar's boat reached a jetty an official approached, bearing a slate. He wore a long black robe and a mask over his mouth. Barmocar disembarked and greeted the official with a smile and a formalized embrace.

"Plague," Rina said. "They're worried about plague, even here."

Alxa, hanging over the rail, struggled to hear what Barmocar was saying. "The man wants us to wait on the ships. We may have to stand off at sea. For seven days! That can't be right."

Nelo said, "They want to wait and see if we're infected with anything. It's sensible if you're trying to protect a city."

Another seven days on the ship! After the trials of the journey, that would finish her off, Rina thought.

But Barmocar and the man were smiling, and Rina saw Barmocar hand the official a small pouch of purple cloth.

Alxa raised her eyebrows at her mother. "Well, we won't be held up."

Rina smiled. "You're getting terribly cynical for one so young."

"That's stupid," Nelo said, visibly unhappy. "That man's supposed to protect the city from disease! What use is he if he's just going to let through anybody who waves a bit of money?"

Rina was an Annid; she had plenty of practical experience of petty corruption. "Nelo, don't worry. It's just a rule being bent. If they were seriously concerned about plague here that man wouldn't be doing what he's doing. He'd be thinking about his own family, his own safety—he probably wouldn't let us land at all. Now come on, let's get our stuff together before we're thrown off the boat . . ."

The quayside was a jumble of passengers and their goods, grimy, weary, eager to get this last leg of their journey over with. The word had evidently gotten around that this was a boatload of the rich, and would-be porters came flocking, hungry for work, a look Rina had come to recognize.

Barmocar and his wife stood by, chatting to a dock official and his ship's captain, while their mountain of luggage was loaded onto carts under the blustering supervision of Mago. Some of the Carthaginians waited while messengers fetched family or servants from the city; others had the dock workers call for carriages. They seemed surprised at how few horse-drawn carriages came in response. But there were plenty of two-wheeled contraptions with weary-looking men in harness—slaves, perhaps, or nestspills, doing the work of horses.

Alxa was growing agitated. "Mother? Everybody is making arrangements. What about us? What are we to do?"

"We," Rina said coldly, "are in the hands of Barmocar, our host. We just wait."

"But he's not paying us any attention. He's not even *looking* at us."

"Wait, child."

They did wait, silent and ignored, until at last the business was done, the carts were loaded. And Barmocar was helped up into the lead carriage.

Rina dropped her bundles, and with all the dignity and command she could muster she strode forward to face the Carthaginian. Even now he didn't look down at her from his perch on the cart. "Barmocar!"

The man laughed, and gave a curt order to drive on. But Rina grabbed the traces of the lead horse. He looked down at her. "Why do you stand in my way?"

Rina summoned Alxa. "Repeat what I say in Carthaginian. Say that we had an arrangement, he and I. A business deal." They were attracting a small but curious crowd, of Barmocar's other passengers, a few passersby. "No, don't whisper it, child. Speak it boldly. Put on a show. I want these others to hear. This man is a Carthaginian. A trader in a city of traders. Is he a man who reneges on deals honorably made? And are there followers of Jesus here? Any Hatti? Shall we discuss why a Carthaginian trader should wish to acquire the bones of—".

"Enough." Barmocar leaned out of his carriage and hissed at her. "The deal was to bring you to Carthage, and that I've done."

"No. The deal was that you should get us established in Carthage. A place to live, work—"

He laughed. "What work? What use is a Northlander Annid here?"

Anterastilis, his wife, touched Barmocar's arm, and whispered something.

Alxa frowned. "I can't quite hear. I think she's saying you're not worth the scandal. 'Send her to . . .' Jexami? 'He might help.'"

"Jexami?" Rina had once known a Jexami, cousin of Ywa. "You're sure that was the name?"

"Jexami," repeated Barmocar, leaning from his carriage. "You heard right. Bought property here years ago. Your countryman. Maybe he'll have something for you. I'll have a carriage-man take you there. Would that fulfill our 'contract'? Now, if you'll let go of my horse—"

She stepped back. The driver flicked a rein, and the carriage rolled away, followed by carts bearing the rest of Barmocar's baggage. The rest of the passengers dispersed too. Rina and her children were left standing, with their pathetic bits of luggage at their feet.

Only one man remained, a tall but scrawny man with big, powerful hands, standing by a two-wheeled cart.

Rina sighed. "All right. Look, I'll take the luggage. I'll get out to Jexami as fast as possible and get things sorted out. I'm sure he'll put us up. Come back here at nightfall. I'll send this man to collect you if I can't make it back. In the meantime stay out of trouble."

"We're not children," Alxa said.

Rina stepped closer to her. "Look after your brother."

Alxa glanced at Nelo with impatience, then resignation. "Just don't forget about us when you start in on Jexami's mead, all right?"

Rina kissed her on the cheek, hugged her son, picked up the rough bags and walked determinedly to the waiting carriage-man and his cart.

34

The carriage-man's cart jolted with every step of his jogging pace, and the bench on which she sat was hard as growstone. Yet she had suffered a lot worse during her long journey from Etxelur; her backside was probably tough as leather by now, and she endured.

Beyond the city wall the North African countryside opened up. They were heading west, toward the setting sun. The road ran dead straight across the plain, and was well built, properly drained—a good road, but there was no sign of an iron rail, and Rina coldly relished that fact. A sandy dust covered the roadway, just like the dust that had blown over the Carthaginian boat from the dried-up plains of Ibera.

Beside the road stood handsome properties, estates of well-constructed stone buildings clustered in rectangular plots. The estates were surrounded by carefully defined fields, and Rina recognized vines, olives, fruit trees. This hinterland, so close to this major route into town, must once have been a lush and prosperous place to live. But the vines looked withered, the fruit trees barren, and the few animals, sheep and cattle, cropped desultorily at sparse, yellow grass. There were some hastily heaped-up stone barriers, with threatening signs hand-painted in the angular local script. On the road there wasn't much traffic—carts laden with produce heading back toward the city, a few carts heading out. And there was a thin trickle of nestspills, all heading to the city, all on foot. It was a sight Rina had become inured to in Northland. It was something of a shock to have come to the other end of the world to see the same thing.

Jexami's property turned out to be a particularly large and well-built group of buildings set back from the road. In scraps of shade, servants watered orange trees. As Rina clambered down, the carriage-man stood by, eyes bright in a dusty face, waiting to be paid. He was thin, evidently underfed, dressed in dusty rags.

"Typical of that crook Barmocar not to pay you in advance," she murmured in her own tongue. She switched to Greek. "Thank you . . . I don't know your tongue, I am sorry." She dug her purse from a fold in her robe and withdrew Northlander scrip. "Is this enough? I'm sure you can convert this to your own currency in the counting houses . . ."

He took the handful of coins, stared at them, then tried to hand them back, speaking in his own tongue.

She closed his fingers over the coins. "This is your fee. If it's not enough—"

He grew angry. He threw the coins on the ground and held out his empty hand, all but shouting.

"I'll take care of it." The voice was cultured Etxelur. A burly, expensively dressed man came walking quietly from an opened gate, a servant at his side. Rina, with relief, recognized him: it was indeed the Jexami she remembered, cousin to Ywa, Annid of Annids, on Ywa's father's side, and so a remote cousin of Rina too. He snapped out questions to the carriage-man and gestured to his servant. *Pay him.* Jexami was shorter than Rina and a little younger, with thinning black hair cropped in the local style, and he wore a purple tunic and tight-cut trousers. He *looked* like a Carthaginian. Even his accent, when he spoke the language, sounded authentic to her. She would not have recognized the man if he had not spoken to her.

She bowed in the formal Etxelur style, ignoring her own grubbiness, and the scattering of coins at her feet. "Cousin Jexami. Thank you for meeting me."

"Barmocar sent a runner to warn me you were coming." He grinned. "Barmocar! That old rascal. How is he? Haven't seen him for too long. Come in, come in, I have no manners left, it seems." He led her through the gate. The man collected her bundles from the road. "You look exhausted, if you don't mind my saying it. Things have become so difficult, haven't they?"

The gate clanged shut behind them. The estate was a series of independent buildings set around a central courtyard. The walls were of stone, with big upright slabs infilled with rubble and neatly finished. In the courtyard a fountain ran, feeding miniature orange trees in pots. The servant stood by.

"Rather impressive, isn't it?" Jexami said, as they crossed the courtyard. "Originally built by an Arabic prince, in the brief interval when this country was overrun by that sort, long ago. They left behind some exquisite architecture. This place is much transformed in the centuries since, but we've restored the hydraulic system. Do you know, this fountain hasn't run dry once, despite the drought. Mind you, the air's so arid the oranges haven't flourished, even so."

She felt bewildered, even oddly dizzy. She found herself staring at the little orange trees. "Jexami, I've come to you because—"

"First I must show you some hospitality," he said smoothly, deflecting her. "Himil—come here." The servant hurried over, and Jexami gave him brisk instructions. Then he led Rina into the courtyard. "Of course dear Ywa is still in Etxelur, is she not? It's some time since she wrote."

Rina frowned. Was he really so out of touch as he seemed? "Things are difficult at home. Ywa is under a lot of pressure."

"Well, of course she is. I've urged her many times to do what you've done, to pack her bag and come here. To fly south for the winter, like a swallow! Look, I insist you relax before we talk. Any of these houses may suit. They all have their own baths, you know, and most have their own bread ovens! For this is the Carthaginian way. You must wash, change—my wife has plenty of old clothes, I'll send a girl to help you. Perhaps you'd like to sleep?"

She felt that if she got to a soft bed she could sleep through a full day. But she must not, not yet. She told Jexami of her children. "Perhaps you could send for them? I was going to send back that oaf of a carriage-man."

It was a simple enough request, and not much of an imposition on his hospitality. Yet he hesitated, to her surprise. At length he said, "Of course." He snapped his fingers and gave Himil brisk instructions. "As soon as he has you settled he will deal with it."

She chose a building at random. As Jexami had promised, it was like an independent house, with its own kitchen, bedrooms, a bathroom just off the vestibule—even its own water supply, from a toy fountain in the bathroom. A girl brought her buckets of water and fresh clothes.

She stripped off her dirty travel garments, which the girl took away, then stepped into the bath. She knew little of Carthaginian customs. Perhaps this bathroom beside the door was meant as a gateway, between the grime of the outside world and the purity of the home. Whatever the symbolism, it was a luxury beyond belief to sponge the hot water over her bare skin. There was even soap, which from its scent appeared to be of North-lander manufacture.

Soon she was warmed through, and scented, and was pulling on the clean clothes the girl had brought her. The need for sleep seemed to wash over her in a flood. Yet she must not succumb, not until she had dealt with Jexami and his odd reticence, not until the children were safely with her.

The man Himil was waiting for her when she emerged. He led her across the courtyard to a west-facing building dominated by a big, airy room. Here Jexami sat behind a desk covered with scrolls and slates, with a scribe to one hand, a clerk to the other scribbling numbers. When she came in, Jexami raised a hand, one finger in the air, without looking up.

The instruction was unmistakable. She waited in the doorway, motionless. She had become used to fielding such slights from the Carthaginians. She had not expected this discourtesy from a Northlander—a friend, a relative. Yet it was so. She began to feel uneasy.

At length he sat up straight, smiled at Rina, and clapped his hands to send the clerks away. He waved her to a seat before the desk. "Are you hungry? Would you like some fruit juice, wine, tea?"

"A little wine would be welcome."

Himil was dispatched to fetch it.

There was a bundle on the desk, neatly wrapped in linen. He pushed it over to her. "Your dirty clothes—properly laundered, of course. Your baggage is outside. Oh, and the coins are in there too."

"The coins?"

"The ones the carriage-man dropped in the dirt. Not worth much of course, but you may as well have them back!" He laughed, as if he'd made a joke.

She frowned. "I don't understand. They are good Northlander scrip."

"'Good Northlander scrip.' Hmm. You know, since I settled here I've come to feel that we were always rather cut off from the flow of events up in Northland. Buried in our great big old Wall. We tend to think that the rest of the world can fall apart and it won't affect us, don't we? Rina, Northlander currency isn't worth the metal it's stamped from these days. After all, what's it backed by? As soon as the cold started cutting the trading links, for the average Carthaginian, Northland has become — nothing. A fantasy country as remote as the moon."

"But you are prospering."

"I was lucky, or we had foresight. We saw that times were becoming hard, the years of flood in the north, the drought in the south. This was even before the cold came, you understand. We thought that Carthage, so much further south, at the center of the world, would be more — secure. We thought ahead, Rina. As you did. It's just that we made our judgments a little earlier.

"We built up a business down here. I handle the import of certain kinds of soft fruit from across Greater Carthage into the city itself. Good sound trade. And we managed to convert most of our Northland currency into the local scrip, just before the crash came." He opened his hands to her. "Do you have any other assets with you? Land titles, other currencies — "

"Nothing but holdings back home. In Northland."

"Which are worth nothing here, I'm afraid. Not even as guarantors of credit."

"No wonder that crook Barmocar asked for payment of the kind he did." And she told him about the Virgin's bones.

He laughed, as if delighted at the man's ingenuity. "No wonder indeed. The rascal! But let me give you some advice. I wouldn't make an enemy of Barmocar — not if you can help it. He's a pretty influential man here. And, let's face it, he's the only member of the Tribunal of One Hundred and Four that you know. If I were you, I would cultivate that. So what will you do?"

She was astonished at the question, and dismayed. *I hoped to find myself under your protection and guidance.* "I can work," she said stiffly. "I was an Annid. I have skills in direction, decision-making. Perhaps I could work as an adviser to the Council of Elders, or — "

He waved that away. "Forget it. The Carthaginians

loathe us Northlanders. Ingrained after centuries of our manipulating their destiny—that's the way they see it."

"The role of Northland has always been to bring peace and collaboration between disparate peoples—"

"And to get rich and powerful in the process. Forget it, as I said. There's no way anybody would *pay* you for your advice. It's best if you can persuade them to forget you're a Northlander at all. Why do you think I dress in this repulsive purple? Is there anything you can *do*? I mean, a specific skill. Weaving, knitting, lace-making, cooking—by the mothers, anything, women do many jobs in Northland, brick-making, growstone-mixing!"

"I am an Annid, from a family of Annids. I was ten years old before I had to lace up my own shoes."

She meant to make him laugh. He returned her look, stony-faced. "Your children, then. How old?"

"Twins, just sixteen now. A boy and a girl. He, Nelo, is a promising artist, in the new deep-look style—"

"How big is he?"

"What?"

"Physically. Tall, short, thin, strong . . ."

"Shorter than me. Quite heavily built. Strong, if he puts his mind to it. But he has a gentle spirit which—"

"He may find work on the labor details. The sewage system, for instance—constantly clogging up. And corpse details when the plagues come. Or the farms."

"No Northlander farms."

"They do here. Now, the girl?"

"Alxa. She's a bright, independent young woman. Stronger than me, I think. She has a facility for languages. She learned Carthaginian on the journey."

"A translator, then? That might have possibilities. Not useful for me, mind you, I have all the staff I need. Good-looking?"

She flared. "Why do you ask that?"

"Because one role Northlander women are popular for here is as companions. Oh, don't look at me so, Cousin. It doesn't have to be—like that. But you can imagine how it gives a Carthaginian pleasure to order around a pretty, stuck-up Northlander, as they see it."

She suppressed her anger. "I am reluctant to rely on the labor of my children. They are too young."

"This isn't Northland," he said firmly. "You are far from home. Nobody wants you here, frankly. The quicker you absorb that fact the better. And the sooner you learn that your preferences are irrelevant—"

"Help us," she said bluntly.

He sat back in his chair, sighed, and rubbed his face. "Rina, Rina. I have nothing for you."

"You have room. Food, warmth. At least let us stay for a few days. Until we can find work, get established somehow. I will pay you back."

He laughed. "What, with Northland scrip?"

"With the money I, we, will earn when we find jobs."

"Impossible. Believe me, with the kind of jobs you'll be taking you won't be paying down loans. Look, Rina, I have my own position in society here to think of. If I start taking in strays and nestspills—"

"You are a Northlander."

"Not anymore," he said coldly. "And since you abandoned the place to come here, neither are you."

"As family, then." She forced herself to say it. After all, she had begged before Barmocar. Was this any worse? "I'm desperate. For my children. Please. I have no other recourse."

He sighed again. "I always was too soft for my own good. Seven days. And then you're gone. Now if you'll excuse me . . ." He bent over his desk. "Send in my clerks on your way out. And shut the door."

A little later Alxa and Nelo, fetched from the city by Jexami's servants, showed up at the estate.

Alxa was wide-eyed. "By the mothers' eyes, this is grand. It's almost as good as the Wall. Does that tap work?"

"Leave it alone," Rina snapped. "Touch as little as possible. *Use* as little as possible."

Nelo frowned. "Are we staying here?"

"Yes. For now. Not for long. But we mustn't impose ..." Nelo's face was bloodied, she saw, a smear from a cut over his eye, and a bruise was rising on his cheek. "Oh, my, what happened to you?" She ran to get a bowl of water and a cloth.

Alxa sat on a chair, testing its softness. "We got into a fight."

"You did what?"

"We went for a walk. The city is teeming, Mother, full of people. We found a tavern. We thought we'd have some wine. But the landlord wouldn't accept our Northlander scrip. And some men had heard us talking, I mean in our own tongue. They came over to give us a hard time. One of them said something—"

Nelo said, "He called Alxa a whore. I know enough Carthaginian for that. He said Northlander women make the best whores, because they're big and healthy. Like wild deer. I punched him."

"You did *what*?"

Alxa said, "It was all I could do to get us out of there in one piece. Those narrow streets, we had to throw them off, we ran and ran!" She laughed at the memory of it, swinging her legs. "Where's our luggage? Is there any hot water? Can I ask for tea?"

Rina held her son's bruised forehead, peering into his eyes, looking for his spirit, seeing only blankness.

35

Rina spent six of Jexami's seven days fruitlessly searching for work.

Then, on the day before Jexami was to throw them out of his house, she swallowed more pride, took Jexami's advice, and approached the only man of position she knew in the city: Barmocar. She used a veiled threat about exposing his possession of the Virgin's relics to secure an appointment.

She was taken into the city by one of Jexami's carriage-men, and dropped at one of the big gates in the landward wall. By now she had learned her way around Carthage, a little. The city within the wall was a neat grid of streets. The building stock was constructed of the local sandstone, and brilliant-white paintwork was common, so that when the sun pushed through the thickening clouds the air seemed to fill with light. The city's complicated history had left its mark too. Alongside the temples to Carthage's ancient gods there were mosques and mu-ezzin towers, relics of the days of Arabic conquest, and more recent churches to Jesus, symbols of Hatti influence, squat buildings whose faces were carved with representations of crossed palm leaves. Mostly, however, the lower city was crammed with residential properties, apartments heaped up three and four stories high, and shops, workshops, taverns and inns open to the street. The people swarmed everywhere, vendors calling, children running, imposing men and women carrying scrolls and slates. She saw no signs of the dispossessed who had washed up against the external walls, but still the city was crowded. She imagined everybody with a place in the city bringing in relatives from the dying countryside, until there was no room left.

Walking through this noisy, off-putting chaos, she never got lost, for her destination was the Byrsa, the tall hill that dominated the center of the town, topped with its mighty statue of Hannibal of Latium, the city's greatest hero, a sight you could see from anywhere in the lower city. She fixed on the statue and headed that way.

At the foot of the Byrsa the street pattern changed. From here, broad avenues ran radially up to the peak of the citadel mound, with lateral crossways between them. She set off to climb a steeply sloping street, lined to either side with apartment blocks that could be several stories high. She passed an open miller's store where grain was ground on a turning wheel, and a jeweler's where the craftsman labored on fine pieces in full view of passersby, and a temple, a fine building with a courtyard where two tremendous statues of men, or perhaps gods, loomed over an altar. At the temple she paused, breathing hard, and looked back over flat rooftops of the lower city. The steep road running down from this point was well maintained and clean, she saw. Vases and jars stood on many roofs, there to catch the rain, she imagined, in a city eager for every drop. From up here at least there was no sign of plague or famine. This was an intact, well-run, functioning city. Perhaps the storm that was engulfing the whole world had yet to break here. But it would break, she thought, remembering all she had seen on her journey. It would break.

Barmocar's office was right next door to the temple. He kept her waiting, of course, and met her in an anteroom, rather than take her into his office. "I thought you'd show up again. Helpless sorts like you always do." He sat at a desk, but she was forced to stand; he had a cup of water, which he sipped, but offered her nothing. "Will this take long? I am, if you haven't noticed, a busy man."

"Busy with what?"

"The temple. Which has always been an important institution in this city, and I'm senior on its governing council." He eyed her. "The temple is the big building next door. With the statues of our gods Melqart and his son Tanit—I don't suppose you know who they are, do you?"

"I need your help," she said.

He sat back, a grin on his face. He was a fleshy man, though even he had lost weight during the long journey from Northland. She had no idea if he intended to help her or not, but he was evidently planning to have some fun. "Jexami warned me you'd show up. How will you pay me this time? Do you have some other prophet's bones hidden up your ass?"

"I have nothing to give you. You know that. Nothing but my labor."

"Yes, but labor doing what? What could you possibly do for me that would justify a salary to keep you alive? Oh, and those kids of yours."

"I am highly intelligent, and educated. Surely you see that." She stopped herself; even in this desperate moment she had slipped into patronizing him. "I can contribute in many ways to your enterprises. As a clerk, a scribe—"

"By Melqart's toenail, you don't even speak the language, woman!"

"I can learn."

"Learn? What, an old stick like you? Look, as far as I can see you have only one salable asset, and that's your son's brute strength. Even the girl's no beauty."

"My son is an artist."

"Ha!"

"There must be something I could do. Work in your office. Your household . . ."

"You really are desperate, aren't you?"

"And you really are enjoying this," she couldn't help but snap back.

"Still the arrogant she-devil! I'll tell you what—only because it amuses me—perhaps there is something. Working for my wife, not for me. She's talked occasionally of needing a woman, somebody less stupid than the cattle that pass for servants these days."

She felt a spark of hope. "I can help with her correspondence, run the household—"

"You'll do what she tells you. Starting with cutting her toenails, I should think."

"I'll take it—thank you—"

"Wait." He held his hand up. "There's a condition. We Carthaginians have a practice. Very ancient, predates the Muslim invaders, even the wars with the Latins I think. We call it *molk*. A gift for the gods, in times of great stress. The greatest gift one can give."

"Molk?"

He leaned toward her. "The sacrifice of a child."

She stiffened. "What are you talking about?"

"Put the boy in the army—if they will have him."

"A Northlander, in a Carthaginian army? It would destroy him."

"No. Starving outside the city walls will destroy him." He picked up a stylus and tapped his teeth. "I have links with the army council. These are difficult times—you know that. We always need recruits. Those wretched Hatti are said to be marching in great numbers. The city will actually pay a small bounty if one brings in recruits.

So, you see, you are worth something to me after all. And it would be good for the city. Good for the boy, probably, too, to get him away from *you*. There's the deal, and it's the best you're going to get. Or," he said casually, "you could prostitute yourself, I suppose. You'd earn a little before they wore you out. What's it to be, Rina the Annid?"

Deep in a black corner of her heart she swore, not for the first time, that she would revenge herself on Barmocar, somehow, someday.

36

Pyxeas' party descended from the land of ice and high meadows. Uzzia insisted they go slowly, for a traveler used to thin air could be as damaged by a sudden exposure to thicker air as easily as the other way around.

Slowly was all they could manage in any case. Having left Jamil under his cairn on the high desert, there were only the three of them now, the three survivors of the shattered caravan. Or four if you counted the mule. Pyxeas, for the sake of his pride, insisted on walking a few steps every day, but it was only a few steps before he had to be loaded up onto the back of the patient mule. He had never seemed older, never frailer, and his energy in the thin air of the roof of the world was a memory.

What was left of their baggage went on the mule's back too, and on the backs of Uzzia and Avatak as they marched along. At least they were reasonably equipped. The robbery hadn't been very efficient, and the panicking thieves had run off leaving a good deal of their own kit behind—clothes, blankets, water sacks, even boots.

Avatak had been all for burning this stuff, but Uzzia persuaded him that if another man's boots might save his life he should take them.

Pyxeas' notes had been soiled and scattered, but were reasonably intact. Avatak saved the scroll on which he had been keeping his journal of the journey, and Pyxeas insisted he make an entry every day. Avatak did abandon his heavy hourglass. The oracle was smashed, but Pyxeas was set on keeping what was left of its case, despite its bulk. Uzzia plucked out a few gears from the oracle's abandoned carcass, saying she might make a bracelet of them for a favorite niece in New Hattusa.

So they continued.

Coming down from the roof of the world didn't mean the journey got any easier. Now they came to a stretch of terrain that Uzzia called "the Desert of No Return." "Except," she said, "it's not a true desert, and it must have been given that name by somebody or other who *has* returned. Make of that what you will." Desert or not, it was harsh, bleak country, where the water was sparse, brackish. It was a comfort to Avatak that Uzzia had come this way before, but everything seemed to be changing as the world entered Pyxeas' longwinter; many of the springs Uzzia looked out for had dried up.

Still, they passed through some spectacular landscapes. There was a dry valley that cut through layers of rock, crimson and black, heaped up like a stack of paper pages. Pyxeas speculated about the process that must have laid down these layers in the earth, and then cut through them like a knife. But his mind, supported by an exhausted, starved, dried-out, failed body, was a feeble flicker these days. Avatak thought this landscape of dead rock was chilling; he longed for life.

Uzzia, more practical, said the valley was a good place to shelter. They laid up for two days in the mouth of a dusty cave, and Uzzia and Avatak set traps for the rabbits and strange-looking rodents that chewed on the dry grass.

They emerged from the desert at a small town by an oasis. Remote as it was, exotic as the people looked, it was a place used to travelers, and it welcomed them briskly and without any fuss. Here they were able to exchange some of their catch for beds for a couple of nights, water, a chance to rinse out their clothing.

A man who claimed a special understanding of horses looked over their mule, for a price. "He's in good condition—you'll get a few months out of him yet before he's ready for the butcher's hook and the glue man's pot. But he has a problem with his left front hoof . . ." It was a jammed stone, a thorn. The mule must have been in constant pain for days. Avatak had never known. While they stayed in the town Avatak made sure he visited the mule in its stable, morning and night.

Then they walked on again. A little way out of town they passed a kind of monastery based in caves in a hillside, with walls of brick and clay set up along terraces. Men, clean-shaven and in dusty orange robes, climbed ladders. Monks, they were, Uzzia said, following the teachings of a god-priest called the Buddha. Avatak had seen some of these in the town. He had thought they were beggars; he had seen them imploring for gifts of food and drink, going from house to house.

Now the country opened up once more, and they found themselves on a broad, grassy plain—flat and endless, it seemed, stretching to the horizon, though as they walked they would glimpse worn mountains looming.

"This is the steppe," Uzzia said as she plodded along. "A Rus word. You're in the very heart of Asia now, the core of the world continent—a place where the writ of even mighty empires like Cathay does not run. And it is this land that has always birthed the savage horsemen. The most powerful of all were the Mongols, under Genghis, the first of the great Khans. Now his descendants rule Cathay itself. You'll see."

Ferocious the Mongols might be, but for now Avatak saw nothing of them. Their progress was slow, though the country was comparatively easy. Avatak insisted on giving the mule time to feed on the sparse steppe grass.

In an island of lusher, greener country, they came to a substantial city, walled, where green gardens within were fed from springs. This was a place called Lop, Uzzia said. She said they should stay here for seven days to feed, rest and water, to prepare for the next stage of the journey, the hardest stretch yet. The city seemed crowded, a tense, busy place. But Uzzia found them an empty house, and a clean stable for the mule, and vendors soon arrived with sacks of water and wine, hunks of meat, dried fruit and vegetables, pots to cook in.

Avatak said, "I don't understand how we're paying. We were robbed—*you* were, they took all your trade goods. And a mountain of trapped rabbits couldn't pay for all this stuff."

She glanced across at Pyxeas, who was limping around the house lighting oil lamps. "I'll take you into my confidence. I suppose if anything happened to me it would be a shame to waste it."

"Waste what?"

She took her quilted jacket from where it hung on a hook by the door. She showed Avatak fine slits in the fabric, pushed her finger deep inside one of the quilt's little sewn pads, and pulled out a gleaming stone. "A diamond," she said. "And I have sapphires, a few rubies, some bits of jade and agate, silver and gold for small change ..."

"Ah."

"This is the best way, in these turbulent times. To convert your wealth into the most portable form. And the most easily concealed."

"Lucky those robbers didn't try to get your jacket off you."

"That's been tried in the past, by lads more interested in what's inside my clothes than the clothes themselves. They end up with slit throats."

"I have a feeling that whatever Rina paid you back in Hantilios to keep us alive wasn't enough."

She laughed. "Well, that's probably true. Unless of course old Pyxeas does after all end up saving the world, in which case it will all have been worth it."

Avatak slept away much of his time in Lop. He did some exploring, but he felt bewildered to be in yet another town, his ears filled by yet another set of unknown and unknowable languages.

At last he saw Mongol warriors, in the town.

They were burly men in armor of buffalo hide, layers of fur, and, some of them, elaborate cloaks woven with gold and silk. They wore their hair oddly, with the scalp shaven, and only a fine mask of beard around the mouth and chin. Most of them carried at least one weapon, an axe, a sword, perhaps a small bow—unimpressive, but Uzzia said it was their use of the bow, their arrows shot from the back of a galloping horse with deadly accuracy, that made them formidable above all else. They were nomad horsemen and war-fighters and they were tremendously rich, all these things at once. Avatak thought he could see the story of their success in the way they dressed, in warrior garb adorned with gold and jewels, the way they walked as others cowered out of their way. Avatak didn't speak to any of them.

He visited taverns, and drank weak beer, and made conversation with locals and travelers in broken Greek and Northlander. The travelers told tales of tremendous fires to the north, as if all the forests in Asia were burning off, and of streams of nestspills all heading south. When he spoke of this to Pyxeas, the scholar looked mournful, and spoke of friends in Albia, their ancient forest, which must be turning to ash too. Lying awake at night, Avatak sometimes imagined he smelled the smoke of the world fires, and that he heard the whisper from a million throats: *"South. Go south . . ."*

He made his twice-daily pilgrimage to see the mule

in its stable. He brushed its coarse coat, and rubbed liniment into its injured hoof. The mule submitted to these attentions in sullen silence, save for the occasional fart.

The seven days over, once again they bundled up their luggage and loaded the mule. Now they had a horse too, a compact, strong-looking pony purchased by Uzzia. They left the city of Lop with gratitude for its hospitality, but without looking back.

Within two days they were in a desert.

This was not like the Desert of No Return, not even like the western deserts they had crossed early in the journey. This was a featureless plain of gravel, dry clay, and a dusty, yellowish sand that tasted salty when it blew into your mouth. At night the stars made a tremendous dome, slowly swiveling toward the dawn. Though it was ferociously hot during the day, in the morning it could be cold enough to leave a frost that the animals licked from their blankets. Aside from the frost the only water, rarely glimpsed in almost dried-up streams, was brackish; even the horse and mule turned away from it. Sometimes a storm would blow up—wind, never rain—and the sand would take to the air, swirling around them, the particles stinging their faces and eyes, sometimes so violent they couldn't make progress at all and they had to huddle in the small tent they had bought in Lop. But then the storms would blow away, and they would move on. They would find the wind had scraped away the earth down to a polished bedrock, and heaped the sand up in dunes like waves on an ocean.

So the next day passed, and the next. Often a day would pass with no landmarks at all, save a shallow dune or two: no mountains looming, no oases. Nothing to see but level sands stretching to the horizon, and the huge sky above. Gradually Avatak lost his sense of time and place, in this land like a dusty tabletop.

Pyxeas had him keep the journal, scratching in the

date, and random observations and speculations. "Perhaps this was once a lake, or a sea," Pyxeas rasped. "A sea that somehow drained away. That would explain the flatness, and the salt. But where are the fish bones, and the wrecks of fishermen's boats?" And he would mumble and mutter, and subside back to his habitual state of halfsleep. Avatak did not care where the salt had come from. He made Pyxeas' notes, but they were another man's thoughts expressed in another man's language; with a little practice he found he could ignore their meaning altogether, even as he wrote them down.

Still they walked, day after day, across a world reduced to its absolute essentials, to land below, sky above. "We walk through Pythagorean dualities," Pyxeas said. Avatak's mind seemed to become as big as the sky, as if trying to fill all that empty space above, yet his spirit was diminished, to become a grain of sand as trivial as those under his feet. Was this how it was to die? To shrink into oneself, to shrivel to nothing, to become a dust speck in a universe grand and ancient that would continue without him, indifferent?

In the dark, during the nights, he would close his eyes and try to shed such thoughts. But he would hear a soft singing sometimes, a low discordant groan, like the calls of tremendous walruses from some far ice floe. Perhaps it was the spirits of those lost in this unending desert. Perhaps it was just a trick of the wind in the dunes. If the others heard it, they did not mention it.

It was a shock when, late one day of walking, they came upon the oasis. There were houses of mud and reeds, and a few sheep wandering. There were even a few trees, their leaves spindly and green. This didn't look real to Avatak, as if it didn't fit into the world.

Uzzia put her arm around his shoulders. She said they had been walking the desert for thirty-six days.

"And this," she said, "is Cathay."

37

For fisherman Crimm, the morning hadn't been so bad. Out on the Northern Ocean, the visibility had been good. There had even been a little warmth in the sun, on this supposedly late summer day. The crew of the *Sabet*, all eight of them who had mustered, had been reasonably cheerful, despite the ice-cold spray that soaked its way through the thickest furs, despite the endless labor of pumping water from the bilge, and despite the lousy catch of cod, a longer-term worry that gnawed at their vitals as they thought of the coming winter, and their families back in Northland.

Of course the ice had been their constant companion all day. Scattered floes scraped against the hull, and to the north fleets of bergs sailed on the swell. On the horizon was a band of whitish light that shimmered and glinted: pack ice, solid, unmovable, much further south even than last year, and much earlier in the year too. It wasn't even the autumn equinox yet! Still, through the morning they had been able to forget about the ice and get on with their work.

But by midday the floes were closing in around them. The men started arguing about when to give up and put into port.

Then the fog rolled in, almost without warning, coming on them with overwhelming speed. That was that. They shipped the nets and made for home.

In a gray cloud they nosed south on a northerly wind. They got close enough to the Northland shore to hear the great steam-powered horns that sounded from the light towers atop the Wall, but they couldn't see the lights. If Crimm stood high in the prow he could barely make out the big square mainsail, let alone the Wall. You could wreck yourself against the Wall if you came on it blind. They had no choice but to head north again, and wait out the fog. They furled the sails and broke out the oars.

Crimm glanced over his crew. None looked happy to be rowing. One man, Xon, the youngest, looked withdrawn, fearful. Crimm said cheerfully, "Call this a fog? Ayto's breath is thicker than this, most mornings." He got grins in response.

They emerged at last into the daylight; the fog was a solid bank behind them. But now the northern horizon was graying too, bubbling into an ominous wall of cloud. At a soft command from Crimm they rested on their oars.

"Told you so," Ayto said to Crimm.

"Told me what?"

"Should have put in before the famous fog rolled in. Told you."

"Yes, but in the next breath you said—"

"Anyhow, now we're stuck out here."

The wind picked up again. Loose corners of the mainsail flapped and cracked. Though the sails were furled, Crimm felt the *Sabet* surge, back toward the fog.

Ayto raised his hands. "And now comes the wind too. You spoil us, O little mother of the sky."

The wind gusted, becoming an icy blast in Crimm's

face, hurling particles that stung his skin and eyes, more like frozen sand than water or ice.

And suddenly, in just a few heartbeats, that bank of cloud to the north rushed down on them, towering high into the sky. It was a storm coming out of nowhere, as fast as the fog had come upon them, or faster. The men didn't need to be told what to do. They lashed down the nets and their barrels of water and dried fish, tried to make fast the day's catch, a pitiful heap of immature fish glistening in the bilge, and grabbed lines, bracing themselves.

The storm hit with a tremendous howl. The wind was a chill blast that tried to drag Crimm off the boat, and dug deep through his layers of clothing to his skin, and drove more of those stinging ice grains into his face, and snow, big fat flakes of it that slapped his cheeks and forehead. The men, the snow sticking to their furs, were like bears, he thought, lumbering in the gray light through the rushing snow. But the spray was coming up too and freezing where it fell. As the ice formed slick on the deck, you had to take care not to slip.

Ayto shouted something, and pointed upward. One hand wrapped in the rigging, Crimm leaned back, holding his hood against the wind, and saw that ice was forming in sheets on the main mast, the furled sail, the rigging. The boat could be capsized by a sufficient weight of ice up there.

Crimm bent, dug in a locker to retrieve an axe, then clambered up the main mast by the rigging and began to hack at the ice sheets. Another man, he couldn't see who, was doing the same at the stern mast. His hands were quickly going numb, and he thought of digging out his mittens, but he wouldn't be able to hold the rigging firmly enough. The boat rolled in a swell, and the men skidded over the deck. Crimm had to wrap an arm around the main mast and nearly lost his grip on the axe.

And the man at the stern dropped from the mast, slid over the slick deck, fell into the surging water, and was gone in an eye blink.

The storm blew over as quickly as it had come upon them. The crew slumped on the deck, exhausted, their breath billowing before their faces. The air felt much colder than before the storm had passed, and Crimm could see the residual wet on the deck frosting up. Suddenly they had sailed into winter.

He worked his way around the ship, passing out water bags and lumps of dried fish, and quietly counted the men. Seven of them left, one lost. He organized a couple of them to start pumping out the bilge, which was awash with icy water.

"We lost Xon," a man called Aranx murmured.

"Yes. Only sixteen, wasn't he?"

"Seventeen."

"I'll tell his mother when we get back."

"I'll do it," Ayto said. "I play knuckles with the father. The stern mast's snapped, by the way. That's the main damage. That and a hundred leaks."

"We can lash the mast," Crimm said. When they got back to the Wall the other damage would be straightforward to repair; the boat's construction was planking laid over a sturdy skeleton, and replacing sections was easy in dry dock.

There was a scraping along the hull, as if they had struck a reef.

Ayto, Crimm and Aranx glanced at one another, and hurried to the rail.

The ice was floating in cakes around them, flat, thick, some of them slushy. The scraping they had heard had been one of the cakes brushing past the stern. The floes looked like lilies on some dismal, colorless pond, Crimm thought.

"In this cold that lot is going to thicken quickly," Ayto said.

"We can get through it for now." The *Sabet*'s high prow was designed to help it weather heavy seas. It was good at pushing through loose surface ice like this. "Break out the oars. If it goes on long enough we'll rotate the man at the rudder."

"All right."

Soon they had the crew organized, and rowing steadily. Crimm worked the rudder for a time, then tied it up and went to work at the bilge pump.

The grinding of the ice against the hull came more often. Soon it was a continuous scrape, and, laboring in the bilge, Crimm could hear the cracking of floes as the boat rose and fell with the swell, and the prow came down heavy on the ice.

Ayto called, "Rest your oars. You might want to take a look, Crimm."

Crimm straightened up from the bilge and walked the couple of paces to the rail. The floes were colliding with one another now, rising up over one another, pushing up ridges of crushed material that quickly refroze. It was a landscape of ridges and mountains, forming before his eyes. There were still leads, open stretches of water, dark stripes between the floes, but further out icebergs towered, floating hills of ice.

"We've seen this before," Ayto said. "Further north."

"Yes. But never this far south."

"No, and not at this time of year. The prow won't crack stuff as thick as this."

"We mustn't get stuck." Crimm glanced around. "There are still some decent leads. We can follow that one, to the west, and then maybe there's a route to the south."

Ayto squinted and nodded. "We can try it. If not that way, another will probably open up."

"You call directions, and I'll take a turn at the oar."

"All right. Tell them to go easy. We don't want any snapped oars."

So Crimm worked his oar with the rest, cautious, breaking his pull at any sense of solid resistance, any sound of scraping on the ice. Ayto stood at the prow, staring out, calling directions, and the men worked or rested their oars accordingly.

"Hold it." Ayto held his hand up.

The men shipped their oars. The boat came to a halt quickly, with a grinding of ice. Crimm got up and joined Ayto at the prow. The lead ahead was still open, but it was narrowing visibly as he watched.

"We can't get any further," Ayto said. "Sorry. It closed up too fast. I was hoping to make a break for it to that one"—he pointed to a wider lane further away—"but it just closed in."

"Maybe we can go back the way we came." They both retreated to the stern to see. The men at the oars sat slumped, still weary from the storm—frost-covered, their clothes, their beards, even their eyebrows. The air was truly, bitterly cold now, Crimm realized; the exercise had kept him warmed against it, even though the sun was still high in a misty sky, even though this was still summer.

When they got to the stern they saw the lead behind the boat was closing up too.

Ayto said, "I'm sorry, Cousin. I fouled up, getting us lost in this maze."

"There was probably never a way through anyhow."

"So what now?"

Crimm was an experienced seaman. His father had brought him up on the ocean; his mother, fond but resentful, said her son had spent more of his boyhood on boats than at home. And at sea, you learned to keep calm. You tried one way. If that failed, you tried another. And if that failed in turn, another yet.

"We get out on the ice. Fix up ropes. We go on foot, and haul the ship back until we find an open lead."

"Hmm," Ayto said. "Look how quick it's closing up. We wouldn't get far."

"So your idea is . . ."

"We wait. Overnight if we have to. Maybe the weather will relent a bit tomorrow. If the leads open up again we might make a break."

Crimm thought about that, looking out to the horizon. Everywhere the ice was solidifying, those great ridges thrusting into the air where the floes collided. Even the drifting bergs were getting frozen into the congealing pack. "This stuff doesn't look as if it's going to give up anytime soon."

"Well, it should," Ayto said, almost resentful. "It's not even the equinox yet, unless I got too drunk to remember. I say we camp for the night and hope the little mother of the sky looks a bit more kindly on us in the morning."

So Crimm gave in. They shipped the oars and set up the mainsail as a makeshift shelter suspended from the main mast. They had a small stock of firewood they carried to warm themselves in the nights at sea, and Aranx started building a fire out on the ice. Another man broke out dried fish and biscuits for a meal. Another, a Muslim, rolled out his prayer mat on the ice and knelt, facing east.

Two more of the crew went on a hopeful quest across the ice in search of driftwood for fuel. Ayto called after them, "Walk where the ice looks blue. That's where it's oldest, thickest. If you fall in through a crack I won't be coming after you."

Crimm walked around the ship, looking for damage to the timbers from the ice scrapes. He could hear the ice around him groaning and creaking as it consolidated. It was an eerie sound, laid over the silence of the enclosed, hushed sea, and the surface shuddered and lurched constantly.

And then, he actually saw it begin, the boat's planking cracked and crumpled inward, under the relentless pressure from the ice, giving way with a snapping, splintering noise. The hull started to tilt.

"Everybody off," he called. "Off the ship, now! Grab what you can ..."

They all got off in time, as the hull crumpled like an empty eggshell. The deck tipped over, and the remaining mast gave way with a snap. It all happened quickly, in heartbeats.

"So, that's that," Ayto said as they surveyed the wreck. "The end of the famous *Sabet*. I've heard of this happening. Far to the north, the kind of stories the Coldlanders tell. Not here."

"Well, it's happened."

"We should have seen it coming. We might have hauled her out onto the ice before it closed."

Crimm asked, "What good would that have done? We still weren't going to be sailing her anywhere soon."

Ayto nodded. "So what now?"

"Now we go in and grab what we can, and see what's what." He glanced around. "May as well build a bigger fire."

"We're going to have to walk home," Ayto said.

"Yes."

"Or at least to the edge of the ice, where we might get picked up."

"They'll miss us. Send boats looking."

"Do we start today?"

Crimm sniffed the chill air. "No. The light will be going soon. We'd be better off camping for the night, sorting out the stuff. We need to carry food, the water. We can make up packs from the sails. Tents, maybe."

"We shouldn't have —"

"We shouldn't have got stuck in the first place. We shouldn't have been born in a time when *this* happens. There's no warmth in shouldn't haves."

"True enough." Ayto aimed a kick at the splintered wreck. "Poor old girl. Come on, let's get set up before it gets any colder."

38

The travelers came to a wall. It was only sod and earth, about the height of a man, with ditches before and behind. But it straggled off across the landscape, heading vaguely for low hills. Its meaning was clear.

Avatak stared. After all their experiences it seemed absurd to find their way blocked by a work of mere humans. "This wall is stupid. You could jump over it! And if I were an invading army I would just go around it, to one side or another."

"But this is what Cathay does," said Uzzia. "Builds walls. There has always been a tension between the nomads of the steppe and the desert, and Cathay with its farms and cities. And over history Cathay has always built walls to control the passage of the nomads, if not to exclude them altogether. Dwarfing even your great Wall, scholar, in length at least."

Pyxeas, on the back of the mule, snorted. "But not matching ours in fitness for purpose. Ask Genghis Khan about *that*."

They followed the wall south until they came to a shabby wooden gate. Two soldiers watched as they approached. Wearing the Mongols' leather armor they were scruffy, dirty, and one had dried soup dribbled down his chest plate. But they had weapons, they were soldiers, and they were manning the wall.

Uzzia went forward to negotiate with the guards. She tried one dialect after another. Their responses were hostile rasps.

She came back to her party. "Basically their orders are not to let anybody else into Cathay, not ever again. Because Cathay is full, and there is famine and plague. Orders of the Khan. They speak about incursions all along the frontier. The Khan is sending troops to the north and west to keep down his own wilder cousins. It sounds like it's a sink of madness out there, where one side builds up a wall only for the other to smash it down again. What this means is that it's going to be expensive to get past these fellows. Your saving the world is costing me a lot of money, scholar."

"Then let me deal with it," Pyxeas snapped, impatient. "Help me down, Avatak." The scholar rummaged in the packs until he pulled out the wreck of his oracle—just the frame, broken open, the little sun and moon snapped off. Now Pyxeas pried at the back of the gadget's face until a panel popped open, and a small golden plaque fell out into the old man's hand. Pyxeas handed the ruined oracle back to Avatak. "Put this away."

Then, limping, he approached the guards, who watched him curiously. "Here! You fellows at the gate! My name is Pyxeas, scholar of Northland, and no doubt you will recognize this." He held up the plaque.

He had spoken in his own tongue. The guards obviously understood not a word. But they stared at the golden plaque, took it, read words inscribed there, their lips moving. They handed the plaque back. They both bowed, murmuring what sounded like apologies, and stood back, opening the barrier as they went.

Uzzia was astonished. "How did you do that? Give me that." She took the golden disc and studied it.

"That is my *paiza*, which is the Cathay word for it; the Mongols call it a *gerega*. The words are written in Mongol and Cathay scripts. It is a right of passage, a guarantee of safety, given me by the great Khan himself. Not the present incumbent—a predecessor. My colleagues in Daidu requested this, and one of them carried it to Northland for me, some years ago. Are you surprised that I possess such a thing, trader? Are you surprised that I, a Northlander scholar, am held in such esteem, even though I have never visited Cathay before? I tell you they are eager to meet me there, just as I am eager to see them. I suggest we get on with the journey. What do you say?"

She handed back the *paiza*. "Lead the way."

Once past the wall they came to a substantial community, a sprawling town dominated by another monastery cut into a cliff. In the end they stayed a couple of nights.

The *paiza* won them food and lodging, in a shabby mud-and-straw hut. The people of the lower town, and, once, one of the monks, brought them food and drink, rather stringy mutton, bitter fruit. Uzzia, urged by Pyxeas, tried to pay, for it was clear these people had little enough of their own. But the townsfolk were evidently terrified by the authority of the Khan and would have none of it.

It was a relief for Avatak to let the saddle-soreness seep out of his thighs. But he found it impossible to sleep indoors, in a box of mud. Something in him was drawn back to the huge emptiness of the desert, and perhaps always would be. So he crept out of the house, to a small kitchen garden at the back, and laid out his roll under the stars.

The second night Uzzia came out to find him there.

She crouched over him, her smile shadowed. "You've got an invitation."

"From who?"

"From the woman in the house next door. Or rather, her husband. I know you've noticed her—she's noticed you."

Avatak knew who she meant. The woman, a good few years older than him, was taller, stockier than most in this country. She had a strong face with a sly grin, and broad hips, and a bust that was heavy, if not firm. She filled her robes well as she went about her chores.

"I know how that type appeals to young men like you. An older woman, evidently fertile, knows her way around a bed—seems to draw the seed out of you just by looking at you."

"What does she want with me?"

"What do you think?"

"But you said, the husband—"

"It is their way, in this country," she said. "To invite travelers into the beds of the women. This is a small place and isolated; there are probably people here who will live and die never traveling as far as the next village. This is their way to make babies who are not the cousins of everybody else. Do you see?"

"Oh."

"You would be doing them a favor. You will be asked to leave a token, a present, to prove that the deed has been done." She sighed. "I remember when you would be asked for a flower, a bit of cheap jewelry. Now they ask for food, which changes the whole nature of the transaction, doesn't it? But these are harder times. Well. We have the food, or can buy it. What do you say?"

He thought about the woman, and felt a warm pressure in his loins. But he thought of his betrothed, and his lover, in far countries. And he glanced up at the cold, unmoving stars.

"What's wrong? Are you missing your betrothed?"

"Not that." He lacked the language to express how he felt. "The desert."

"Hmm. I've seen this before. All right. But better to lose your soul between the thighs of a woman than to the emptiness out there. I will say you're ill, so nobody's feelings are hurt. May I give her the food anyway?"

"If you wish."

"Of course in *my* arms she would explode like a Northlander eruptor. But I cannot give her a baby, and, for this one night, that is my deepest regret. Good night, Coldlander." She bent, kissed his forehead, and passed into the night.

So they moved on, leaving behind fearful guards and wombs not impregnated, and with a fresh horse, new blankets and saddles, and their surly mule trotting behind.

They headed ever east, into the Mongol empire.

Avatak's feet, and his arse when he rode the horse, noted the better surface of the trail here, a straight and narrow track that arrowed to the east. But Pyxeas bewailed its condition. "This is one of the Khan's post roads. He united his empire, and all of Asia, with roads straight and fast and true so that messengers could cross a continent as fast as a thought crackles through your small head, Coldlander. Look at it now! Covered in dust from this desiccating farmland all around, and with the trees cut down—mighty trees they were, purposefully planted along the route so a rider could never lose his way no matter what the weather—cut down for some peasant's firewood, no doubt!"

The deeper they walked into Cathay, the more densely it was farmed. But workers thin as shadows toiled at dried-up fields, there was only a scattering of green even though the harvest must soon be due, and the bare ground was turning to dust that blew over the roads.

And, in the middle of the farming country, they came

upon Mongol camps. These were not princes of Daidu and Karakorum, or traders, or border guards; these were common folk, herders like their ancestors, with their horses and a few cows and fat-tailed sheep. They lived in yurts, battered houses with their door flaps all set to face the sun at midday, like rows of shabby flowers.

The travelers stopped one night, close to an extensive camp. The nomads showed respect for the *paiza* of the Khan, and the travelers were invited to stay in a yurt, but they declined, wary of imposing on what might be a fragile hospitality. They sat by their own small fire, eating a bit of mutton and sheep's tail they had been given by the Mongols, and watched the conquerors of the world at play. The adults wore colorful clothes, trousers, tunics and hats. Their children ran around and shouted and fought as children always did. They seemed to have slaves, plenty of them, skinny-looking folk of Cathay who went barefoot. Mostly the slaves cooked and cleaned, but Avatak glimpsed one girl writing something down, as dictated by her owner. As the night drew in, the adults gathered in a circle and danced, and sang, and passed around cups of drink and smoky pipes.

Pyxeas grunted. "This dancing, the pipes and the strong stuff they seem to be drinking—this is the old culture, when spirit men would talk to their sky god and the ninety-nine junior deities he controlled. The spirits of the deep steppe, coming back again. When times are hard, people go back to what they know best. The Mongols own half the world, but even they are in thrall to the weather."

He was dismissive. But something in the way the Mongols celebrated their evening reminded Avatak of home, his own people, nomads too. He said nothing.

"Once they would not have been here at all," Uzzia said."They would have driven their herds to the summer pasture in the hills; it must be too cold up there this year. And they would not have camped in farmland at all; this is not the steppe. But the land is so dry—it is as if the steppe itself is shifting south, and driving the people with it. There will be conflict. Probably there is already. The farmers will lose, of course."

"And the city dwellers, in the short term," Pyxeas said. "But in the long term everybody will lose, when the Mongol empire turns on itself. Once, you know, a khan threatened to obliterate Cathay altogether, and use the land to pasture his herds. Perhaps in time to come — and not very far in the future — that promise will at last be fulfilled. But the irony is that nomadic herders will be far better suited to the conditions that will prevail than city folk, than civilization."

"If war is coming to this place we must press on to Daidu."

"Mmm," said Pyxeas. "And will we find safety there?"

In the morning they moved on once more, working their way ever further east, passing towns and villages and more dried-out farmland. They had to use the scholar's *paiza* to get past more layers of guards, more walls thrown across the roads, even this deep into the heart of the country.

Gradually the road grew busier, and Avatak noticed that much of the traffic was heading the same way they were, eastward — traders and merchants with wagons full of goods, but an increasing number of ordinary folk, adults with children, old folk riding carts, horses heaped with furniture on their backs, even rolls of carpet. Nestspills, folk from failed farms or imploded towns, all heading, Avatak supposed, in search of the succor of the emperor.

And at last, late one morning, they crested a rise and faced the formidable walls of Daidu.

Pyxeas leaned down from the mule's back and murmured to Avatak, "Coldlander, to reach this place you and I have traveled almost a third of the world's arc. *And* we got here before the equinox—just. Quite an achievement."

Uzzia snorted. "Just remember this mule has come almost as far, and he's not bragging about it. Come now, let's see if your magic *paiza* will get us through this last set of gates." She gave the mule's stirrup a tug, and let the animal lead the way toward the city.

39

At the Wall, more snow had fallen overnight, and indeed it was still falling as the morning broke.

Thaxa needed to see Ontin, to ask him to come treat some fishermen caught by the cold. The doctor's lodge was only a short walk down the Etxelur Way from the Wall, but Thaxa wasn't going to try it until the snow eased. So he made himself comfortable in the linen shop that fronted his Wall-front home. He told his servant, Moerx, to let the fire in the hearth die down a little. You were always aware of the need to save fuel, even kindling. The shop cooled quickly, and he wrapped himself up in layers, leggings and trousers and waterproofs, a couple of tunics and a heavy sealskin coat, three layers of socks over which he would later pull his hide boots. Then he sat in a window seat in his house's south-facing wall, and looked out, watching the snow fall.

The house was in one of the most prized neighborhoods in Greater Etxelur. A modern stone structure backing onto chambers cut into the face of the Wall itself, it directly faced the big, rich estates that in this age encrusted the old earthwork called the Door to the Mothers' House—and of course, being south-facing, it was blessed with good light for much of the day. Rina had always loved this house. It was a legacy of a favorite uncle and a place she had often visited as a child. She had spent an inordinate amount of time and money on it to make it a home for their two children as they had grown, as well as an establishment suitable for one of the richest and most powerful couples in Etxelur. Yet it had been a lonely place for Thaxa this summer, since his family had gone south.

Well, that had been the deal they had struck back in the spring, he and Rina, during those difficult, sleepless, guilt-ridden nights. She would get the children to safety; he would stay behind and help prepare the Wall and Etxelur and all of Northland for the difficult days to come. That was the deal, a compromise between their primal need to protect their children and their wider duty. Rina was, after all, an Annid. And if the weather didn't let up next year, if Rina couldn't come home, then Thaxa would make his own way south to join her. But after the summer they'd had here, and now the horribly early winter, Thaxa was starting to wonder what would be left of the world by the spring, and whether he would ever be able to get as far as Carthage.

And still the snow fell, big fat flakes of it from an eerie sky, a sky that glowed with a kind of silver light. Perhaps it looked so odd because the autumn sunlight was strong; he was used to snow in the low light of midwinter, not at this time of year. He had loved snow as a boy, for it had been rare then. Close to the Wall snow would often not fall at all, for the great bulk of growstone blocked the northern winds, and its heat warmed the land at its foot. Experts like Pyxeas said the Wall created its own weather. Yes, once he had loved the snow, when it was a rare treat. Now he hated it, like the rest of Northland, he suspected. The only consolation was that the chill was never too deep while the snow was actually falling. It was in the clear nights between the snowfalls that the cold really bit deep, and walls could crack and windows frost up and the piss in your night pot would freeze over, and old people and little babies would die in their beds.

Finally the snow relented, the fall dwindling to a few scattered flakes, that odd silvery glow fading from the sky. Thaxa dragged on his boots, checked the bone toggles on his coat, pulled up his hood, stuffed his hands in his mittens, and opened the door. The new fall, about as deep as his kneecaps, came spilling into the house. He kept a snow shovel behind the door, an expensive tool made from the scapula of a deer and an ash pole. He got to work shifting the snow from the doorway, lifting rough blocks of snow on the blade and dumping them to either side. It wasn't so difficult this time; this particular deposit of snow was powdery, and it was easy to slide in the blade. They were all getting used to the different kinds of snow that could fall depending on minute differences in temperature and the dampness of the air. The worst kind was the slushy wet stuff that clung to your blade; that could be like shifting wet sand. But however it fell, if you didn't clear it, it would consolidate, setting at last to a layer of white ice over the hard ground, lumpy, hummocky stuff, treacherously slick underfoot and hard as rock if you tried to break it up.

As he worked, falling into a now familiar routine of scoop and throw, scoop and throw, being careful to favor his back, he warmed up quickly, and he loosened the toggles of his coat. Of course many of his neighbors left this sort of thing to the staff, but Thaxa liked to pitch in. For one thing he only had old Moerx as a permanent servant. And besides, this was Etxelur, not a land of princes and rulers like Carthage or Hatti—a land of equals, in theory at least. But he tired quickly, he always did; there was never enough to eat, not even for the husband of an Annid, never enough coal in the engine.

He didn't have far to dig, however. There were already

parties out clearing the Wall Way, the main road that ran along the foot of the Wall, men and women with shovels like his, their voices oddly deadened by the blanket of snow. A team of bony horses, a rare sight in Northland, dragged a heavy blade that cleared great swathes of snow, dumping it in dirty banks by the road, just as it was heaped up alongside all the main drags in Northland. All these people were out working for the state, backbreaking labor in return for a dole of salted fish and perhaps a little frozen peat for the family fire.

He was relieved to see a guard patrol walking slowly along the road, bundled in fur-lined cloaks. Crime wasn't as bad as it had been, the harsh penalties imposed by the Water Council during the summer had seen to that, but there was always somebody desperate enough to loot an abandoned property for food, firewood, warm clothing, even snow shovels.

When he had cleared a path to the road he put his shovel back in the house, locked the door carefully, and followed the cleared road toward the heart of Etxelur, making for the junction to the northsouth Etxelur Way. The Wall itself loomed over him. Ice clung to buttresses and balconies, and gigantic icicles dangled. After every snowfall there were unusual forms, sculpted drifts, shapes strange and unexpected, created by the wind swirling around the Wall's complex frontage. The world was full of complexity, Thaxa thought, of pointless beauty that came out of nowhere, from falling snow and moving masses of air and a growstone wall. Nelo's artistic eye might have been caught by these strange winter visions. But there were uglier sights too, great scars in the growstone core where the frost had gotten into it. It had been a long time since it had been safe to send up repair crews, and even when they tried, the growstone wouldn't mix or set properly in the cold.

He turned down the Etxelur Way, the main route south. This too was being steadily cleared by more bands of workers, slumped, laboring people. There was some traffic on the road, carts laden with ocean produce heading south from the Wall, the usual steady trickle of nestspills coming the other way. They were *people*. Desperate parents, struggling children, infants in arms. Nestspills.

Beyond the banks of cleared snow, beyond the dense suburbs of the Bay Land and Flint Island, the land was flat and eerily featureless. Northland was a tremendous plain anyhow, and now the fallen snow had erased the detail, with only faint lines where the dikes ran, and clusters of shapeless hillocks that were houses or flood mounds. Even the canals had frozen over and were becoming lost in the snow, and it was rare to see a tree that hadn't been cut down for firewood.

Not far down the Way he came to the lodge of Ontin, standing on a very ancient flood mound, a modern house with a square floor plan, wooden frame, and steeply pitched roof. Ontin greeted him at the door. The doctor, wearing heavy outdoor clothes but with his boots off, had evidently been out clearing the snow himself. Once inside, Thaxa stamped the snow off his own boots. He saw that Ontin's wife and sons were tending to a family huddled by the fire, husband and wife, a pair of infants close in age. One child, a boy, had the swollen belly of deep hunger.

"Here." Ontin handed Thaxa a mug of heady Gairan beer. "I feel like I need it, though it's not yet noon." He took a deep draft himself. "What brings you here, my friend?"

Thaxa drank gratefully. "Fishermen. A party came in last night. The frost got to them." The sea before the Wall had been frozen solid for a long while, few boats had made it out since Crimm had lost the *Sabet* before the autumn equinox, but the fishermen were going out anyhow, walking out to try their luck at ice fishing.

Ontin nodded. "I'll come."

Thaxa glanced at the family. "They're from your estate?"

"Yes, from a wet-house." A house on stilts, built on a foundation of boulders and logs sunk into a wetland.

"You should see it, looks very odd now, stranded high above ground that's dried out and then frozen—you have to use a ladder to get to the door. When the cold set in, their eel catch died off . . ."

In Northland landholding was frowned on as a disreputable practice of farming kingdoms. Here, most of the land was held in common trust, for it was a shared larder for a people who still at bottom relied on an economy of gathering and hunting. But there were instances of temporary landholding for management purposes—for example, when a stretch of land needed leadership in developing. After the rainy years had flooded swathes of Northland, some land had been allowed to revert to ancestral wetland, and the people who lived there, like this family, had needed investment and guidance in a way of life that was very ancient, but new to them. That was the job of Ontin, as much a duty as a privilege, for which he was paid a proportion of the land's bounty. The family would be expected to give up the land on his and his wife's death; there was no inherited property. But no guidance had been enough for this poor family, it seemed.

"We had to take them in," Ontin murmured. "What else could we do? I can treat that one for her hunger, and the other has diarrhea I'm treating with salt and honey. Thaxa, I've seen it before, all over my estate and beyond. The growing season was just too short, just a month or so between the last frosts of spring and the first of autumn."

"The dole of salted fish—"

"Gone in a flash. And all this, Thaxa, within a morning's walk of Etxelur itself. What is happening deeper in the country? We may never even know."

Thaxa touched his shoulder. "We must do what we can. As you are helping these poor people. Come with me to my house at the Wall this afternoon; I'm having the fishermen brought there for you to see to. And there's to be a discussion this afternoon on how to cope with the winter."

Ontin laughed hollowly. "Cope?"

"It will be informal, but under Ywa." He smiled. "The Annids like coming to me for their meetings, because I make good nettle tea. Stay the night. Forget all this, for a time. We'll talk, eat, drink, get warm. I think you've deserved that much."

The doctor smiled back thinly. "I'll pass on the nettle tea, though. You have any Gairan ale? For that's the best, you know."

"I'll lay some in . . ."

But Ontin was looking over his shoulder, out of the window, at fresh flurries of snow that fell from a graying sky.

40

They made it back to the Wall, just, through the closing mouth of the latest blizzard.

Despite the storm, Thaxa couldn't help but glance with pride at his shopfront as they struggled up to it. He was still well stocked with exotic linen and cloth, from Albian wild-cattle wool to Cathay silk and Carthaginian purple, even fine-spun wool from the llamas and alpacas of the lands across the Western Ocean — precious indeed, since trade across the ocean had been sundered by the icebergs. But nobody was shopping today, and the snow was heaped up in banks before the shopfront.

An archway on the left-hand side of the shop led to a courtyard laboriously swept clear of snow, surrounded by a cluster of buildings: a hall to the left, a pantry and kitchens to the right, and the main living quarters at the rear, with parlors, bedrooms, bathrooms, privies, and the household shrine to the little mothers. All this backed onto the Wall, which loomed over the shop. Thaxa's property actually extended into the Wall itself. There were chambers cut into the growstone, much older, abandoned now, behind the elaborate structures that had been built onto the face—Thaxa himself wasn't sure what there was back there.

Much of the property was shut up now, for the difficulty of heating it. But a light gleamed in the window of the largest parlor, and Thaxa led Ontin that way.

The parlor was deliciously warm, thanks to a roaring fire in the hearth. Thaxa and Ontin stripped off their heavy outdoor clothing in a small anteroom. They were later than Thaxa had planned. The fishermen were already here, some of the crew of the lost *Sabet*, Rina's cousin Crimm, his partner Ayto—and Aranx, who was nursing a badly damaged hand. Ywa was here too, Annid of Annids, sitting close to the fire with Xree, another cousin of Rina and another Annid. Moerx was serving drinks, a hot nettle tea, a speciality of Thaxa's—hot to banish the cold, and made of nettles as a kind of expression of sympathy for all the ordinary Northlanders who had nothing *but* nettles to keep them alive. Thaxa smiled easily at his guests. This was what he had always been best at: hospitality, a kind of talent for making people welcome, letting them relax.

Ontin went straight to the fishermen, who sat around a table looking slightly out of place. Aranx held out his hand, wrapped clumsily in a strip of cloth. "Got it wet, didn't I? Another lad fell in a lead, through a crack in the ice. Didn't notice it was wrong; it got so cold I couldn't feel it anyhow."

Ontin carefully peeled back the bandage, to reveal swollen, broken flesh. A stink of corruption filled the room.

"Sorry, Doctor."

"Don't apologize. It sounds as if you were a brave man." Ontin took a scalpel from a deep pocket, and began to probe at the damaged flesh.

"Don't know about brave. We got old Tabilox out of the water all right, but he didn't make it back."

Ayto said evenly, "The bravest thing you did, mate, was to go tell his widow when you got back. And his kids."

"We miss our boats, that's the truth. We're rubbish out on the ice, cutting holes and that. We'll never be Coldlanders."

Ywa said, "All of Northland appreciates what you are trying to do for us. And you've managed to bring home more than a bit of fish."

Xree smiled. "We were talking about you earlier. Of your marvelous return from the dead, so to speak, a couple of months back, when the *Sabet* went down. I was actually there on the Wall when you showed up. Walking out of the cold, dragging that improvised sled with your injured crewmate and the carcass of that seal, and your families waiting for you at the dock. Remarkable."

Crimm sounded embarrassed. "We didn't do anything but live through it."

"Oh, believe me," Ywa said, "you did more than that. You brought back a bit of good news, for once, and you've no idea how rare that has been over the last year."

"But I didn't bring back my ship," he said heavily. "Or one of my crew. Or any of the catch, save the little bit we'd been eating ourselves. What kind of achievement is that?"

Thaxa saw Ywa flinch. Crimm backed off, reddening. There was an awkward silence.

And for the first time Thaxa saw there was some kind of connection between the two of them, the Annid of Annids and the weather-beaten fisherman. Well, whatever it was, they were entitled to it, and he suppressed his curiosity.

Crimm said gruffly, "Anyhow, you're here to talk about the future, not the past."

Xree sighed. "True enough. The problem's simple to state. We have to get through the winter."

"The issue being—"

"The issue being too many people, and too little food . . ."

As they spoke Thaxa discreetly refilled their teacups. At least you couldn't accuse *his* family of consuming

more than their fair share. One reason he hosted these
meetings was as a kind of polite, unspoken penance for
the absence of Rina and the children. Everybody knew
they had gone off down south, and had sneaked away in
secret. You could see it as a betrayal, or as an example of
devotion to a wider cause, to leave your home and risk
the unknown to reduce the pressure on the Wall's resources, depending on how generous you felt. But as Rina
wasn't the only one to have fled, the social disgrace he had
feared had never materialized, not quite. And people had
more to worry about than that.

"In fact," Xree was saying, "there are more people
showing up all the time, from Northland and beyond,
even Gairans, even Albians."

"Turn them away," Ayto snapped. That won him a few
glances of distaste.

"We try," Ywa said. "But there are always more. And
some have a claim to be let in—some of them have relatives in the Wall. Those we do turn away may simply become bandits and even more of a problem than if we had
fed them in the first place.

"Then there's the issue of the food itself. There's more
of your salted fish, Crimm, and other comestibles in the
storehouses than you might think," she said softly. "But
even so, not enough."

"How much 'not enough'?"

Xree said, "Unless we cut the ration again we'll run
out before the midwinter solstice."

Crimm nodded. "Then you must cut the ration."

Ywa said, "I've asked Ontin and the other doctors to
come up with recommendations on the absolute minimum people can survive on. We must get as many
through the winter as possible, and hope that the spring
is kinder."

Ayto said, "And if it isn't? No, forget that. If we don't
survive the winter it won't matter. You may have to go
further."

"What do you mean?"

"If there's not enough to go around, stop the ration altogether for some. The very sick, the already dying."

There was a shocked silence at another blunt remark from the fisherman.

"People won't stand for it," Thaxa said instinctively.

"They may have to."

"We have considered such options," Ywa said grimly. "Believe me. But even if we could make it acceptable—how do you choose, fisherman? Do you cut out everybody over fifty, say? Or the very young, on the argument that their mothers can always have more babies?"

Xree said smoothly, "In any event, food is only one problem. There's also the question of heating . . ."

It had been a month since the last of the Wall's great engines had seized up, of a lack of fuel, of lubricating oil, of damage caused to the piping by the cold. Thaxa knew the first such engines had been developed by the school of engineer-philosophers founded by émigré Greeks. Those primitive mechanical beasts had solved Northland's perennial problem of a shortage of manpower; Northlanders' numbers were comparatively few, for they did not farm, and they did not keep slaves. But the Wall had become dependent on its engines, and now they had failed. If the heating couldn't be restored, the Wall might not remain habitable. And in the longer term too, there would be problems out in the country; the whole of Northland was an artificially managed landscape, dependent on labor: human, animal and mechanical.

Xree and Ywa spoke of efforts to find fuel sources in the Wall itself and its environs. Even the wooden frames of buildings like this house of Thaxa's might be sacrificed, the inhabitants taken into the growstone womb of the Wall. The Wall would have to consume itself to stay alive, thought Thaxa.

"Then there's the problem of the Archive," Xree said.

Ayto looked puzzled. "The Archive?"

"It is rather exposed," Ywa said. "It is housed in chambers built into the forward face of the Wall. It was done that way, by our predecessors two centuries ago, to provide a light and airy environment for the scholars to work in. Now we're working through a program of moving the Archive back into older housing deeper within the Wall, the growstone core."

Xree said brightly, "And we're taking the opportunity to convert some of the more fragile records to permanent forms. On baked clay for instance."

Ayto leaned forward in his chair. "I can't believe I'm hearing *this.*"

Crimm said warningly, "Ayto—"

"People are starving, freezing to death, dying out on the sea, all over. And you're worried that your famous Archive might get a bit of damp?"

Xree bristled. "The Archive is at the center of our cultural identity."

"Will you have folk eat words?"

Crimm sighed. "Take it easy, man."

Ayto looked at him sternly. Then he said, "Can I have a word with you?"

Crimm hesitated. Then he stood, nodding apologies to the Annids, to Thaxa. The two fishermen left the room.

Xree and Ywa talked on about their Archive project. And Ontin, the doctor, spoke slowly and patiently to Aranx, who, realizing he was going to lose a limb, was beginning to weep.

Ayto led Crimm through a smaller, windowless parlor that ran off from the back of the room they'd been in, took an oil lamp from the wall, and then went on through another dusty door, down a darkened passageway, and into another sitting room, or office. There was a desk piled with curling paper, a smell of must and dust, and an unlit hearth like a gaping black mouth.

"I did some exploring back here earlier, before you showed up with Aranx."

"It's not too cold in here," Crimm observed.

"We're already inside the Wall. Old Thaxa's property goes on further into the growstone. I don't think anybody knows how deep these old chambers go, or how much Thaxa actually owns. But according to Moerx, the servant, there should be another door at the back here ..."

The rear wall was covered by a tapestry bearing stylized Northland icons, concentric circles with stabbing radial lines. Ayto pulled the tapestry down to expose a heavy wooden door. This wasn't locked, but was stuck in its frame, perhaps the wood had swollen, and it took the two of them to shift it.

Then another corridor. And another room and corridor, and another.

And they emerged into a much larger space. Ayto lifted the lamp high. The walls were just rough growstone, the floor bare and roughly laid, the roof so high it was almost out of sight, but Crimm saw that it was well constructed, of vaulted domes of growstone. He thought he saw a glimpse of daylight from the roof. He pointed. "An air vent?"

"I think so. Moerx said there was a hearth—look, over there."

Crimm walked a bit further, away from the circle of light cast by the lantern. The hearth looked very crude, just a heap of bricks in the corner, set up under the vent. There were shadowy heaps in the corners and by the walls: bits of canvas maybe, wooden pallets. And Crimm made out stains on the walls, greenish-gray, that ended in a band some distance above his head.

"Must be an old warehouse," said Ayto. "Something like that."

"No, I don't think so. Look at those stains. It looks as if water was kept here. It's some kind of huge cistern. Or was. Maybe the system it was part of was abandoned. And then it's been reused, by somebody camping here— whoever built that hearth."

"That might have been a long time ago. And then it was forgotten, and the Wall has sort of grown out around it. Moerx told me about it because I asked him how deep the house went into the wall. Just being nosy. He's looked around before — well, you would, wouldn't you? When he described this place it gave me an idea."

"Hmm. I don't always like your ideas, Ayto."

"We could use this place."

"There's certainly some firewood we could use —"

"No." Ayto walked over to him, his footsteps echoing in the empty space. "You're not thinking big enough, my friend. Listen to me. You heard the rubbish the Annids talked back there. Rations that are going to run out. How they can't even keep out the Gairans and the Albians and other useless stomachs. How they're wasting time copying old tide tables onto clay tablets."

"What's your point?"

"*The famous Annids can't cope.* Like you, they aren't thinking big enough. That's obvious. This is Northland! That's what they think. The whole world speaks our language, and accepts our scrip. We won't be beaten by a few flakes of snow! But we will be beaten, my friend, when the cold closes in and the food runs out. The Annids can't face it, the reality."

"And what's that, according to you?"

"When people get hungry enough they'll rip each other apart, and the Wall." He shrugged. "You know it as well as I do. And after that there'll be no food left for anybody, and we'll all die."

"So . . ."

"We can't save everybody. So we save ourselves."

"In here?"

Ayto glanced around, at the doors leading off from all the walls, the air vent. "Think of it as a fortress, like the Carthaginians would build. We bring them in here."

"Who?"

"Our families. Friends, lovers. Whoever we want — up to a limit. We'd have to work out what that limit is. We bring in enough food to see us through the winter."

"You mean steal it."

"Just our share. Salted fish, dried vegetables, stuff that will keep. And water—we'd have to think about that. Storage tubs, or maybe there's a working pipeline, if you're right that this is an old cistern. Firewood. Everything we need to stay alive. And weapons. We establish some kind of perimeter, out from here, in all directions. Barricade it, defend it when they come."

"Who?"

"The starving mob. We fight them off, until they die of cold or hunger."

"You're talking about Northlanders."

"Northlanders can grow hungry. And when they do, they'll behave like everybody else. It's this or die," Ayto said.

Crimm, overwhelmed, felt as if he was having some waking dream, in this dry, echoing place, by the light of the single lamp, talking like this while just a short walk away the Annid of Annids, his lover, was drinking nettle tea and discussing the preservation of old books. But this was Ayto, who always had been a much tougher thinker than Crimm, always the first to call the warning about the coming storm, when the rest wanted to carry on for just a little more catch. Even so . . .

"It seems dishonorable."

Ayto shrugged. "Thaxa's wife has already cleared off to Carthage, without telling anybody. How honorable is that? And she's not the only one, by the way. Look, we don't have to do this yet. It's a fallback—that's all. Every smart man has a fallback. Are you in, or not?"

Crimm wondered if he could betray Ywa. She was Annid of Annids; he could not discuss this with her. "I need to think."

"Don't take too long."

"Or what?"

"Or you might find yourself on the other side of the barricade, my friend." And Ayto began to prowl around the old cistern, sniffing, scattering dust, peering up at the walls.

41

Avatak learned that the capital of Mongol Cathay had several names, given it by the many peoples who lived and worked here. The Turks called it Khanbalikh, which was a rendering of the phrase "city of the Khans." The folk of Cathay called it Ta-tu, which meant "great capital." The Mongols themselves had adopted the Cathay name, "Daidu."

On the day they arrived, thanks to Pyxeas' *paiza* they were escorted safely through scrubby outer suburbs, through gates in a double layer of city walls, and into the city itself—and Avatak, who had seen too many wonders during the long journey, was overwhelmed once more. Daidu was huge, clean, bright, opulent and luxurious. Even the roofs of the lesser buildings, lacquered and glazed, were visions in brightly colored green and yellow and blue that seemed to float in the air. Thinking about what a Mongol city might be like, Avatak had vaguely imagined a huddle of yurts—tremendous yurts, perhaps, made of expensive felt encrusted with jewels and set on golden platforms, but yurts nonetheless. Uzzia told him that the capital of Genghis himself, the first great conqueror, called Karakorum, had not been altogether unlike that vision. But Daidu was different. Kublai Khan had eschewed his ancestors' habits of burning down cities, and had built his own to match the best.

They were given three days' rest before they would have to meet the scholar Pyxeas had come so far to speak to, and had a small apartment near the western city wall to rest in. Avatak chose the smallest, plainest room he could find. Even so, the couches were so soft he felt as if he were drowning when he lay on them. So he unrolled his own blankets on the carpeted floor, and slept away most of two days.

On the third day he found a sanctuary that would take the mule. It was a place where sentimental and wealthy Mongols retired their favorite ponies. It wasn't cheap, but Uzzia said she was happy to pay. The mule was dismissive of the whole affair.

On the fourth day they were summoned to the Khan's palace.

Pyxeas insisted they dress as smartly as they could.

Uzzia had somehow preserved a decent set of clothes through the vicissitudes of the journey, even the robbery. But she stuck to her own style. She wore a tunic and breeches with a wide belt and boots with turned-up toes, the way a Hatti prince might dress in New Hattusa, but she pinned back her hair with a golden comb, and applied cosmetics to her face, a white base with bright red spots on forehead and cheeks. Avatak couldn't help but stare at the result, and she grinned. "I am what I am," she said. "I am Hatti. I am Uzzia. I like to show both sides."

Pyxeas and Avatak wore clothes loaned by their hosts. Avatak found himself in a brightly colored blouse and breeches, and a round felt hat. The material felt impossibly soft against his skin. Pyxeas dressed similarly, but, oddly, the clothes fit Avatak better. His round Coldlander frame was more like a Mongol's than Pyxeas' was, and the scholar speculated about some ancient relationship between their peoples. Uzzia complimented them both gravely, but Avatak could tell she was laughing inside. As a reminder of who he was, and despite Pyxeas' protests, he tore a strip of sealskin fur from one of his blankets and tied it around his waist like a belt.

So they were led to the palace.

The palace compound was a city within a city, enclosed within its own substantial walls. Avenues paved with shining mosaics were filled with neat houses, and grand tree-lined ways led from the walls to the central square where the palace itself stood. Avatak spotted a tremendous lake, contained by the walls, formed by the damming of a river; tall, elegant birds waded among reeds.

Ferocious-looking guards at the doors, both Mongol and Cathay-born, scrutinized Pyxeas' *paiza*.

Once inside the palace itself they were instructed to remove their boots and shoes, and don soft white slippers to protect the floors, all of which were carpeted. They walked almost noiselessly down a long corridor, and Pyxeas murmured that they must keep their voices down for fear of disturbing the Khan. But Avatak had been told the palace had a thousand rooms, and he thought it unlikely the Khan would be close enough to hear them.

They were brought through a grand set of doors to a tremendous room, so vast that to Avatak it was almost as if he had stepped outdoors. The room was brightly lit by tall windows and by lanterns on the walls; the carpet, brilliant white, was so wide and empty it was like a snowfield; and the walls were crusted with vivid paintings, of birds and dragons and lions, warriors and half-naked women. The walls were many times taller than a man's height, and, looking up, Avatak saw a ceiling similarly coated with dazzling art.

Much of the floor space was empty. But to the rear of the room was a collection of domes and boxes of clear glass, big structures that towered over the servants that fussed around them, adjusting bits of tubing, peering at instruments, making notes on clay tablets. A man came walking toward them from this assembly, not tall, middle-aged, with the round face, olive skin and tonsured hair of a Mongol. Servants trailed him, eyes respectfully downcast.

Pyxeas hurried forward, his gait clumsy, almost a limp. After enduring such a journey the old man could barely make the last few paces, and Avatak felt a stab of affection for the brave, vulnerable scholar.

"Bolghai! My dear fellow. It has been much too long, too long." Pyxeas grasped the Mongol's hands in his. "Ten years, is it, since you graced us with your presence?"

"More like fifteen, old chap," said the Mongol, grinning.

Uzzia murmured to Avatak, "Even here the scholar speaks in his native Northlander and expects to be understood and answered in the same—and he is!"

Pyxeas introduced his "dear traveling companions," and Coldlander and Hatti bowed to the Mongol. "My good friend Bolghai, with whom I have corresponded for many years, is one of the finest scholars of his generation—no, Bolghai, do not be modest—and he is a Mongol! A cousin of the Khan—"

"A rather distant cousin. But Buyantu is kind to me, as you can see from the facilities he grants."

"Bolghai is a Mongol prince but educated by the best teachers the court could find, and he has further broadened his mind by traveling far beyond the reach even of the Khans' conquering armies. All the way to Northland, in fact. The result is a fine intellect."

"Fine for a Mongol, you mean." For an instant there was tension, before Bolghai grinned.

Pyxeas scolded, "Now don't you go trying to trip me up like that, you rascal. Show me your investigations into fixed air. I've come rather a long way to see them."

Led by Bolghai, who walked slowly to allow for Pyxeas' pace, they headed toward the cluster of apparatus at the rear of the room.

"Ah, how I have missed you, scholar," Bolghai said, in his lightly accented Northlander. "Our talks of this and that, of men and stars, of the fate of the whole world and the precise shape of a grass seed, late into those long Northlander nights. But, as you may know, I have since commissioned some research into the biography of the great engineer Yu, who designed and built flood defenses in Cathay some three thousand years ago. There are gaps in his biography, and I have come to suspect that he traveled in his youth—why not? And why not to Northland? Which was a great civilization even then. I have come to suspect that the design of your mighty Wall could have sprung from Yu's fertile mind. The similarities are striking when you consider such works as—"

"Oh, now, you're trying to provoke me! What a lot of nonsense. It's far more likely that this upstart Yu came to Northland to study a Wall which was already ancient long before he was born . . ."

"They're good together," Uzzia murmured as she walked with Avatak. "Two bantering scholars. Pyxeas needs to make sure he doesn't go too far, however. Even this Bolghai must have his Mongol pride."

Avatak was staring up at the ceiling, at a panel where Mongol warriors on horseback shot tiny arrows at a rampaging dragon. "What a room this is."

"That's what plundering a continent earns you."

They came now to the scholar's facility, and Avatak saw that it was a series of glass-walled compartments—domes, square-walled boxes, some a good deal taller than he was. Tubes of some flexible material led from each box to a complex apparatus of brass and glass, fussed over by attendants.

And in each of the boxes there was something alive, he saw. Something growing. A tray of soil bearing grass shoots in this box; in the next, what looked like wheat; in the next, potatoes; in the next, rice. These boxes were bathed with sunlight from open windows in the walls above. In the very largest boxes there were animals, one to each compartment: a horse, a cow, a sheep—*a man*, Avatak saw with shock, a small, skinny, youngish man of Cathay, sitting naked on a mat, his eyes averted, bowls of piss and shit beside him. Beside each container was a similarly sized box, quite empty, but fitted with tubes and valves. The largest dome contained a tree, of a kind unfamiliar to Avatak, with wide branches and bright green leaves, growing from a big ceramic pot. A tree, taller than he was, in the middle of this vast room.

Uzzia stared, amazed. "By the Storm God's left buttock, what under heaven is this?" Then she remembered herself, and she bowed hastily to Bolghai. "My apologies, lord. I am a simple trader; I am overwhelmed by this evidence of your mighty learning."

Bolghai looked amused. "Oh, get up, madam. Overwhelmed, even though you understand not a jot of it, I suppose?"

Pyxeas snorted. "Uzzia, Bolghai is studying properties of the air. We are all at the mercy of the weather, yes? And though I, Pyxeas, and the generations who went before me, have shown that the great cycles of the weather are dominated by astronomy, by the dipping and nodding of the world as it orbits the central fire, it is nevertheless the air that delivers that weather to us. So we study it too.

"After all, invisible though it may be the air is *real*; it has weight and substance. You can feel it dragging into your lungs, you can use pumps to evacuate it from a chamber—we all felt its lack up on the roof of the world. And the air is made up of several component parts, which can be separated with sufficient ingenuity. This was first achieved by Northlander scholars. We know there is *vital air*, an air full of energy, which we suspect is the agent that supports combustion—and indeed the slower fire that burns in our bodies to sustain life. And then there is *fixed air*. This was first identified by a scholar at Etxelur called Cleomedes, of Greek descent, who studied the burning of charcoal in a closed vessel."

Bolghai said, "The scholars of Cathay have long shared their knowledge with Northland, a tradition I have sought, in my time, to maintain, or rather revive. I with my party was the first to travel to Northland after the conquests of the Great Khans. And, given the importance of the air to the weather which shapes all our destinies, as Pyxeas points out, we have continued its study here. Although Cathay scholars are perhaps of a more practical bent than those of Northland."

Pyxeas sighed. "True, true, but the first Wall-builders would cringe to hear you say it. That's the legacy of Pythagoras and his Greeks, who could be a bit contemplative."

Bolghai gestured at his apparatus. "We have found ways to measure the presence and concentration of fixed air more precisely. For instance here, you see, the air from this chamber is fed through lime dissolved in water; it precipitates a kind of chalk whose weight we can determine . . . The details are unimportant."

"Not to me, they're not!" thundered Pyxeas. "I want to examine every tube and valve, every seal and measuring gauge. Excellent experimental design," he said now, walking around the boxes. "Can you see it, Avatak? Why these empty boxes, for instance?"

That was easy; Avatak had seen similar setups in Pyxeas' own studies. "They are for comparison. A horse in this box, not in that box that's otherwise the same; you can subtract one from the other to see what difference the horse makes."

"Exactly!"

Bolghai said, "Of course the emissions and absorptions vary depending on the plant or beast enclosed, and indeed on its conditions—if the horse is agitated or not, resting or exercising, for instance. All these things we can study."

Uzzia asked, "Who is the man in the box?"

Bolghai seemed puzzled by the question. "*Who?* Why—he is the subject. I sent specifications to the slavers regarding size and weight and general health. I hope to extend the studies to compare different ethnicities, ages, health conditions—sex, of course. I am not concerned with *who*.

"What is most important is the conclusion. Which is this." With the air of a showman he walked them past the compartments containing the grass, the grain. "Vegetables, plants, trees—as they grow, these things *absorb* the fixed gas from the air. But if they are burned they release that gas again. Whereas animals, from sheep to pigs to men, they *release* the fixed gas as they breathe. All of this in the processes of their lives, you see—it seems accurate, as you say, Pyxeas, to think of life as a kind of slow burning, animal life at least. Plants and animals, absorption and release—"

"Yes, yes. And together they shape the atmosphere—and *it* shapes *them*. But to what end, what end? And how does this relate to the longwinter? For somehow it must . . ."

"Quite so," Bolghai said. "To explore that I am also running studies of the physical properties of fixed air. Perhaps that will offer some clues. But the properties are subtle, the apparatus unwieldy and preliminary. Nevertheless I have some first results. We can proceed to that when we're done here."

"Good, good," Pyxeas murmured. The two scholars wandered off, talking, debating.

Servants stood by Uzzia and Avatak, heads bent, waiting for instructions.

"I want to get out of here," whispered Avatak.

"Yes. And I've got deals to do. We've delivered Pyxeas to his scholar; we've done our jobs for now. Let's go."

42

zzia wandered through Daidu, reacquainting herself with a city she'd visited once before. Avatak followed her, gradually finding his bearings.

Within its double walls the city was laid out like a board game played by giants, the rectangle of walls enclosing a grid-pattern of streets, with tidy blocks of houses and inns and manufactories, temples and schools, all on a tremendous scale. Avatak, a boy from a chaotic land of ice and water, even having visited Northland's mighty Wall, felt utterly out of place in this vision of stone and geometry.

But the vision could be pleasing. You would turn a corner and come upon a park gleaming green in the late autumn sunshine, with animals apparently roaming loose: squirrels, ermine, deer, even stags. A river ran right through the city, and people walked its banks and crossed delicate bridges. The people were both Cathay and Mongol, the latter in their colorful silk tunics and coats. People spoke Mongol, or one of the tongues of Cathay, or a rapid language that Uzzia identified as Persian, a common tongue for the traders who came here.

Some of the grander folk went on horseback. The cultured Cathay folk seemed to flinch at seeing horses inside a city, but the Mongols' bond with their animals was indissoluble. Avatak saw one man ride along under a canopy of gold, carried by bearers who had to run alongside. Uzzia said this was probably a baron, one of the Khan's top generals, who would command a hundred thousand men or more.

In one place by the river Avatak saw a tower, four or five times taller than a man, with a small waterwheel at its side. On the top was a brass construction, a ring showing the constellations, models of sun and moon. It was a representation of the sky, driven by the waterwheel, like a tremendously expanded version of Pyxeas' oracle. Perhaps the links between Cathay and Northland really were deep and ancient, Avatak thought.

Uzzia said she wanted to go out of the city proper and into the suburbs, where the livelier markets were to be found. So they made their way to the northern wall, heading for a gate. The gates themselves were huge, like fortresses built into the walls, each hosting hundreds of soldiers. Uzzia spoke in her cursory Mongol to the guards, ensuring they could get back in later, even without Pyxeas' *paiza* in their pockets. Beyond the gate they had to pass through the city's outer layer of defenses, over a moat filled with brackish water and then to an outer wall. There seemed to be a whole army of soldiers in rough camps in the space between the walls, with heaps of weapons, herds of the Mongols' stocky ponies. "Not so much a city," murmured Uzzia as they walked, "as a fortress, and designed by Kublai to be that way. Well, I suppose it is inevitable; Old Hattusa was a fortress-city too, another capital of conquerors."

The suburb beyond the outer walls was a city in itself, but much more disorderly, crowded, with a pall of greasy smoke rising from a hundred fires. There was a steady stream of traffic through the gates, of pedestrians, horse riders, and carts drawn by bullocks and horses. Avatak noticed a line of people, men, women and children, all of them shabby-looking, strung out along the length of the outer wall, leading away from the gate. They were waiting for something handed out at the gate itself by a team of soldiers; more tough-looking troops patrolled the line, weapons ready, prepared for any trouble.

Uzzia, evidently feeling more at home in this bustling market town, plunged into its narrow alleys. The houses here were of mud or sod bricks, and roofed by turf or wood slats. There was business being done everywhere, in inns, stores selling food or clothes or spices or precious goods, and brothels with exotic whores, both female and male, beckoning from doorways. Uzzia soon found a tremendous central marketplace, crowded with stalls. Avatak was baffled by the masses of porcelain, silks, plums, watermelons, and a blizzard of paper money. But the marketplace backed onto a stockyard where animals, distressed and calling out, were being lined up in huge numbers for slaughter in the open air. Corpses dangled from hooks, and the cobbles were sticky with old blood. Avatak had gutted seals and flensed walruses; he was far from squeamish. But the sheer scale of this slaughter, however necessary to feed the hungry city, repelled him.

With a word to Uzzia, he turned away and began to walk back toward the gate. He was curious about the line of people at the wall. When he came to the line he backtracked, trying to find the end, but the line stretched all the way to the corner of the wall's rectangular layout, and back down the next side, and on out of his sight. There must be thousands of people in this one line, perhaps tens of thousands.

He walked back along the line toward its head. Every so often the waiting horde would move forward in a great rippling movement that spread along the line, and people jostled, making sure their neighbors didn't try to jump a space. There were always fights somewhere, and soldiers would leap in with clubs raised to sort it out. Whatever it was these people were waiting for, they needed it badly.

The line ended at a simple table, manned by two officers and heavily guarded by a circle of troops. They backed onto a kind of storehouse built into the wall itself. The soldiers made a note of each supplicant's name on a paper scroll, and then a bundle was handed over, wrapped in paper. The supplicant would hurry away with nods of obeisance and gratitude.

"Bread," Uzzia murmured in his ear.

Avatak glanced around, surprised she'd found him. "Bread? That's all?"

"A daily handout from the Khan. And they send grain from the city stores to the provinces too. Apparently they have been feeding twenty thousand people from the city alone this way. But the granaries are emptying and every day the dole is cut down a little more. Of course the soldiers are always well fed. We need to get back inside the city."

"Why?"

"A messenger found me. There's been an explosion at the palace."

"There's been a *what*?"

She grinned. "That rascal Pyxeas. You can't leave him alone for a heartbeat, can you?"

They were brought to another corner of the palace, a smaller laboratory. Here another elaborate experimental apparatus had been set up, on a lesser scale—stands and tubes and flasks and pipes, mirrors, small oil heaters. But this equipment had been scattered around the room. The carpet was scorched, the paint on the wall blistered. One servant seemed to have been injured, a weeping woman, and a doctor was tending to her burned arm. Soldiers stood around, looking shocked, dismayed, as well they might, Avatak supposed. The explosion, deep inside the home of the Khan himself, must have made them fear assassins, and, worse, the punishment they would receive if any harm came to the Khan or his family.

And here was Pyxeas, a blissful smile on a soot-stained face, the fringe of white hair around his scalp vertical, his robe smeared black. Bolghai stood behind him, equally begrimed, rather more shamefaced. "Avatak!" Pyxeas cried. "I hope you enjoyed your walk. You missed a bit of fun."

"I can see that. What were you making here—eruptors?"

"Nothing of the sort! Though I can see you might have difficulty working it all out given that it's lying in pieces everywhere ... Where is the gas tube, Bolghai?"

"Over there," said the Mongol. "And there. Oh, and there's a bit stuck in the ceiling, I think."

As the philosophers and their servants gathered the fragments of the broken apparatus, gradually Avatak pieced together what Bolghai had been attempting here.

"What controls our weather?" Pyxeas asked. "The sun, whose position in the sky as determined by astronomical considerations fixes the amount of heat delivered to the world—and the air, through which that heat must pass. But *how* does the sun's heat pass through the air? How much of it is blocked—and how much trapped, as the thinnest linen blanket will trap some of the warmth of the body? That's what this apparatus seeks to determine."

The core of it had been a long brass tube, held horizontally. One end of this was heated, either by reflected sunlight or an oil lamp. At the far end of the tube was a thin, upright glass flask containing oil; by seeing how the oil expanded and climbed up its flask you could tell how much heat was passed through the tube—or rather, through whatever was trapped inside.

"Can you see?" Pyxeas said, holding up a fragment of smashed-open tube. "The ends are sealed with rock salt, which passes heat without diminution. The tube can be evacuated altogether, emptied of any kind of air, or it can be blocked with metal plugs, so that virtually no heat passes. Thus we have a maximum and a minimum for the heat transfer. Then we can fill the tube with, well, whatever we like — ordinary air, fixed air, water vapor. And we can see how the various components of the air trap the heat differently."

"I think I see. And the conclusions?"

"That the fixed air, even a trace of it, makes a very efficient blanket for the trapping of heat. Very efficient indeed."

Uzzia was scowling. "Bits of gas in a tube, mirrors and flames — how *did* you manage to make all this blow up?"

"That took some doing," Pyxeas admitted ruefully. "And on my first day here too. But — patience, my dear. Philosophical understanding grows as a child learns to walk, with one uncertain step at a time. Of course all these results are preliminary and need to be confirmed, which we can begin to do once we get this apparatus rebuilt. Where is that craftsman of yours, Bolghai? Got something better to do, has he? And can't we get these wretched soldiers out of here?"

43

High on the Wall, fisherman Crimm didn't want to get too close to the balcony rail. The day was clear and bitterly cold, and the balcony was thick with ice, slick and slippery and bright in the low winter sun that hung in the southern sky, shining straight in his eyes. Plenty of opportunity to go tumbling off this balcony, to go skimming down the length of the incongruously cheerful banners that had been unfurled down the face of the Wall, and to smash his head open on the heaps of rubble at the foot, thus getting himself killed before the day's action even started.

Ayto, though, wasn't troubled. He rested easy on the rail, arms folded, mittened hands stuck under his armpits, staring south, oblivious of the drop below. He waited calmly at Crimm's side, just as they had so often faced a storm at sea about to fall on the *Sabet*.

Now there was motion on the ice-bound land, far to the south, black specks crawling under a clear blue sky. People approaching the Wall.

Ayto murmured, "Is it them?"

"Not sure."

"They are coming up the Way, straight to Etxelur . . ."

Despite the obvious approach there was no call yet from the lookouts on the Wall parapet. Crimm wasn't surprised. You didn't last long at sea without sharp eyes, and the lookouts would do no better than a couple of fishermen, stranded since the loss of the *Sabet*. And of course there was always a chance of snow blindness on a bright day like this. To the south, as he looked out now, all of Northland to the far horizon was locked under a covering of ice and heaped-up snow, a panorama in white and black and blue and streaks of silver-gray where ice lay on deeper water. Across a world locked in ice the Wall itself strode, its tremendous face frost-cracked and strewn with icicles, yet standing against the winter as it had defied the sea for millennia. But perhaps it had all been for nothing, Crimm thought, for those whom the Wall had been built to protect were now preparing to attack it.

Ayto stirred. "It's them all right. It's not just more nestspills. You can see the organization. They're moving as a pack. And there's metal glinting."

"Weapons."

"That would be my guess," Ayto said drily.

The lookouts woke up at last. Calls went up all along the Wall, from the roof scouts, across the balconies and galleries. People emerged to take their places at the rails, grim-faced, scared, shivering with the biting cold, and yet determined to play their part in saving the Wall.

Ywa joined the fishermen, coming out from the inner Wall to the balcony. The Annid of Annids' quilted coat was open to the waist so that her bronze chest plate could be seen, a very ancient and battle-scarred relic. She allowed herself one glance at Crimm. He took her arm, squeezed it, out of sight of the rest. They rarely had time alone nowadays.

"So they come," she said. "The scheme is working. They've ignored the other Districts and are heading straight for us, for Etxelur."

Ayto said, "They're cold and they're hungry, and even if they've got anybody with military experience they aren't much more than a starving mob. They're heading for the obvious signs of life—"

"Which we kindly provided for them," Crimm said.

The Wall had been closed to incomers for a month now, a dreadful truncation that had cut off Etxelur and the Annids from the population of Northland. There had been petty assaults on the Wall, easily repelled, but as the hunger mounted in the country everybody had expected a more substantial attack, and plans had been laid, strategies discussed. A central stretch of the Wall had been prepared. With much labor, elaborate stone buildings built onto the Wall's growstone face, themselves centuries old, had been smashed up and prized away to lie in rubble at the foot of the Wall, to make a defensive barrier against the invaders. With the superstructure gone, the older growstone core lay exposed, pocked with holes and pits like eye sockets—and a bank of slogans had been revealed, in an archaic dialect, slogans written tall enough to be seen across the countryside:

THE WALL STANDS!
THE LOVE OF THE MOTHERS PROTECTS US ALL!
THE TROJANS CANNOT PREVAIL!

On seeing this, some historically minded folk had expressed nostalgia for the age of Milaqa and Qirum, when Northland had been able to unite against an easily recognized human enemy. Now the enemy was the world itself, and Northlanders turned on one another.

And, built into the fabric of the Wall, the searching scholars had uncovered weapons, a relic of a later generation than those who long ago had defied the Trojan Invasion.

When the scouts reported that a large force appeared to be massing to the south, the Annids ordered banners to be draped down the Wall's face. The banners, meant for days of celebration, for the midsummer Giving, were incongruous splashes of color in an ice-bound world, brilliant red and green and purple against the gray-white of the frozen growstone—and in this bleak winter they would surely attract the dispossessed and desperate. The banners, though, had a second concealed purpose, and as he glanced down now Crimm saw engineers and volunteers crawling behind the banners, making frantic final adjustments to the ancient, little-understood weaponry built into the face of the Wall and hidden by the banners. The whole District had become a trap.

"It should work," Ywa murmured. "It has to work. I could not bear a war as the farmers wage, not Northlander against Northlander, hand to hand."

Ayto, still leaning casually on the rail, glanced back at her. "Annid, I'd be a lot more sure of success if you'd let us use the fire-drug eruptors."

"I told you," Ywa said coldly. "That's not acceptable."

"I know how you feel about this," Ayto said. "But—look at them all! If they break through today they will swarm through the Wall like maggots through a corpse and eat all there is to eat—"

Crimm touched his arm. "Leave it. It's the mirrors or nothing." Crimm shared many of Ayto's doubts about the wisdom of the Annids' strategy. Who wouldn't? But even if all was lost today, as Ayto knew very well, the two of them, and their families, had their bolt-hole, in the abandoned cistern deep inside the Wall. Though Crimm still had not decided how he would deal with his relationship with Ywa, if that dire choice had to be made.

"They're getting close!" somebody called, higher up the Wall face.

They all stared out, shielding their eyes against the glare.

The mob was making slow progress, struggling in drifts that could be waist deep. The fresh-fallen snow had been purposely left uncleared before the Wall for many days now—another line of defense. The attackers were just bundles of filthy cloth and fur, armed with hunting knives and clubs and spears, breathing hard, as Crimm could tell from the misting of their breaths. There was no sign of any military discipline, any formation. But there were an awful lot of them. Folk the color of mud against the snow.

Crimm turned to the Annid. "Ywa, it may not be safe here much longer."

"I will not leave. Whatever the outcome, Crimm, something of old Northland dies today. Never before have we turned on each other on such a scale. And I must be here to witness it . . . I cannot believe it has come to this so quickly. But then, I suppose, each of us, however grand, has only ever been a few missed meals from the animal."

Crimm glanced up at the sun, at the position of the advancing crowd. "Time for the scholars' weapon, I think. We're lucky with the sun being so bright."

Ayto snorted his contempt. "We'll be lucky if this stunt makes any difference at all. Typical scholars! Strike at a distance and hope you never have to close with the enemy at all."

Crimm understood his cynicism. Yet he hoped in his heart that the scheme worked, and the horror of a close fight could be averted.

It was time. He heard the clear voice of Annid Xree calling out final instructions. "Be ready to cut the banner ropes . . ."

Crimm leaned over the rail. All over the Wall face people came forward to the balcony rails, ordinary folk, clerks and cleaners and barkeeps, looking down nervously at the approaching horde, whose angry cries could already be heard. They held their places, their knives and axes poised.

Xree called, "On my three. One—two . . ."

A hundred arms, raising axes and blades.

"Three!"

With a roar the volunteers chopped at the ropes before them. The banners fell away, billowing, some trailing from stray threads. The sunlight struck the Wall, struck shining surfaces exposed for the first time in centuries—tremendous concave mirrors—and was thrown back at the advancing mob, in tight, precise splashes that glared brilliantly from the white of the ice. Those caught in the light threw up their hands to shield their eyes, and cried out in pain. Steam rose from the melting ice, itself brightly lit.

Crimm, dazzled, tried to see. "Some are fallen, burned. A lot more are running from the light. Scared out of their wits!"

Ayto shook his head. "Never believed this old gear would work."

"Those Greeks were clever. It's said they used mirrors to fry enemy ships in battle."

"Yes, but I've been to Greece, and the mothers know the sun is a lot stronger down there than it is here. But still, I bow to the scholars. Has it made any difference to the battle, though? I mean it's not as if we can aim this thing. We can only fry those who kindly wander into the hot spots."

"Yes. Others are coming on."

"We've a fight before us yet." Ayto drew his sword from its scabbard, an unfamiliar weapon for a fisherman despite their hasty citizens' training by the guard.

Now more voices started calling up and down the face of the Wall. "Be ready! Here they come!"

Crimm leaned over the rail again. He saw that advance parties of the invaders had reached the tumbled rubble at the base of the Wall. It took them more effort to clamber over the heaped, ice-slippery stuff, and the hungry fighters were already exhausted. And they were greeted by chunks of rubble, frost-smashed thousand-year-old growstone thrown from the balconies higher up and from the roof of the Wall, and a sparse hail of arrows.

Yet they came on. Now the leaders were clambering

up the face of the Wall itself. Slick with ice it might be, but the ancient growstone was so rough and frost-damaged that it offered plenty of handholds. Crimm saw a man climbing up directly toward him, knife in mouth, arms and legs bare, ruined boots on his feet, so thin he looked like an animated skeleton. Yet he climbed with purpose and strength. His eyes met Crimm's.

The Annid of Annids was right beside Crimm, looking down as he was. He took her arm. "Please, Ywa—get back into shelter. It's not safe."

She shook him off. "I must be seen, in the Armor of Raka. I must be seen!"

Ayto hefted his sword. "Forget about her. Be ready—"

There was a yell from above. "Look out!"

Crimm twisted and looked up. Heavy stone blocks were hailing down from the roof, meant for the invader, bouncing down the face of the Wall. Ayto grabbed him and pulled him back.

But Ywa hesitated. And one falling block, carved basalt from some smashed sculpture, caught her neatly on the back of her head, smashing her skull like an egg. Her body slumped over the rail.

"No!"

Still Ayto held Crimm back.

That skeletal man came over the rail with a roar and hurled himself forward. Crimm raised his sword to parry the man's lunge, pushed him back, then swept the weapon at knee level, making a satisfying contact with ropy flesh and muscle. The man fell, blood spilling vivid on the growstone surface. Crimm finished him with a swipe that cut his throat.

But before he was still, another came over the rail. And then another.

Crimm charged forward, and beside Ayto fought for his life.

44

The note was brought to Rina by Thuth, in the room they shared in Barmocar's servants' house. The big Libyan barged the door open with her hip—in Carthage there were no locks or latches on servants' doors—and spun the note through the air. "For you."

Rina sat up, clutching the blanket over the ragged remains of the undergarment from Northland that she used as a nightshirt. "A note? Who's it from?" They spoke in the patois of the servants' quarters, a clumsy amalgamation of Carthaginian, Greek, Libyan—no Northlander in the mix, for Rina was the only one of her kind in the house.

Thuth said heavily, "Who's it from, I don't know, I'm not the Face of Baal." Her tongue could be sharper than her chopping knives. "I do know I need to get to work, and so do you." She hooked the door closed with her foot on her way out.

Rina sighed and tousled her short hair. She felt as if she hadn't slept at all. She shared her bed with one of Anterastilis' night-duty maids, a spiteful young Libyan.

Until the maid left for her shift Rina had to try to sleep on the floor. But the night was already over, the light was bright through the muslin stretched over the empty window frame. There would be no more sleep; Rina faced another day's work.

In the meantime here was this note. She turned it over in her hands. It was a simple folded page sealed with a blob of wax; she didn't recognize the pressing.

A note! She didn't get notes. Servants of Barmocar and Anterastilis didn't get notes, or got them rarely. And the seal, of course, was already broken. Anything written down that came into the household that was not marked for the attention of the owners was routinely scrutinized by the head of house. In these increasingly difficult times Barmocar was concerned about security.

Rina opened up the note, shedding fragments of wax from the cracked seal. It was written in the Carthaginians' angular alphabet, in a neat hand in a dark blue ink, presumably by a scribe. But Rina saw, intrigued, that a few hasty amendments to the text had been made, crossings-out and additions, in the swirling script of Northland—as if the note had been dictated to a Carthaginian scribe, and then the author had marked up corrections in Northlander on the copy. She scanned down to the signature. It was from Jexami! It was signed with a looping scrawl, beside an envoi in Carthaginian: "Your ever-loyal cousin."

Jexami had not written to her before, nor had he made any attempt to contact her since the few days he had put her up in the late summer. Nor would she have expected him to. Jexami's survival strategy was to pose as a Carthaginian gentleman. It was hard to believe he would risk all that with a note to a servant, especially one with an embarrassing Northlander past, and a relationship to Jexami himself.

She went back to the top and began picking out the Carthaginian letters. Her understanding of the tongue was still poor. It didn't help that the blocky Carthaginian alphabet, in which you broke up the words into letter-particles and wrote them down, was so unlike the ancient Etxelur script she had grown up with, in which each word was represented by a single symbol of concentric arcs and bars—a written language that, according to scholars like Pyxeas, had more in common with the languages of Cathay than with the bitty scrawls of the Continent's farmers. But she made out the words, and read them to herself one by one: "Greetings to my cousin Rina, Annid of Etxelur! I send you news of home. Recently I received a long missive from my much-loved cousin Ywa Annid of Annids …"

But Rina had heard a rumor, passed on spitefully by one of Barmocar's men, that Ywa was dead, killed in a revolt.

She saw, reading on, that the "news" in the note was a lot of jumbled nonsense. Of a Giving feast in the late summer, but Givings were always held precisely on midsummer day. Of the good health of Rina's own husband Ontin, the priest, but Ontin was a doctor, and her husband was Thaxa. This was a clumsy fake! But good enough to have fooled a Carthage-born-and-bred head of household who knew nothing of such a remote land, or of her personal business.

Well, then, what was its purpose?

She turned to the "amendments." The Northlander script would have been utterly incomprehensible to the head of household. He must have judged that the additions were minor enough not to pose a problem. But his judgment had been wrong, for the message they picked out had nothing to do with the nonsensical "news" from Etxelur:

"Mother. Go to the back wall now. Alxa."

Rina was scarcely able to breathe. She had not seen her daughter for months.

She did not hesitate. She got out of bed, used the room's communal piss-pot, washed quickly with what was left of the jug of water on the nightstand, and changed into her day clothes, the cleanest of the two sets of the uniform-like tunic and skirt Anterastilis ordered her to wear. She ripped up the note and fed the pieces to a small lantern that burned high on the wall.

Then she pulled her cloak over her shoulders and slipped out of the room.

She knew a way to the compound's back wall that she could take without being seen. Every servant in the household knew of such routes. You learned to live like a rat, in such circumstances as these. The house's servants, staff and slaves had a covert life of their own that went entirely unnoticed by Barmocar and Anterastilis and their circle—and no doubt the same had been true of her own household in Etxelur, she ruefully realized.

She did check the time on one of the big Greek water clocks. She had a couple of hours free. Today Barmocar and Anterastilis were hosting members of the overlapping assemblies that governed Carthage, the Tribunal of One Hundred and Four and the Council of Elders, no doubt debating such crises as the rationing, the plague, and the growing rumors of a vast Hatti horde on the way. These sessions, crowded with drunken young men, were always raucous affairs lubricated by generous helpings of Barmocar's wine. A greater contrast with the grave councils of Northland, which tended to be dominated by older women like herself, could scarcely be imagined. Rina would not be needed during the session, but afterward Anterastilis would no doubt require her "special comforting." All that for later.

The estate's back wall was a crude affair, just heaped-up blocks, hastily improvised in the early autumn. Hurrying along it, Rina soon found a gap that even an old woman like herself could easily step through.

Waiting on the other side was a young man she faintly recognized, dressed in a tunic and trousers that might once have been smart. He grinned and beckoned. "This way, lady." He spoke in crude Northlander.

She stepped through the wall, taking his hand for support—but she caught her fingernail on a jagged stone and snapped it painfully. Biting it to neatness, she hurried after him as he made his way along a narrow street down the slope of the Byrsa. The way was lined by the homeless, ragged bundles slumped in doorways, outstretched skeletal hands. Troops would come through later in the day and clear the track, but the people would return later, or others of their kind would, filling up the empty spaces like mercury settling in a cracked bowl; you could move them around but you could never get rid of them.

Meanwhile the rising sun caught the fronts of the grand buildings of the Byrsa, and from his column at the summit Hannibal, hero of Latium, stood proud, surveying his decaying city.

Rina remembered who this man was. "You're Jexami's servant. That's how you know Northlander."

He shrugged, grinning easily. "Easier for me to learn the master's tongue than for him to learn mine, though he would beat me if he heard me saying it."

"I'm sorry. I don't remember your name." Nobody remembered servants' names—nobody of the class to which Jexami belonged, and Rina herself, once.

"Himil. My name is Himil."

"Thank you for coming to get me, Himil. How do you know Alxa?"

"Who, sorry?"

"My daughter. I suppose you remember her from our arrival in Carthage."

"Not so much. She helped me. The master threw me out."

"He did? Why?"

"Heard there was blood plague in my family." The Carthaginians were terrified that the awful infection they called the "blood plague," which had left scars in their history before, was on its way back to the city, brought by the endless nestspill flows.

"He threw you out just for that? And was there plague? In your family, I mean?"

"No. Father died. Not plague. Just died. Hungry, got sick. I had nowhere to stay. Got work cleaning sewers, and bought food for the family, little brothers and sisters, but still nowhere to stay. Sleeping in streets, like these folk. Then I heard a rumor about the Ana."

"Who?"

"Your daughter, mistress. The Ana was helping people find places to live. I went looking, I asked and I asked, found the Ana and she remembered me, said I'd been kind when she came to the master's house. But I think she'd have helped me anyway. Got me a bed in a house, outside the walls, but that's all right."

"Alxa did all that? How?"

"Ask her yourself."

They had come to a tavern, an open door, a counter fronting the street, a dingy interior behind. The wall bore a hand-scrawled sign in chalk:

NO ALE. NO WINE. NO WATER. NO FOOD.
NO OUT-OF-TOWNERS.
NO SEWAGE WORKERS.
NO DOCTORS.
"ALWAYS A FRIENDLY WELCOME AT MYR-
CAN'S!"

"Hello, Mother." Alxa came forward from the shadows of the tavern.

Rina rushed to her, and hugged her daughter. Through layers of much-patched clothing, she could feel Alxa's shoulder blades.

Alxa led her to a table at the back of the tavern. It was a dismal cave, Rina thought, which must have seen better days with a location this close to the Byrsa. But despite the chalked denials outside, a barman produced a jug of wine and two pottery mugs. "Always we serve the Ana," he murmured, pouring the wine.

Rina sipped the wine. It was sour, the grape crops had evidently been awful for years, but it was the first mouthful she'd taken in months—servants in Barmocar's home didn't drink wine. "Ah, that's good. Thank you. So—'the Ana'?"

Alxa seemed much older than when she had come to Carthage, her face lined, her once-habitual smile gone. She was still just sixteen. "It's a long story, Mother. But first, Nelo? I've not heard a word since the army took him."

"Nor me. From what I can tell from overhearing Barmocar's conversations, they're anticipating a clash with the Hatti, but it's not come to that yet."

"Maybe he lives," Alxa said grimly. "As long as disease, hunger, or the sheer stupidity of the military haven't killed him yet."

"We have to hope."

"Here's to hope." Alxa raised her mug, and touched her mother's.

"I've heard nothing from home either, incidentally," Rina said now. "From your father. Which is why the note you sent was such a shock."

Alxa grinned wickedly, suddenly seeming more like her old self. "It evidently worked. My ruse, I mean. Maybe I'd make a good spy, do you think?"

"You'll earn me a whipping."

That wiped away the smile. "They whip you?"

Only once ... She changed the subject quickly. "So now you're the Ana, are you?"

Alxa shrugged. "Carthaginians have trouble pronouncing 'Alxa,' believe it or not." *All-sha.* "They've only heard of one Northlander, most of them, who is Ana, who they think lived a hundred years ago and built walls on the seabed by hand. So now I'm 'the Ana.'"

"What have you been up to, Daughter? The last time I saw you, you were doing translation for a member of the Tribunal of One Hundred and Four."

"That didn't last long. I made a couple of mistakes ... There are so many people flooding into Carthage, you can find whatever skills you want, if you just look. Lawyers, doctors, even priests. It wasn't hard for my boss to replace me with someone better and cheaper. And prettier," she said with a grimace.

"You should have come to me."

"Oh, Mother, that's ridiculous. What could you have possibly done? No, I found my own way."

"Doing what?"

"Nothing too terrible, don't worry." On impulse she took her mother's hand. "I'm still a maiden of Etxelur. Still chaste."

With great care, Rina showed no reaction.

"But I got to know Carthage. I mean, the real city. Not as it exists in the imagination of the suffetes and the elders and the tribunes. Not even the priests know what's going on, I don't think. Mother, the bread ration, such as it is, doesn't reach half the people it's supposed to. There's a whole population who have been simply abandoned. Yet they're still there—many of them in a huge slum city outside the walls beyond the western gate. There is terrible corruption out there, terrible cruelty.

"But most people are *decent*. I started to see the ways they help each other. One has room to take in an orphan, and does so. Another has a sort of food that her own child can't eat because it sickens her, so she gives it to the family next door. There's no fresh water but for a couple of dried-up springs, and even they are polluted by sewage, but they get organized, and dig latrines and sewage channels. Now we have doctors and nurses who can at least advise the sick. Of course it all depends on food, and there's a dwindling supply of that, and in the end . . . Well, I suppose it's best not to think about the end."

"So this is what you're doing. You're in the middle of this network of—of helping."

"I'm educated, Mother. I can organize things on a bigger scale than most. Write things down, work out the numbers. And I'm a Northlander. I'm not in any of Carthage's factions or cliques. That helps, I think."

She had become a woman Rina barely knew, so much had she grown just in the few months they'd been in Carthage. She was still not seventeen. "Oh, Alxa! The risks you must run, of disease, of robbery . . ."

Alxa smiled. "Mother, there's always a risk. But people know me. I'm the Ana. If anybody tried to hurt me there would be a hundred to step in and protect me." Alxa patted Rina's hand, as if she were the parent, Rina the child. "Besides, what choice is there?"

"The family would be proud of you. But I wish I could spare you this!"

Alxa pulled back and stood up. "What would you do, hide me in a broom closet? I wanted to tell you—well, that I'm fine. Now you must go. Himil told me about your demanding boss."

Rina could barely bring herself to stand and leave her. "Give my love to Nelo if—"

"If I hear from him, I will."

They embraced again, and it was over. Rina let Himil lead her out of the tavern and back up the hill toward Barmocar's residence.

It was only then that it occurred to Rina to wonder why Alxa had arranged to see her *now,* and not before.

Rina returned to the Barmocar property without being spotted. She presented herself on time at Anterastilis' bathroom, where a maid had already filled the mistress' deep sunken bath with hot water sprinkled with salts and balm. Anterastilis herself was not yet present. Rina took the time to change into the sheer shift she used for this work, and to wash her face and neck.

Anterastilis bustled in, staggering slightly, evidently drunk. "By Melqart's left ball, that rabble on the council go on and on. And the way they drink! Oh, help me with this, you dozy woman."

Rina clapped her hands to dismiss the maid, who closed the door behind her, and helped her mistress loosen her robes, held in place by pins and buttons. Soon the folds of hugely expensive purple-dyed cloth slipped to the floor, and Anterastilis stood revealed in the girdle of bone and linen that held her figure in something like the shape it had been when she was younger, Rina thought cattily, with a prominent bosom and tight waist. Now this garment was unlaced from the back and discarded. Anterastilis, who was a little over forty and perhaps ten years younger than Rina, was full-breasted but flabby, with folds of flesh rolling from her belly, and sagging buttocks and thighs dimpled with fat. Not for her the privations suffered by the rest of Carthage, Rina observed, not for the first time.

Anterastilis stretched, yawned, belched, and allowed Rina to lead her by the hand to her bath, where she climbed down the steps into the hot water, sighed and settled back. Rina took sponge and pumice stone and rubbed at her flesh. Rina could smell spiced meat on her breath, and wondered what the meat could possibly be. Dog, perhaps?

"That rabble on the council," Anterastilis murmured sleepily. "Only come here for my husband's cellar, I'm sure of it. And because he lets them fight . . ."

The way the young dominated life in Carthage had been among the most profound shocks for Rina on arriving here. Back in Northland she'd known the theory, of course. Farmers routinely died young. The women died of backbreaking toil and relentless childbearing, the men died in the course of hazardous sports like hunting, or of fighting in wars, and everybody just died of famine or the diseases they caught from their animals. Even in the cities, even in the long-gone good times, more had died than were born, and the population depended on immigrants from the countryside. The result was a city that felt to fifty-one-year-old Rina like a playpen full of squabbling children. Even their councils fizzed with youthful aggression. Barmocar, in fact, was among the most elderly still serving—

"Ow!" Anterastilis slapped her face with a wet palm, hard enough to sting. "You pinched me, you useless sow!"

"I am sorry, sorry," Rina mumbled, head lowered.

Concentrate, Rina—concentrate! For if you earn enough disfavor you will be banished from here, and then how will you live?

With the bathing done, Rina helped Anterastilis out of the bath. Rina took special care, wary of the woman's drunkenness; a fall would be disastrous, for Rina. She walked Anterastilis to the massage table. This was a slab of marble heated from beneath by a system of furnaces and pipes that circulated hot steam—a primitive contraption by Northland's standards, but effective enough. Anterastilis lay on her back, a pillow under her head, naked, and closed her eyes.

Rina warmed her hands on the slab, and took oil jars down from the shelf. These were exotic products from the mysterious countries of the east, and even now Rina had no real idea what most of them were, but she had quickly learned which her mistress preferred, and how they were to be applied. She began with handfuls of a gelatinous oil applied to Anterastilis' heavy stomach, Rina's strong hands kneading the flesh. Then another handful for Anterastilis' collarbones, and then the breasts themselves, which sagged to either side as if deflated.

This was the moment when Anterastilis would let her know how she wanted the session to proceed.

Sure enough, Anterastilis pushed Rina's hands away, and as she massaged her own heavy breasts, Rina moved down to her thighs, which parted softly. Rina worked the oil into the flesh of the thighs, teasingly, slowly moving up to the folds of her sex.

Rina had no idea if this was merely sexual, if Anterastilis was a woman unsatisfied by her husband who demanded such services from all her maids, or if it was the kind of power display Rina had endured from Barmocar. Anterastilis' motives made no difference to Rina. She had to perform these hateful acts anyway, for it was that or the street. She was an Annid! But the sheer repetition of it had taken her to a numb space beyond degradation.

Anterastilis seemed tired, as well as drunk. The session

was proceeding more quickly than usual, and maybe she
wanted to get it done before she fell asleep. Rina was relieved. There were times when her mistress asked her to use
a variety of aids, expensive items carved of ivory, applied to
her vagina or anus. Now, as Rina pushed her fingers inside
her, Anterastilis moaned, and reached up to grab Rina's
small breast, squeezing it painfully through her thin shift.

Then Anterastilis yelped, slapped Rina's hands away
and sat up, the oil glistening on her bare flesh. "You
scratched me!"

Rina cringed. "Madam, I promise—"

Anterastilis pulled at her crotch, her legs akimbo.
There was a slight red line on the inside of her right
thigh. "Look at that! By Tanit's mercy, I am bleeding."

There was a stinging cleansing lotion on the shelf.
Rina reached for that.

But Anterastilis grabbed her wrists so the bottle fell
and spilled on the floor. "Show me your hands. Show me!"

It took her only a heartbeat to discover the nail Rina
had broken on the wall.

"Look at that claw! Look at it! How dare you bring
that anywhere near my body? And these nails! They are
filthy. What have you been doing, woman?" She peered
at Rina's face, and abruptly grabbed her neck. She was
surprisingly strong. Rina resisted for a heartbeat, she
couldn't help it, then suppressed her instincts and yielded.
Anterastilis dragged Rina's face to hers, and sniffed noisily. "Wine! I can smell it on your breath. Where does a
woman like you get wine from? From whoring—is that
it, Northlander?" She released Rina.

"Madam, please—"

"Out." Anterastilis began throwing jars at Rina's
head. They were too solid to smash, and rolled noisily to
the floor. "Out! You will be whipped for this. Wait until
my husband hears of it. Flayed! Get out, woman, out!"

Rina fled, in no doubt that Anterastilis meant every
word she said.

45

er punishment was delivered by the head of house: ten strokes of the whip. Rina had suffered three the time before, delivered by a former soldier who seemed to enjoy punishing non-compliant women. She forced herself not to cry out, not to weep—not to beg.

Later Thuth, the Libyan cook, rubbed in a solution of salt and unguents that she said would help the healing and maybe reduce the scarring, all the while berating Rina for her stupidity in fouling up such an easy job.

She had the evening to recover.

But when she showed up for work with Anterastilis the next day, the head of house sent her away. Instead she was put to menial work, sweeping floors, clearing the courtyard of the debris of yet another dust storm. It was harder than her work for Anterastilis, but not so degrading. And the steady labor might or might not help her back heal.

She slept little, those first nights after the whipping. She had to lie on her front, or try to sleep sitting up. The lack of sleep gave her time to think. You had very little time to think as a servant of the Carthaginians; your workload was heavy, your sleep and rest times short, the patterns of your days chaotic. Now she had time to reflect back on her brief meeting with Alxa, those unimaginably precious moments, worth ten times the whipping she'd suffered as a consequence. And time to puzzle out again exactly why it was Alxa had chosen to contact her mother at just the moment she had.

It was when she overheard grim reports delivered to Barmocar of authenticated cases of the blood plague not far from the city that she began to suspect the truth. Alxa had wanted to see her because she knew, from her own network of informants, that the plague was coming. And Alxa, following her own self-appointed mission, was not going to stay away from the afflicted.

It was a month since her meeting with Alxa. One night, while her bed was still occupied by the snoring night maid, Alxa once more pulled on her cloak, and her Northlander boots, about the only worthwhile possession from home she had left, picked up a small purse with a few treasured Carthaginian coins, and slipped out through the grounds. That gap in the external wall had been roughly patched up, but the dry stonework was loose—mortar was in short supply like everything else this dismal winter—and she easily pulled a few stones loose, clambered over the wall, and slipped away into the dark. There was an abandoned property not far away, a small warehouse, used by some of the younger staff for love-making. Tonight it was empty save for the scuffling of rats.

She sat, favoring her back, wrapped herself in her cloak, and waited for dawn. It wouldn't be long until her absence was discovered. The night maid who shared her bed might tell on her; she was the kind who liked to win favors that way. One way or another Rina would be in for another whipping, or maybe this time just a chucking-out to join the starving in the streets. Well, what came next didn't matter. She had to see Alxa again; she had to know.

When the light of the African morning was strong in the sky, she slipped out of the warehouse and walked down the narrow street.

She soon came to Myrcan's tavern. He was just opening up, throwing open the doors, sweeping half-dried vomit into the street, setting out his chalkboard of exclusion and welcome.

"The Ana," she said to him in Carthaginian.

He eyed her cautiously. "What did you say?"

"Forgive me. My speaking is poor. I am her mother . . . I was here. You remember? You gave us wine, a month ago."

He nodded, still cautious. He probably thought her accent was oddly upper crust, since she'd learned it from Barmocar and Anterastilis. Was she a spy, here to check up on black markets in food rations? "Why do you want her?"

"I am her mother." She longed to shake him, to make him understand. "Is she here?"

"Not for days."

"Then where, where?"

He shrugged. "Out of town, maybe."

"Outside the walls?"

"Yes. Maybe. I don't know. You look."

The western gate. Alxa had said there was a big community of the excluded outside the western gate.

She nodded her thanks and hurried on down the hill, following one of the main drags that ran radially away down the Byrsa, and headed straight for the western gate.

It wasn't hard to get out past the guards and through the gate. It might be harder to get back in. Well, she would use her bit of money.

She was shocked by what lay beyond the city wall.

Once again this was something she had known about intellectually from Alxa's descriptions, from complaints from Barmocar's guests about the grubby crowds they had to pass through on their way into the city. The reality of it was astounding. It was another city, she saw, grown up out of nothing, a ramshackle metropolis built from spare stone and sagging bits of canvas and piled-up turf blocks—no wood, for that had all long gone to the hearths. Smoke rose up from desultory fires of peat or dung. Everywhere she looked she saw men moving list-lessly, mothers holding silent infants, children playing in odd, aimless ways. Gaunt faces and stick limbs and swol-len bellies. It was *quiet*. There was nothing like the noise you would have expected from such a crowd. But flies buzzed everywhere, and carts moved along the rough tracks that threaded between the hovels, carts that bore heaped-up bodies towed by skinny men with their faces masked.

She felt a stab of anxious fear. But she must find Alxa.

She strode forward boldly, asking everybody she met if they knew about the Ana, the Northlander, Alxa. She got a few replies, listlessly given. They all pointed her away from the city, away, further out. The shantytown stretched out along the main road out of the city—the result of beggars competing to be first for the cash of arriving visitors, perhaps. She followed the road until the shacks and hovels began to thin out.

She came to a kind of compound, set aside from the road, marked by a loose ring of stones, a scratched mark in the earth. A handful of huts stood here, and smoke curled up from a central open fire. She saw men in masks and heavy gloves digging a pit.

As she was about to cross the line into the compound, a man limped over. "You don't want to come closer," he called, his accent a thick country brogue, obscured by his mask. "Not unless you're ill yourself."

"I'm looking for somebody," she said as clearly as she could. "The Ana, they call her. The Northlander."

Above the mask his eyes narrowed, suspicious. "Who wants to know?"

"I am her mother. Please, if she is here—tell her I have come."

He hesitated. "Wait here." He hurried off to one of the huts. Not running, nobody living outside the city walls seemed capable of running any more.

Here came a slight woman, walking stiffly, with mask and gloves and heavy brown clothing that covered most of her skin, her neck and arms and legs, her face. It was Alxa. Rina would have run across the boundary, taken her in her arms.

But Alxa stepped back. "Don't, Mother. We don't know how it passes from one person to the next. It may be by touch, or by fluids, blood and spit and snot . . ."

"The plague. You're talking about the blood plague. That's what you're doing here." Rina had guessed as much but the thought still filled her with horror. "Tending to the victims of the blood plague."

"Tending . . . Yes. We serve a double purpose," Alxa said wearily. "We take in the afflicted. At the city walls they are simply cut down, you know. Here we allow families to die together." She seemed to stagger slightly. "And we keep the city that bit safer. For it is a terrible illness, Mother. There are two manifestations. The first is a fever, and a spitting of blood. That can kill in less than a day. The second is less vicious, but it kills just as certainly in a few days. If you catch this plague you die, either of the first manifestation or the second. Your only hope of survival is not to catch it in the first place. If it got loose in the city—"

"So here you are protecting Carthage. A city that wouldn't give you a gutter to lie in."

"This is where I am, Mother. Perhaps that is part of the mothers' plan."

"And is it part of their plan that you should sacrifice your own life so eagerly?"

"I knew the risk. We hope to bring doctors here.

Scholars. From Carthage, Egypt, even Hatti. Have them study the disease. Find what spreads it. Find how to cure it. Why not? For this thing is surely the common enemy of all mankind, whatever our political differences, or religious . . ." Again her voice tailed off.

A heavy dread pooled deep in Rina's stomach. "Alxa—let me help you."

"Mother, stay back."

"I will not—"

"It's too late!" Alxa pulled open her tunic, slipped it off her right shoulder, and raised her arm. There was some kind of swelling in the armpit, purple-black.

"What is that?"

She whispered, "The second manifestation." She lowered her arm. "I'm sorry, Mother."

"Oh, my child—" And though Alxa stumbled back again, Rina crossed the space between them in a few strides and took her daughter in her arms. "If only we could have stayed at home—if only you had had a chance to grow into this woman I see before me in Northland— what might you have done, what an Annid you might have become! Oh, child, I'm the one who's sorry, so sorry . . ."

46

This hour it was Thaxa's turn to make the piss run.

He rose from the corner of the huge old cistern, where he'd been reading a scroll by the dim light that came down the air shaft at midday. It was the only light in the room save for the increasingly rare intervals when they lit the lamps. He stood and pulled on his outer clothes, his heavy hooded coat and his waterproof leather trousers and his boots.

Then, carefully avoiding the prone bodies on the floor, he made for the door leading to the passages out to his house at the face of the Wall. It was the time of day when the small children were laid down together to nap. "Time to sleep now," the mothers were whispering all across the chamber. "Time to sleep." Some of the adults slept too, if they could, in the muggy air. Sleep was the best way, the only way really, to use up the empty, point-less hours in this growstone box. There was the usual stink of fish, their staple food, on their breath and in their farts, though you would think he would have got used to that by now. In the dimness he recognized Crimm the fisherman, a few other faces.

The people here were not exactly friends; the jealousy over food and floor space was too strong for that. But they were his guests, that was how he thought of them. He had been astonished to learn from Crimm and Ayto that this huge abandoned cistern buried deep within the Wall behind his own house was, in theory, his property. He hoped that if they survived this dreadful winter they would remember his contribution, the last gesture of hospitality from a hospitable man.

At the door he picked up the latest slop buckets. Aranx, the young fisherman who had lost an arm to the frost, was on guard this hour. He offered Thaxa a weapon, a stabbing spear with a rope sling, but Thaxa had never used a weapon in his life and he saw no point in pretending he could now. Aranx shrugged, opened the door, let him pass through, and closed it after him.

After the human fug of the cistern, the corridors and empty rooms he passed through were dark and bleakly cold. In the circle of light cast by his candle, Thaxa walked softly. Crimm and Ayto had endlessly stressed to those who they had brought into this refuge that as the Wall burned itself up this winter their best hope was to stay concealed—not to be discovered at all, because that way they wouldn't have to fight again, for their food, their lives, as they had had to already.

Ayto himself was waiting for him at the exit from the growstone: another guard on duty, heavily armed with sword and spear and stabbing knife. "Go carefully," he whispered to Thaxa. "And look out for Xree."

"Xree? What about her?"

"She didn't come back from a piss tour yesterday."

"I didn't notice." It was shameful but it was true.

"Well, there's nothing we can do for her. But if she's been made to talk about where we are—"

Lurid rumors were always running through the little group about what might be going on in the world outside the sanctuary of their fortress. Ayto and some of the others had been out there, dealing with whatever was going on in the rest of the Wall. Sometimes Ayto returned splashed with blood, and he would not say what he had seen, what he had done. There was nothing to do, Ayto always said, but to sit here and try to survive, while what he called "the big sorting-out" ran to its conclusion elsewhere. But if Xree, a gentle scholar and good Annid, had fallen into the wrong hands ...

"Perhaps she got lost."

Ayto raised his eyebrows. "Yes. Maybe she got lost. Just take care, all right?" He opened the door to Thaxa's old house, beyond the Wall.

Thaxa hurried through with his buckets.

Suddenly he was in his old courtyard, in dirty, knee-deep snow. The sky above was a slab of blue, and he breathed deep of the fresh air, but the cold felt like a blade in his lungs. The winter had done its damage to his home, of course. The snow had smashed in the roof of the big hall, the very walls were cracked by the frost, the ice had got in through broken windows and coated every surface in the parlors and reception rooms, on the abandoned furniture. But still, this was home, and it was odd to be back out here, after all that had happened. It was not long, he realized, only a few months, since he had sat in these chambers with Ywa and others and discussed the darkness to come, as if it were all a game, a story.

He put these thoughts aside and hurried across the courtyard, where the snow never piled deeply even though no servant swept it anymore: an odd effect of the shelter of the surrounding buildings. When he returned he would have to kick the lying snow around to mask his traces; he knew the routine by now, rigorously imposed by Crimm and Ayto.

He came to his linen shop. The light was dim, silvery, for the accumulated snow was piled high against the panes of the shop's glass front, higher than he was tall, leaving only a strip of blue daylight visible at the very top. The shop was mostly untouched, though his guests in the warehouse had robbed some of his cloth swathes for clothing and bedding—and, he had discovered, some of it had been nibbled by desperate rats or mice. The shop had a privy, with a drain beneath that you could reach by lifting a tile. Here he dumped the contents of the buckets. The drain was surely blocked and frozen, but they hadn't managed to fill it yet, and this was a better solution for disposing of their waste than any other they had found—at least it couldn't be detected by any others still surviving in the Wall.

As he worked, he thought of Rina. Wondered what she and the twins were doing right now. If he knew Rina, she would have landed on her feet; she always did; she was probably running Carthage by now. And he wondered what she would think if she could see her husband on his hands and knees, pouring the shit and piss of forty people down this old drain in the back of the shop.

The buckets emptied, he wiped them with a scrap of outrageously expensive Carthaginian cloth, and threw it aside into a gathering heap. He made for the front door and pulled it open slightly—he always flinched when he did this, expecting to be buried by the infall—but the fallen snow had frozen to a hard wall that blocked the doorway almost from top to bottom, and he was in no danger. A few flakes drifted down from the looser, fresher stuff at the top, though, and this was what he had come for. He reached up with his mittened hand and scooped handfuls of loose snow into the buckets. This was the only way to get fresh water; the piped supply to the old cistern had, miraculously, worked for a while, but the water had soon turned foul, then failed altogether.

"Thaxa!"

The whispered voice came from above his head. He dropped the buckets and stumbled back, heart pounding. "What? Who?"

A face appeared above the snow, from outside the

door, surrounded by a hood from which gray-blond hair curled. "Thaxa! It's me!"

"Xree? What are you—we thought you were lost! What happened to you? Where did you go?"

She lay flat on the snow, grinning, pleased with herself. "There's more than one way out, you know. I wanted to check on the Archive."

"The what?"

"In its new store, deep in the Wall. To see if it's safe. Dry. No mice or ice or other problems."

"That's insane."

She frowned, evidently surprised by his tone. "Not at all. It's a duty. I found that apart from a little ice on the walls—"

"Why didn't you come back?"

"Well, I did get lost then. Found myself wandering around empty corridors." Now she looked as if she had been badly frightened, despite the front she was putting up. "Nobody to ask for help, of course."

"By the mothers, Xree, if you'd been found—"

"So I thought, I know, I'll go to the Wall front and find Thaxa's shop, and get in that way. How clever! Wasn't I?"

"But were you followed? Oh, never mind, never mind—get in! Come on, climb through the snow, I'll catch you."

"Yes. All right." She held out her arms.

But she was snatched back with a muffled cry, pulled out of his sight. He heard voices, a struggle, torn clothing.

"Xree! Xree!"

He jumped up at the ice blocking the doorway. Of course he couldn't climb its slick surface. He fetched a short ladder, used for accessing high shelves in the shop, propped it against the ice, climbed, and thrust his head through the gap at the top of the doorway and into clean, fresh air.

Dark shapes, looming over him. Hands grabbed him immediately, his shoulders, arms, even, agonizingly, his hair, and he was dragged out through the gap. He should have gone to get Ayto, he thought now, too late.

He was flipped on his back, in the cold snow. There were forms all around him—legs, hands reaching for him, a stink of blood and piss. They didn't even seem human. It had happened in a heartbeat, from the security of the shop, to this.

He saw Xree; they had her on her back and were pulling at her clothes, her coat. He tried to roll that way. He bowled into them, two, three, four, and they staggered, stumbling in the snow. "Xree! Get away!"

The first kick was to the mouth, knocking him onto his back again. He felt broken teeth, agonizing. Yet he raised his arms, tried to fight. Make them come to him, and give Xree the best chance she had to get away, to squirm into the shop, to get to Ayto. But he was weak, ineffectual, he always had been, and there was no force in his punches. His reward was more kicks, more blows.

Then they surrounded him. They got him pinned down, on his back, five of them, one on each limb, one sitting on his chest. He bucked and squirmed in the soft snow, but more punches and kicks rained in; he felt something crack in his chest, more horrific pain in his mouth that might be a dislocated jaw. And the cold dug into him, aiding his enemies. What little energy he had drained away, and he started to grow limp, blood filming over his eyes.

They pulled at his clothes, stripping him of his good coat, his waterproof leather trousers, his boots. Even his mittens went. These were Northlander citizens, he thought, as he was. Maybe he knew them. They might have been customers. Friends. Even relatives. And what would come next, when they had divided up his clothes? *The taking of human flesh for the lack of alternatives is actually a logical outcome of our situation.* He'd said that himself, in some polite forum in the Wall, or his shop. Drinking nettle tea. *Not me. Not me.*

When they had stripped him to his grimy underwear

they pulled away. The cold of the snow against his bare skin was intense. He rolled, tried to stand in the deep snow, fell forward. Hands grasped after him, but they were still squabbling over his clothes, and he got away. The snow was deep, and as he tried to run his legs sank into it. He lunged forward and fell into a deep drift, the snow bright around him. Still he thought he heard their voices. He burrowed, bare hands working at the snow—by the mothers it was cold—he dug his way into the snow as a mole would dig into the earth. On and on, the snow compacting around him, heavy and dark, until his strength was all gone.

He gave up and lay quietly, breathing raggedly, pain flaring, encased in the snow. He could see nothing. Hear nothing. He lay still. Even their voices were gone now. The snow, pressed up against his bare, wet skin and packed all around him, seemed to suck away his heat. It occurred to him he must be only a few paces from the front door of his own shop.

The shivering began. He pulled his limbs to him, arms against chest, legs up, a child in this womb of ice, his whole body shuddering. He hadn't been able to see if Xree had got away. Even if she had got into the shop, the others might have followed her. But Ayto would have stopped them. Ayto was strong, resourceful. She would be safe with him . . .

Perhaps he fainted, or slept.

The shivering had stopped. The pain in his chest and mouth was still there, but distant, somehow separate from himself. And his hands—he couldn't feel his fingers, his toes. He tried to move them; there was no response.

The pain ebbed further. It wasn't uncomfortable. He wished he was able to tell Doctor Ontin that; it would console his patients. It wasn't painful if you just gave in to the cold. Ah, but Ontin had fled before the winter locked in, fled south to Carthage, where Rina had gone . . .

There was ice in his mouth. Actually inside it. And on his eyes, he thought, he could no longer close them.

He listened to the deep, slowing beat of his heart, beat, beat. He thought he heard Rina, calling to him, and his children, Nelo and Alxa. And they became the three little mothers in their shrine deep in his house, his proud house with the linen shop that fronted right on to the Wall Way. *Time to sleep now,* whispered the little mothers. *Time to sleep.*

47

Snug in the old cistern, Crimm tried not to doze off during the day. But there was nothing else to do for long hours. It was so comfortable to lie back, he could hear the soft snores of the others around him . . .

He forced himself to sit up. Something was wrong. What?

It was dark. Too dark for the middle of the day. The cistern was lit only by the glow of the fire in the hearth. There should be light coming down the air vent. There was not. His chest dragged as he tried to breathe. The air felt stuffy, thick, even more redolent of fishy farts than usual.

He got to his feet. He felt even worse when he stood up. He made his way across the room toward the vent, treading on people in the dark, and they squirmed and moaned and growled insults at him. Nobody woke fully. It wasn't usual for *everybody* to be asleep. There was generally some brat or other squalling. Something wrong. He got to the air vent and peered up. Nothing but darkness, but, directly underneath it, water puddled. The vent was blocked, by snow or ice probably. It could have happened naturally. Maybe the snow had covered over the whole Wall by now.

Or somebody could have bunged up the vent with snowy handfuls on purpose. Ever since they'd lost Xree and Thaxa a few days ago—they'd seen traces of the struggle in the snow—they'd been aware of being hunted. This would be a good way to flush them out, he thought, to stop off the air they breathed. He wished he'd thought of it.

Where was Ayto? Ayto, a difficult man to work with, but a clear thinker if you gave him the chance, he was the one who had come up with the idea of using this cistern, this fortress for the winter . . . Ayto went missing a lot, though. Off on self-imposed missions, into the darkness of the Wall. Sometimes he went alone, sometimes with others. Often he came back bloodied. Once he came back wearing a man's *face*, like a bloody cap on his head. Crimm had made him hide it before he scared the children and women. But Crimm never asked him what he was doing out there. He was doing what needed to be done, he always had, and Crimm trusted him that far.

The world grayed. He held on to the door, stood straight, shook his head. He could figure it out with Ayto. But Ayto had gone. Now he remembered. This time he'd picked one of the blocked doors at the back of the warehouse, smashed it in, discovered a corridor, and gone looking to see where it led.

Seeking another way out. Now Crimm needed a way out too. He had no better idea but to follow Ayto.

He lit a candle at the fire, and made for the back of the warehouse.

The door Ayto had opened was ajar. Crimm pushed it wide. Beyond was a dark corridor, bitterly cold, the growstone slick with ice. But already the air was a bit fresher.

He needed a coat. To get his coat meant crossing the room again, and he wasn't sure he'd make it without passing out. There was a heap of blankets by the door, good alpaca wool shipped very expensively across the Western Ocean to Thaxa's shop. He grabbed one, draped it over his shoulders, and walked down the corridor. Thinking more clearly, he tried to establish a sense of direction. He was heading deeper into the Wall, away from the landfacing side, toward the ocean face. He didn't know how thick the Wall was here.

He came to the end of the corridor, and a choice of doors, to left, right, straight on. Which way would Ayto go? There was a mark on the door straight ahead, a few concentric squiggles. Ayto's signature. This way then.

Another corridor, doors branching off, and then a fork, a narrower tunnel off to the right, a broader way straight on. Another scribble: straight on.

The latest corridor opened out into a larger chamber. It was warm, lit by a single oil lamp—and there was a stink of corruption that made Crimm recoil. Blankets and bodies on the floor, a kind of liquid mess.

Nobody moving. He was tempted to back out immediately, just shut the door. But there was an Ayto mark on the far wall; this was the way he had come, and evidently out through a door on the far side.

Crimm forced himself to follow, crossing the floor, trying not to touch the dead, their filthy blankets and clothes. Everything was covered with dried-up shit and vomit. Somebody had had the same idea he and Ayto had, to ride out the winter in the belly of the Wall. But one or more of them had come in here sick, and it had spread between the people, and got onto their clothes and their blankets and spread even more. It would have been much worse in here, he thought, if not for the cold, the lack of flies to attack the bodies.

The room itself was smarter than Thaxa's cistern— smaller, the walls better cut, presumably older. Halfway along the wall there was a kind of shrine, cut into the growstone, supporting two urns, side by side. Writing was neatly etched into plaster around the alcove with the urns, and Crimm, despite the bodies all around him, lifted his candle to see. These were the remains of Milaqa and Qirum, he read. *Doomed by love and ambition . . . Milaqa was a heroine as great as Ana or Prokyid, but none must ever know the truth of their story . . .* Milaqa. He remembered something about that name. The Black Crime. Oddly, in a room full of corpses, the etched words made him shiver. The Wall was very big and very old and none knew all its secrets. He hurried on.

Beyond the far door was a corridor, then another door marked with Ayto's sign, and still another corridor. He was heading almost directly away from the Wall's landward face, as far as he could tell. Ayto had been unimaginative and dogged in his choice of directions. But this corridor ended in a rectangle of blue light, pale, cold, clearly daylight. Crimm hurried on. The air grew increasingly cold, and there was slick ice on the growstone under his feet.

He reached the exit. A door, heavy, very ancient, its outer surface crusted with long-dead barnacles, lay open, revealing brilliant light that dazzled his dark-adapted eyes. He stepped forward cautiously, under a pale blue sky. He was outside the Wall, in its shadow. He was standing on a rough ledge of growstone, matted with green-brown fronds of dead seaweed, coated with ice. The Wall towered above him, a rough-finished surface deeply pitted and shining with rime. The sea lapped at the growstone ledge, covered with sheet ice that spread to a knife-sharp horizon, crisp and white. There were ice blocks piled up at the sea's edge, perhaps a relic of the tides.

Somebody sat on the ice, cross-legged, beside a disc of dark blue, a hole in the ice. There was an animal beside him, inert, the head blood-splashed: a seal.

Crimm stepped forward carefully, and found himself standing on sea ice that creaked, a little ominously, reminding him of the end of the *Sabet*. He saw a place where the ice looked a little darker, a little bluer—older. He stepped that way. Rope sections had been fixed to the soles of his boots, and he could walk without slipping, if he didn't rush.

He stepped out of the shadow and into direct sunlight, the first sunlight on his face for many days. He turned, hand raised. The Wall was silhouetted. He saw complex sculptures cut into the upper surface—docks, he realized, quays and piers cut into the growstone and now stranded far above the water level. And above that the light towers stood proud, blind, and the great heads of dead Annids looked out at a frozen sea. The cold was bitter. Crimm pulled the flimsy blanket tighter around his body.

The man on the ice was, of course, Ayto. He held a hand up when Crimm's creaking footsteps got too close. He didn't move, didn't so much as look around. Crimm waited obediently.

A pale shadow passed through the water.

When it had gone, Ayto relaxed. "Ah, you scared him off."

"You might have come back. We're choking in there."

Ayto glanced around. "And you might have put a coat on—you'll freeze."

"This is the ocean side of the Wall."

"Obviously."

"It's all exposed. The sea can't be much higher than the level of the land on the other side." Crimm found it hard to think that through; the fresh air was making him groggy. "How did the sea get so low? Ah. Because all the water is heaped up as ice on the land."

"Just think, these are stretches of the Wall's face nobody's seen for generations."

"What do you think we should do? With everybody in the cistern, I mean. The vents are blocked. We can't really stay there if that's going to happen."

Ayto looked around and sniffed the cold air. Crimm saw there was frost on his roughly cut beard. "Bring them out here. Or at least, find somewhere in the Wall closer to the ocean face."

"Why?"

"Because we can find food here." He patted his dead seal. "Seal, fish. Maybe other animals." He glanced at the sky. "Spring's coming, it must be, but the winter's not done with us yet. Maybe it never will be. If the ice doesn't clear, we won't be able to use the wetlands, the forests. But out here . . ."

"The Coldlanders survive, and it's always winter where they live."

"That it is. Maybe folk from the other Districts will find a way out too, if any of them live through the sorting-out. Let them. But they can stay away from here; this is our bit of coast." He looked around, at sea, ice, sky. "Different way of living, this will be. Makes you feel different just to think about it, doesn't it?" He glanced up at the Wall. "That's all gone now."

"Civilization?"

"Yes. We've gone back to an older time, before Ana and the Wall. Back to the ice. That's how it is here in the north, and soon it will be the same everywhere else. Maybe we'll have older thoughts. Ice thoughts." He poked at his own ribs. "Maybe we'll all start to change shape. We'll look like Pyxeas' Coldlander runt. What was he called?"

Crimm couldn't remember. He found himself thinking of Ywa, months dead now, and he wondered what she would make of this conversation. Of what Ayto was becoming.

He remembered the others, with sharp urgency. "We've got to get back and sort out that air vent."

"Agreed. Come on."

Arguing, bickering, speculating, they worked their way back into the deep shadow of the Wall.

Three

48

The Third Year of the Longwinter:
Spring Equinox

*T*he ice spilled off the growing continental caps, and gathered in sheets over the open sea. From the mountains too the ice descended, the glaciers flowing down valleys gouged out by their predecessors millennia before. When they reached the lowland the glaciers spread out and flowed together, merging into sheets of ice that covered the ground, covering the traces of forests, farms, cities.

Across swathes of the northern continents, there were few people left to mark the latest equinox.

49

The woman was waiting for Sabela under the Gate of the God of Light.

Situated next to the Exaltation of the Sky Waters, a square-cut pyramid that was the greatest monument in Tiwanaku, the Gate was only nominally an entry to the city. Not attached to any wall, the Gate was the frame of a door that led nowhere. Yet this was traditionally where supplicants came to ask for residence in this holy city, the highest city in all the world, enclosed by its finely cut stone walls and surrounded by raised, carefully irrigated fields of maize.

This was the High Country. The day was bright, the lake, a day's walk away, was a plane of brilliant blue under the sky, and the snowcapped mountains beyond gleamed. The city was a jewel set in the great mountain chain that stretched down the spine of this southern continent.

And here was this woman, round-shouldered, her clothes layers of grubby rags, a clutch of children around her, the oldest a boy who might have been fourteen, a couple of little girls, an infant in arms, all of them staring at Sabela. One of the girls was laboring, having trouble breathing. Sabela had no idea how old the woman was. Younger than she was, probably. Broken down from toil, child-rearing, and maybe years as a nestspill.

Sabela held out the note she had been sent, written on reed paper, scrawled in a soldier's hasty hand. It had found her eventually at her mother's home on the other side of the city, where she had been visiting with the twins. "You sent me this? Your name is—C'merr." The click in the back of the throat, characteristic of lowlander tongues, was alien to Sabela's own language.

"C'merr—yes. And you are Sabela, wife of Deraj."

"You claim we offered to take you in."

The woman frowned, perhaps puzzling at her speech. "Yes. Not you. Husband, Deraj."

Sabela found that hard to believe; Deraj, busy running a wool business that spanned swathes of the highlands and thousands of llamas and alpacas, was not given to making sentimental gestures to unfortunates like this nestspill. Especially not to a grubby, unprepossessing— *ugly*—woman like this one. Deraj, for better or worse, had always had an eye for beauty. "You understand that the city is crowded."

"Crowd—yes."

"Many people come here for refuge." It had been a one-way flow from the lower lands for years. "We have no room."

"Deraj. He say."

Sabela said coolly, "We never spoke of it."

"Deraj say."

Sabela studied the woman. Her features were nondescript, the tone of her skin hidden by dust and the stains of sweat. "Where are you from? Were your family alpaca herders?"

"No. Fisher folk."

"From the river valleys?"

"Ocean."

Sabela was shocked. If that was true, it was no surprise the little girl was having trouble breathing; not
everybody born by the sea adapted well to the thin air
up here. "You lost your living there."

"Fish died. Years ago. Only one baby then. We moved,
and grew beans."

That would have been in the river valleys, above the
coast, marginally richer land where folk grew beans and
squash and cotton, in farms irrigated by summer meltwater from the mountain glaciers. "And then?"

"No water. No rain. No rivers in summer." Because
the summers had got so cold the glaciers stayed frozen,
and there was no meltwater. "Then more babies. We
grew potatoes." In the mountain foothills, probably. "Not
bad." She grinned, almost wistfully. "Grew fat, one summer. But then, no water. Then came here."

"Where's your husband?"

"Died. Fighting in war."

Sabela had no idea which war she might be talking
about; the whole region, the mountain country, the coastal
strip, even the borders with the forest nations to the east,
had been convulsed by raids and petty wars for years. So,
after fleeing step by step from her home by the ocean,
climbing gradually into the highlands, the woman had
ended up here, at the summit of the world, the home of
the gods, like so many others.

"C'merr—I'm sorry for your troubles. But Deraj
never said anything to me about you."

"Met him in . . ." A name Sabela couldn't make out,
so thick was her accent. "He came to trade, wool for potatoes. Deraj say," said the woman stubbornly. The boy
nudged her, whispered something. The woman dug into
her grimy coat and pulled out another scrap of paper,
handed it to Sabela.

Sabela took it reluctantly; the woman wore skin gloves
from which blackened fingernails protruded. When she
opened the paper she saw it was a note in Deraj's hand-

writing. "Why didn't you give me this straightaway?"
C'merr had no reply. Perhaps she was not used to written
notes, Sabela thought. It hadn't occurred to her.

The note was scribbled on a bit of reed parchment
that was stained in one corner by what looked like spilled
wine. Sabela's heart sank. Her husband got drunk a lot
these days. Much of his export business was with the Sky
Wolf nations, to the north, and times were hard there—
tremendous forest fires, drought, whole cities buried by
dust storms, so the travelers said. And he had a way of
making deals when drunk that he later regretted. But the
note was in Deraj's hand, undoubtedly. And it promised
C'merr and her family refuge in Tiwanaku as long as they
needed it.

She studied the woman, the grimy, tired face, the fixed
eyes. Why would he do this? How could a woman like
C'merr have possibly bought refuge from a man like Deraj?

"You'd better come with me," she said. "We'll find
Deraj and sort this out."

The nestspills goggled as they walked through Tiwanaku.

Today the city was as busy as ever, with crowds of reed
boats working the lake waters beyond the jetties, the
streets jammed with street-sweepers and porters, bearers
leading llamas laden with goods or drawing carts. A
temple was being torn down, one of the grandest in the
city. There was always building going on somewhere in
Tiwanaku, a cycle of demolition and construction as the
city endlessly renewed itself to attract the next season's
pilgrims, who came to worship the God of Light in his
citadel in the sky. If anything the pace of life here had got
more frantic in the last few years—and of course the
place was ever more crowded with nestspills. Sabela
sometimes thought it was like the frenzied last dances at

the parties she used to go to when she was young, everybody working harder to squeeze out the last bit of enjoyment before the cold light of morning.

For every year the winter was harsher, the summer shorter. Today, this spring day, sheet ice still lay on the lake waters, and frost blighted the maize fields. And while the likes of C'merr and her family came washing up from the lowlands like a rising tide, so the ice on those beautiful mountains on the horizon was creeping down to the plain. It was as if Tiwanaku were being crushed between two great fists, from above and below. No wonder people danced.

So why, in such circumstances, would Deraj have promised a nestspill family refuge in their home?

The answer, when she got home, was immediately obvious.

The girl might have been fifteen, no more. She lay naked on the thick llama-wool carpet in the middle of the room, pale body limp, legs folded to one side, arms lying loose. She looked barely awake; perhaps she was drunk, or drugged. She was none too clean, but she had good breasts, wide hips, a full mouth. The type Deraj had always liked. She even looked a little like Sabela, at that age.

And here came her husband, naked too, his penis limp and glistening, a skin of wine in his hand. He started when he saw Sabela standing there, and the nestspill woman behind her—obviously C'merr was the girl's mother. But he was too drunk to be guilty. "Shut the door, by the god's shade, you're letting all the heat out."

Sabela pushed past the nestspill woman and stormed out.

Deraj came to the door, naked, the wine in his hand, and called after her. "Sabela, wait! Where are you going?"

To the twins, she thought, at her mother's home. That was where she was going. And then away from this place. Where, though?

Far from here. To the friends she had made that had nothing to do with Deraj. To the River City to see Walks In Mist, or the Altar of the Jaguar, where she would find Xipuhl. She would go all the way to Northland, perhaps. She would wait for the ships with her friends as they had promised, and go back to that little growstone bar in the Wall, at the heart of the greatest civilization in the world, where she had drunk potato spirit from Asia. Where she had been happy. Where she would be safe again.

Deraj continued to call after her. Neighbors were laughing at his nudity and drunkenness. She broke into a run, to get away.

50

On the battlefield south of Carthage, Nelo was in the reserve. He and the rest of his unit were kept back while the main phalanxes stood firm against the last ragged charge of the Libyan rebels, and then when the Carthaginian cavalry was unleashed at the enemy.

It was the afternoon of what now passed for a spring day in North Africa, dry, dusty, cool. The battlefield had once been an extensive farm by the look of it, but after years of drought it was abandoned, the olive trees withered, the stubble of the last grain crops dry in the fields, the fences of the stockades robbed for their wood. It had taken the Carthaginian force half the day to ride out here. The scruffy Libyan rebels, numerous but disorganized, had showed rudimentary military thinking by clinging to a scrap of high ground in the hope of gaining some advantage. General Fabius had ignored this, had drawn up his army in the ruins of this farm, and had simply waited.

And as the Carthaginian command had evidently expected, the Libyans lost their nerve and attacked.

"You see?" Gisco, Nelo's sergeant, had said, always ready to draw a lesson to deliver to his ragtag troops of conscripts, levies and volunteers. "What have I told you? It is sometimes harder not to fight than to fight. Braver to wait than to charge in. You must pick your moment. Watch and learn, if you ever want to be a general like Fabius."

Now it was only a question of time, as the Carthaginians steadily pressed. Nelo stood at the center of his phalanx, with his sword and spear and the hand-me-down helmet that pinched his brow, hoping to be spared his first real action for one more day. Dreaming of the sketches he might make of the scenes before him if he got the chance.

At last the Libyan formation broke and the survivors started to run. The Carthaginians cheered. Fabius raised his sword, horns blasted, and a ripple of commands spread out through the Carthaginian army.

Sergeant Gisco grinned and raised his thrusting spear. "Our turn, lads! After them and finish them off!" The men of Nelo's phalanx surged forward after the fleeing Libyan survivors, running across a field already strewn with corpses.

But Nelo didn't have a chance to move before a hefty shove in the back pitched him onto his face. Suniatus, of course. The big man peered down at him. "Too slow, aurochs!" And he gave him a kick in the head for good measure, and ran on.

Naturally, in the midst of the advance, Gisco saw this and pointed his sword tip at Nelo. "Northlander! You're on a charge! Get to your feet!"

Nelo struggled up, shook his head, hefted his sword and stabbing spear, and ran with the rest.

As Gisco never failed to remind them, the men of this unit were the dregs of the conscripts and levies that the suffetes, the executive officers of the city, had raised to swell out the Carthaginian army, as rumors swirled of the advance of the Hatti horde by land and sea. Even Suniatus was a poor soldier, for all his bullying: strong, fearless, but evidently too stupid to obey the simplest order. But the men around Nelo seemed keen enough as they charged—keen to get among the killing at last, especially if it could be against an opponent already beaten and demoralized, and keener, perhaps, to get their hands on some booty.

Already they closed on the Libyans.

The Carthaginians descended with a roar. Sergeant Gisco himself went in with sword swinging, cutting down rebels like a sickle in a field of wheat. Suniatus threw himself on the back of a fleeing Libyan, forcing the man to the ground and stabbing him brutally in the side of the face with his sword, over and over as the man writhed and blood spilled. Nelo had got used to the noise of battle, or so he thought, but he had always been out of it before, held back from the fray. Now he was in the midst of it, and the noise of men screaming in anger or pain all around him was astonishing. It was like an abattoir.

Suddenly there was a hiss, a blur, and something shot past his ear. A javelin!

Shocked, heart hammering, he turned to see an enemy warrior, wounded, blood streaming from his leg, but with a round wooden shield in one arm, sword in wooden scabbard. He wore a crude leather tunic as a herdsman might wear, but he had no protection at all for his bare arms or legs or face, and if he'd ever had a helmet it was long lost. He hardly looked like a soldier at all. But he had some kind of loop of leather around his fingers, which he was fitting into a notch on another javelin. He was fumbling, pale from loss of blood.

Gisco knocked the man's javelin aside, and he stumbled back onto one knee.

"He could have killed you!" the sergeant screamed in Nelo's ear. "That javelin missed your stupid melon of a head by a thumb's width. If not, you'd be lying in the dirt already, Northlander. Dead! Everything that you are, have ever been, or ever might have been, spilled out into the Dark Earth for all eternity, for that's where bad soldiers end up, believe you me, never mind what the Jesus botherers will tell you. All because of him! That man in the dirt, who never saw you before today! And now he's trying again. Are you going to stand there and let him? Are you, aurochs? Are you?"

It was Gisco's screaming that drove him forward as much as the shock.

Still the fallen warrior fumbled with his gear. This time Nelo knocked the javelin aside with the shaft of his own spear. The man fell back on the ground and raised his sword, but Nelo, remembering his training at last, fell on him, straddling his torso and pinning the man's sword arm with his own gloved fist. For one heartbeat his eyes met his enemy's. The man was dark, even darker than most Libyans. Nelo smelled blood, and dust, and sweat, a richer stink of horses and cattle and hay. He looked older than Nelo. His face was lined and heavily weathered, as if he'd spent much of his life out of doors. He was *strong*; Nelo could feel it in the way the man struggled in his grip, but he was too exhausted to break free. All this in a heartbeat.

Nelo swept his sword across the man's throat. Skin and cartilage resisted, but he dragged the blade through. Blood spurted, shockingly bright, and the man choked and spewed blood from his mouth. Still he stared at Nelo.

"Again!" yelled Gisco. "Again and finish it!"

Nelo swung his sword once again, this time a chop as if he were severing an ash branch, and he felt the sword cut into the bone of the neck. The man shuddered once, and his eyes rolled, and he lay still. Nelo's sword was stuck in the bone. He had to drag at it to release it.

Then, suddenly filled with revulsion for the bloody corpse under him, he scrambled to his feet.

"There." Gisco clapped Nelo on the back. "You did it,

aurochs! You took a life. No worse than sticking a pig in training, was it? And now you've done it once you can do it again, you'll see, it gets easier every time. And look at this." He leaned over and with a brisk chop of his own sword he severed the man's right hand. Gisco lifted the hand by its little finger, almost delicately, as its stump dripped blood. There was a fine leather strap around the first two fingers. "See those loops? To help him throw his javelins. Libyans don't do that. This isn't a Libyan bastard, he's an Iberan bastard. This is what Iberans are good for." He threw down the severed hand. "*All* they're good for. Now, we use Iberan mercenaries for they're useful in specific situations, but we don't expect the ungrateful bastards to start chucking javelins at us, do we?"

"No, sir."

"But here he is."

"I suppose they are hungry in Ibera as well, sir."

"I suppose you're right. The whole world's hungry, and they've all come here to pinch our grub, the Iberan bastards from across the strait, and the Libyan bastards who live around the corner, and the Hatti bastards who are on their way across the Middle Sea. But they aren't going to succeed because we're going to fight them and stop them and kill them, aren't we, aurochs?"

"Yes, sir."

"Right, there's still a few Libyans left. Get stuck in. If you find a helmet that fits you, take it; that acorn shell on your head looks ridiculous." For a moment he glanced down at the mutilated Iberan, at blood-splashed Nelo. "An Iberan and a Northlander, fighting to the death on a scrap of Carthaginian soil. I don't suppose either of you wanted to be here, and we don't want you here, but here you are, and this is the way it has to be."

"Yes, sir."

"You're still on a charge. Go, go!"

Nelo ran off, after the fleeing Libyans and his own jubilant comrades. Already the crows were gathering overhead. Even the crows were hungry this spring.

51

Nelo's force got back to camp at noon the next day.

The army of Carthage, swollen by levies, conscripts and mercenaries, was gathered on the plain to the west of the city's landward walls. The camp wasn't much to look at, just tents, a few buildings of mud brick or sod. The ground was scored by drains and pitted with latrines, a system Nelo had come to know very well, for digging out the latrines and emptying them was the kind of detail that devolved on units like his own.

Still, Nelo had already been a Carthaginian soldier long enough to witness the changes that had come upon the camp since Fabius the Roman, the favored general of the moment, had taken command. Once it had been a dusty shambles. You couldn't even have told where it began and ended, and traders and whores had come and gone unchallenged, along with a few Libyan assassins. Now defensive ditches and barriers marked the camp's boundaries, and Fabius had had stubby watchtowers built and manned, and sent patrols riding far out into the country beyond. In the camp, on a day like today after a bit of action, you could hear the blows of the smiths as they fixed battered armor and weapons in their workshops, and the cries of the wounded as the surgeons tended to their injuries, and the multilingual chatter of this force gathered from many nations: the mostly Carthaginian officers, tough black warriors from the southern empire of Mali; pale blond men from as far north as Scand; and men of the Middle Sea from Ibera and Gaira to the west, and the Muslim kingdoms to the east. It was a mixed-up army in a mixed-up world, Gisco would say, shaking his head.

Sergeants like Gisco applauded Fabius' competence. The men grumbled at the extra work he created, and were annoyed when a change meant they suddenly found themselves downwind of the latrine trench rather than up. But then, Nelo was learning, soldiers always grumbled, if things stayed the same or if they changed, at the prospect of action or the lack of it. And the wise old heads predicted it could all change again when the suffetes or the Tribunal of One Hundred and Four decided that Fabius was nothing but an upstart Roman after all, and kicked him out in favor of some other strutting tin hat who would turn everything upside down once more.

For Nelo the best part of each day was the evening, when the soldiers gathered by their fires in the open air and prepared their bread for the evening. Following an ancient tradition Carthaginian armies on the march carried grain, not finished bread, and every unit had its own grinding stone. Fabius had insisted on the same discipline in camp, even though they were not far from the walls of the city itself. So you would grind out your barley by hand—and it was always barley these days, though this was looked down on by proper Carthaginians, who preferred wheat—and you would knead up the meal in a scrap of leather with a little wine or oil if you had it, then flatten it into wafers. You roasted it quickly on the fire, and ate it quicker, for it was unleavened and would set hard as rock if you left it to cool. But the fresh, hot bread at the end of the day on an empty stomach, along with a little meat or cheese and wine if you were lucky, was always delicious, and the soldiers, gathered around their fires, kneading and roasting and eating their own bread, were at their most companionable. Even Suniatus tonight, who sported a ridiculous plumed helmet he had looted from the corpse of a Libyan officer, left Nelo alone for a while.

After the meal, as the dusk drew in, Nelo took himself off to a corner by the wall of a barracks house, dug his paper and crayons out from his satchel, and started to sketch. Soon the face of the Iberan he had killed took shape on the paper. The grimacing mouth, the eyes oddly defiant though he must have known death was near. Nelo had long ago given up his formal experiments, though when he drew larger scale scenes he still tried out his look-deep techniques. Now he just tried to capture the immediacy of the moment. The extraordinary experience of risking one's life, and taking another man's.

"Nelo."

The voice startled him, and he scrambled back into the shade, clutching his sketch to his chest. He had had enough of his work being trashed by Suniatus and his cronies. But the man who stood before him, silhouetted against a sterile, cloudy sky, was portly, swathed in a grimy tunic, stooped slightly. And the accent, when he had pronounced his name, had been Northlander. "What do you want?" Nelo asked in his rough Carthaginian.

"Don't be alarmed." Northlander words. The man came forward and squatted in the dirt. His scalp was bare of hair, and he was old, Nelo saw, fifty or sixty at least. He had a leather pouch slung from his shoulder. His tunic and upper arms were splashed with blood, but his forearms and face were washed clean. "Do you remember me? My name is Ontin. I used to treat your family. Your mother knew me well. I'm a doctor, you see."

"I remember you, I think."

"I came down to Carthage after your mother pioneered the way. Left it a bit late—didn't leave until the autumn, and we were lucky to get through—but it seemed the sensible thing to do. Imagined I would set up a practice like the one I had at home. Instead, I was drafted straight into the army. Strange, isn't it? Here we are, Northlanders both, you serving in Carthage's army, and me patching up its wounds, which is why I'm such a mess, by the way. Trauma wounds are so much less *civilized*. Well. And how are your mother, your sister?"

"I don't know. I mean, we're not allowed into the city. My mother writes. I don't hear from my sister, and my mother doesn't mention her." Which made Nelo fret that something bad had happened to his twin. It was strange to hear himself speak Northlander again; his own voice sounded odd in his hearing.

Ontin nodded. "I'm not surprised they keep you out of the city. It's overfull as it is, stuffed with famine and fear. The last thing the city needs is a bored army roaming the streets looking for trouble."

He spoke quickly, almost anxiously, as if he was relieved to have someone to talk to as an equal. Doctors weren't much respected in the Carthaginian army; they could even be killed by the companions of a wounded man if they botched a job. But Nelo could think of nothing to say to the man, and the silence between them stretched.

Ontin pointed. "Is that your art? I remember that about you, always scribbling as a child."

"What about it?" he said defensively, clutching his drawings.

"It's not a secret, is it? I mean, your sergeant knows all about it. Can I see?"

Nelo forced himself to calm down. This was just some old doctor his mother had known at the Wall. He opened his arms and handed over the sheaf of drawings.

Ontin flicked through them. "Very vivid. Not that I

know anything about art." He turned around one image of an amputation, the doctors and their slaves holding down a writhing man. "You've even got the details of the instruments right. You should be proud of this, not hiding it in the dark."

Nelo took his pictures back. "There are lads in my barracks who would wipe their asses with them. Or wipe *my* ass."

Ontin stared, and laughed. "Well. I suppose an army isn't the place for a budding artist. You mustn't let them grind you down, you know. Reduce you, as you crush your grain on the quern. Remember who you are, Nelo. You are a Northlander. And you always will be—"

"What do you want?"

Ontin was nonplussed. "Ah. So, to business." He looked oddly regretful. "I have something for you." He opened his leather pouch. "Do you know a man called Pyxeas?"

The name came out of a mist of memory. "He's my uncle. Or maybe he's my mother's uncle. He's the one my mother took to Hantilios."

"One of our greatest minds, my boy. I mean Northland's. In this or any age. He's far from home too. Well, he, or rather one of his students, gave me letters to bring to your family, if and when I got to Carthage." He dug a packet of papers out of his pouch, and glanced around before handing them to Nelo. "Taken me a rather long time to deliver it, I admit, but it hasn't been too easy to find you, boy—and I can't track down your mother and sister at all. But I've had fair copies made, for your mother and sister when I find them, and other exiles from home. Best not to tell anybody about this, I mean nobody outside the family. Something of a Northland secret, or it has been so far."

Nelo opened the papers and scanned the neat writing. It was boldly addressed "To My Family," and signed as "On Behalf of Your Loving Pyxeas, May the Blessed Mothers Protect You in Your Exile." The rest of it was densely written in long convoluted sentences. There were no headings, no summaries—no pictures, which Nelo would have fallen on immediately. He was aware that Ontin was watching him. He picked out a few words:" 'Hazel or alder or willow . . . sulphur from the volcanic pools of Kirikland . . . scrapings from the urine-soaked floors of barns and latrines . . .' Latrines?"

"That's where you collect the solve stone. And the wood types are the best kind for making the charcoal that's needed."

"Needed for what?"

"No, it's not clear, is it? Ah, these academics. So poor at expressing themselves, for all their wisdom. Mind you, I suspect Pyxeas is too wily to say it straight out. I'm only guessing myself, Nelo. I was never in Pyxeas' confidence after all. But I've had to read it through to have it copied, and I think I know what it's about.

"Look, boy—have you ever heard of the House of the Crow? One of our more secretive orders, who kept their knowledge hidden in chambers deep within the Wall. Knee-deep in espionage they were. And hidden programs of study and scholarship, too, out of sight of the rest of the world—indeed the rest of Northland. I think this is one of their secrets."

Nelo found a more comprehensible passage, about making some kind of great barrel. " 'In the absence of cast iron, for none in the world between Etxelur and Cathay have that secret, have the craftsmen take iron rods and hammer them flat around a wooden former, and then bind them with white-hot iron bands which will contract when cooled, gripping tightly. Then remove the former. The barrel should be thick-walled at its base . . .' " His imagination caught, he immediately began to sketch the iron device, as best he understood it. "What kind of secret?"

"A devastating secret. A destructive secret. A secret that Northland has gathered to its growstone bosom for millennia, to be kept from the rest of the world to avoid harm being done—and, frankly, when necessary, to be used to save us. So it was in the time of the Cursed Milaqa, it is said, and so, perhaps, it is now. Look, Nelo, even if I never find your mother, you must take this knowledge and use it. Talk to other Northlanders. Find an engineer—you know, someone who used to work on the Wall pumps or the Iron Way engines, who will understand all that about making the barrel. There must be some here. *Start the work.* In secret, of course, but there are plenty of Northlanders here and many of us have the resources to do it."

"I still don't understand."

Ontin smiled. "We are far from home. Your great-uncle is even further away, by all accounts. None of us can go back, perhaps not ever. But, I think, even so, your uncle is trying to save us all . . ."

"The general!" Nelo heard Gisco's peremptory orders, and then the trumpet blast. "The general is coming! Out, out, on your feet, and you can put that away for a start, Suniatus . . ."

Ontin looked confused. "General Fabius?"

"A snap inspection." Nelo scrambled to his feet, stuffed the letters and his sketches into his satchel, and without another word ran out to join his comrades, as they lined up before the barracks hut.

52

abius walked before his troops, this unit of scrubby
reserves. Caught unawares, half of them were barefoot and none wore their helmets or armor. But they
raised their spears and swords and yelled a welcome for
their commander.

Fabius wore an iron breastplate over a scarlet tunic,
with a plumed helmet of bronze and a purple cloak
thrown back over his shoulders—but it was the purple of
the Roman kings, not the Carthaginian shade. He had a
full beard and mustache cut in what was apparently the
Roman style. His legs and arms were bare, despite the
chill of the day. He was not tall, not handsome, but he was
stocky, he looked strong as a bull, and his face bore one
deep scar that told of his own experience in the field. Behind him walked his staff, his senior commanders in their
own armor and cloaks, and a couple of civilian scribes.
The other commanders, Carthaginians all, looked with
disdain on the reservists before them. But Fabius grinned
widely, and when his glance fell briefly on Nelo, even the
Northlander conscript swelled with pride.

As the cheers died down, somebody called out cheekily from the Carthaginian ranks, "What's it like to lose a war, then, sir?"

"Ha!" Fabius stopped dead, hands on hips, and scanned the ranks. "We've got a historian, have we? Who's your sergeant?"

Gisco stepped forward. "Sir. The man is called Suniatus. Tough sort from the back streets. More mouth than brains if you know what I mean. I'll sort him out later—"

"You won't, you know. Because he asked a fair question. Who's Suniatus? You? I'll tell you what it's like to lose a war. You know why I'll tell you? Because I'll promise you something. Unless I tell you, you'll never know, not *you* or *you* or *you*, because no Carthaginian is ever going to learn what it's like to lose a war, not while there's breath in my body to lead you, that's what I promise you, that's what I promise!"

The end of this invective was drowned out by cheers, and Nelo, borne along, joined in.

"A boy from the streets, eh?" Fabius eyed Suniatus again. "We've all had our journeys. I'm from the back streets of Rome myself. When I was a boy I sold pretty pebbles in the forum by day, and fought to stay alive by night. Yet here I am, standing before you now. Some of you have come even further. Where's the Northlander?"

Nelo was frozen with shock. Those around him had to shove him out of the line. He stood shivering, exposed.

But Fabius' smile was like the sun. "Here we stand, a Northlander, a Roman, and my good friend Suniatus the historian from Carthage. But wherever we're from, whatever gods we follow, *we're here*, together.

"And I'll tell you this. It's a special war we're here to fight, when the Hatti come, thick as a swarm of locusts. A war like none other in history. Because this is a war that will *end* history. It's not about glory or the ambitions of kings or booty or even about our gods. It's about who lives and who dies—as simple as that.

"The world is ending, you know that, you've seen the

winter close its fist on the land. And whoever loses this war will end with it. But whoever *wins* will build a new world, when the sun returns once more. That's what I want you to remember when the Hatti come, as you whet your blades and polish your armor. You are the last warriors, fighting the last war in the world. And you will fight to win!"

Again the men cheered at these terrifying, inspiring words.

Still Nelo stood before this formidable man, trying not to tremble.

The general said more softly, "A Northlander, eh? You folk dismay the likes of us—oh, dismiss your men, Sergeant. Not you, Northlander. Do you know why you dismay us?"

"No, sir."

"Because of your cursed history. Such a weight of it, as massive as your Wall, or so I'm told as I've never seen it, which hangs around the neck of the world like a slave's shackle. And makes the likes of us, Latin and Carthaginian, look like children at your feet. Well, that's all to be scrubbed away by the ice, isn't it? Leaving the world bare, and ready for a new race to build a new world, fit for the gaze of the gods." An impulse seemed to strike him. "This is the same Northlander who's the artist, is he, Gisco?"

"He is, sir."

"Oh, don't look shocked, boy; a good sergeant knows all his men's secrets, and their hiding places. I think Gisco is proud of you, in his way. I was taken by the scribbles he showed me, I must say.

"Listen to me, Northlander. I think I have an interesting assignment for you. I want you to join my staff. You can be my official artist. You'll find me an unusual sort of soldier. Like my good friend Suniatus over there I fancy myself as something of a historian. I want future generations to witness what's to be done, here on the plain before Carthage. And it's through your eyes, perhaps, that they will do that witnessing. Hmm. I don't suppose you have any epic poets hiding in your ranks, do you, Sergeant? Never mind, never mind." He walked on, turning to his aides. "What's next?"

When they had gone Nelo just stood there, staring after the Roman.

It was Gisco who broke the spell. "Well, get a move on, lad, what are you waiting for? You heard the general. Pack up your kit and go after him. And don't forget your crayons."

53

In Daidu, it was not yet dawn when Uzzia came to Avatak's room to wake him, with a not-so-gentle kick in the buttocks. "Get up."

Avatak, lying on his blankets and furs on the floor of his room, rolled on his back. The room was cold—cold enough for Uzzia's breath to mist in the gray early light, cold enough to leave a rime of frost on the window ledge. It was spring here in Daidu, he was assured, but you wouldn't know it. Well, Avatak liked it this way.

But he smelled smoke. His nose wrinkled. "What's that?"

"None of your business."

He rolled easily to his feet. "Why am I awake? I thought you Hatti liked to sleep until noon."

Uzzia grinned. "You're learning cheek. I should have kicked you harder. The Khan is going to his hunting grounds in the south."

He frowned. "So late in the season?" In the months they had stayed here in Daidu, he had learned that the Khan preferred to take out his mighty hunting parties in the depths of winter, when the land was open, bare, the game easy to spot. "What does that have to do with me?"

"We're invited—you and I. Pack a bag, have a piss, and meet me at the south gate."

Daidu, that cold, clear spring morning, seemed more tense than usual to Avatak. There were fewer people in the wide streets, but more soldiers, watching nervously from doorways and gates. The gates of the palace compound were sealed shut. To the north a pall of brown, greasy smoke rose from beyond the city wall. In moments of stillness, Avatak thought he heard distant shouting.

He found Uzzia at the city's south gate, in a milling crowd of Mongols and Cathay. Some were dressed in expensive breeches and tunics, cloaks and felt hats, the hunting gear of rich folk, slapping gloved hands, their breath steaming. The rest were servants and slaves, dressed drably but as warmly as they could manage. Uzzia wore her traveling clothes, including her precious quilted cloak. She carried a couple of throwing spears. She handed one to Avatak; it was a light, well-balanced javelin.

They made their way through the gate. Outside, on the wide, well-made road leading south from the city, more attendants had assembled horses—a whole herd of them, saddled, or harnessed to carriages. An attendant from Bolghai's household brought Avatak and Uzzia a horse each. The man had more weapons strapped to his back, including stout stabbing spears.

Avatak started to see the scale of this expedition, stretching off down the road. There had to be thousands of riders here, thousands of horses and attendants, and carts bristling with weapons, with javelins and stabbing spears and blades. Back in Coldland hunting parties were no more than a few men and boys, gathered together on a whim. This was more like an army assembling for war. And Avatak saw an expensive-looking pavilion, bright colors under the clear blue sky, mounted on top of what looked like a rock, a fat gray boulder. No, not a rock—it moved, slow yet oddly graceful. It was some tremendous beast.

Again he smelled smoke as the wind shifted. Heads turned to the north, and faces wore worried frowns. He suspected there were plenty of folk who would rather not be riding off with the Khan to play at hunting on this particular day. But the Khan's whim overrode all other considerations, and the hunters began to mount their horses and carriages.

Horns sounded, and there was a cheer, noisy if unenthusiastic. The Khan's great gray beast was the first to move. It really was like a boulder, walking on legs like cut-off tree trunks, with flapping ears and a long nose that trailed to the ground. A boy, dark, slight and skinny, rode behind its huge head, slapping the beast's ears with a switch to make it go this way and that. The Khan himself was invisible inside the tent of silk and wool strapped to its back, but the tent tipped this way and that as the animal plodded, and Avatak could not imagine that it would be a comfortable ride. The beast was an astonishing sight, and would have been even if it had not had the most powerful man in the world in a box on its back. But Avatak had seen nothing but astonishing sights since he had been brought away from Coldland.

"Where is Pyxeas?"

Uzzia, riding beside him, shrugged. "With his colleague Bolghai, I imagine. Immersed in his numbers and his theories. As happy as he ever is."

Avatak knew that the old man was agitating to be away, to return to the west. It would be a journey back over the roof of the world, Avatak supposed, and the sooner they started, the better. But meanwhile, here he was hunting with the Khan. "Why are we here? You and I."

"Because we have both been observed to fare well in the games in the palace, I with the javelin, you with the stabbing spears."

He grunted. "None of those sleepy, overfed beasts we faced in the games would be a match for the great bears of Coldland."

"Be that as it may, you have caught the eye of the Khan's attendants. And today we are here as the guests of Bolghai."

"Why?"

"So that Bolghai himself does not have to travel. I suspect Bolghai has more pressing business in Daidu. Most people do."

"Not the Khan, it seems."

"No. Not the Khan."

The procession was a great crowd, trailing the Khan on his boulder-beast. The ride continued through the morning, across a landscape of woodland and open plains, a land dotted with farms—though the plain looked parched, many farms abandoned, the woodland hacked for firewood. Twice the progress was interrupted for hunting. Horns sounded, scouts rode off—and then the animals would appear, to great excitement. The first was a band of wild boar, ugly, bristling creatures that ran squealing across the road. The Khan had his curtains thrown back so he could see, and allowed his barons to run down the boar. Then a magnificent stag was sighted. A cage was revealed on a cart, and opened to release a hunting animal, a lithe cat that Uzzia believed had been brought from Africa. The cat was ferociously fast, and Avatak saw the Khan stand up in his pavilion so he could see it chase down the stag.

Uzzia was not impressed. "I spoke to the attendants. They go ahead into the country, hunters, beaters, trappers. They flush out the game, round it up. They even cage the beasts to be released when the Khan rides by. This is not true hunting. This is a rich man's indulgence. This particular Khan is a man of civilization, of letters, and there's nothing wrong with that. But he plays at being what his ancestors once were, a wild man of the steppe. I hope he remembers his limitations."

As noon approached there was a commotion ahead. The progress of the caravan was not slowed, but Avatak heard shouting, brisk, impatient commands, and the unmistakable ring of swords being pulled from scabbards.

He saw a band of people beside the road, adults, old folk, children, families. Some of them had carts or mules laden with carpets, furniture; others carried goods on their backs. Avatak saw one thin old woman in a neat floor-length silk gown, expensively made but very dusty, with a bird in a bronze cage perched on her head. To let the Khan pass they had been cleared from the road.

"Nestspills," Uzzia murmured.

"From where?"

"Daidu, of course. Or its suburbs. Where else? There have been rumors about this all winter, in the taverns and the suburbs, that as soon as the winter relented half the population would be off, heading south."

There were cries of "Crane! Crane!"

All eyes turned to the sky, where a pair of the big ungainly birds were flapping over. The Khan threw back his curtains once more and released a bird from his arm, a huge, muscular-looking falcon. In Daidu, only the Khan was allowed to keep birds of prey, and this was a breed of falcon unique to Cathay. The falcon shot into the air and dived down on one of the cranes. There was an explosion of feathers, and the birds, locked together, tumbled from the sky. The watching nobles whooped and applauded, the nestspills utterly forgotten.

At the end of the day Avatak at last glimpsed the Khan's lodge, in the middle of the great hunting ground. It was a band of brilliant color along the southern horizon, tents and pavilions and yurts; it was as he had imagined Genghis' yurt-capital of Karakorum to have been, before it was broken up. There was much activity, smoke rising from a hundred hearths, men on foot and horseback moving everywhere. Uzzia said there were traders in these districts who raised huge nations of dogs, to be ready to provide thousands of hounds at a time to the Khan on demand. The great hunts could span an area as wide as Northland itself, she said, though Avatak wasn't sure he believed that.

But in the event he saw no more of the Khan's hunt. No sooner had they reached the lodge than messengers came riding down from the north, from Daidu, demanding an audience with the Khan. The rumors spread quickly of trouble in the city. The bulk of the party turned around immediately, led by the Khan on his boulder-beast. Nobles hurried to change their horses, and attendants sparked torches.

As dusk gathered, Uzzia and Avatak joined the ride. Uzzia murmured, "So much for this foolish jaunt. Stay close to me."

Behind them, Avatak heard thousands of dogs howl at the rising, ice-ringed moon.

54

Having ridden all day, now they rode through the
night back to the capital. Avatak wondered how
many plans were being curtailed and abandoned
like this, around the world, because of the weather.

It was almost morning again when the van of the
hunting party approached the gate in the southern wall.
That great plume of smoke from the north loomed taller
than ever, and flames leapt high in the dawn light. As they
neared Daidu, the Khan's caravan had to battle through
a thickening crowd of nestspills pouring south from the
city, a flood compared to the trickle they'd overtaken yesterday. Some of the nestspills actually jeered at the Khan,
and shook their fists. All of these were Cathay, Avatak
saw. But the protestors melted into the crowd when the
Khan's guards drew their weapons.

At the city gate, the soldiers gathered around the Khan
as he was lifted down from his litter, and formed a tight
party around him as he was hurried through the outer
wall. Behind him, the great column broke up into smaller
parties, each noble with his own little band of warriors.

"Stay close to the Khan," Uzzia said to Avatak.

"Why?"

"Because each of these nobles has his or her little pack of retainers. We have none. Best we are protected by the Khan's own men, if we can manage it. I have this." She pulled Pyxeas' golden *paiza*, his safe-conduct pass, from the neck of her tunic; she wore it tied to a thread. "It ought to get us inside the palace."

"And then?"

"We find Pyxeas."

"Yes, and then?"

"I'm making this up as I go along, boy. Wait and see."

They hurried after the Khan, through the city. Even inside the palace compound there was pandemonium, courtiers and warriors running everywhere. In the palace itself, one of the Khan's senior advisers was waiting for him at the door, a slender Cathay who trembled with fatigue and terror as he prostrated himself before the ruler. The Khan kicked the man to his feet and stalked on into the heart of his palace, with the guard from the hunting party following. Maybe the Khan trusted them more than his palace guard at this moment, Avatak thought. The Khan was unmistakable in his brilliantly colored silk hunting gown, and the soldiers, grimy from the march, were dark, lumpen figures in the palace's brightly lit opulence. Avatak noticed racks of the soft white slippers you were supposed to wear to protect the carpets; now they were ignored, and trails of muddy, dusty footprints were everywhere.

All the way the adviser jabbered to the Khan in rapid Mongolian.

Uzzia murmured, "I can't hear it all. He's talking very softly, very fast, and these warriors around us aren't exactly keeping quiet. It sounds as if it's all falling apart. The smoke we saw to the north, the flames—"

"Yes?"

"Warriors from the steppe. More nomadic horsemen. I can't make out if they are Mongol or not. I don't suppose it matters. They got through the border walls, and here they are at the gates of Daidu. Some of the men are muttering that the city walls have already been breached."

"No wonder the people are running away."

"Yes. Those that aren't rising up. That's the other thing. The Cathay are taking the opportunity to rebel. The Mongols are marauding conquerors, after all. Some of the soldiers around us are muttering about conspiracies; maybe the Cathay rebel leaders have been in touch with the nomads. But there are more unpleasant surprises for the Khan to come, I think. I keep hearing a name: Kokachin, who they call the Wind-Rider."

"Kokachin's a woman's name. A Mongol woman's."

Uzzia grinned. "So it is."

They turned corners, following the increasingly agitated Khan, until Avatak was quite lost in the belly of the great building. They came to a tremendous hall, yet another of this palace's gigantic chambers, packed with milling people. And, under a roof of lacquered blue, he heard the hooves of a horse, oddly muffled. A horse?

The Khan ascended a podium on which stood a huge, elaborately carved throne. He glared down the length of the room—and faced a rider sitting boldly on a horse, Avatak saw now, a short, squat beast, one of the Mongols' own tough ponies from the steppe. The rider was a woman, wearing light Mongol armor, a chest plate of boiled leather stitched with metal pieces, a small bow slung on her back. She wore no helmet, so all could see her face. She was handsome, severe, her straight black hair pulled back from her brow. And she was laughing as she turned the horse around, making it prance and nod.

Around her men were gathered, on foot, warriors all, brandishing weapons, spears and swords and axes. One of them was waving a bit of smashed furniture at the Khan, carved wood and pale pink silk, a ragged scrap of a chair that must once have been exquisite. At least as many men surrounded the Khan, many from the hunting party. Cowering from these posturing warriors were courtiers, Mongol grandees with their shining cloaks and tonsured scalps, nervous-looking Cathay officials in silk gowns. There were hundreds of people all jammed in this one huge room together, and their voices rose up like the cawing of gulls on a cliff face.

"Oh, dear," Uzzia said, looking at the mounted woman.

"What?"

"The Mongols are horse warriors. I'm guessing that to ride your horse into another man's yurt is a grave insult."

"So, along with the assault by the steppe warriors, and the Cathay uprising in the city—"

"Yes. Now the Mongols are turning on themselves."

There was a hiss, a soft impact. A single arrow had been shot into the air to thud into the roof, high above. The woman on the horse had fired it. The clamor in the room stilled, and all eyes turned to her. She sat straight on her horse, and spoke directly to the Khan, in rapid-fire Mongol. For his part he replied angrily. Their two voices filled the room.

Uzzia murmured, "She says she is Kokachin, called the Wind-Rider. He says he knows who she is; she is a niece gone to the bad. (Not a niece—something like that.) She says he has shown his weakness by allowing the brutes from the steppe to penetrate the empire. He tried to buy them off, it seemed; it did not work. He says matters of state are not hers to judge. She says her own father was disinherited by the Khan's father, who was a camel turd. (A Khan cannot accept such insults! Ah, that's the nub of it. It's a family dispute. The descendants of Genghis Khan are as numerous and as disputatious as the royal family of New Hattusa.) The Khan is offering a conference to settle it. (That's what the Mongols do, the clans gather on the steppe and talk it out.) She says the time for talking to the likes of him is over. He is demanding she kowtow—"

"Look! There is Pyxeas, with Bolghai."

The two scholars stood together, Pyxeas frail but defiant, Bolghai agitated. The Mongol was clutching the Northlander's sleeve, as if for protection.

"Come." Uzzia slipped through the crowd toward them.

By the time they reached the scholars, the Khan and his niece were shrieking at each other, and their followers were growing restive, their voices a rumble. Bolghai was murmuring to himself, distracted. Pyxeas was dismissive. "What a scene! What savages these fellows are, under the veneer of civilization they stole from their Cathay subjects."

"That's as may be, scholar," Uzzia said, "but a small war is about to erupt in this room, and we don't want any part of it. We are going to get out of here, and fast." She pointed. "That door."

Avatak nodded. "Why that one?"

"Because it's the quickest way to the city's south gates. We have the *paiza*. If we move fast enough, maybe we can beat the spread of the bad news from Daidu."

"And then?"

She was distracted by the gathering row, tense, nervous herself. "It's always 'and then' with you, isn't it, Coldlander? And then we will get out of this insane place and find a way to get the two of you home."

Kokachin jumped up onto the back of her pony. Standing straight on the stolid beast, she called out, waving her bow in the air.

" 'To me, to me,'" translated Uzzia. " 'To me, my cousins!' This is it. Now the barons and the rest of the Mongols have to choose, Khan or challenger."

Bolghai hid his face in his hands. Then he straightened up, looked regretfully at Pyxeas, and walked toward Kokachin on her horse. He had made his choice, Avatak realized; at heart he was a Mongol like the rest.

The fighting erupted. It broke out across the whole room, all at once, as if somebody had given a signal. Suddenly there were struggling figures everywhere, screams, and blood splashed on the rich carpets.

And a warrior took a measured stride toward Bolghai, swung an axe, and beheaded the scholar with a single stroke.

"No!" Pyxeas rushed forward, but Avatak held him back. "No, no! That such a scholar, such a mind, should be destroyed like this—"

Uzzia held his shoulder. "He was a Mongol, and he died a warrior's death. His children will laud him for it. Come now, we must go—" She grunted, staggered, her eyes wide.

Avatak said, "Uzzia? Are you all right?"

She straightened up, determined. "Go, go! Get Pyxeas out of here."

So they hurried for the door, Avatak using his broad shoulders to push through the crowd. Once out, Uzzia led them through the network of corridors and rooms. Warriors and courtiers ran both ways in the corridors, drawn by the clamor of the battle in the great hall, or fleeing from it. And Avatak started to hear the rumor, spread in a dozen languages, some of which he understood: "He is dead! The Great Khan is dead! Buyantu slain, and so is the she-wolf who challenged him . . ."

They reached the gate in the palace wall. Already small battles were breaking out in the city beyond. And now they were out in the open air, Avatak noticed for the first time the short Mongol arrow that stuck out of Uzzia's shoulder.

55

The travelers left Daidu almost as lightly equipped as when they had arrived. They used some of Uzzia's money, Mongol scrip acquired by selling her own gems and gifts from the court, to purchase a small cart and three horses. Even Pyxeas had sensed trouble coming; he had already packed up the essentials of his work with Bolghai in a trunk, along with personal effects.

Before noon on the day of the rebellion they were already out of the city and heading down along the road they had just traveled, south toward the Khan's hunting grounds once more. Uzzia drove the cart behind two of the horses, with Pyxeas and their gear. Avatak rode the spare horse. He wondered what would become of the mule, and wished he had had time to say good-bye.

Only when they were well clear of the city would Uzzia permit a stop so Avatak could treat her wounded shoulder. Pyxeas remained in the cart, sipping sullenly on a skin of wine. He had barely spoken since the death of Bolghai; he seemed in deep shock.

Avatak plucked out the arrow, making Uzzia wince.

She said she was lucky; it had not penetrated deep enough for the barbs to dig into her flesh. But she warned him against touching the arrowhead, or the brown stuff smeared on it. She loosened her tunic, and let Avatak dab cleansing unguents on her broken flesh with scraps of cloth. The medicine's scent made his nose wrinkle. The wound was not deep, did not need stitching, and the blood was already clotted. But there was a patch of discoloration around the wound, not purple like a bruise but an ugly, faintly green color.

"Don't worry about it," Uzzia said when he described this. She pulled up her tunic. "We must get on. The sooner we can put some distance between us and Daidu, the better."

"Heading south."

"Yes."

"Why not west? That's the way we came—the way back home."

"But we can't go back that way." She sighed. "Look at Pyxeas, Avatak. Do you imagine he could stand another journey like that? Even if it could be made at all, after another year of his longwinter!"

"South, then. How?"

"By ship. We're heading for a port called Quinsai, a few days' ride from here. There we'll find a ship. You'll sail home in comfort." She wiped sweat from her brow, though the air was far from warm. "You'll like Quinsai. It's just like Hantilios."

So they hurried on.

Beyond the Khan's hunting grounds the country changed, becoming more dominated by farmland, and Avatak stared out curiously at wide flooded fields where the people waded amid their crops of rice. Toward the end of the day they found a way station, deep in the old heartland of Cathay, a handsome wooden building with dry, comfortable rooms. Avatak thought they would not have stopped at all if Uzzia had had her way. But they had to rest the horses, and they were all exhausted; even before the rebellion Uzzia and Avatak had ridden through a day and night with the Khan. So they stayed the night. They were served country food of rice, meat, freshwater fish and mollusks—delicious, at least compared to the overelaborate concoctions of the Mongol city to the north. Avatak concluded that the Mongols had poorer tastes than their subjects.

Pyxeas barely ate. He did as he was asked, and he looked after his own personal needs. But he seemed to have withdrawn deep within himself, to a place where, perhaps, he felt safe. Uzzia grew weaker. She would not let Avatak look at her wound again. But she was pasty, pale, sweating.

She roused them all at dawn, and drove them on.

Thus was the pattern of their days, until, ill, bedraggled, withdrawn, bewildered, they arrived at Quinsai.

They found rooms on the outskirts of the city, for an exorbitant rent, and they got a lousy price when they tried to sell their horses. Avatak concluded that despite their haste the rumors about the Khan's fate had reached this city, and things were falling apart. Uzzia disappeared to find a ship. Pyxeas withdrew to his bed in the rented room.

Avatak cautiously explored Quinsai.

Yes, it was like Hantilios, as Uzzia had promised, but so overwhelmingly larger in scale it made comparisons with that city seem specious. Like Hantilios, Quinsai was built on a lagoon strewn with islands. Canals ran everywhere, crowded with waterborne traffic and crossed by many bridges. These canals were straight and clean, with none of the fetid stink of Hantilios. A freshwater lake embraced one side of the city, and a river to the other side kept the canals clean of stale water.

The city itself was an artificial landscape of wide squares, and broad, straight streets paved with baked brick, and magnificent houses, most of them built of wood. There were pavilions, temples, palaces. Every day the great squares were full of market stalls where you could buy foodstuffs, clothing, heaps of shoes and bales of silk and wool, racks of jewelry—and full of crowds, Cathay and Mongols and many others, Persian, Muslim, Carthaginian, Rus, even Northlanders, and exotic folk Avatak had never seen before, perhaps from further east. And full, too, of entertainers, jugglers and magicians and acrobats. Avatak heard a rumor of a man who had trained *a fish* to wear a hat and perform various tricks, but never saw him.

Far though he walked in his brief time in Quinsai, Avatak knew he did not get a sense of its true scale. He suspected that a western city like Hantilios could be lost without trace here.

"Of course it is beautiful." Pyxeas whispered when Avatak described all this in the evening. "A beautiful and ancient city built by a beautiful and ancient people. This is how Cathay was, before the Mongols came along to build their temples to vulgarity and greed, like Daidu. And of course it is crowded. We are a good way south of Daidu—that much further south of the eventual march of the ice. This place will not be spared—*nowhere* will be spared—but comparatively, Quinsai may prosper, and so people will flock here like migrating birds. But this is an occupied city despite its beauty, as you can tell from the number of soldiers on the streets—Mongols all, I'll wager." And he fell silent again, retreating inward to his own inner mesh of calculation.

He was right, of course, and the soldiers became more obvious when night drew in. Toward midnight great drums were beaten to signal the curfew, a pulsing rhythm that crossed the city air.

And every night, too, part of Quinsai burned. The buildings were of wood, and dry as tinder after years of drought. Avatak heard rumors that some fires started because people recklessly built bonfires to battle the cold of the spring, and perhaps there was some rioting over a shortfall of the city dole. But the city was organized; engines would rush through the street, and pumps would pour water into the latest conflagration, even as the rebuilding began in last night's disaster area.

Avatak was bemused by Quinsai, the crowding people, the endless carnival, the whirlwind of buying and selling, the nightly blazes and frenetic rebuilding. An insane city, a city at the end of the world. He was relieved when, on the third day, Uzzia said she had found a ship.

"Here are the details." She pushed a slip of paper across the table to him. "Berth, all the way to Carthage, if the gods spare her, and the pirates. Remember, the ship won't wait. I'll leave it to you to get the old man ready." She stood up, leaning for a moment with her fingertips on the table; she looked very pale, her brow slick with its customary sweat.

"Are you going out again?"

That's my business," she snapped. "Just don't miss the ship." She went to the door and gathered her cloak. "And finish the journey. For, you know, it might be a journey no one else will be able to make, not for many generations. That's something to tell your grandchildren, isn't it?"

She did not return that night, despite the curfew.

The next day he waited almost until noon. Still she did not come back. When he went into her room, he found her sparse luggage gone—all save the quilted coat, with its sewn-in treasure.

He donned the coat, and began to get Pyxeas ready for the sea voyage.

56

A month after the first Hatti landings on the African shore, Fabius suggested to the councils of Carthage that the time was ripe for an attempt at negotiation. He kept Nelo at his side during his sessions with the councils, so the boy could sketch the scene, the general in his Roman-purple cloak standing before the Tribunal of One Hundred and Four in their chamber on the Byrsa, or in a private office in deep discussion with the two suffetes. Nelo's crayon captured expressions and body postures in rapid, silent sweeps.

"I will lead the party myself. Let us show these Hatti that we are strong and determined. Honor must be served. They tread on our sacred land—"

"It's not your land, Roman."

"My apologies. And already blood has been spilled."

"Yes, because you failed to drive them off."

"We could not defend the entire coast. And the Hatti are a mighty host."

"A host of locusts."

"If we must fight them to the finish there will be a

great war—the kind of war which both sides lose, a veteran of too many wars might say. If we can turn them away with words, we may be spared great destruction."

"He is a soldier who would sue for peace. And a Roman too!"

"The Hatti want Carthage. We know that. They want to destroy us so they can gorge on Egyptian wheat. They won't accept peace, they won't accept anything short of our obliteration."

"But it's worth a try, brother. Talking may buy us time for the siege that is sure to come."

"Well, you may be right. What have we to lose? We can spare a Roman and his Northlander runt . . ."

The great men of Carthage, Nelo quickly learned, were very suspicious of their generals, even as they relied on them to fight and die on their behalf. It was the way the Carthaginian system worked, with a split of powers between the civilian and the military, neither one dominant. The Tribunal of One Hundred and Four particularly was charged with keeping the soldiers on a tight leash. In history, it seemed, it had not been unknown for generals to win famous battles, against the Romans or the Persians or the Muslims or the Mongols, only to return home to face trial for a lack of loyalty or other perceived crimes, with the penalty often being execution, which was traditionally by crucifixion. They were especially suspicious of Fabius, because he was brilliant, popular, and a Roman. But he was the best they had.

"You may proceed, General. One of us will travel with you. But go with caution. And don't make any promises."

"I understand. Come, gentlemen; come, Nelo."

On a late spring morning the mission to the Hatti formed up outside the city gates: Fabius and his officers, one of the suffetes, a man called Carthalo, with his own advisers, and a small squad of soldiers as guard. They gathered under a banner especially made for the occasion, an ornate image of Jesus Sharruma, Son of Teshub Yahweh, the Storm God of the Hatti, with the crescent moon sigil of Baal Hammon over his head: a gesture of peace, the gods of Hattusa and Carthage intertwined. The details had been agreed by ambassadors exchanged between the two nations.

The party was slow in forming up, the horses being harnessed and saddled, a few wagons loaded with rations and water, the soldiers checking their boots. The day was fine, bright, and though the winter snow was long gone nothing but scrubby grass and weeds grew away from the roads. Another hungry summer was coming, Nelo thought gloomily.

Sergeant Gisco was here, to add to his burden. And then he learned that the escort as a whole was under the nominal command of a man Nelo knew: Mago, nephew of Barmocar, a scion of one of Carthage's great families, appointed to lend a bit more weight to the party.

Mago soon spotted Nelo. He was more grandly dressed even than Fabius himself, with a spectacular crimson plume on his helmet. "Ha! When I heard the general had adopted a Northlander runt who could scribble a bit, I thought it must be you."

Nelo thought it was a long time since the two of them had worked together in the aftermath of the Autumn Blizzard in Etxelur. As soon as he was back home, the worst of Mago had come to the fore once more. "What do you want?"

"What do you want, *sir.*" Mago stalked around Nelo, inspecting his quilted tunic and light mail coat and cloak, his pouch with his paper and crayons for the sketching. "Treats you well, does he, the general? I don't hold with the rumors that he's bumming you, though Romans are notorious for it. Greek influence, you see. No, you're not pretty enough. You're his little pet, though, aren't you? Feeds you on scraps from the table, does he? And how's your mother? And that tasty sister of yours—"

Nelo faced him. "My sister's dead."

They faced each other, eyes locked.

Mago sneered, contemptuous, arrogant. "You're no soldier."

"I agree."

"What?"

"I agree. *Sir.* I never asked for it. I do my best."

"And it's a poor best from what your sergeant's told me."

Something in Mago's arrogance struck Nelo in that moment, his complacency, his absolute certainty about his place in the world. Nelo had been around Fabius long enough to see the Roman's point of view, to believe it: whatever was to come this campaigning season, the world was changing, utterly and irrevocably. He had a sudden vision of Mago in two or three or four years, standing in the frozen ruins of Carthage. How arrogant would he be then? How complacent? He tried to think how he could capture this insight on paper.

Mago seemed to sense there was something going on inside Nelo's head that he couldn't reach, couldn't touch. "Pah! You are a waste of grain, you Northlander cur. And if the protection of your precious general ever wavers, I will make sure you are cast down where you belong."

"Thank you, sir."

Fabius said they would travel north along the coast roads. He wanted to see again where the Hatti had first landed, he said—and where they were landing still, according to his scouts—and then they would come upon the city the Hatti were building on African soil. And, he told Nelo, he wanted his artist to see it too, for even the landing was an exercise on a scale never before seen in the history of the world.

The march was easy. The weather was cold but calm, and the breeze fluctuated between a wash off the sea and a drier breath from the interior. The little traffic on the road cleared at the advance of Fabius' party under its banner; there wasn't much, a few mean carts pulled by skinny donkeys or bullocks. The road was lined by farms, but the ground was parched and lifeless. And as they passed, the people would come out and run alongside, skinny wretches in rags, hands out, begging. Fabius allowed his troops to give them bits of silver, but none of the party's own rations. This was the breadbasket of the city, Nelo reminded himself. These starving beggars were supposed to be supplying Carthage with its food, not the other way around.

Then the wind shifted again, coming from the south, whipping up grains of hard sand. The soldiers muttered complaints and covered their faces with their cloaks. Nelo had heard the soldiers talk of vast empty deserts to the south, nothing but bone-dry sand. If the country kept drying out, maybe the desert would wash up and cover Carthage itself.

The march was made in good order, the overnight camps efficiently set up and struck. And on the third day out of Carthage, they came upon the Hatti's landing site.

Guided by scouts, Fabius took a small group forward to a headland, for a first view. Nelo went with them, his pouch at his side. From the headland the view to the north opened up, a vista of shore and sea. They were close to a river estuary, a sprawl of mudflats and braided waterways. A Carthaginian city called Utica lay a little way up the river; it had been abandoned and burned on the approach of the Hatti. Before the landing there had only been a scatter of fishing villages here, all now obliterated in the battle at the first landing site. Now the country had been transformed.

A tremendous arc of growstone dominated the estuary, an artificial harbor and groyne—an almost perfect circle. There were warehouses and other structures around this harbor, hasty constructions of turf and mud but huge even so. From the harbor, tracks trodden into the earth led inland. Looking that way, to the west, Nelo could see a new city being laid out around a low hill, for now not much more than a sketch of banks and tracks on a straight-line plan, but with the smoke of many fires feathering in the low breeze. Traffic moved on the tracks between city and harbor, carts, people on horseback and on foot. There was motion everywhere, and a distant clamor of voices—a sense of industry, of purpose about the scene.

The harbor itself was crowded with ships. And, look-ing north out over the sea, Nelo saw more ships, a scatter of them on the breast of the ocean as far as he could see—a snowstorm of Hatti ships, a countless number, descending on this shore.

"Draw," Fabius muttered. "Draw, boy!"

Nelo fumbled for his paper.

Gisco said, "I'm surprised there wasn't a Hatti scout up here. I'd have placed one."

"Oh, we've been seen." Fabius pointed. "Notice that party? Moving this way. That's a Hatti war chariot. Not used in anger in a thousand years or more, and now the carriage of a prince."

"Look at all those ships," muttered Carthalo. He was a tall, angular man with a high forehead and a cool man-ner, evidently used to command, yet he seemed over-whelmed by the sight. "It's as if the whole of the northern Continent is draining into Africa."

"Try not to be awed, sir," Fabius said sternly. "This is still your country, remember."

"True," Carthalo murmured. "And these Hatti are no more than a band of vagabonds and raiders, no matter how many there are."

"Quite right, sir."

The Hatti party drew up below the headland. The sin-gle chariot was escorted by a hefty troop of soldiers dressed in the Hatti style, with their conical hats, and peculiar boots with the toes upturned.

Fabius muttered an order, and the Carthaginians be-gan the gentle descent to meet the Hatti. Gisco made sure none of his troops raised a weapon. Still, Nelo could feel the tension rise as they approached the Hatti; a great deal of blood had already been spilled on this shore.

Nelo was surprised to find he recognized the man who led the Hatti party, dismounting now from the chariot. A young man with an air of command, with a queue of hair like a soldier's, dressed not in armor but in a richly embroidered ground-length robe; this was Arnuwanda, prince of New Hattusa, who had come to Northland two years ago, and had been stranded there when the first bad winter closed in.

Arnuwanda spoke in clear, stilted Hatti, and the man who had driven the chariot proclaimed a translation in Carthaginian. "You may bow in the presence of Arnuwanda, son of Arnuwanda, who was nephew to My Sun the King Hattusili, the sixteenth of that name."

Fabius bowed deeply but waved aside the translation, and replied in Hatti himself. Arnuwanda looked surprised, then grinned.

Aides muttered a hasty translation for the benefit of Carthalo and the rest. "The general says he knows Nesili and will address the prince in his own tongue."

Fabius spoke again.

"What did the Roman say?" Carthalo snapped.

"He asked, 'How was your journey?' "

The two parties merged, cautiously, and began to make their way down toward the Hatti port. Fabius and Arnuwanda continued to speak, translated for the benefit of the Carthaginians.

"Roman, the journey was dramatic," Arnuwanda said. "First came the March of the Hatti, as history will know it, across Anatolia to the southern ports. That in itself was an epic adventure that will be remembered as long as mankind lives, in the blessing of Jesus Sharruma. You may know that our cities were always stocked with seal-houses of grain—granaries dedicated for the use of the King's war-fighting. We planned the route to pass from one city to the rest, meaning to use the seal-houses. We found almost all of them looted, barren. And, rather than acquiring grain, we generally found ourselves acquiring more people, as each town emptied out and the people followed their Lord Jesus Sharruma. So we progressed across the country, stripping it of whatever food we could find—you can imagine how it was, the country was already starving. We left the country strewn with graves like poppy seeds. We did all this in the full gaze of Jesus Sharruma Our Lord, and built shrines, and kept a careful list of those who died, for they will be remembered when the Hatti return to take back the old lands.

"It was a mighty throng that left New Hattusa; it was a much greater host by the time we reached the southern ports. There we began the process of transport across the sea. This was led by our allies of Hantilios, who as you know are expert seafarers."

Fabius grunted. "I know my history, sir. That city was founded under the protection of the Hatti kings in the first place. It is no wonder its leaders serve you now."

"At a price, as you can imagine, good Fabius, I expect our grandsons still to be paying it off in installments. But Hantilios served us well. Their shipwrights built special vessels for the first landing here on the African shore, which I myself led."

"Ah. The famous flat-bottomed boats that drive up the beaches."

"An ancient design, revived and reworked."

"My men resisted fiercely."

"Yes. As you know, even the first landing was a battle that would dwarf most in human history. Then it was a question of securing our position, of building the harbor to accommodate the hordes who followed us, and preparing for the greater war to come."

"Your harbor is impressive."

"We used Northlander engineers, and their expertise in growstone. We are involved in tremendous undertakings, General."

"Indeed. You spoke of the King. Uhhaziti is the crown

prince, as the whole world knows. Since the death of My Sun the King Hattusili—"

"There will be no coronation until this migration is done," Arnuwanda said. "Uhhaziti has insisted on it. He will be crowned in Carthage, on the Byrsa, and anointed by the Father of the Churches when your greatest temple has been rededicated to the worship of Jesus Sharruma. Not until then."

Fabius nodded gravely. "And I, of course, will stop that from ever happening."

"We understand each other," Arnuwanda said. He glanced curiously at Nelo. "Do I recognize this boy?"

"He serves me."

Mago took the chance to push himself forward, and spoke in Carthaginian. "The boy answers to me; I am his commander. He is a Northlander. You may remember him from that chilly place. And me, perhaps, Prince?"

Arnuwanda stopped, and studied Mago, and replied in the same tongue. "I think I remember you. Your name, though . . ." He hesitated, an obvious bit of playacting.

Mago, infuriated, snapped out his name. "My father is—"

"Yes, yes. So we meet again. Fate draws us all together, it seems. Well—" and he switched back to Nesili, "—let us walk on and talk some more, Fabius. It's refreshing to hear a Latin accent, frankly. So much more melodious than the coarse Can'nai tongue of these fellows . . ."

57

The Hatti's new city had no name. This, it seemed, was
deliberate, a signal of its impermanence; it was an
undertaking the size of New Hattusa itself, but it
was only a way station on the road that led to Carthage.
The core of it, however, was a military camp, and Arnuwanda led Fabius' party through the wider suburbs to that
austere heart. They had to leave the bulk of the Carthaginian force outside, including Mago, who fumed as Nelo
walked on at Fabius' side, with the Carthaginian dignitaries and under the great banner of the joined gods.

The camp itself was surrounded by fortifications,
ditches and berms. Perhaps, Nelo thought, the Hatti rulers
feared their own restless people as much as they feared a
Carthaginian attack—after all, there was an awful lot of
them. Within the fortification, tents and sod huts housed
the soldiers. In some ways it was typical of any military
camp, with many of the troops at ease this morning, or in
training. Wagons trundled, laden with loaves of tough-
looking bread; unlike the Carthaginians, Hatti troops did
not routinely bake their own bread. In one open area

horseback archers were training, and the party stopped to watch the spectacular sight. The men, fully armored, would run their steeds at a target and fling off their arrows without stopping.

Arnuwanda grinned. "I've had a go at that myself, in my time. The rewards are graded. You get a cup of wine if you hit the god's eye in the center, a cup of horse's piss if you miss altogether."

"And which vintage did you sample, my lord?" asked Fabius.

Arnuwanda laughed.

They walked on to an area where more archers were working on their equipment. Evidently these men made their own arrows and bows. They stared at the Carthaginians.

"This is a fine art that I find fascinating," the prince said. "Making the bowstave itself, for instance. You must use the right kind of wood, of course, and not just that, wood from the right part of the tree for each component. Heartwood for the belly of the bow and sapwood for the spine, so it flexes, you see. A delicate business. And here they are making arrows . . ."

The men worked with chisels, adzes and knives, fine tools of iron, bronze, even flint. They fixed arrowheads of various kinds to shafts with silk thread and glue, and tied on feathers as flights.

"The arrowheads have different shapes for different purposes," Arnuwanda said. "I know that much. One kind is designed to pierce armor. Another sort—like that fellow's, with the deep flanges—will knock down a deer."

"Or a warhorse."

"Quite so."

In another open area carpenters and teams of soldiers and slaves labored over large wooden structures that Nelo could not recognize.

"Siege engines," Fabius murmured to Nelo. "Or bits of them. I wonder where they got the wood? Maybe they took some of their ships apart. Rather an ominous sight—and one I'm sure we're meant to witness. Make sure you draw this well, boy; the information may be valuable, in advance of the day we see these beasts trundling up to Carthage's walls."

Nelo sketched busily.

As they walked on he was always aware of the wider city beyond the core of this military camp. In blocks defined by gullies for drainage or sewage, buildings were being put up, sod huts, occasionally structures of stone, perhaps robbed from abandoned Utica. The place was unfinished but had already taken on a kind of human life, with people coming and going, slave-women with baskets of washing going down to the river, old folk sitting on porches, children running and laughing. There were even marketplaces with a few dusty heaps of shoes, tunics, potatoes, cabbages for sale. He had seen the straight-line layout of the place from the rise. Evidently the new city had been planned and laid out before the first inhabitant had moved in, and set out like a sketch on the countryside. Now that outline was being colored in by this muddy mass of people. But in this first rushed impression, Nelo thought there were few babies or old folk, few very young or very old, who must have been winnowed out by the March. He wondered how to capture all this on paper.

Then he saw two laughing boys, no older than five or six, mock-fighting with wooden swords, copying the soldiers. It had taken the Hatti a year to complete their March from New Hattusa to this place, and a year was a long time in the lives of these boys. Perhaps they barely remembered the great city they had left behind. And they were what Nelo chose to sketch, with the strange temporary city in the background, capturing their moment of innocent play forever.

A group of soldiers sat beside a fire, with a pail of water before them. They set pebbles and olive pits on hot rocks by the fire, every so often prodding them to see how warm they were. They glanced up at the Carthaginian party with blank hostility.

Fabius said, "Tell me what these men are doing, sir."

Arnuwanda said, "Just a little ritual our soldiers go through to boost their spirits. These men are scouts; they have seen Carthage, and your ferocious soldiers and your towering defenses. These men must see the enemy truthfully, and report on his strength, truthfully. But truth crushes the spirit, do you see? And so we give them this. The enemy's strength is like the heat of that olive stone. It spits and roars as the stones will when they are put in the water. But it will subside quickly, as will your resistance when the war comes."

"Our soldiers have rituals. Different, but the same idea." Fabius glanced around, squinting. "Sometimes I think that if you could put every soldier in the world in a tremendous camp like this one, and if you kept them all fed, and provided a little wine, a few whores, and let them burn up their energy in a few wrestling contests and such, there need never be war again."

"You have a sentimental streak, Roman. I don't agree. War is in our hearts. We Hatti know that; my dynasty has survived millennia by waging constant war against our enemies. War is what we are *for*, Fabius. It is why the gods created us. That's my view, anyhow, though you'll find some of Jesus' more weak-mouthed apologists with differing ideas. And this war, in particular, is inevitable."

"How many people have you brought over?"

"Now we are settled we are trying to count them. My guess—perhaps as many as a million."

Fabius had to check he understood the Nesili word. "A *million.*"

"We did drain all the Land of the Hatti, Fabius. And there are more on the way; you saw the ships."

"And, whoever wins or loses this war—how many must die, on either side?"

"That is in the hands of the gods."

"Literally so, perhaps," Fabius said. "The Trojans used to see war as a kind of trial. Before the fight you would argue your case before the gods, your own and your enemy's. And then the war itself was a resolution of that trial."

"You know your history."

"In such an age as this, I find it helps."

The soldiers scooped up the hot pebbles with their bare hands and chucked them into the water, where they created a hissing of bubbles, an evanescent rage, before quickly subsiding. Fabius watched this little ritual, and grinned, showing his teeth. Nelo sketched the soldiers and the water and the pebbles, and Fabius' grinning face.

58

The smoke from the burning suburbs of Quinsai billowed across the water as the small boat bearing Avatak and Pyxeas pulled away from the jetty, rowed by a scrawny young Mongol. The harbor was crowded with rowboats and tenders, all trying to leave the city. Small sounds carried over the water, the calling of the crews, the lapping waves, the splash of oars and the snap of sails — and graver sounds from the land, the crump of a collapsing building, throatier roars that might be the firing of eruptors.

Further out, outside the harbor, the great ships floated on the still ocean water. Some were magnificent, serene, their decks crowded with masts like spindly forests — serene at least compared to the frantic scenes in the city. Avatak wondered which of them was waiting for him and Pyxeas.

Pyxeas himself was huddled over, wrapped in a coarse blanket against the unseasonal chill of this early summer day, and with one liver-spotted hand resting on the small trunk that contained his treasure, the records of his study with Bolghai in Daidu. He muttered to himself, barely audible. He seemed to take no notice of the scene around him, the burning city, the crowded harbor.

The Mongol boy was grinning at Avatak as he rowed. "He sick?" He spoke in heavily accented Persian.

"I don't have much of that tongue."

"Yes-yes-yes. Nor me. Ha!" His open mouth revealed gappy teeth, as if the rest had been knocked out. He looked no older than twenty. He was skinny for a Mongol, and the clothes he wore were filthy rags. "We get by, you and me."

"His name is Pyxeas. He's a . . ." Scholar. Avatak tapped his head. "He thinks. Better than other people."

The Mongol shrugged. "Not sick?"

"He's just old. If you're old you're sick all the time."

"Yes-yes-yes. My father, his father, his father, the same. Safe on boat. Listen. Bayan. My name—Bayan. You want anything on the boat, you come to me. Bayan. You remember, yes-yes-yes."

Avatak studied him. Ever since they had come to Quinsai they had been surrounded by people trying to sell them something. "You're a Mongol. What's a Mongol doing at sea?"

Bayan grinned again. "Never liked horses. Horses kick me. I ran away to sea, made some money. Came back, lost money, back to sea. Make more money. Ha! My bad luck, the only Mongol in the world who doesn't like horses. You need anything, ask for Bayan. Remember."

"I'll remember."

Pyxeas was stirring. He raised one hand to point, but his fingers would not fully extend.

Avatak switched to Northlander. "Scholar? What is it?"

"Our ship."

The craft was not the largest, but big enough, Avatak thought, as Bayan rowed the length of its hull—big enough to have dwarfed the fleets that sailed from ports like Hantilios into the puddle of the Middle Sea, even most of the craft that sailed from Northland's Wall harbors to take on the Western Ocean. And, of course, it would have utterly overshadowed the little fishing boats of Avatak's people.

Bayan's boat was only one of a dozen that crowded around the great ship now, bearing passengers, bales of goods, even animals. The crew worked from the top deck and leaned out of open hatchways, hauling up stuff with ropes and pulleys, or carrying it on their backs up ladders. The ship's hull was blackened by fire and much patched; you could see the joins where whole sections had been replaced, fresh planking hammered home and sealed with grayish paste. Close to, the wooden flank smelled of deep-ingrained brine. It was not a pretty ship, like the yachts that had sailed the tame lakes of Daidu for the pleasure of the Khan's courtiers. But Avatak felt reassured at its very roughness. This was a working vessel that had seen tough times before, and survived them; there was every chance, then, that it would survive a little longer, and its passengers along with it.

Bayan brought them to a ladder, dangling in the water. Their few goods were easily transferred by Bayan and a couple of sailors. Avatak would be able to clamber up the ladder easily, but it was soon evident that Pyxeas would not. There was a brief, farcical scene as the stubborn old man tried anyhow, but his gnarled hands would not grip the rope rungs, his booted feet slipped, and he could not raise his weight—he could barely stand, let alone climb. So Bayan and Avatak tried to help him, the Mongol pulling his arms from above, Avatak pushing from below. Other crew gathered on the deck above, offering ribald advice in a dozen tongues.

Eventually a sterner, older man came to investigate. The captain, Avatak supposed. He glanced down at the scene in the boat, and looked out at Quinsai, and Avatak saw the burning city reflected in his black eyes. Bearded, wearing a turban and a crisp white gown, he had the look of an Arab—this was an Arab-owned ship, though of Cathay manufacture. He snapped a quick order to Bayan, and turned away.

Bayan shrugged. "Al-Quds is the captain and he wants to be gone. 'Get on with it,' he says. Poor Bayan! Now then, master—"

Without ceremony he caught Pyxeas by the legs and lifted him over his shoulder. Pyxeas struggled feebly, but seemed too weak to protest. Thus laden, Bayan made his way up the rope ladder. Avatak was impressed by his skill, pushing one-handed from one rung to the next so that with every step up he had to balance without a handhold, and managing Pyxeas' not inconsiderable weight as if he were no more than a sack of feathers.

Once on deck, Bayan set Pyxeas upright. The scholar seemed bewildered, disoriented. Bayan headed for their cabin, while a couple of the crew carried their trunk and baggage. Avatak led Pyxeas gently by the hand across the rocking deck.

From up here, the ship looked even more substantial than from the ocean. Its four masts were laden with sails of matted bamboo, furled for now, and two more great masts lay like tree trunks, lashed to the deck. There were structures on the deck like little wooden houses, and hatches were thrown open to show the interior below, great holds where goods were being stored, sacks and jars and barrels. From some of the holds came the sounds of animals—lowing, bleating, clucking—and a stench of straw and dung. Despite the noise and the chaos Avatak could see the crew were working methodically, moving goods around the holds to balance the weight on either side of the ship. He wondered how many crew there were—hundreds perhaps. There were many passengers too, like themselves, Cathay, Mongols, Arabs, most of them presumably traders, hurrying across the deck and in and out of open doorways.

"Watertight holds," Pyxeas murmured unexpectedly.

"What was that, scholar?"

"Watertight holds. A feature of these great vessels.

See? Hole one of them and it will flood but the ship won't sink. The shipwrights of the west have got a lot to learn." But then his eyes clouded, a look of confusion returned to his gaunt face, and he retreated inside himself.

They had to clamber down a short stair, Pyxeas managed with difficulty, to the small cabin that had been allotted them. There were two narrow bunks, one table, a few shelves with rails to stop their possessions falling off when the ship rolled, and a tiny glassless window through which a stiff breeze pushed, bearing a scent of smoke from the fires on land. Bayan and the other crew crowded around, their hands held out. Avatak had a pouch of coins at his waist; he doled out one to each man. He had spread his wealth around a number of pouches and satchels and pockets, including a few of Uzzia's gems, most of which were still sewn into the quilted coat, which he wore. He hoped that these layers of deception would distract thieving fingers enough to enable them to reach Carthage with some of their wealth intact.

Now the turbaned captain pushed into the cabin, carrying a slate. His nose was strong, his face masked by a gray-flecked beard, but his large, dark eyes were oddly gentle as he inspected Pyxeas. "You are the scholar? And his man." His Northlander was passable.

Pyxeas stood and drew himself to his full height. "I am he, Pyxeas," he said in rich Northlander, and repeated the words in Persian. "The boy is called Avatak."

The captain made tick marks on his slate. "Good. You may call me al-Quds. It is not my name, which nobody in Cathay can pronounce, but it's the name of the holy city where I was born, and it'll do."

"I will need quiet," Pyxeas said sternly. "I have work to do—vital work. I must not be disturbed. You cannot comprehend the importance."

"Can I not?"

Pyxeas glanced around at the cabin, the tiny table. "I suppose this must suffice." He sat uncertainly on one of the bunks.

The Arab raised his eyebrows at Avatak.

Avatak shrugged. "He's a scholar."

"Well, for the next months, he's to be a scholar and a sailor." He eyed Avatak. "What are you, a Mongol? Not a Northlander."

"Not a Mongol. From very far west."

"Do you know the world? Perhaps you can explain it to your scholar friend. We are making for Carthage. To do that we must sail south and west and across three oceans, of Cathay, of Indh, of the Arabs. If we survive all that we will pass through the Gulf of Africa, and then through the Canal of Hasdrubal, if it is still open, if it hasn't been clogged up by war or piracy, to the Middle Sea. And on the way I'll do my very best to keep the noise down," he said drily.

"I will explain it to the scholar. He has family in Carthage; he is eager to return to them."

"And I have paymasters, and I'm eager to return to *them*. You're among the last to board. What of the city?"

"The siege will be over soon, I think." Since the spring Quinsai had been assailed by rough armies of Mongol factions, Cathay dissidents and steppe nomads. "Every night it burns. Quinsai has always burned. Now they are failing to douse the fires before they spread."

"Then it will all be up soon."

Avatak felt motivated to try to explain, to this evidently thoughtful, competent man, the man who now held Avatak's own life in his hands, and Pyxeas'. "It is the longwinter. People fleeing the weather, on the move. My master says we must expect war this year. Across the whole world, wherever we go."

"That's a cheerful thought. Let's hope *we* have nothing but the sea to contend with." He nodded to Pyxeas and withdrew, closing the door.

Pyxeas was already picking at the clasps of his trunk. "Help me with this thing, would you? I must make a start, I must."

59

The Third Year of the Longwinter:
Midsummer Solstice

This time the Hatti raiding party tried to get into Carthage from the northwest, near the suburb of Megara. Gisco was given a corps of men and ordered to stop them.

The Hatti were probing at an acknowledged weak point in the ancient defenses of the city, Gisco knew, where the land wall approached the shore and cut eastward to follow the line of the coast. The shore itself was protected by barricades of tremendous growstone blocks on the land, and nasty hull-ripping traps underwater—but there was no assistance from the Carthaginian navy, which had been bottled up since early in the siege, when the Hatti had blocked Carthage's main harbor with their mole across its mouth. Even so it had cost the Hatti a lot of lives to land on that lethal shore. But land they had, according to the Carthaginian scouts, and had immediately begun burrowing under the city wall.

Gisco had no way of driving the Hatti off from the seaward side of the wall, or of stopping them tunneling. So instead he formed up his own men to dig counter-tunnels *under* the Hatti workings, the idea being to come up from below and attack them. Gisco joined in the digs himself; it seemed only right.

They couldn't be sure where the Hatti were digging, and had to proceed by guesswork and surveys. Every hour or so the officers would have the men stop work, and listen for the thud and hammer of the Hatti. Gisco knew these intervals of silence would always be vivid in his memory: the gaunt, hungry men stripped to the waist in the light of the candles and oil lanterns, the muscles of their arms like knotted rope, panting, filthy, hot, hearing the scurrying of the Hatti above, like huge mice in a loft.

In the end the climax came unexpectedly.

One moment the Carthaginians were digging calmly—the next the roof fell in with a roar, and earth, broken timbers and struggling soldiers and slaves tumbled down on them. The lamps were extinguished immediately, and Gisco found himself in the pitch-dark, in a compressed mass of men, slipping on mounds of earth and rubble. And a huge, heavy man fell right on top of him, arms and legs splayed, knocking him to the ground. Gisco could smell the horse stink of the man's sweat, and the tang of some kind of bread on his breath. The man seemed briefly stunned, shocked. The Hatti must have had no warning of the collapse.

So Gisco raised his steel dagger and slammed it into the man's neck.

The blade scraped on bone. The man convulsed and spewed hot blood, and inadvertently butted Gisco, his forehead slamming into Gisco's nose. Gisco's face became a mask of blinding pain, and he swore out loud. Enraged, he hauled out his knife and dragged the blade through soft tissues and cartilage, cutting the man's throat. The man quivered and died, not having landed a single conscious blow.

Gisco shoved him aside, and on he fought. At first, in the dark, he could only tell who was friend or foe by subtle signals, by muttered curses in an exotic language, or prayers to Teshub or Jesus. He tried to bring his men together, calling out, "With me, Carthaginians! With Gisco! With me!"

Then the Hatti workings collapsed altogether, with another rush of earth. The pit was opened up to the night sky, where a half-moon hung, tinted orange by the dusty air of this dry summer. Even by moonlight the men looked alike, all half-naked, none of them wearing uniforms or much in the way of armor. It didn't help that such a variety of races fought on either side, the Carthaginians with their Libyan levies and Iberans and Balearic herdsmen, and on the Hatti side Scand. They were men from across the known world dumped in a pit to struggle for their lives, like playthings of some malevolent god.

But gradually, Gisco perceived, the Carthaginians were prevailing. They had had the marginal advantage of knowing what to expect; it must have been a great shock for the Hatti when the floor fell out from under them.

Finally a Hatti officer cried out in his own tongue, and repeated the word in Carthaginian. "Yield! Yield!" For a time the killing went on, of its own momentum, and Gisco thought he heard the officer himself take a blade in the chest.

But at last it was done.

Gisco, panting hard, slippery with blood and sweat, tried to organize his surviving men to round up the captives and see to the wounded.

A man came up to him with a lantern. It was Suniatus, a grinning brute. Blood leaked from a long cut on his forehead into his eyes, but he didn't seem to be aware of it. "Good scrap, sir."

Gisco clapped the man on his bloody shoulder. "It was indeed, Suni. Carthage is saved, for now."

Suniatus turned and whooped. "Hear that, boys? We're heroes. The tarts in Megara are going to take some punishment today! Even from you, sir, despite the mess some bugger has made of your face."

Gisco reached up to touch his imploded nose, and a wave of agony convulsed his face. "Yes, all right, Suni—"

There was a tremendous groaning crack from aboveground, and the earth shuddered as if massive weights had tumbled down. The men started shouting. What now?

"A ladder, Suniatus. Quickly, man!"

Gisco worked his way up the ladder to the level of the Hatti digs. He had time to be briefly impressed by how well constructed the Hatti tunnels were, the walls and roof of packed earth, the tunnel wide and spacious. There was even timber to prop up the roof, although widely spaced, for timber was desperately scarce. But he reminded himself that his own more modest mole runs had done their job in the end. He clambered on up above the Hatti works to ground level.

When he emerged into the air he was surprised to find how close he was to the city wall, still within its protection on the Carthaginian side, but he was no more than twenty paces from its massive base; his surveyors had got that wrong, and not for the first time. But the Hatti digs, or maybe a combination of their work and the Carthaginians' own counter-digging, had undermined the wall. It slumped visibly, and the cracking he heard had been the beginning of a tremendous split that looked as if it cut right through the wall's fabric. Massive facing stones, blocks half his own height, had fallen away to slam into the ground, leaving a looser core of rubble that was shattering and spilling as he watched.

And he saw a helmeted head pop up over the widening breach: a Hatti scout. Gisco flung a dagger, and the head ducked back down.

In the runs below Gisco, Suniatus and another ladder-bearing friend stood looking up. Gisco kicked the second man on the shoulder. "You. Run to the next watchtower and tell them to get a message to the commanders."

"What message, sir?"

"What message?" Gisco was maddened by the pain

of his smashed face. "What message do you think? Oh, tell them Sergeant Gisco wishes the great General Fabius a restful night. Tell them about the wall breach, man! Go, go." The man ran off. "As for you, Suniatus, the thighs of those whores in Megara are going to have to remain untroubled a little longer, for until reinforcements arrive it's going to be you and me and whoever's left alive down there to hold off the Hatti that are soon going to be coming over that wall."

"The prisoners—"

"Oh, slaughter them. Just get the men up here."

A single arrow came arcing over the wall. Gisco ducked into the dirt. The arrow thudded harmlessly to the ground to his right. Dawn was breaking. This was midsummer day, he remembered. More arrows hailed down.

"Suniatus! Get your ass up here!"

60

Three days after midsummer day, three days after the Hatti's latest attack on the walls of Carthage, Hastayar the Tawananna herself led the Hatti party that approached the city's great gate, in response to the Carthaginians' latest offer of negotiation. Thus went this war, Kassu thought, a huge oscillation between bouts of bloody warfare and stiff, usually futile attempts at reconciliation.

A pall of smoke, yellowish, hung over the city as the Hatti party approached, and Kassu, walking in the train with his wife, Henti, at his side, wondered what could be left in that hulk of a city to burn. The day was bright and the sun high, though the air was no hotter than usual, and the Hatti queen walked under a canopy carried by four favored servants—including Pimpira, Kassu's "nephew." The awning itself was a spectacular tapestry, a minor masterpiece of Hatti art, and a great banner of Jesus Sharruma with crossed palm leaves went before Hastayar. The invitation to serve had been an honor for the relative of a serving officer, but Kassu wondered what Hastayar would think if she knew the boy's true origin.

Pimpira limped bravely, compensating for the deformity of his foot. The sight of him there made Kassu obscurely proud. He had failed at many things in his life, but at least he had saved this one boy.

Kassu himself, in brightly polished mail and his best cloak, walked behind the main Hatti party. Henti carried a bowl of potatoes, gathered from the bit of farmland they had been granted, a day's walk from the Hatti camp-city, dispossessed from a Libyan family. Fifty soldiers' wives in this party were carrying such bowls. The potatoes were a symbolic gift for the Carthaginians, to show them the Hatti besiegers were not starving, that they could afford to be generous. The bowl was heavy, and Henti looked hot, weary, displeased. They barely spoke. They rarely did these days. Kassu had saved her life, and Palla's, but he had not been able to save his marriage, it seemed, apart from the outer form.

Then the wind changed, and the smoke from the city wafted over them. Kassu smelled meat, grease: the smoke of funeral pyres. Henti winced and turned her head, but with her two hands holding the bowl she could not cover her face.

Only a handful of advisers walked with the queen under the awning: Tiwatapara, who had once been Hazannu of New Hattusa, the general Himuili with a small, carefully selected guard—and Palla, the young priest, dressed in elaborate robes of purple embroidered with gold. It sickened Kassu to his stomach to see Palla there. But he had to admit Palla was doing well during this extraordinary war, filling the gap left by his superior, Angulli Father of the Churches, who was usually either insensible with drink or raging because of the lack of it.

The Carthaginians themselves waited before the gate, the dignitaries on a spectacular podium under a white linen roof, bright in the sunlight. Perhaps a thousand troops had been drawn up in parade order before the gate, a show of strength; Kassu recognized Libyans, Iberans, Franks, Balearics, in among the Carthaginian phalanxes. But despite this splendor the ground before them was scarred by defensive ditches and berms, and the face of the great wall behind the Carthaginians was blackened by fire. Once there had been fine suburbs out here beyond the city's protecting walls, the homes of the rich, even hunting palaces. Now all that had been demolished by the Hatti, stripped and burned, any inhabitants caught outside the walls driven off, sold into slavery or slaughtered. Even the Carthaginian army had retreated to within the walls of their city now, despite the crowding inside.

In the Carthaginian pavilion, chairs and low tables had been set out on a huge ornate rug. After an elaborate formal ceremonial the Tawananna and her advisers were seated in the pavilion, facing their hosts. Servants circulated with trays of sweetmeats and jugs of wine. Of the Carthaginians, Kassu recognized only Fabius, the Roman general, who had made sure the enemy troops knew his name and reputation. The rest, mainly men, mostly dressed in elaborate robes, were evidently courtiers—or whatever the equivalent was in Carthage, which was a strange city that had no king. The group broke into huddles of conversation, while interpreters and aides murmured in their ears. Around the dignitaries, soldiers on both sides stood with their cloaks held back and their hands hovering over the hilts of swords.

Kassu could hear his own general Himuili speaking to Fabius, and he could understand, for the cultured Roman spoke the Hatti's Nesili tongue. They made a contrast, though. While a huge ferocious Rus stood behind Himuili, Fabius' only close companion was a boy, unarmed, who sat on a low stool, scribbling, drawing, writing.

The pyre smoke was the first thing Himuili mentioned. "By Jesus' mercy, Roman, you're roasting the pork this morning."

Fabius grinned, not offended. "The clear-out of the night's dead. We've long run out of anywhere to inter them, trapped within our walls as we are, and so we burn.

As do you, for my scouts have spied out your daily pyres, Himuili, so you needn't deny it."

"Of course we burn to get rid of the plague victims — and you have it in Carthage as well as we do, *and you* needn't deny *that.*"

"Must it be like this, Himuili?"

Himuili nodded. "You and I know what a siege is like. You begin with trumpet blasts and bright banners and dreams of glory. Before long it's disease and hunger and filth, and latrine trenches running with liquid shit and vomit."

"But do our masters know this?"

"At least my lord the prince Arnuwanda has served on more than one battlefield. Whereas the fat old men who command you, Roman — what are they, merchants, landowners, farmers? And, I hear, when they get bored with their generals they put them on trial and nail them to the nearest tree."

"We haven't reached that point quite yet."

Himuili shrugged. "Spare yourself that fate. All you need do is persuade your merchant bosses to open the city gates to us, and the war will cease."

"Really?"

"We have not come to destroy, or slaughter. The Hatti kingdom has always been open to people of all kinds — New Hattusa was always a land of a thousand tongues, under the mercy of Jesus Sharruma. We don't want to destroy Carthage. All we wish is to *share.*"

"You are a million strong! Come to *share* a land already starving?"

"But what choice is there? After all, we can't withdraw, for we have nowhere to go. Your merchant princes must understand that. And even if you were somehow to manage a victory over us, what would you do with us all?"

"Sell you as slaves in return for wheat. Egypt is a big country. Always lots of work for slaves. You could build a new mausoleum for the Pharaoh, perhaps."

Himuili laughed. "You do amuse me, Fabius. Are all Romans comedians?"

Fabius grunted. "Since we've been the butt of jokes by the all-conquering Carthaginians since before your Jesus walked the world, we have to be."

"Ha! I've heard some of them. What do you call a Roman raising a cup of victory wine? The waiter! But time is running out for you, comedian." Himuili leaned forward, intent. "My own spies tell me that. Factions at your court are pressing you to come out of these walls and give battle."

"You know as well as I do that you Hatti would probably win such a battle. Which is why it won't happen. Besides, there's an equally vocal faction on the councils who want to negotiate some kind of peace."

"And you, what passes for a military commander in this city, must try to satisfy the contradictory demands of your rulers."

"This is the Carthaginian way, Himuili, and it's served them well for a long time."

"Hmm. If you ask me, they've already got you crucified, Roman."

Fabius drily raised his cup of wine to his opponent.

Now the event reached some subtle milestone. The servants withdrew and more formal negotiations began, with the Tawananna directly addressing the senior Carthaginians, amid a buzz of translators and assistants.

The talks lasted hours. Kassu and Henti stood in stiff silence, with the silent ranks of aides, servants, slaves and soldiers.

It was fruitless, of course. Despite the courtly politeness and the elaborate exchange of gifts, there could be no peace; the Hatti could not withdraw from the field, and the Carthaginians could not afford to open their gates. The meeting ended in pleasantries, and no agreement. This had been the pattern of the whole campaign season.

The very next day the Hatti launched another attack.

61

I n Carthage, the cry of alarm went up before dawn.

Nelo, in the barracks he shared with a hundred soldiers just inside Carthage's walls, heard it echo from watchtower to watchtower, and then within the city itself, along the streets and alleys, in the market squares and temple places. And he thought he heard shouts and screams.

Gisco was on his feet, fully armed. It was as if he never slept. "Up! Up, you buggerers, up you get, on with your boots and your scabbards."

Suniatus rolled out of bed and belched, and from paces away Nelo could smell the stale wine on his breath. "Those Hatti ball-sacks sound like they're having another go, Sergeant."

"So they are, lad."

"What's our assignment?"

"We're going up one of the gate towers. The scouts have been here with the news. Lads, this time the Hatti have managed to get the gate itself open, and they're already swarming in the city like maggots in a corpse."

"What? How? Those gates have stood all summer."

Gisco laughed as the men hurried to piss in their night pots, to dress, to find their boots and helmets. "All summer! That's what I like about you, Suni. A real sense of history, just as the general once said to you. Lad, those walls have stood *a thousand years* without being breached. Even the Muslims couldn't knock them down when they came calling. And they haven't fallen now. The problem is somebody has conveniently *opened* the gate. Just a crack, but that's all that was needed."

"Who did it, Sergeant?"

"Doesn't matter. What does matter is that the Hatti have to be stopped. And they'll be stopped by us. You too, Nelo, get that coat of mail on, I'm sure your lord and master will want a scribble of what's to be done today. And, you never know, you might decide you'd like to share in a bit of fighting after all. Right. All ready? To the gate—this way."

Without looking back, he led the troops out of the barracks. The men, some still buckling armor or fixing their helmets, followed Gisco at a trot through crowded streets. Nelo ran with the rest.

They were at the south side of the sprawling suburb of Megara. Their barracks was actually an old warehouse, requisitioned when the army corps had had to abandon their camp and move inside the safety of the city walls, a transfer that had made Carthage even more crowded, even more tense, even more dangerous. It was barely dawn, and Nelo smelled the tang of desert sand in the air. Another dust storm must have blown over in the night, but at least it muffled the stink of the ever-burning funeral pyres.

The alarm had been raised. As they hurried to the gate, they had to push through crowds running the other way: men and women, mothers carrying infants, old folk, the ill and feeble being helped or carried along, and in a city riddled with disease and hunger there were plenty of them. Gisco's troops had to push their way through the fleeing mob.

Then they turned a corner—and Nelo was confronted with the sight of enemy troops, *inside the city*, standing and fighting before the half-open gate. But they weren't Hatti. These towering men, fighting knots of hastily assembled Carthaginian troops, were Rus or Scand, with long tunics over baggy trousers and leather boots, and caps and coats lined with fur. They wore their red hair, beards and mustaches long, and any exposed skin was dense with tattoos, intricate scribbles over faces, hands, bare arms. Some of them fought with barbed stabbing spears, some threw javelins. But the most ferocious of all used axes, each longer than a man's arm and fitted with a single crescent-shaped blade tapered to widen back from the edge, a design that made it horribly efficient in its function. Nelo, staring, saw one man get in a clean blow at his Carthaginian opponent, a single downward swipe that cut through the man's mail coat and tunic and splayed open his breastbone and ribs, lodging in a mass of intestines before he fell forward.

Before such warriors, wave after wave of Carthaginian troops pressed forward only to fall in their turn, and the cobbles already ran with their blood. A horrific battle, taking place within the walls of Carthage itself. Was the city lost already?

Suniatus and some of the others would have dashed straight into the fray, but Gisco roared commands. "Not here! Not yet! You'll do no good to be cut down like these poor lads. Follow me, and we'll win the day. This way, this way!"

The gatehouse was one of a pair of massive stone towers that sat on either side of the gate itself. Gisco led a dozen men up a stone staircase; soon they were panting with the exertion. Through slit windows Nelo saw the battle opening out beneath him, a pool of struggling, fighting, dying men before the open gate, and a greater Hatti force outside the wall, pressing to enter. At the top of the tower was a small chamber with glassless windows that looked out at the plain beyond the city, where the fires of the Hatti sparked, as innumerable as the stars in the sky.

Nelo was bewildered by what he saw in this crowded room. On the stone flags stood massive wooden barrels, brimming with what smelled like pitch. Under the command of an army officer, two harassed-looking slaves were using buckets to transfer this sticky slop to a smaller container set in the middle of the room. This container was connected to what looked like a two-handled pump, a lever fixed over a single pivot; Nelo had seen similar gadgets used to clear minor floods in Northland. And from the container ran a kind of hose, with its nozzle dangling out of the window over the Rus and Scand and their foe.

Gisco nodded to the officer in command. "Here's the muscle you asked for, Sili."

"You took your time!"

Gisco hastily dumped his helmet and weapons. "Get these slaves out of the way. You two!" He pointed to Suniatus and another man. "Work this pump. See?" He grabbed the handle and, with an effort, raised and lowered it. Nelo heard the pitch gurgle in the hose. "And you"—he picked two more—"get the hose. Hold it out of that window so you can get the stuff all over the Hatti and their Rus attack dogs. Understand?"

"No, Sergeant."

"Just do it. The rest of you stand by. Watch that door, the stairs—don't let *anybody* in until this is over. Got that? And be ready to replace the others at the pumps and the hose. And you, Northlander. Watch. Listen. Draw. Show your Roman master how clever we Carthaginians are."

The man Sili muttered, "Or at least the Syrians, from whom we long ago stole this trick."

"Shut up, Sili. Just have the wick lit and ready. All set, lads? Get pumping. Hold up that hose. Hold it up!"

Soon black liquid was squirting fitfully out of the hose. Nelo saw it rain down on Carthaginians and the

Hatti and their colleagues alike. It was just mucky, oily sludge, and none of the fighters even looked up from the work of slaughter as it fell on them.

But Gisco called down in his own tongue, "Fall back! Down there—fall back!" To the blank astonishment of the Hatti, the Carthaginian soldiers broke and ran, as if leaving the way into the city clear.

Sili brought forward a lit taper. At arm's length, cautiously, he applied it to the sludge as it emerged from the nozzle.

And the stream turned into a jet of fire, liquid, dense, brilliant, yellow-white, that poured from the hose and rained down over the Hatti and their allies below. Where it touched a man it burned furiously, and though the men rolled on the ground and beat at the flames with their bare hands, it would not be doused. One man hurled himself into a horse trough, but even water would not quench the flaming liquid, which clung and scorched and blazed.

The men holding the hose had been terrified when this fiery breath had leapt from the nozzle. They would have abandoned their place if not for Gisco's roar. Now they yelled in triumph, as the Hatti below screamed. But then the hose burst, just behind the nozzle, showering the men's hands and arms with burning stuff. They fell back howling, burning.

Gisco pushed them aside and ordered two more men forward. "Bring that fresh hose! Bring it now!"

Nelo stared at the carnage outside by the gate, where screaming men were turning to human torches, and inside this gatehouse, where soldiers he had barracked with just last night rolled and writhed in agony, and Suniatus and the other man pumped, terrified, and he drew and drew.

62

n the Sea of Indh, the ship was struck by a great storm.
There had already been trouble, from bandits in
the water and boats and rafts full of nestspills, all imploring passage. The great continent of Indh, to the
north of here, was in turmoil as Mongols invaded from
the north, fleeing the cold, to meet ferocious resistance
from the Hindu population and the Turkish sultans who
ruled them. Avatak had watched Bayan and the rest of
the crew fend off skinny, half-starved nestspills with
oars and pikes as they crowded around on their water-
logged craft, some of them holding up infants for sanctuary. All this added to the anxiety of the crew, who,
Avatak learned, were much perturbed by the disruption
of wind and weather patterns, which had always been
predictable on these great ocean highways. Even without human threats, sailing had become a much chancier
business.

And now, the storm. It took days to gather. The first
sign Avatak noticed was a steadily rising swell that
lapped against the ship's hull, gathering into white-

flecked waves that rocked the vessel. That was all: the air was calm, the sky clear of clouds; only the sea was restless. But the sailors watched the weather anxiously, muttering in the coarse Persian that was their common argot that it was not the season to expect such conditions. Then a lid of feathery cloud covered the sky, and descended, horribly quickly. Lost in gray fog, the sailors began to make fast the sails and lash loose goods and fittings in place. The captain brusquely told the passengers to stay in their cabins, and they were given a couple of days' ration of biscuits and beer to keep them happy.

Pyxeas had barely stirred from the cabin anyway, and complained only when the rocking of the ship, the howl of the wind, disturbed his concentration. Avatak spent a lot of time standing at the window, holding down the scraped leather cover to keep the draft out of the cabin. He watched the sea surge, and the wind tearing at the crests of the waves, scattering spray that flew horizontally. He began to see strange sights in that sea, trees uprooted, a dead cow floating with its legs stuck up in the air—debris from the land where the storm must already have struck. He saw nestspills too, their fragile craft smashed, bloated bodies drifting in rags.

Still the seas rose, still the winds gathered until no man could stand on deck, still the clouds raced over the sky, dark and menacing. And suddenly the rain lashed down, coming in horizontally, hammering against the hull, leaking through the slightest gap. It washed into the cabin and over the scholar's pages, evoking furious complaint, unless Avatak held the leather cover firmly in place with both hands.

Then, suddenly, the storm went away. The sea was calm again, the rain vanished, the winds dropped. Avatak and Pyxeas exchanged puzzled glances; this did not seem natural. The air felt warmer than it had done for days, warm and humid, sticky. Avatak cautiously peered out of his window. By a peculiar golden light he saw a flat sea littered with debris, some of it having come from the ship—barrels, what looked like a snapped mast—but, further out, there was a mass of cloud, low, racing by.

"The eye of the storm," Pyxeas said, marveling. "Remarkable. I've heard travelers tell of it; I never expected to experience it myself. But don't relax, Avatak; the storm is not done with us yet."

He was right. Soon that wall of cloud roared toward the ship, and they were plunged back into the storm as abruptly as they had left it.

The ship survived the storm, thanks largely, Avatak suspected, to the clear-thinking command of al-Quds, although if you listened to Bayan's bragging it was all down to him. A handful of crew had been lost, one passenger, and one hold had been broken open and flooded, drowning a few pedigree goats.

On the first calm day, Avatak went down to the ship's galley and returned with a small tray. A *very* small tray. It bore two biscuits, flour and fat baked and compressed until they were hard as fired clay, and one sack of weak beer. Thus their ration for the day.

Pyxeas, as was his wont, had spread his work over the cabin's two bunks, the small table, the open trunk, even the floor, and Avatak had to be careful where he stepped. He found an empty spot on one of the bunks and set down the tray. Then he sat on the floor, his back against the closed door, and got to work at mouthing one of the biscuits, hoping to soften it a little before a first attempt at biting into it.

The ship rolled, and Pyxeas looked around uneasily, as if remembering where he was. "You're back! I didn't see you return."

Avatak was used to that. "Scholar, when you work, you see nothing else *but* the work."

The wind shifted, and a slaughterhouse stink drifted up from the holds.

Pyxeas pressed a cloth to his nose. "The ability to concentrate is a rare gift, boy," he said. "One you would do well to acquire. I myself would never have dreamed I would be able to achieve substantial work in conditions like this, in this, this *cage*."

"Yes, scholar."

Pyxeas noticed the tray with the single remaining biscuit, and the sack of beer. "What's this, breakfast?"

Avatak sighed. "Dinner, scholar. It's later than you think. But actually that's breakfast, lunch, dinner, supper, rolled into one. Not even bribing Bayan helped this time."

"I thought the captain promised to reprovision. Fresh fruit, he said! Fresh water!"

"He's not been able to put into the ports, scholar."

"Why not?"

"Plague," Avatak said simply.

Pyxeas grunted. "It would take a brave king to put his people at such risk for the sake of stocking up a few hungry sailors. Well, the spread of plagues is to be expected—I wrote it down in my notes some years ago, you can check it. When people are stirred up and on the move, and animal populations too, plagues are carried from their natural reservoirs, even carried between continents. It's about time al-Quds sacrificed a few of those prize cattle down in the holds to feed us. I must have a word with him, I must . . ." He gazed at the biscuit, picked it up, then set it down again, as if puzzled by its very presence. Then he glanced at Avatak. "The numbers, boy—it's all in the numbers. It always was."

"What numbers?"

Distracted, the scholar cast about, shifting in his chair, and brought together lists of numbers, either in the hand of a scribe or his own spidery writing, some set out neatly on scrolls or books, some scrawled on scraps of paper and parchment. "Thank the mothers Bolghai was good enough to have his results translated into the North-lander system. Here now—can you see?" He pointed to two lists of numbers.

"See what? I'm sorry, scholar."

"Of course you won't see it, of course not, it's been staring me in the face for years, it *still is*, and I can make no firm conclusion, not yet... Look! What drives the weather, I mean the grand changes like the coming of a longwinter?"

"The sun in the sky," Avatak said promptly; he had absorbed that much.

"Yes. Good. The world bobs about like a duck on the Khan's ornamental ponds in Daidu. The higher the sun is at midsummer, the warmer the world is that year. But *how* high, *how* warm? We Northlanders have been keeping records of the weather for millennia. And in those records I, Pyxeas, have found a good measure of that changing warmth.

"Look here—*this* is a list of years, and *this* is a list of solar elevations at Etxelur at midday on midsummer day on each of those years. And *these* dates, Avatak, record the last spring frost of each year and the first frost of winter. Pieces of information easily and unambiguously recorded, and though they vary with circumstance, the overall trend is clearly related to the warmth of the year. Can you see the correlation between the two? Oh, it takes a trained eye. Avatak, these tables show conclusively that the elevation of the sun drives our climate, as indicated by the span of the frost. *But.*"

"But, scholar?"

"But the tidy patterns break down! Centuries, millennia back, you can see it. The world should have got colder, quicker. The longwinter should already be here! I had long suspected this, from historical accounts, anecdotes. Now, after intensive study, I have assembled quantitative proof."

"Then there is another agent, acting to postpone the longwinter."

"Yes. Good! And that agent is?"

Avatak considered before answering; he had fallen into Pyxeas' verbal traps before. He said carefully, "You *suspect* that the agent has something to do with the various airs Bolghai was studying."

"Yes! Especially the fixed air, which holds back the heat. Good. But how? And why? That is the question I wrestle with. And I *still* can't see it, I can't. Though I suspect I edge closer to the truth." He glared at Avatak. "Suppose I fell over the side of this wretched tub tomorrow. Would you be able to communicate all this to the scholars of Etxelur?"

"No," Avatak said frankly.

Pyxeas nodded. "And could they progress the work without me? No! Those dolts in Etxelur have always been too busy questioning me and my methodology rather than *listening*. Than *thinking*. Very well! I, Pyxeas, must resolve this planetary conundrum, or go insane in the attempt. Yes?"

"Yes, scholar." Avatak took a moment to pop his biscuit into the sack of beer, hoping it would soften a bit more, before he bent with Pyxeas over the tablets, scrolls and books.

63

Nelo saw it all, that fateful day, the day that everything changed, for Fabius, for Carthage—for everybody. Saw it all from beginning to end. Drew it all, and remembered.

It began before dawn, on another chill late summer's day. Nelo, in his barrack, was woken by a shake from Gisco, unexpectedly gentle, not the usual boot in the back. "Out you get, aurochs," he murmured. "Got a special job for you. But keep quiet about it. No need to disturb the other cock-pullers in their slumbers. You too, Suniatus."

"Sergeant—"

"What did I say?" Gisco snapped, in a whisper. "Keep that mouth of yours shut."

The barrack room was dark, with only a single sputtering lantern burning in one corner. After another night in here the air was thick with beery farts, the acid stink of rotting feet. Only Nelo and Suniatus were moving; the rest of the troop slumbered on.

Suniatus pulled on socks and boots. "Just us, Sergeant?"

"Just you."

"Why? I mean, why me and *that*?" He jerked a thumb at Nelo.

"Because I can trust you two. Yes, you as well, Northlander, I know I can rely on you to follow an order while keeping your mouth shut, and you can do this little job for me and still be free to scribble your drawings for the rest of the day. This army of ours is full of useless Libyans, and useless sods, and useless Libyan sods, and two reliable men are hard to find."

Suniatus grinned. "Hear that, aurochs? You're reliable." He picked up his sword in its scabbard. "So what's the job, Sergeant?"

"To save Carthage."

"What, again?"

"Just get on with it."

Nelo grabbed his weapons and satchel and made for the door. Suniatus couldn't resist clowning; he walked on exaggerated tiptoe and shoved Nelo in the back, trying to make him stumble. But they got out of the barracks without disturbing anybody else.

They emerged onto a silent street. The sand that had blown in from the desert scraped on the cobbles under Nelo's boots. Gisco had left a lantern by the barracks door; he raised this now and scrutinized a bit of paper. Nelo saw it was a list of addresses, all in Megara. This barracks, by the city wall, was on the periphery of the suburb.

Suniatus glanced over the sergeant's shoulder. "I know the first address, sir. That street anyhow. There's a whorehouse where they have these Balearic women who—"

"All right, Suni. Just lead the way."

The soldier strode confidently through the darkened streets. With experience Suniatus was becoming a good soldier, Nelo realized, for all his bullying and bluster. The word in the barracks was that he would already have had a few promotions if not for his habit of punching out his comrades when drunk.

The sky was a lid of cloud, the city all but pitch-dark save for the occasional gleam of a lantern in the houses and shut-up shops and shrines. Nelo wasn't sure what time it was, but these were the hours of the curfew the suffetes had imposed months before, and the streets were empty—silent save only for distant soft whistles, the signals of the patrolling guard. One of Fabius' iron rules was that the streets had to be kept clear—there could be nobody sleeping out in the open, in alleyways or doorways, as had become common since the city had filled up with nestspills. The rule seemed to be working well. Occasionally you would hear a scurrying in the dark, a rustle, perhaps footsteps, a rat or wild dog, or maybe some human scavenger. But Nelo, eyes wide open, saw nothing.

Once they passed a cart hauled by a couple of beefy-looking Libyans, perhaps slaves, and led by a soldier in a dark cloak, his face hidden. The cart's load was covered by a thick, bloodstained cloth, and Nelo did not need too much imagination to know what was under there. The deaths continued in a steady trickle, from hunger, from the blood plague and other diseases that swept like fires through the city's crowded tenements. Nelo had found these deaths horrific when he had first come to live inside the city walls. But Fabius had once told him that cities were always like this, even in the good times, even with plentiful food and water. It made Nelo sharply homesick for the wide, empty, orderly landscape of Northland, where people did not die like *this*.

They came to a darkened property that had once, according to a faded sign over the door, been a manufactory of jewelry. Now the frontage was scarred by fire, and the door had been broken down.

Gisco checked his bit of paper. "This is the one." He gestured to Suniatus. "No need to knock."

Suni grinned, drew his sword, kicked the door in, and led the way inside.

If this had been a manufactory, it had long been

stripped bare, the contents looted. Now in two, three, four ground-floor rooms people huddled, whole families crammed into one corner or another, mothers clutching infants, cowering back from Gisco's light. There was a complicated stink of milk, piss, shit, sweat, and deep in-grained dirt. Gisco, without a word, stalked through the rooms, blade in hand, holding his lantern so he could see faces. Eyes gleamed bright from heaps of rags. He still hadn't told Suni or Nelo what he was looking for.

"Not here," he said once they had gone through all the rooms. He saw that Suniatus had grabbed a bit of bread from some wretch, and was biting into the hard crust. "Oh, give that back, Suni." Suniatus cast the fragment over his shoulder, and the huddled forms scrambled for it. Gisco looked around. There was an upper floor, but the ceilings of the rooms were flimsy and cracked, and the dawn sky showed through, a reluctant gray.

"Nothing up there, Sergeant," Suniatus offered. "I saw from outside. Top floor pulled down, for the wood to burn, I guess."

"All right." Gisco stalked through the rooms again, ignoring the people who had to shrink back out of his way. At length he found a hatch in the floor. "Aha! A cellar." He gestured at Suni, who found an iron ring fixed to the hatch, and hauled it up. Gisco held up his lantern over the hole. Nelo glimpsed a wooden ladder, a floor of packed earth beneath.

Gisco nodded to Suniatus, his finger to his lips. "You first, Suni. Quiet, now."

Suni grinned, settled into the hatch, and let himself down the ladder one-handed. Gisco passed the lantern. Suni looked around, then headed off determinedly to one corner, moving out of sight.

Nelo waited with Gisco. Somewhere an infant murmured, and was hushed. Nelo wondered what happened to these people when it rained, under that roof. But then it rarely rained in Carthage nowadays.

There was a brief sound of a struggle, a surprised grunt. Then Suni called up, "You can come down, sir."

Nelo led the way down the ladder.

The cellar, whatever it had once stored, was stripped as bare as the rest of the house. In one corner a man lay face-down on a pile of blankets, with Suni grasping one twisted arm and kneeling on his back. There was a heap of clothes, a discarded mail coat, and weapons—a battleaxe leaning against one wall. And there was a woman, Nelo saw, cow-ering in the corner, grasping a blanket to her chest.

Gisco took in the scene at a glance. "Good work, Suni." He strode across to the man, got a handful of hair and pulled his head back, making the man grunt. Nelo saw the hair was bright red, and that the man was bearded. Gisco dropped the man's head casually, as if dropping a sack of potatoes. "This is the one. Who's she?"

The woman sat up straighter. "Sir. My name is Satilis. My husband owns this shop. Owned—I have not seen him for some time."

Gisco leaned down and peered at her in the lantern light. "She's older than I thought."

Suni grinned. "Maybe this fellow likes 'em wrinkly."

"Sir—are you acting under the orders of the suffetes? Of the Popular Assembly?"

"Aren't we all?"

"I demand my rights. We have always paid our taxes and tolls, officer. My husband's father once served on the Tribunal of One Hundred and Four. It was bad enough that my shop, my home, was forced to open its doors to stinking farmers' families from the country. Now this man has come, he just walked in here, he doesn't even speak our tongue, but he had a letter demanding asylum, a letter from General Fabius, and, and—"

Suni guffawed. "General Fabius? Sure he did."

Gisco stood straight. "Get out of here, madam."

"What?"

"You won't want to see what's to come. Get out. Shoo, shoo." And he chased her as he would a reluctant dog.

The woman got up and scrambled for the ladder, which was hard to negotiate in her blanket. Both Gisco and Suniatus stared as she climbed, revealing thighs, buttocks, ample hips.

Gisco sighed. "That will keep me warm tonight."

Suni laughed again. "Now what, sir? What do we do with this fellow? Haul him in?"

"No time for that, Suni. He's an obvious saboteur. Placed here to open the gates and let his brutish comrades into our city, along with their Hatti overlords. Finish him off."

"With pleasure. How?"

"Behead him. Make it neat, would you?"

Suniatus lifted his blade, yanking the man's head back; the man began to struggle, his teeth grating.

"Oh, by the left bollock of mighty Teshub, kill the man first. Have some manners, Suniatus."

"Sorry, sir." Suniatus efficiently slit the man's throat with a scrape of his blade, held him down while he bled out, and then sawed off the head, grunting and complaining as his blade got stuck in the vertebrae.

Meanwhile Gisco turned to Nelo. "You. Find a sack, a bag."

"Yes, sir. What for, sir?"

"Our keepsake. This brute's crimson head, boy. We're on a mission to root out agents of the Hatti princes, like this one." He said this absently, while perusing his list by the light of the lantern. "You still here? Go, boy, go!"

So they proceeded through Megara. Nelo had to carry the sack, which dripped blood as they walked, and was surprisingly heavy. It got heavier yet as they visited a second house, and a third, each time finding a solitary Rus or Scand warrior living among fearful Carthaginians, each time coming upon him without warning, each time coming away with a head. The whole business, the stink of the heads, sickened Nelo.

Yet it puzzled him too. Even when the warriors saw them coming they made no attempt to resist, not until it was too late and they realized their fate at Suniatus' hands. They did jabber out pleas in their own harsh tongues, but that was to be expected, and none of the killing party understood a word.

On the fourth killing Suniatus whistled as he sawed at the man's neck. "This is the life for me, aurochs," he said to Nelo. "Killing these brutes is as easy as picking olives off a tree." He threw over the head for Nelo to catch.

They came upon the fifth man in an upper room of a small abandoned temple. By now the day was bright, the curfew lifted, and in the streets outside, the wagons of the dead continued their mournful progress amid the gathering noises of the city day. This time Suniatus struggled to get the Scand on his back before dispatching him. Gisco was forced to help, sitting on the man's legs while Suniatus pinned his chest.

And the man saw Nelo. His eyes widened. "Northlander."

Nelo was startled. He had said the word in the tongue of Etxelur.

"Northlander. You are a Northlander. I can tell, the hair, the eyes. I visit—I have visited—" Suniatus punched him in the mouth, knocking his head to the side. But he stayed conscious, and spoke from a bloody mouth. "Please. Mistake. They make mistake. I am loyal, loyal to Fabius!"

Suniatus recognized the general's name, and sat back, panting, pinning the man's arms. "What did he say? Something about my general?" And he slammed the back of his hand into the Scand's face.

"Get on with it, Suni," growled Gisco, pressing on the man's legs.

"Sir." Suniatus made a more determined effort to contain the man's struggles.

But the Scand still tried to talk to Nelo. "Please! Fabius, his men take us, he speaks to us. Offers us gold and bread, more than the Hatti, if we fight for him. He will give us back to our families, when Hatti are gone. That's what he said."

"Shut up!" Another blow with the back of the hand.

"That's what he said! Gold and bread! Look, look—"
But, pinned, he could not reach whatever he was after.
Some proof of a contract with Fabius? "That's what he
said—"

At last Suniatus drew his blade across the neck. The
man died, choking on his own blood, gaze still fixed on
Nelo.

As Suniatus removed the head, Nelo said, "Sir. He
was speaking Northlander."

"What of it?"

"He said the general recruited them. General Fabius,
sir."

"No, he didn't."

"He gave them gold and bread, and told them—"

Gisco stalked over to Nelo and loomed over him.
"No, he didn't, aurochs. You didn't hear him say any such
thing. Because if you did I'd have to cut off your precious
artist's hands, and then I'd let Suni finish you off like the
rest of these treacherous scum, and maybe I'll do that
anyhow because you annoy me, Nelo, you're a waste of
good muscle. Now. Did this man say anything to you?"

"No, sir."

"Good. Right. Where to next?"

64

There were two more items on Gisco's list, two more addresses. Two more heads to collect. By the time they were done it was mid-morning, and Suniatus had to take three of the heads from Nelo to carry in a separate sack.

Now they had a fresh appointment, Gisco said.

He led them through the streets of the lower city to the ancient inner wall that enclosed the Byrsa, the citadel. People were going about their business, to work if they had it, or to queue for the daily dole of gray bread and water if not. Nelo was aware of the glances they attracted, for the sacks dribbled blood, but people knew not to stare at soldiers.

They reached a gate in the citadel wall where more soldiers had gathered, with more bloody sacks. Comrades hailed one another, and made black jokes about what their sacks contained. Gisco spoke quietly to other officers, and they scrutinized one another's lists, comparing notes. Nobody asked why they were waiting, or what for, or why the heads were needed. You weren't supposed to ask such questions.

With permission, Suniatus went off and bought shriveled apples from a trader in a sparsely populated marketplace nearby, and handed them around. Suniatus made a pretense of offering one to Nelo, then threw the fruit in his sack instead. "Let these Scand fight over it in Valhalla."

Then there was a gathering noise, the murmur of a crowd, along with footsteps, some laughter and cheers, and the rattle of wheels. The soldiers dumped their apple cores and straightened up, fixing helmets and mail coats.

A war chariot, a big two-horse machine stolen in a raid from the Hatti, came clattering into view around a bend. With driver and spear man, Fabius was aboard, resplendent in a polished breastplate, scarlet tunic and purple cloak. With his helmet off he was unmistakable, and the men cheered as he approached. A couple of carts followed behind him—and they were laden with severed heads, Nelo saw, dozens of them heaped up like turnips on farmers' carts. They were all men, all bearded, all red-haired—all Rus or Scand. A guard detail jogged along beside chariot and carts.

Behind Fabius came the crowd, citizens of Carthage. They were a ragged, grimy lot, Nelo thought; not only was there no food to be had but there were no new clothes to buy in the market, not even soap and fresh water to spare to clean the old. But today the great general Fabius was putting on some kind of spectacle, and on impulse the people came out to see what was going on. And it helped, Nelo saw, that a few more soldiers followed behind the guard, carrying satchels from which they threw stuff out to the crowd—peas, beans perhaps, small items that people leapt for and scrapped over.

The chariot pulled up at the gate. Fabius beckoned Gisco over, while Nelo and Suniatus emptied out their own sacks onto the heap on the carts. "More fruit for my harvest I see, Gisco."

"I've spoken to the other commanders, sir. I think we got them all."

"Good, good, a thorough job. The city thanks you for it—or it will, before the day is done. Ah, there's my scribbling Northlander. Up here, boy, ride with me. Do you have your satchel? By the gods, what's that mess on your clothes?"

"Sir—"

"You. Give him your tunic, man. Just do it! He can't be facing the Tribunal of One Hundred and Four with Rus brains all over his bib."

The soldier, picked out at random, reluctantly stripped down to his breeches and handed his tunic to Nelo. His companions whistled and mocked.

Nelo climbed onto the chariot, hideously self-conscious. He dared to ask, "The Tribunal, sir? What are we going to do there?"

"You'll see, boy. Just record everything, Nelo, regardless of how well you understand it. Once again we are going to witness history. No—we are going to *make* history." He stood on his chariot, and turned to face the crowd and the soldiers. "Did you hear that? Did you hear what I said?" He had the leathery lungs a commander always needed, and at his bellow the murmur of the crowd subsided. "I said that today, we, all of you, are going to make history!"

That won him a ragged, slightly bemused cheer.

Fabius dramatically pointed to the Byrsa. "There are men up there, old men, men who are fat in these times when even a soldier goes hungry, men who would today hold me to account. That's their job, you might say. That's the purpose of the One Hundred and Four. Well, so it is. That's their duty. That's their privilege. That's their right. But such duty requires immense wisdom. And what wisdom do they show? They question the conduct of the war. *My* conduct of it."

"You've not won it yet," somebody dared call out.

There was a mutter, people looked at one another, and soldiers prowled menacingly.

"No!" shouted Fabius. "No, let him be. He speaks the truth, after all. This war is not yet won. The siege is not lifted. It might take months yet. Years. *But*, if it were not for me, if not for my vigilance and the vigilance of my men, *the war would already have been lost.*" He turned to Nelo, and murmured, "Pass me one of those heads, boy. And for Jupiter's sake keep the innards from spilling on your clean tunic."

When he had the trophy, Fabius held it aloft, its red hair grasped in one strong fist. People gasped and turned away.

"Do you see?" Fabius cried. "Do you see what my men found in your city? Do you see what we are up against? If we had not rooted them out, these infiltrators would have opened up the gates in the night, and slaughtered you men in your beds—your children next—and then they would have fallen on your daughters and your wives. This is the horror that I have averted. This very morning!" He pitched the head into the crowd, and people flinched back out of its way as it bounced and rolled. "I cannot promise you a quick victory. Nobody could. But I can promise you there will be no quick defeat. I can promise you that Carthage will throw off these wolves at the gate, and will rise again. I can promise you all this. Here, you see the proof! What can the old men on that hill promise you, but to bring me down?

"Well, this morning I have been summoned to account for my actions. I am a good Roman, and a good Carthaginian. I will obey the summons. But will you come with me?"

"Yes."

"Will you be at my side?"

"Yes!"

"Will you, will you?"

"Yes! Yes!"

At that moment Fabius' driver whipped his horses, and the chariot lurched forward, through the gate and into the Byrsa. The cart followed, the piled-up heads rolling and rattling perilously, and then came the gathering crowd. Nelo saw Gisco take brisk command, ensuring that the general was secure, and that the chariot was escorted by flanking soldiers.

The chariot rolled up a broad avenue toward the summit of this central mound, passing through the Hannibal Quarter, a district that Nelo had heard of but had never visited before. There were shops, temples and grand government buildings here, all in shining stone, some faced with marble, and in much better order than the lower city. Yet, as in the rest of Carthage, those shops that weren't selling essentials, such as shoes, clothes, food and oil, seemed mostly to have been turned over to habitation. These days even the Byrsa was crowded with nestspills. As Fabius passed, some of these folk came out to follow him too, joining their grubbier counterparts from the lower city. Whatever Fabius was up to, this was a chance for them to make some noise, to vent their frustration, and maybe to smash a few windows and crack a few skulls in the process.

Soon a great tide of people was washing up the slopes of the Byrsa, carrying Fabius to the house of the Tribunal of One Hundred and Four at the summit. Nelo sketched and sketched.

Fabius glanced at what had been drawn, smiling, folding the pages back. But he frowned when he got to one sketch, of himself holding up the severed head before the crowd of the lower town. "What's this?"

"Sir?"

He had to shout above the noise of the crowd. "The head of this Scand—he's looking at me. And the heads in the barrow too, all turned—all looking at me!"

"It's what I saw, sir. I mean—"

"What your heart saw?"

"The dead Scand and Rus are asking why you betrayed them."

"Betrayed?" His voice was deep, ominous.

Nelo knew he was talking himself into trouble. But he said, "One of them spoke to me, sir. Before we managed to kill him. He told me—"

"That I had invited them in."

"Yes, sir."

"And so, you conclude, this is all got up by me. A stunt to impress the rabble."

"Yes—no, sir—"

"It's all right. I took you under my wing because I believe you see the truth, where other men fail. I can't complain if you see the truth about me, can I? But it is only a partial truth, Nelo. Only a necessary lie. Greater truths lie beyond."

"Sir?"

"These fellows, with their ridiculous red hair and their inability to hide, are of course a fiction, a plant. But the city is riddled with spies, informants, would-be traitors. That's the greater truth. And it's only my strict control of the city, my soldiers' thorough rooting-out of it all, that keeps us safe. It's hard and it's not pretty, but it's the truth.

"The Tribunal of One Hundred and Four think this isn't enough. Some of them are impatient for war. They want me to ride out with the phalanxes and meet the Hatti on open ground. That would lose us the war for sure, and I suspect some of them know it in their hearts, but the siege has so ground them down that they'd rather lose it than carry on. I have seen sieges, I've laid them, I've survived them. Most sieges last *years*—that's what they don't understand.

"Others, meanwhile, want to clip my wings. They are envious of my power, my position, and so on. Such envy is a constant in the affairs of human beings. Some, indeed, think my appointment with the cross is overdue." He glanced at his hands, flexing them, as if his palms itched. "Again, they want this, even though they know it will lose them the war, or at least they suspect it. They want me downed even so. But I, you see, cannot allow that, Nelo, for my duty is to save Carthage, despite the difficulties I am having with some of the Carthaginians.

"So it is true that I have rigged this business of the redheaded saboteurs. I'm sure you won't be the last to spot it. But I am doing it to force the Tribunal, and the elders, the suffetes and the rest, even the *s'rnm*, the ordinary folk of the city, force them to accept that they need me if they are to survive this war. And that they need to give me a free hand."

Nelo thought he understood. "You're going to take over the government."

Fabius grinned. "It's happened before, as I know very well, for all literate Romans are perforce taught a great deal about Carthaginian history. A man called Bomilcar, for example, back in the days even before Carthage went to war with Rome. Not that his coup succeeded, but he had the right idea.

"It is quite a feat I am attempting," he said now. "A foreign general who won't call his troops out to fight the besieging enemy. Hardly a basis for great popularity with the people, you'd think. Yet here I am, strolling up the Byrsa with a mob at my back."

"And if you win today, sir? What then?"

"Two things. I'm going to want to talk to your people, Nelo."

"My people?"

"The Northlanders. I'm aware there's quite a community of you here, having fled from your own frozen country. And I'm also aware you've brought treasure with you."

"Treasure?"

Fabius rapped his temple. "Up here. Secrets. That's what I intend to acquire next."

Nelo thought of his enigmatic conversation with Ontin the doctor, his talk of secretive House of Crow projects, work Nelo had never been able to progress but perhaps others had . . .

"That's the first thing," Fabius went on. "And the

second—I will rewrite history, for all time. A Roman defeating Carthage at last! In a manner of speaking at least. How the Carthaginian historians of the future will spit and fume as they are forced to copy out my name, over and over! And all of this, my boy, you are going to capture with your clever scribbles. Scribbles that will some day be etched into stone friezes that will cover the walls of the new buildings that will flourish in this miserable old city."

"Yes, sir."

Now they approached a grand, square building, sitting on a stone pavement on the terraced summit of the hill.

"Is the Tribunal of One Hundred and Four in session, Gisco?"

The sergeant jogged up to interrogate the guard at the door, then turned. "Yes, sir."

"Then get those big doors open."

"Yes, sir." Gisco snapped commands to a soldier nearby. Soon a group of men were running at the doors, swords in hand.

When the doors were open Fabius urged his driver to drive the chariot right into the great palace, into the central chamber itself, to shouts of outrage from the white-robed men who sat in their rows within. The cart with the severed heads followed too, its wheels leaving trails of blood and mud on the marble floor. Fabius leapt down, ignoring the shouts and pointed fingers of the outraged Tribunal members, and he started hauling the heads from the cart and throwing them at the members. "This is why you need me! And this, and this! This is what I protect the city from!" The delegates flinched back, as blood and gray skull-matter splashed over their white robes.

Nelo saw it all, everything that came about that day, and fixed it all on paper, scribbling, scribbling.

65

The ship sailed on, heading west, making for the Sea of the Arabs. The crew toiled to repair the storm damage. Pyxeas grumpily put his notes in order and rewrote those that had been spoiled by water from the leaks. The weather, for now, was calm.

Then the pirates struck.

Avatak and the scholar were immersed in a deep technical discussion on the absorption of fixed air by a given unit area of farmland, and its production by the burning of the same unit area of forest. "Once men hunted the worldwide forests," Pyxeas said. "Now they farm—not in Northland and its hinterland, but elsewhere, they farm. It must make a difference. It must! I nearly have it, Avatak—I nearly have it—"

Bayan burst into the cabin, and slammed the door shut behind him.

Pyxeas glared. "What's this? I left clear instructions not to be disturbed."

"Pirates," said the boy. His eyes were wide, he was bathed in sweat, and Avatak saw that his shirt was stained red with blood. "Yes-yes-yes. Hide me!" He dived at the floor, into the heaps of scrolls and books, and burrowed in like a rat into garbage.

"Get out of there!" Pyxeas ineffectually pawed at the papers.

"I've never seen pirates like these. Monsters. Killers! Yes-yes-yes!"

Avatak was bemused. *Pirates?* "Bayan, come on. Al-Quds has beaten off pirates and nestspills before—"

"They killed al-Quds! Slit his throat with a single swipe—near enough clean took his head off—they killed him, yes-yes-yes, the first heartbeat they were aboard! Oh, they're coming, they're coming . . ."

Avatak heard it now, heavy footsteps, shouting, the scrape of steel—screams. He tried to think. "Maybe we can block the door—maybe if we hide—"

It was too late. The door crashed open, smashing off its iron hinges, sending Avatak tumbling back into the little cabin, landing on top of Bayan in a mess of scrolls and parchments.

Pyxeas stood and faced the intruders. "You have no business here—"

A gloved fist slammed into the scholar's mouth, and Avatak heard the crunch of breaking teeth. Pyxeas fell back, landing against the outer wall with a thump, his mouth a bloody mess.

Two men pushed through the door. They seemed huge, their arms and necks bare, their trousers blood-soaked leather, their hair tied back. They had weapons at their waists, cruel-looking swords and axes. Each had his face covered in intricate tattoos, like a tracery of black-walled veins. Avatak scrambled back against the bunks and reached for his own weapon, a blade hidden in his mattress. Before he got there one of the pirates grabbed him by the shirt front, raised him with one un-believably strong arm, and drove his fist into Avatak's belly. Avatak fell back, doubled up, hollowed out by pain.

Bayan took his chance. The little Mongol scurried on all fours through the men's legs and out of the cabin.

As Avatak and Pyxeas lay helplessly, one pirate brutally rummaged through the cabin, lifting the bunks, ripping through heaps of paper, shaking out bundles of clothes. Uzzia's coat, with the jewels sewn into the quilting, hung unnoticed on the back of the sagging door.

The other man, who had punched Avatak, grabbed him again. "You! The old man's bum boy, are you?" He spoke a guttural Persian. With his free hand he roughly frisked Avatak, soon finding his pouches of coins. "That what you are? Bum boy?"

"Take it," Avatak said, his voice a mumble.

"What? What's that?"

"It's all we have—"

The pirate slapped Avatak. "All? Where's the rest of it? An old man like this, a ship like this—where's the rest of his treasure, boy? Up your ass? Because if it is I'll slit you open to get it."

"Not rich. He's a *scholar*." He had used the Northlander word. He tried again, in Cathay, Mongol. He didn't know the Persian. Maybe he could make them understand. Make them spare the old man, even if only through pity. "Not rich. His treasure is what he knows."

The pirate slapped him again, almost routinely. "What treasure?"

"Inside. It's inside him—"

But the pirate grinned, and threw him down, and Avatak realized he had made a horrible mistake. "Ha! That old trick." The pirate called over his shoulder. Avatak recognized the words "tamarind" and "brine."

A third man came, carrying a filthy, heavy sack. Avatak's captor threw this over to the man with Pyxeas.

The scholar lay unmoving on a heap of bloodied manuscripts. The pirate cradled Pyxeas' neck and raised his shoulders, so that his head was tipped backward. Then he forced open the scholar's injured mouth with his fingers, making Pyxeas moan with renewed pain, and held Pyxeas' nose, and he poured a thick crimson liquid from the sack into the scholar's mouth. Pyxeas gagged, choked and struggled feebly, but the pirate held him firmly— almost skillfully, Avatak saw, wondering, almost like a mother in a winter house with a willful infant—and Pyxeas had no choice but to swallow, to take in great mouthfuls of the stuff. Then he convulsed and doubled over. With a bark he vomited out a mass of crimson fluid laced with half-chewed ship's biscuits, a foul-smelling pool that spread out over the mess of papers under him. The pirate laughed and stood back from the pool, making a show of trying to keep his feet dry. Now there was a fouler smell, and the pirates laughed again. The man dragged at the old man's breeches, pulling them down with a casual rip, and Avatak saw shit dribbling from between the scholar's skinny buttocks. Soon both men were rummaging in the vomit and shit with their bare hands—looking for Pyxeas' treasure, which they thought he had swallowed because of Avatak's own foolish words. And, he saw, they would keep on doing this in their frustration until they had squeezed the old man dry of every drop of fluid in his body, and perhaps finish the job by slitting him open. All because of Avatak's mistake.

He had one pouch the pirates hadn't found, sewn into his shirt, under an armpit. In here he kept one of Uzzia's gems—just one. When both pirates were distracted, their backs turned contemptuously to him, he dug his fingers into the pouch, pulled out the jewel and swallowed it. Then he called out, "Me. Not him. In me. He made *me* swallow it."

Immediately the pirates were on him. One of them punched him again, as if in greeting. "Swallow what?"

"His gem," Avatak gasped. "The family treasure. He made me swear—"

But he got no further. While one man held him down, the other forced the sack of liquid to his mouth, pinching his nose hard. He could taste Pyxeas' vomit on the bag. Now the fluid was coursing down his throat, thick and fibrous and rank-tasting. He was gagging almost before he'd swallowed.

They found the jewel easily, but they kept on until he was spewing and shitting as helplessly as the old man.

At last they decided he had no more to give. On the way out one of them kicked him in the head, almost casually.

He woke with a kind of tunnel of pain passing through his body from throat to ass, and a foul taste in his mouth, and a fouler stench in his nostrils. He was lying facedown with his cheek resting in some cooling liquid. His own vomit, probably. He rolled on his back, to more pain from his tortured gut. Pyxeas' work was scattered around the cabin, soaked in blood and vomit and shit. But the quilted coat still hung from the door, apparently undisturbed.

And he saw Pyxeas, on hands and knees, crawling toward him. His mouth was a ruin, his lower front teeth smashed out. But, unaccountably, he was smiling. His speech a slur, he whispered, "I have it, Avatak. The secret—the link—the mechanism of the world. I have it!"

At that moment Avatak knew that Pyxeas was mad, that his quest for learning had made him so. Though Avatak would always cherish the old man for that deep wound of grief in his heart, a grief that encompassed the whole suffering world, he would have no more to do with the scholar's numbers.

That was how it was for the remainder of the voyage, all the way to Carthage.

66

n his last days Jexami summoned Rina.

In the tiny servant's room Rina read the note he had sent, over and over. It was a simple request for her to visit. The note was written out, evidently in his own hand, in an elegant but wavering Etxelur script, though he had signed it in both Northland and Carthaginian styles. No pretense now, no more hiding his origins. And no subtlety about the pleas he made with the desperation of a dying man.

The note filled her with contradictory emotions. She had not seen Jexami since he had first expelled her and her children. To know he was dying gave her a kind of vindication. Jexami had been the man who had turned her away in her darkest hour, her and her children. Now the blood plague had come for him: *let him die*. Yet such pettiness seemed meaningless in the context of the plague. It was said that in Carthage perhaps half had died—Jexami, walking with the dead, would soon have more company than among the living. What did past slights matter in such circumstances? And he was family. Of course she had to respond.

She begged time away, from Barmocar himself. She rarely saw Anterastilis these days; there were rumors in the household that she was ill. Barmocar consented with a curt nod, not speaking to her.

It was not far to walk to Jexami's town house. He, like Barmocar, like the rest of Carthage's privileged and wealthy, had abandoned his country property and flown to the safety of the city at the approach of the Hatti horde. The house, smaller than she had expected, seemed shut up, empty. This was a plague house, of course. Rina pulled on gloves, and a mask that covered all her face but the eyes, before she knocked on the door.

An elderly maid answered. There seemed to be nobody here but the maid, and her master.

In a small room, alone, Jexami lay on a thick pallet. The stench was terrible, and Rina went to push open a window. There was a water jug by his bed, empty. Rina summoned the maid to get it refilled. She knelt by the bed and took Jexami's hand. She would not have recognized the burly, confident Northlander. His eyes were closed. He looked as if he had been drained, leaving only a sack of flesh. Only the swellings at his neck, thick and purple-black, looked healthy, ironically.

He stirred, his eyes fluttering open. When he tried to speak, his voice was a rustle like a moth's wing. "Who is it?" He spoke in Carthaginian.

"It is me. Rina of Etxelur." She spoke in their own tongue, but she would not lift the mask to show her face. She squeezed his hand. "Your note reached me."

"Ah." His dry mouth opened with a pop. "Water—"

"Coming."

"That villain Drubal did that for me, at least. My head of house. Brought me water. While robbing me of everything else. Now you have come, although I turned you out when you needed help. I regret—regret—"

"What's done is done. And I might have done the

same. I, too, was arrogant and complacent in the days I lived in Etxelur."

"Your children? Twins?"

"Alxa is dead," she said bluntly. "The plague. Nelo is at the war. I've heard nothing of him for months." Strange to think, when she summed it up like that, that she had come here in the first place to protect her children.

"Alxa," he whispered. "I heard of her. The work she did to support the dying—remarkable. And you are untouched."

"Some are spared, for no reason that any can see."

"I thought that of myself . . . I had lasted so long. But then it came for me, it came. I heard Pyxeas is alive. That he is here, in Carthage."

"Yes. Though I have not been able to see him myself. He made it to Cathay and back! He got here just before the equinox, he and that Coldlander boy of his. He had to talk his way through the Hatti siege to get into the city. How did you know?"

Jexami's face twitched; perhaps he was trying to smile. "His was an epic journey, though I never saw the point of it myself. News of it traveled—something to admire, an achievement to light up a time of blackness."

The maid returned with the water. Rina wet a cloth, and sponged drops into Jexami's mouth.

"You wonder why I summoned you," he whispered.

Summoned. Even now, that haughty term.

"Listen to me." His hand closed on hers, the last of his strength. "I don't want to die and finish up as these Carthaginians do. Oiled up and stuck in a hole in the ground. And nor will I be thrown into a pit with the poor people . . ."

He wasn't alone in obsessing how he would die; she had seen it a hundred times. And, she saw, he was to remain a snob even beyond his death. "What, then?"

"I want to die a good Northlander, as I believe I've lived like one, for all I have been seduced at times by the ways of the city folk. *Take me home*, Rina. Don't leave me here.

Take me home and bury me in the Wall, facing the sea, like all our ancestors back to the age of Ana and Prokyid. One day this weather will relent, or even if it does not there may be a way ... Say you will do this for me."

"Of course," she murmured. "Rest now. You will sleep forever in the Wall, with your mother, your father, all your family, under the care of the little mothers ..."

His eyes fluttered closed. Perhaps he slept.

She stayed with him until the daylight started to fade.

She emerged from the house into a soft, early evening light. For once the sky was clear, and the sunset was spectacular. The remarkable skies had, for the last year, been a small consolation for the disruption the world had suffered, a bit of beauty amid the misery. But she suspected that Pyxeas would say that even this was merely a symptom of the world's agony; she was looking at the sun's light reflecting off the dust that had once been all the farmland in North Africa, now dried out and blown high in the air.

The maid said that when the master died she would have the corpse cremated, send the ashes to Rina, shut up the house. Rina nodded, thanked the woman—wondering vaguely what would become of *her* when Jexami was gone—and set off back across the city to Barmocar's household.

Where Barmocar himself was waiting anxiously for her. For a second time that day she had been summoned.

67

Carthalo, one of the two suffetes, had asked to see her. They would meet at an expensive cemetery on the flank of the Byrsa.

"I will accompany you," said Barmocar.

"I am summoned by the suffetes," she said, unbelieving. "Me. A runaway servant. A middle-aged Northlander with whip burns on her back and my fingers worn out from working your wife's slit—"

"My wife is dead," he said bluntly. "Two days ago."

"The plague?"

"Of course the plague. And now she lies out in the cemetery. You will see. That is why we are going there."

"Anterastilis was a foolish, indulgent woman, who used me, and others, cruelly. But nobody in this world deserves to die, certainly not of the blood plague. Still— she is gone. Why should I help you, who took advantage of my weakness and vulnerability?"

"I brought you to Carthage," he snapped with a trace of his old anger. "I took you in when no other would. Times were already hard, or have you forgotten that?"

He made a visible effort to regain control; he seemed to be under huge stress. "It is not me who asks for your help. You and your uncle, actually."

"Pyxeas?"

"He is to attend too. It is important, Rina. Will you attend or not?"

The next morning Pyxeas himself came to the house, with Avatak, his Coldlander companion. Rina was over-joyed; it was the first time she had seen her uncle since his arrival at Carthage. But Pyxeas was silent, withdrawn, and seemed much older than she remembered, drained by his journey. He had trouble talking too; there were bloody gaps in the teeth of his lower jaw. Yet he was gathering his strength for whatever was to come today, she saw.

The four of them, Barmocar, Rina, Pyxeas and his boy, together with a servant, were loaded onto a carriage drawn by a single elderly horse, and they crossed the city.

Carthage, these days, woke slowly. On the landward walls the sentries' fires were sparks against a sunrise that towered pink, and carts bearing the dead rolled in dole-ful caravans, heading for the big, ever-burning pyres. Pyxeas stared at the slow carriages, and his lips moved slowly. He was counting, Rina realized, counting the carriages, perhaps hoping to estimate the number of the night's dead. And, as they began to climb the Byrsa itself, a series of upright crosses was thrown into relief against the sky, the dangling bodies silhouetted. Thieves, looters, murderers and other criminals, punished in an ancient Carthaginian style. At least the crows didn't go hungry anymore, the Carthaginians bleakly joked.

At length they came upon the cemetery, a place of grand tombs, some of them evidently ancient. Here was an open grave, a wound in the ground. A pavilion of some weighty fabric had been set up beside the tomb. Solemn folk had gathered here wearing heavy purple cloaks, while servants fluttered around bearing trays of drinks and bits of food. A ring of soldiers watched warily, in case any hungry citizens took offense at this display of ostentation by their leaders.

Inside, the pavilion was opulent, with an Etruscan tapestry hanging from one wall, a Persian carpet covering the dusty cobbles. A table had been set up along the pavilion's axis — and the body of Anterastilis lay on the table, dressed in her finest clothes, washed, anointed with oil, her hair and cosmetics carefully made up. Beside her was an altar of stone laden with food, drinks, and gifts: perfumes, herbs, expensive-looking bits of pottery, amulets. A priest murmured prayers, reading from a scroll. Rina couldn't help but remember the last time she had seen Anterastilis lying on her back like this. Well, she looked better now than she had back then, even at the peak of sexual ecstasy. They had even put her in a girdle, judging by the prominence of her bosom.

Carthalo of the suffetes approached them. He was a tall, angular man with a high forehead but a full head of dark hair, and blank gray eyes, and an oddly sinister, soft smile. And, trailing him, Rina was astonished to see Mago, Barmocar's nephew, healthy, well fed — uniformed, but not at the war. He grinned, insolent, when he caught her eye.

Carthalo bowed formally. "Rina of Etxelur. Thank you for coming on this sad day. And you are Pyxeas the sage, sir?" He spoke Greek; perhaps he had prepared for this visit sufficiently to know that Pyxeas could follow Greek but not much Carthaginian.

"I am he, I admit it." Pyxeas' speech was slurred by his damaged teeth. He rather spoiled the moment by absently helping himself to a biscuit from a plate on the altar.

Rina had to slap his hand to make him put it back. "By the little mothers' tears, Uncle, that's for Anterastilis!"

"Oh. Well, I don't suppose she'd have missed it."

Carthalo smiled. "I follow a little of what you say. I once visited Northland, you know, many years ago. When the world and I were both much younger. Fascinating place. But your customs are quite different from ours. Your treatment of the dead, for example. You inter your dead in the fabric of your mighty Wall, so that your ancestors may add their strength to the unending war against the sea. Inspirational."

His tone sounded mocking. Rina's reading of his Greek was too uncertain to be sure. She wondered if this man, used to manipulating those around him, was too clever for his own good.

"We of Carthage do things quite differently," he said now, waving a hand. "As you can see. We believe that the afterlife is similar to the life we have lived on earth. Hatti missionaries of Jesus argue that this is a childish notion. But really, which is the simpler assumption—that the afterlife is like the world we know, or like a world none of us has ever experienced? We believe, however, that at death a person's spirit splits in two. The spiritual embodiment of Anterastilis, the *rouah*, now resides in the world of the dead. But the physical embodiment of her spirit, the *nepesh*, stays with the body—and as you can see she requires nourishment, just as a living person."

"Biscuits," Pyxeas said.

"Biscuits."

Rina faced Carthalo squarely. "You brought us here for a reason, I presume."

Carthalo gave her that thin, intimidating smile. "It's true that I thought it would be appropriate to have our discussion in the context of this solemn farewell to a woman who was your employer and your friend."

Barmocar looked away.

"This, our most ancient rite, is central to our culture, we Carthaginians."

"This and crucifixion," said Pyxeas. "And child sacrifice—"

Rina hushed him.

"We have retained the semblance of an orderly society, despite our terrible losses, losses nobody would have believed a few short years ago. This is still Carthage, we are still Carthaginians. We asked you here today—indeed, at the command of Fabius himself—because I wanted you to see us at our best. For there is something I must ask of you. Something that Carthage must ask of Northland."

Rina flared. "More than you have already asked? The gods took my daughter's life, but Carthage took my son, to fight in her wars. Speaking of which"—she pointed at Mago—"why is *he* here?"

Mago grinned again. His face was scarred, she saw, the length of his right cheek. He blew her a kiss. "Glad to see me, Grandmother?"

"Get him out," Carthalo murmured to Barmocar.

"But I brought him here—the funeral—"

"Out. Now."

Barmocar turned and gestured to his nephew, who left the tent gracelessly.

"I know why he's here," said Rina. "And the sons of the rest of you, I daresay. *Because you are losing your war with the Hatti.* That's the truth, isn't it? And you privileged ones are pulling your sons out of the killing fields."

Barmocar seemed prepared to deny it, but Carthalo raised a hand. "It's true enough," he said softly. "Not that this is news we want to shout out. We are *not* withdrawing our sons, not all of us. My own two boys, as well as a nephew already dead . . ." He hesitated, apparently overcome with emotion, but it could have been a skillful act, Rina reminded herself. "Rina, we fight valiantly—our sons do. But the plague is cutting through our young men like a scythe through wheat ripe for the harvest. It has even reached the troops in the field, that and other diseases and blights."

Pyxeas said, "The plague has afflicted the whole world. The losses must be affecting the Hatti too."

"Of course. But the Hatti's sheer numbers overwhelm us."

Rina's eyes narrowed. "Are you asking us to help you fight this war?"

"You, and Northland."

"We don't speak for Northland," Rina said. "Besides, all the resources of Northland are locked up in the snow."

"Actually not all," Pyxeas said. He tapped his liver-spotted temple. "*This* is where our real resource is. Knowledge. And that's what this Carthaginian wants to get his hands on. Am I right?"

Carthalo nodded. "We need to win this war—or at least stop the Hatti. And to do that we need, frankly, a weapon they don't have. That's what I hope you can give us. What Fabius hopes for."

Rina shook her head. "Why should we help you? The Hatti have been our allies for . . ."

"For two millennia," Carthalo said smoothly. "I know my history, you see. And do you know how that came about? In a different time of crisis, long ago, there was an exchange. Etxelur gave Hattusa the potato to feed a starving population. And in return Hattusa gave Etxelur a plague. An invisible demon to wipe out an invading army. You see, this sort of arrangement has been made before."

"But if the Hatti have been our allies for so long—"

"Why betray them now? But what of the long-term interests of Northland? If Carthage were to be overrun, even destroyed, you would have a Hatti empire dominating the Middle Sea. When the world recovers from this longwinter, would such an empire not have further ambitions? Why should it not look north? Would it not be in Northland's best interests to keep a balance of the continental powers?"

Pyxeas laughed. "That's a good argument. Or would be, if not for the fact that the longwinter *never is going to end*—not in our lifetime anyhow. And that kind of petty human calculation is going to be scrubbed out by the ice. You'll have to do better than that, sir, if you're to get what you want from us."

Rina felt left behind. "But what is it they want, Uncle?"

Pyxeas tapped his temple again. "He wants me, Pyxeas, to tell him how to make the fire drug of Cathay. And eruptors, weapons to exploit it."

"Ah. And can you tell him?"

"Oh, yes." He stepped closer to Carthalo, intense. "In fact, I can do better than that. I, Pyxeas, have long anticipated this moment. I have put in place a plan—I had my students send letters to Northlanders in Carthage. To you too, Rina, though I don't think you ever received it. But others did. House of Crow studies. And they have been working, in secret, for months."

Carthalo's eyes narrowed. "What do you mean? What kind of work?"

"We already have the weapons. We Northlanders. We have the fire drug. We have the eruptors. *In this city.* These could be in your hands in days—a month at most. I, Pyxeas, have organized this."

Carthalo was clearly stunned. But he was a good politician and remained in control. "If you were to grant us this—"

Rina touched Pyxeas' arm. "We would be making a decision on behalf of all Northland."

He turned to her with eyes huge and sad. "I'm afraid we must, my dear. For Northland, the old Northland, is already lost—save for us. What we must face now is the future. And the building of that future begins here and now."

Carthalo smiled. "Quite right. Name your price."

Pyxeas glanced at Rina. "This is your moment."

"Bring him home," she snapped. "Bring him back from your wars."

Carthalo nodded. "Your son. I understand. Consider it done."

But even as he spoke, Rina saw Barmocar sneer at her, a sly smile he didn't trouble to hide. She saw his opinion of her there and then. She might have the power of life and death over him and his kind, but to him she was small, a petty woman obsessed with family, and always would be so. She had been abused by this man's wife. Humiliated for his amusement. She had sworn revenge on them both. That little smile, she thought. That little smile was going to cost this man so much.

Pyxeas, meanwhile, had greater prices to exact. "You may have the fire drug. But you will use it to make *peace* with the Hatti, if you possibly can."

"What? They are barbarians," Barmocar said. "One may as well try to make peace with a rabid wolf—"

"No. They follow Jesus. Warlike they may be, but peace is at the heart of the creed of their god. And they too have suffered with the plague. You may have the fire drug, to threaten them with overwhelming destruction, but you will offer them the chance of peace at the same time. Stop the bloodshed. And to symbolize that"—he glanced at Rina—"you will give them the bones of the Virgin Mother of Jesus, which Rina took illegally and gave to Barmocar in fair payment for her passage here."

Carthalo raised his eyebrows at Barmocar. "I knew nothing of this."

"It was private business."

"Not anymore. You will deliver the bones to the Temple of Melqart in the morning. Consider that done too, Pyxeas."

"Good. And there is more."

"I thought there might be."

"You will help us build a New Northland," Pyxeas said.

Carthalo smiled again, more cautiously. "And how are we to do that?"

"Give us a city. Somewhere in your hinterland. By the little mothers' tears, man, don't balk at that! You must have a dozen tomb-cities emptied out by the plague and ripe for reoccupation. As for our people, they are scattered across the Continent, the cities of the Middle Sea . . . You will help us find them. Send agents throughout the known world, wherever the ice has spared. Bring them home—bring them to their *new* home. That way, at least something of our culture, our values, our learning, may survive, until the longwinter passes, and we can go home again, for we will not forget where we came from." He looked at Rina, and held her shoulder. "This has been done before. I, Pyxeas, have seen the mark of Northland, or of our ancestors—the three rings, the bar, the form like the Mothers' Door—on rock panels in Coldland, even in the Land of the Sky Wolf. *Put there before the last time the ice came.* Northland has endured the ice before. Now it is the task of our generation to ensure it endures again."

Carthalo said, "You realize you are asking me to nurture a rival close to my own hearth. For I have no doubt that you Northlanders will rise to greatness again."

"It's either that or have the Hatti crush you," Pyxeas said with uncharacteristic bluntness.

"Consider it done," Carthalo said softly. "I must prepare a presentation on this to the Council of Elders. In the meantime, the fire drug—"

"One more thing," Rina said, and she faced Barmocar.

Barmocar looked fearful, as well he might, she thought. He glanced at Carthalo. "Our business is surely done—"

"This woman is the niece of the man who is going to give us the fire drug," Carthalo said smoothly. "And a woman who has a grudge against you, Barmocar, my friend, and from what I've heard I can't say I blame her. I suggest you listen to what she has to say."

She smiled. "The *molk*, Barmocar."

"What?"

"A word you taught me when I first arrived in this country, having all but reneged on your deal to deliver my family to safety. Do you remember, Barmocar? 'We call it *molk*. A gift for the gods, in times of great stress. The greatest gift one can give.' Do you remember saying that to me? And then you made me send my son off to war."

He glared back at her. "What is it you want?"

"To see you perform the *molk.*"

Carthalo said smoothly, "The *molk* has long become a merely symbolic practice. Today we sacrifice lambs— sometimes a carving is burned—but children—"

"*I know it's done,*" Rina said. "When you're desperate enough, you Carthaginians. You murder your children to please your antique gods, in secret, so I have learned. After the year I've had, I suspect I know more about your city than you suffetes do yourselves. Now I want to see it done again. By you, Barmocar."

"Mago," Barmocar whispered. "You mean Mago. You want me to send him back to the war."

Pyxeas touched her arm. "Niece, you don't need to do this."

She shook him off.

"Please," Barmocar said. "I've lost my wife—we were childless, you know that—the son of my sister is like my own—"

"And this is the end of it," Carthalo said sternly. "No more demands?"

"No more," said Pyxeas with finality.

Carthalo turned to his countryman. "Barmocar?"

But the man, head dropped, could not speak.

68

On the night that word came down that the Car-
thaginians were ready to give battle at last,
Kassu and Zida hurried to their homes in the
Hatti's temporary city.

Zida was exuberant. "They say Carthage's priests
chose tomorrow for its auguries. A near-midwinter night,
and the moon has just waned past its half, and for days
to come the sky will be dominated by the crescent moon,
the sign of Baal Hammon—or some crud like that. Ha!
They can have the moon; we have Jesus Sharruma who
will crush their puny testicles in His holy fist."

Kassu grunted. "Don't get your hopes up. Years of
drought, months of siege, the plague . . . we're all worn
out."

"I'll take my chances." They reached Zida's shack, a
kind of cone of turf heaped up on poles. "Anything's better than this shit." He aimed a mighty kick at the wall,
and a chunk fell in with a dry rustle.

There was a high-pitched squawk, and out came the
burly Libyan woman Zida had taken as his slave, mis-

tress or third wife, depending on how drunk he was when he was telling you. She had bits of straw in her crisp dark hair, and dried mud in the bowl she was holding. "Look what you did to supper, idiot!"

"We're fighting in the morning, Roofa, my love. Fighting those Carthaginian pustules at last! Won't you Libyans be glad to see the back of them?"

"Never mind Carthaginian pustules. Look what you did!" Still holding the pot, she stalked around the house, and pulled at the wrecked wall. "Now what's going to keep the rats out?"

He laughed. "The rats are more at home in there than we are. Oh, I'm a fired-up warrior tonight and you'd better be ready for the passion that's coming your way, woman!"

"And you be ready for the pots and pans I'm throwing at your empty head. Get in this house. Get in!" And she shoved him with the flat of her hand toward the crude gash of the door.

"See you in an hour," Zida said to Kassu.

"An hour."

Roofa delivered one final mighty shove to the small of Zida's back, and he fell into the house, weapons clattering, mail coat rustling.

Kassu walked on, grinning. But, as usual, he had lost his good humor by the time he had got home.

His own house was a marginally tidier, marginally better-built box of sod, in a rough street of similar properties. He stood before the house, looking at the old worn-out blankets that hung over the door, the patch of ground where they had tried to grow peas and beans but the plants had been devoured by rats and rabbits before they had a chance. It was hard to imagine a more depressing prospect, even if you hadn't known what the atmosphere was like inside. Angrily he pushed indoors.

In the single room within, one lamp burned. Oil was

expensive; all you could get was thick, gloopy stuff that was said to come from some animal of the sea. Henti was sitting cross-legged under the lamp, stitching an expensive-looking officer's cloak, dyed deep purple. The cloak wasn't Kassu's, but that wasn't unusual. The whole Hatti nation had pitched up on the plain before Carthage for this end-of-the-world war, and the whole nation was contributing to the effort. Kassu knew women who worked in the man-ufactories, even in the forges.

In the corner, meanwhile, Pimpira was grinding grain. He kept his head bowed, his eyes averted, subservient. He lived with Kassu and Henti as a slave once more, though he slept with his parents in a big barracks during the night, both of them having survived the March. The only sound in the room was the soft, repetitive, scratching rasp of Pimpira's grindstone — and under that, a soft, breathy singing. Henti, murmuring an old Kaskan lullaby. Kassu had heard it before, it had been taught her by her grandmother on her mother's side, who had come from that region. She probably didn't even know she was singing it.

Kassu leaned over his wife. Her head was bowed, and he saw the neat parting in her long dark hair, the tight bun at her neck. "You've been with him," he said softly.

She didn't look up. "Have I?"

"I know. I always know. I can see him on you. Smell him. Hear him in the songs you sing."

"Why don't you stop us, if you still care? Oh, I forgot. You had your chance, and you weren't man enough to take it."

"We fight in the morning."

Now she looked up at him. "What?"

"The Carthaginians are coming out. Our scouts have sent word."

Uncertain, she bent her head and kept sewing. "I thought that general of theirs who has taken over the city, the Roman, has been refusing to give battle."

"Evidently he changed his mind. That's Romans for

you—probably why they always lose. Indecisive. So you see, my dear wife, this might be the last time we will be together this side of the grave."

She looked up again. "Do you want—"

He laughed and pulled back. "I only have an hour. We're to muster and advance on the city, to be ready before dawn. I'm to report to Himuili himself. So unless you can do something quick—has Palla taught you any more whore's tricks?"

She put aside the cloak she had been mending. "I'll help you prepare. Pimpira, food for the master, now."

Kassu was deflated at her calm. She always had been the stronger one.

He began to pull together his kit.

So, before the dawn had fully broken, the Hatti army drew up on the desiccated plain, west of Carthage. Kassu reported to Himuili, his general.

And he was handed a horse. The beast was a nag, bony and limping slightly, but it was, undoubtedly, a horse. Somewhat to his surprise he found himself riding with Himuili and other senior commanders, even including Prince Arnuwanda himself, as they inspected their forces. In the often chaotic months since the siege had been laid Kassu had enjoyed a kind of promotion that wasn't necessarily reflected in his rank. He seemed to be recognized as one of Himuili's more literate and numerate junior officers, and was therefore useful in great feats of organization, such as the running of the Hatti's military camp-city, and now in drawing up the army in good order, ready for this climactic battle. So here was Kassu in the dawn light, passing before tens of thousands of men ready for battle, *on a horse*.

Himuili watched him, amused. "Comfortable, soldier?"

"Yes, sir. Well, I can feel this nag's bones through the saddle. I thought I'd come no closer to a horse again than a hoof boiling in a stockpot."

Himuili barked a laugh. "Well, it's your lucky day. We've been keeping back the surviving beasts for today, for the battle that we knew would come—keeping them out of the sight of hungry scumbags like you, Kassu. You can guess how many men have gone to their graves because we kept a horse alive instead, but that's something we will have to sort out in the afterlife."

"Yes, sir."

"Shut up. Look along the line." He pointed.

Kassu looked north. On the Hatti army's left flank he made out cavalry units: men and horses, some mounted, some leading their horses.

"So what do you see?"

"Our own cavalry." The men were each equipped with lance and sword, and a small round shield. "And light archers. Mongols?"

"Good, yes."

"Others equipped with Frankish bows." These were gadgets of wood and iron; you turned handles to wind a thick cord back across a frame. They were awkward to handle but the bolts they delivered could pierce thick armor. "What about the Almughavars?"

"On the right wing."

Kassu turned to see. These riders of the steppe were lancers; they carried four or five iron-tipped javelins that they would hurl one by one, and then they would drive forward at an infantry unit with a long spear. Once they closed, they would snap the spear to use it as a shorter thrusting weapon.

"All these lads of the steppe have worked out their own way of fighting," Himuili murmured. "Godless wretches who drink their horses' blood by day and hump them by night, but formidable fighters if you use them right. If we get one good charge out of them I'll be happy. Well, it might be enough, for the Carthaginians are probably in a worse state than we are."

He turned his horse's head to the east, toward Carthage, and led Kassu a little further away from the line.

The plain before Carthage was turning yellow-brown, like the desert, from all the sandstorms, but you could still see the hummocks and ridges that had once marked out farms and orchards, and the ruins of broken-down buildings stuck out of the dirt like broken limbs. And beyond all that, on the horizon, Kassu could see the walls of the city itself, a line of dirty white, studded with towers.

Himuili grunted. "A formidable sight."

"Yes, sir. But even from here you can see how the walls have been blackened by our fires. Anyhow, Carthage itself isn't the prize. Carthage is just an obstacle on the road to Egypt, and all its lovely grain."

Himuili grinned, leaned over and slapped his back. "Good response. You should talk to Palla about putting some of this stuff in his sermons to the troops, which for me are a bit heavy on the suffering and submission of Jesus. Ah, but you and Palla have history, don't you? Well, forget I mentioned him."

He turned his horse again so they looked back at the army of the Hatti, drawn up for battle, blocks of men, their armor and polished weapons glittering in the light of the rising sun. Kassu could see the restless rustle of the cavalry units on the left and right wings. Arnuwanda with his party was galloping before the line, under a great banner of Jesus Sharruma, a colorful little knot of motion. Jesus Himself had been brought out of His temple and positioned on a cart just behind the central phalanx, a towering statue encrusted with precious metals and jewels, shining in the low sunlight.

"So you see the formation," Himuili said. "Our best troops in the center, the Bodyguards and the Golden Spearmen, before Jesus, to be led by Arnuwanda himself. The other central units have been handed to the Chief of Bodyguards, the Chief of the Wine Cellar, the prince's brothers and cousins . . ."

In the Hatti system the King was always the commander in chief—but as the Hatti nation had no king just now, with Uhhaziti's coronation postponed until after the fall of Carthage, Prince Arnuwanda took that formal command, while relatives, more men of the royal blood, filled the other senior posts. Kassu suspected that Arnuwanda would be allowed to lead the initial advance, but would be whisked to the back of the lines by his own guards before the real action started. "Who have they given you, sir?"

Himuili pointed to his right, and spat between his helmet's cheek flaps. "That bunch of bears." They were a unit of Scand and Rus. Bristling with fur and in their horned helmets, from this distance they did look like animals. "I've learned enough of their language to order them about. Mostly obscenities. You should see them in their quarters, Kassu. Hairy as my left bollock, every last one of them, but when they strip naked to scrape off the filth, you see that their entire skin is coated in tattoos. If I were a Carthaginian I'd take care where I pierce such a fellow when I kill him, for his flayed hide would make a good souvenir to hang on the wall. But they're ferocious, I'll say that.

"Well. There you see it, soldier. What do you think of our chances today?"

Kassu thought carefully before answering. Himuili was quick to anger, but he knew the general wanted the truth. "There's a lot of us, sir. But a lot more have died since we got here. And we look . . ."

"Say it, man."

"Weakened. Even before the fighting starts. By the hunger, the thirst. Many of us have had a brush with one sickness or another, even if we haven't succumbed to the plague, and every dose of the shits weakens you a bit more."

"You're not wrong about that. Ten days back you'd have observed me attempting to spew up my own asshole. Look how scrawny they are—even those cursed Rus, for all their bluster. Look how *slowly* they move. I think we've prepared as well as we can today. But even so, here we are, Kassu, the last army of the Hatti, and it's an army of skeletons, of wraiths."

"Perhaps. But it's the Carthaginians' last chance too . . ."

Now there was a trumpet blast, cries of warning, fingers pointing east. Turning their horses, they saw that the great gates of Carthage had opened.

Himuili grinned. "The game's on. Good! Come on, soldier, let's get back to our line before it blows away in the desert wind." And he flicked his horse's reins and galloped away.

69

n the early morning of the very day of battle, a courier came for Rina, sent by Barmocar. To her bewilderment she was summoned to join a party that would go into the field ahead of the Carthaginian army, to meet the Hatti leaders in a last-ditch negotiation. Her—a Northlander matron and outsider in this city, summoned to this most historic of events! But, she thought with a kind of grim pride, a Northlander should be marching with the Carthaginian army today. After all it was a Northlander weapon that might win the day for Carthage. And, short of beating out the iron carcass of an eruptor herself, in the days since her meeting with Barmocar and Carthalo she had used long-dormant skills of leadership to do as much as anybody to ensure that the project had been completed.

So she dressed quickly, donning a smart but sensible robe, and pulled a cloak over her shoulders. For walking on the rough ground outside the city, she dug out the stout boots she had worn for the journey from Northland. Here in the small town house given her by the suffetes, she had no servants to help her. She could not bear servants in her presence, not anymore. Having checked her appearance in a brass mirror, she hurried out of her house and to the city gate.

The army pouring out of Carthage was an extraordinary sight. It was an army of scarecrows, Rina thought, after months of siege, all but the officers dressed in ragged uniforms and armed with rusty blades.

Fabius' carriage was more extraordinary yet. He called it his "truce wagon." The great vehicle, specially constructed, rolled on four pairs of mighty timber wheels, each hooped by iron and fixed to tremendous axles. The wagon was drawn by teams of Hatti prisoners, harnessed like oxen, but Fabius had promised them their freedom when the job was done, and so they pulled willingly. On the wagon's bed sat a great chest, a huge wooden box nearly as tall as Rina, so long that the custom-made wagon barely fit it. The chest was covered in expensive cloths and tapestries bearing images of the city's gods. But the most extraordinary aspect of the whole thing was what lay on top of that chest: human skulls, all lacking their lower jaws, a heap of them arranged in an orderly pyramid. You could see that most of the skulls were small, most of young children; the larger ones supported the smaller, until at the apex of the pyramid was fixed the smallest of all, tiny enough to have fit into Rina's palm. It was the skull of a newborn, its little throat slit at the moment of its birth. This was a *molk* cart, and the city's primitive sacrifice was horribly visible. And that, of course, was the point.

As the truce wagon rolled out of the gate, followed by the columns of troops, Fabius with his senior officers walked ahead. The great and the good of Carthage had been summoned to follow behind the general, and Rina hurried to join them. Here came Carthalo, following in the Roman's wake, along with many others of the councils, even the Tribunal of One Hundred and Four, whose constitutional function was to keep generals like Fabius in check. None dare resist him now. Some of Fabius' soldiers walked beside the general, whether to protect him from Hatti or Carthaginians it was hard to say.

Barmocar, his expression dark, worked through the small crowd of dignitaries toward her. "So you came, madam."

"You summoned me. It was only courteous—"

"Courteous? I brought you here to see what you have done, woman. The skulls, Rina—the skulls!"

She took a breath. "And Mago—"

He turned away from her, his face working. "*His skull is here*, on the carriage with the rest, not ten paces from where you stand. He did not die on the grisly altar of the temple, however. He died well, in combat, fighting off a Hatti raid. I hope that whatever you imagine I have done to you is now compensated." He leaned closer and whispered, "And if we live through this day I will make sure the rest of your life is blighted as mine is." He withdrew.

Alone, Rina walked on, trying to show no emotion.

Outside the city walls, the Carthaginian army began drawing up in battle order, the men gathering in great blocks within which the men were all dressed and equipped similarly. These formations were called phalanxes, Rina had been told. The truce wagon rolled forward, accompanied by Fabius and the nobles, advancing beyond the lines. And now, Rina saw, a party of the Hatti came out to meet the Carthaginians. One man was mounted, and the rest walked under their own truce banner, of Jesus Sharruma with the crescent moon.

Rina was close enough to Fabius to hear one of his aides muttering advice to him. "The mounted man is Arnuwanda, their prince, chief of the armies, though it's said it's his aunt the Tawananna who makes the big decisions. The soldier at his side is Himuili, one of the smarter generals. The young priest—I don't recognize him, I was expecting Angulli . . ."

"Mother?"

She whirled. She had not heard that voice in months. *"Nelo?"*

It was him, her son, a soldier in his tunic and mail and helmet, standing beside the Roman. He was armed with nothing more lethal than a crayon and his sketch paper. For a heartbeat they stared at each other, both disbelieving. Then they broke and ran to each other, regardless of the rest of the world, the two foreign armies before and behind them.

"I didn't know you were here," he stammered out at last.

"Nor I you. I spent an awful lot of money paying for news of your progress." She laughed, but it was as much a sob. "I tried to save you, to get you out of there. It was part of the deal—I thought Barmocar had cheated me—"

Nelo glanced at Fabius. "His man came for me. I refused to leave. I could not leave him, Mother. The general. This is history."

Fabius heard all this. He growled, "There won't be much more history for you if you aren't back by my side this instant, boy."

Rina clung to him. "Forgive me," she said frantically. "For what happened in the beginning—it was Barmocar, again. We could not have survived here in Carthage if I had not let the army take you. Forgive me!"

Nelo shrugged. "I thought it had to be something like that. It wasn't your job to protect me, I was old enough. If you'd just asked, I'd have gone anyway, to save you and Alxa."

"Oh, Nelo—"

He broke away. "Later, Mother."

There was no more time. For now, in the middle of the field, the enemy commanders met.

The Hatti prince dismounted. With the general and the young priest, and trailed by aides and wary soldiers, he walked boldly toward Fabius.

"Roman," Arnuwanda said. "We meet again."

Fabius bowed. "I am honored to be in your presence again, sir, My Sun, whose integrity is known to all the world."

They both spoke Hatti and Carthaginian, and aides murmured translations.

Arnuwanda grunted. "I don't deserve that title, and Crown Prince Uhhaziti won't have it, not until this day is won. Why are we speaking? Why are we not fighting? And what is that grisly contraption? What are you going to do, pelt us with skulls?" He was rewarded with a ripple of laughter from his own men.

Fabius waited patiently until they were quiet. "I am a Roman. But I work within the traditions of my adopted city. And these poor bones represent one of those traditions. It is the *molk*, the sacrifice. In this lore, the gods' favor is won by the sacrifice of children."

Arnuwanda paced. "What barbarism is this?"

Some of his men were disturbed, and they muttered prayers, and made the symbol of Jesus Sharruma, the crossed arms over the chest. Every eye was fixed on the heap of skulls, which, Rina knew, was its true purpose, to distract.

"Not barbarism, Prince," said Fabius evenly. "If I had a son myself I would have given him up willingly, to the gods of the city."

"Well, *our* gods will have something to say about how effectual that has been. What else, Roman?" He peered at the huge covered casket on the wagon, on which the skull heap stood. "I yield to curiosity. What is in the box?"

Fabius smiled. "Another tradition of the Carthaginians, sir. A gift. They are a trading people, remember; they would always rather trade than fight. So here is this offer—a gift for you, after the receipt of which, they hope, your will to fight this day will be eliminated."

"Are you trying to buy us off? Is it gold, silver, jewelry? Is it so banal? My men can't eat gold. And besides, every coffer in Carthage will be open to me by the end of the day."

"Not that."

The Roman seemed to be enjoying the game, Rina thought uneasily, and she prayed he wouldn't push his luck too far. Already some of the men behind Arnuwanda looked suspicious.

Now one tough-looking soldier stepped forward and grabbed Arnuwanda's arm. "There's something wrong here. Sir, step back—"

"Oh, be still, Kassu—"

Fabius roared, "Now, Gisco!"

In an instant Carthaginian soldiers leapt at the cart and hauled aside the drapes, scattering the skulls carelessly on the dusty ground, to reveal the wooden crate. With a few tugs on rope loops the walls of the crate fell away—and the eruptor was exposed to the air. It was a great bulb of cast iron, reinforced with bound hoops, and with a gaping mouth pointing straight at the Hatti lines. Men huddled around the eruptor, blinking in the sudden daylight; they too had been hidden with the weapon inside the crate. One of them was a young man called Thux, a Northlander engineer who had once worked the pumps on the Wall. The rest were Carthaginian soldiers.

Already they were in action. Rina had witnessed endless rehearsals with this team since the casting of the barrel, and she knew that the loading must already be complete, the powdery fire drug itself shoveled into the barrel and rammed home, the muddy loam paste pushed in after it, and then the stone, a rock roughly chipped into shape. And the wick, a tube of paper filled with the drug, would have been pushed into a hole drilled into the eruptor's metal flank. Now Thux himself approached this wick with a lighted candle.

Arnuwanda and the Hatti stood and stared. "What is that?"

"A thunderbolt from Jupiter," snarled Fabius in Latin. "Now, Northlander!"

As Thux lowered the candle to the powder tube, Rina screamed to her son. "Get down, Nelo! Oh, get down!"

Kassu saw the iron contraption, and the flame, and the scattering Carthaginians. *This was a weapon.* And he stood right before it. He was nowhere near the prince—Himuili had already dragged Arnuwanda away—but Kassu stood beside Palla. He grabbed the priest and hurled him to the ground.

The eruptor exploded.

That was what it felt like, sounded like. He glimpsed a dark mass flash from its mouth in a plume of fire and smoke, with a noise like thunder—it seemed to brush his foot even as he fell over Palla—and then it plummeted into the Hatti lines, and scattered the men, and he saw a kind of bursting of blood and bone.

When the roaring was over he found himself down on the ground, on top of the priest, Palla's face below his. Smoke billowed around them. Men were screaming, but it felt as if his ears had been stuffed with cloth. He looked around. The central phalanx had been scattered, men lying smashed and broken. The statue of Jesus was gone too, shattered, only a stump remaining. And high on the walls of Carthage he saw dark mouths, more eruptors, aimed at the Hatti lines.

Then the pain hit him, a great wave from his right leg. He looked down. The leg was gone, from beneath the knee. Oddly no blood spurted. Perhaps the heat of the stone had cauterized it.

The priest beneath him grinned. "You're crippled."

"Your god is dead." He had to shout to hear himself.

"You should have killed me while you had the chance." And the priest drove a blade into Kassu's side, under his mail coat.

More pain, exploding in him like the Carthaginian weapon. The priest twisted his blade, and Kassu could feel it pierce his muscle and pull his guts, feel it as it scraped on his backbone.

But Zida was here. He rolled Kassu aside. "This story ends now." He brought his axe chopping down on the priest's neck.

Kassu, lying on his back, tried to speak. "Pimpira . . . I leave my estate to Pimpira, not to that whore of a wife. To Pimpira . . ." But he saw no more, heard no more, save a rush like thunder that rose up and enveloped him.

Four

70

In the north the snow was still falling. The great ice sheets continued to spread across the continents, merging, pressing south. As so much water was locked up in the newly formed ice, all around the world sea levels dropped, and the land grew arid. Even the tropical forests withered back.

One day new kinds of terrain would coalesce south of the ice sheets, belts of sparse tundra, grassy steppe, barren desert, stretching all around a colder, dryer planet. The chill oceans would be fecund too. New ways of life, in the future.

One day. For now, there was only the death of the old.

Still this was only the beginning.

71

The Hatti negotiating party was to be met by Barmocar at the Byrsa gate.

Pyxeas and Rina had been invited to join the official Carthaginian response as representatives of Northland in exile, and as embodiments of the knowledge and power that had crushed the morale of the Hatti siege forces. Rina insisted that Nelo should attend too, to see the end of the story that had had such an impact on his own young life.

So Nelo met his mother and great-uncle at the gate. Waiting for the Hatti, they were all wrapped in their winter cloaks for, despite the arrival of another spring, it was a cold, blustery morning, with flakes of snow driven on a swirling wind. This was a part of Carthage Nelo rarely visited, much too grand for Northlander exiles, even now.

And Fabius still dangled from his cross high above the gate, bones and flesh and cartilage, wrapped in his cloak of Roman purple.

Carthalo of the suffetes was here too, waiting with

Rina. He regarded Nelo blankly. "You are the soldier boy who scribbled at the whim of the Roman."

Pyxeas flared. He was an old man, bent, weary from the long journey from which he would likely never recover, yet he straightened with dignity to face Carthalo. "A boy who was ready and willing to fight in the army that defended this city. Perhaps he deserves a little respect, sir." He glanced up at Fabius. "And perhaps the Roman does too. I'm sorry if it troubles you, Nelo, to see him abused like this."

Nelo shrugged. "I've seen worse on the battlefield. Fabius is gone. His people believe that when you die you cross a dark river to the next world." But you needed coins to pay the ferryman, and Nelo knew that some of Fabius' soldiers had sworn that when the body was finally cut down they would bury it with Roman honors, with coins on his eyeless sockets. "That's not Fabius up there."

"No," came a wheezing voice. "Not Fabius, but a symbol of him. And that's what counts, isn't it?"

They turned, and saw that the party of Hatti dignitaries was approaching, processing up a cobbled street toward the gate. The party was small, just a handful of Hatti nobles in their brightly colored court robes, with one senior military officer, flanked by an escort of wary Hatti and Carthaginian soldiers. The street had been cleared for the day, to be sure that nobody got a chance to have a swipe at the Hatti in revenge for the long siege.

The man who had spoken was old, stooped; he wore a long robe decorated with the crossed palm-leaves symbol of the Hatti god Jesus, and boots with toes upturned in the Hatti style. Everybody was looking at him, and he smiled. "I seem to have spoken out of turn, before the introductions were done. Well, I don't imagine we need rely on protocol overmuch today, do we? My name is Angulli. I am a priest; my title is Father of the Churches." He gestured to the woman he accompanied. "And this is My Sun Hastayar the Tawananna."

Carthalo stepped forward and gravely welcomed the queen. She looked magnificent, Nelo thought, her hair lustrous, her face painted white with vivid red spots on cheeks and forehead. Gold thread shone bright in her robe of rich crimson, despite the clouded sky.

The senior Hatti officer, a general, stepped up to Nelo. "I know you."

This was Himuili, who had commanded the Hatti forces in the field, under the prince, Arnuwanda. "Yes, sir, I—"

"Shut up. You're the Northlander who Fabius insisted on bringing to his parlays." He glanced up at the crucified Roman. "Much good it did him, eh? Standing here today you'd never believe that *he* won and *I* lost. This is how Carthage treats its victorious generals, is it?"

"Carthage is always suspicious of its generals, successful or not. And Fabius did take over the government."

Himuili grunted. "Smartest thing he ever did. And so there he dangles with his guts hanging out. As a symbol, of course. The question is, a symbol meant for who? Other uppity Carthaginian officers? Or us, the Hatti? 'Look how strong we are, we Carthaginians. We can defeat you *and* afford to string up our winning general.' By Jesus' armpit, I hate diplomacy."

"Yes, sir."

"Shut up."

Now the party were led through the gate into the Byrsa district. This was the first formal visit of the Hatti leaders to Carthage since the day of the aborted battle nearly half a year earlier. As Angulli had suggested, it didn't seem to be a day for excessive formality, but a certain precedence emerged anyhow. The Tawananna walked flanked by the city's two suffetes, while Pyxeas and Nelo's mother escorted Angulli the priest, and Himuili walked with senior Carthaginian officers. Nelo and the rest of the party followed on behind, with soldiers of both nations flanking them. Interpreters hovered, murmuring into their masters' ears like bees seeking pollen.

The Hatti were to be taken up to the formal buildings at the Byrsa's summit, where treaties between the nations would be outlined, to be formally written up by scribes on both sides and sealed at a later date. Those Hatti who had not visited this place before visibly tried not to stare at the striking layout of the citadel, the radial avenues leading up to a summit crowned by monumental buildings, and Hannibal's column at the very apex.

Once there had been shops, offices, fine expensive residences, many buildings rising two, three, four stories over the streets. Now the shops were closed, the offices empty. But several buildings had been knocked through to make room for new functions. They were manufactories, here in the most secure quarter of the city. As they neared, Nelo could hear the shouts of the workmen, and a hammering noise, metal struck by metal. The suffetes and their aides had been determined that the Hatti should see these workshops. And now through the open doors of one great building they glimpsed the components of more fire-drug weapons being cast. There was a fully functioning forge where workers hammered at lumps of iron, and a carpentry shop where giant wooden formers were constructed, and then a series of great benches where cast-iron strips, white-hot, were hammered flat to be fitted around the formers. Nelo could see the way the manufacture of the weapons went, from one step to the next. And at the finish stood a complete eruptor, the bulbous belly with the stubby nozzle, just as had been unveiled on the plain of battle. The men who labored in the forge heat were stripped to their loincloths, but they wore gloves that stretched up to cover their forearms, saving their skin from red-hot splashes.

"More symbols for us to gawp at," growled Himuili.

Hastayar gently chided him. "Now, General, we're here on a mission of friendship, and we must be polite.

But he's right, of course," she said to Carthalo. "You clearly intend to impress on us your capability to churn out these fire pots of yours. You drive home your dominance, like a booted heel driven into the back of a fallen soldier."

Carthalo smiled. "A little crudely put, madam."

"But I am right."

She was, but since the day of the battle Nelo had learned more of the truth. The eruptor that had fired its fatal shot at the Hatti ranks that day was only the fifth to be successfully constructed by Pyxeas' conspiracy of Northlander engineers here in Carthage—and only the third to have been fired without blowing itself up, turning its firing crew to an expanding cloud of blood mist and bone shards in the process. Although Nelo supposed that in itself would have been a spectacular demonstration. Most of the eruptors that had been pushed to the crest of the walls of Carthage had been harmless dummies. Some weren't even cast iron.

Himuili grunted. "These big iron beasts are all very well, but I see no sign of their lethal breath. I mean this substance you call the fire drug."

Pyxeas smiled. "That's kept under lock and key elsewhere. I, Pyxeas, offer my apologies. It has been a state secret of the Northlanders for centuries, and now is a secret shared only with Carthage."

"I do know it came from Cathay originally," Himuili said, probing.

"That's true," Pyxeas said. "In fact Cathay scholars discovered it entirely accidentally. They were seeking an elixir of life, a drug to banish death forever. Well, what they came up with is an elixir of death, I suppose. A quirky gift of their gods. And that is why it is known as a 'drug' to this day.

"General, I heard you talking of symbols to my great-nephew. Of course you're right. Carthage seeks to impress you today. You are a military man. Think of the future, sir. Imagine a more powerful eruptor, capable of smashing down a city wall with a single stone. Imagine an eruptor that can fly through the air like a bird. *Or imagine an eruptor small enough to hold in the hand of a single warrior.* You think this is fanciful? Soon Carthage will have all this, as you never will."

"We know we are beaten, scholar," murmured the old priest. "Speak gently."

Now, after the weapon manufactory, the party was led past another workshop, where a much more positive symbol was under construction. In a lofty hall a dozen artisans worked on a tremendous statue of Jesus Sharruma, the Hatti god. For now it was a rough marble form, but Nelo knew the plan was to decorate the god as richly as had been the holy image brought from Hattusa. Old Angulli made the crossed-arms sign of the palm leaves, and bowed down, muttering a prayer.

Carthalo said smoothly, "You can see how we labor to heal the wound we inflicted. The new god will include the smashed fragments of the old."

"It's true," Angulli said. "I supervised the collection myself, especially of the remains of the core wooden sculpture created by the hands of Him. The fragments are splashed with the blood of our soldiers—but that only sanctifies them further."

"We have invited your best sculptors and artists to work with our own—we have given you every facility. And when it is done, you understand, we will offer you the statue of your god—together with the bones of His Mother, which treasure has been saved from Northland and the ice."

"I have heard of this," Angulli said. "It is an extraordinary gesture. On behalf of my people, of my god, I thank you for this."

"When He is complete, Jesus Sharruma can lead you to your new home."

Hastayar said restlessly, "It's easy to say that. But where are we to go? We had no plans beyond the conquest of your city, I admit."

Carthalo said, "We are not monsters. We will take your sick, your young, your old, all those who cannot walk, even though our own resources are strained. *The rest of you must go.*"

"But, I say again, where? I don't imagine you'd welcome it if we marched east into Egypt, your breadbasket."

Carthalo glanced at Pyxeas, who stepped forward. "Not east," the scholar said. "*West.* Go west from here, along the coast—"

Himuili snapped, "Until we run out of land and find ourselves facing the ocean. Then what?"

"Then go west again," Pyxeas said. "Take ships across the ocean."

"We will help you," Carthalo said.

Pyxeas smiled. "Though I've never made the journey myself, we Northlanders have been crossing the Western Ocean for millennia. We will guide you."

Hastayar seemed baffled. "And when we have crossed the ocean—what then?"

"There are new lands waiting for you," Carthalo said. "Whole continents, where you can build your next Hattusa."

Himuili scowled. "Lands with people in them already, that's what I've heard."

"But with room for more," Pyxeas insisted.

And Nelo, looking at him, wondered if that was the first time he had ever heard his great-uncle tell a flat lie.

At length the group walked on, heading for the great buildings at the summit of the Byrsa, and the formal sessions.

Nelo walked with Pyxeas. "You didn't tell the truth," he said accusingly. "You told the Hatti that the western continents have room. No, they don't. Especially now the winters are taking their grip, for they must be suffering over there as we are over here."

"Well, true, that was a lie I told the Hatti. But I balanced it by telling the Carthaginians a lie too."

"What lie?"

"That the Hatti will never have the secrets of the fire drug. As soon as their great fleet of ships is ready to sail, I intend that they should be given the secrets of the drug. With that advantage none of the peoples of the western lands will be able to resist them."

Nelo stared, shocked. "Why would you do such a thing?"

Pyxeas sighed. "It was a difficult decision to make. Of course it is difficult. The suffering that will follow from this act, the thousands that will die. I—we, for the other Northlander elders in exile concurred—we are playing games on a continental scale. But we have to be rid of the Hatti, you know. *There isn't room for them here*, especially not if we are to build our own city, a New Etxelur. Sharing Africa with the Carthaginians will be bad enough. And then there is Mali, south of the desert, rich from its gold mines, which has been relatively spared by the longwinter so far. Now the *mansa* is making what some regard as aggressive noises oward its northern neighbors. We have enough to handle here. Let the People of the Jaguar deal with the Hatti."

"I can't believe you will give away precious Northlander lore."

"But the Hatti would probably soon steal it anyway. And besides, the fire drug knowledge is nothing. A shiny bauble, a whiz-bang toy that distracts small minds, like those of princes and generals. Once, you know, the great treasure of Northland was flint, a particularly fine lode that was mined from Etxelur. That was what men crossed the world for! Now nobody cares for flint at all. But since the age of Ana our true treasure has been Northland's deep and ancient collective memory, our profound understanding of the world and its cycles—even as those cycles scatter us across the globe. Which is why I must return to Northland, by the way."

"What?" Nelo stopped and stared at him. "Uncle, are you mad? The weather was bad enough last year when I traveled down with my mother. It may not even be possible to make the return journey now. Your journey to Cathay nearly killed you!"

"Ah, but I live on."

"Now you want to do it again?"

"I must, Nephew. I brought back much lore from Cathay. I have since reached certain conclusions . . . I must consult any scholarship that survives at Etxelur, and I must reach the Wall Archive before it is lost to the ice altogether. For we must build an Archive in New Etxelur, wherever it is founded, and we must stock it with the heritage of the past. To preserve the *idea* of Northland, and our learning and scholarship."

Snow swirled down, thicker, heavy flakes that beat like chill butterflies against their faces. They walked on, side by side.

"I will come with you," Nelo said impulsively.

Pyxeas studied him. "Are you sure? I have Avatak."

"He is a good man. He will be better with me at his side. There is nothing for me here."

Pyxeas, limping as he climbed, clapped Nelo on the shoulder. "Very well. But make sure you secure your drawings first. They must be preserved too. That mad Roman was right, that they are a true first-hand record of the last war in history . . ."

Talking, arguing, they climbed the hill, cloaks clutched tight around their bodies. The snow fell thicker, settling on the rooftops of Carthage.

72

As soon as the epochal deal was done with the Hatti, the party that would take Pyxeas back to Northland prepared for their departure.

Rina tried to help. At least she could do that much, given that she had failed to get the old man to abandon this foolish idea and stay in the comparative safety of the city.

Avatak would go, of course, the old man's constant companion. As a Coldlander he possessed the skills needed to survive in a world gripped by the longwinter, if anybody could. And, Rina suspected, he was the only man Pyxeas really trusted. Himil wanted to go, which was a surprise. Once a servant to Jexami, he was now a capable young man with enterprises of his own in a much-changed Carthage—and who seemed to feel some loyalty for Rina, because of Alxa. He still had to support his own family. "But," he said, "everybody says the world is shutting down because of the longwinter. I want to see a bit of it while I still can. Something to tell my own kids." Rina saw he would certainly be useful in the early stages of the journey; he knew Carthage and its dependencies and allies as none of the rest did.

And then there was Nelo, artist-soldier, who had had enough of Carthage, he said, and wanted to go home. Rina felt it was good for Pyxeas to have family with him on this jaunt—and Nelo, in the course of his time in Carthage, had certainly toughened up.

But Nelo was Rina's son, her only surviving child.

She could not dissuade him. And, thinking it over, she gave him a special commission—a small case to carry, containing the cremated remains of the Northlanders who had died here in the months and years since the great flight from the north, all she could assemble. They could be interred with their ancestors in the Wall growstone, ready to continue the millennia-long fight against the sea. Thus she discharged her debt to the dying Jexami.

The most basic question was how they were to travel, and by what route. It was clear that Pyxeas could not walk far. Himil the Carthaginian wanted to go by sea, probably sailing north along the shore of the Western Ocean as far north as they could, putting in to surviving ports to reprovision. Avatak the Coldlander wanted to go overland, through the heart of the country, then across the Northland ice all the way to the Wall. They would carry most of what they needed; they would hunt on the way. Nelo had no opinion.

Rina asked around Carthage for advice; this was a city of travelers and traders after all. In the end she talked to the innkeeper called Myrcan—not for the first time, for it was in his dingy bar that she had had one of her last meetings with her daughter, and she had come back many times since, as if in search of the echo of Alxa.

"People tell me the truth," he said. He poured her a cup of wine. "Make the most of this, by the way, the last really good vintage we got before the weather turned to shit. Pardon my language."

"I've heard worse," Rina said drily.

"The truth. Every traveler is expected to file a report with the suffetes. It's not just scholars who need to know what's becoming of the world. And when they've reported to the suffetes most of them come here, and report to me—or rather, to the best listener in the world," and he rapped a fingernail against the neck of the wine flask.

"Well, I want the truth, as best you have it," she said grimly.

"Then tell your uncle he must travel overland. That Coldlander boy is right. The interiors of the countries are emptying out. This has been going on for years. By now the people have either fled south or to the coast. So if you travel by sea you have these crowded coastal ports full of starving nestspills, and everybody's out on the ocean fighting for the catch, and you have pirates who've got bolder and bolder. Why, I'm told the market for slaves from the west, shipped over to what's left of the countries in the east, is one of the healthiest businesses in the world.

"So your son and his party want to avoid all that mucking about. Go across country. That way they'll only have to deal with a few starving farmers, and wild animals who are as confused as we are. Tell them Myrcan said so. Now, do you want some more of this reasonably priced nectar or shall I stopper it for you to take home?"

From such recommendations, and partly because of all of them it was only the Coldlander boy who seemed to have any idea of how this journey might actually be achieved, the decision was made: overland it would be, after a short sea crossing to the southern shore of Ibera.

The Carthaginian authorities were lavish in funding Pyxeas' expedition, in a mood of nervous gratitude. Or perhaps the city just wanted rid of him, he joked. So the party gathered equipment and supplies, heavy jackets, breeches, hats and boots made from the fur of seals and bear, meat and fish dried and salted, pickled vegetables in clay pots—and a carriage.

Pyxeas took a great deal of interest in helping Avatak design this carriage. In its initial incarnation it would be a heavy horse-drawn cart with stout iron-rimmed wheels. It would bear a small canvas shelter at all times, so Pyxeas could stay in the warm and the dry while they traveled. Pyxeas even had a metal plate installed in the floor so they could build a fire in the back. But when they had to travel across snow and ice, the carriage's wheels and axles could be detached, and long polished runners exposed so the cart became a sled. Pyxeas had a lot of fun with this, devising little mechanisms whereby the axles could be detached by loosening a few bolts and pulling levers. Rina saw a side of him she had never known before. All her life he had essentially been an old man. This was how he must once have been as a child, a bright boy tinkering with gadgets, just as the scholar would one day try to take apart the mechanisms of the world itself.

Suddenly they were ready to go.

A good crowd assembled by the dock in the great Carthaginian harbor to see them off. Pyxeas' fame as a scholar had been wide even before his monumental trip to Cathay. Avatak too, a sturdy, exotic-looking young man, was an object of curiosity, though he seemed completely unaware of it. As the small ship was loaded with their goods Nelo made a few last sketches of Carthage's astonishing harbor, the low light catching the long stretches of docks, jetties and warehouses, the crowd of spectators, and the vendors who, as ever, turned up from nowhere to sell people stuff they didn't know they needed.

Rina struggled with her feelings. She thought she had lost Nelo emotionally because of the blood sacrifice she had had to make of him, and then she feared she had lost him altogether to the war. Now she was going to lose him again, to the ice, to the longwinter, to Pyxeas' strange ambitions. Even as she had worked on the preparations, her mother's heart had been ripped apart, shred by shred.

In the end she could not bear to wait for the final departure, the last embrace, the waving from the shore as the ship pulled away. She couldn't help it, even if it was yet another betrayal. She fled to her office in the city and buried herself in work, until Nelo's ship had sailed.

73

The ship out of Carthage took them west, through the strait into the Western Ocean, and then to a Carthaginian port in southern Ibera, at the mouth of a mighty river. The port was working, the harbor crowded with shipping, the town itself bustling. But Avatak, having seen a dozen ports on the way back home on the Arab trader, had learned how to read a town, a countryside. He quickly saw that the ships were bringing in food, armor, other supplies, and they were taking out people, more nestspills, all heading south. The country that had once sustained this port had become a threat to it; the landward city walls were heavily armed against rough camps of nestspills beyond. But that was the country across which they must travel.

They spent three days spending Carthaginian money on what they needed for the next stage. They hired a riverboat to take them deep into the interior of the country, and a troop of the port's city guard for protection. Their elaborate carriage was loaded on board the boat.

They sailed out beyond the protection of the city

walls by night, to minimize the threat from the great band of nestspills, bandits and warlords that surrounded the walls. The weather inland was cloudy, blustery, cold, and it frequently rained, the water pooling on the hard earth. The soldiers from the coast huddled under leathers and gambled over games played with broken bits of bone. Pyxeas spent much of his time working in the little shelter on the carriage, or dozing.

They passed by empty towns on the riverbank, and huge plantations where once olive trees had grown in great numbers. Now it was all gone, the weather too wet and cold for the olives, the people bankrupted, fled or starved. But the land was not barren, Avatak saw; in places swathes of grass glowed green in the rare sunlight. Nelo sketched all this compulsively, on Egyptian paper scraped so thin you could almost see through it.

Pyxeas, on one of his rare ventures out of his tent, nudged Avatak in the ribs. "Remember the steppe? One day soon, it may only be centuries, this place will be an ocean of grass too, just as we saw in the heart of Asia. The great-grandchildren of these boatmen and laughing soldiers will be horse-riding nomads, and herds of fleet beasts will cross these plains like the shadows of clouds. I, Pyxeas, predict this."

Himil looked baffled. "I do not question your conclusions, scholar. But how can you know all this?"

The scholar smiled and tapped his temple. "From observations of the world—from patterns deduced, and stored in my memory—from understanding the superhuman rhythms of the ice."

Himil just stared. Then, when the scholar had withdrawn, he turned to Avatak. "*You* must know what he's talking about."

Avatak shrugged.

But Nelo said, "I thought he was trying to teach you. I know he's come up with some big idea about why the longwinter is happening."

"Yes. We were on a ship when he said he got it, the

final solution. Pirates were smashing in our heads at the time."

"Didn't he *tell* you?"

"I stopped listening. It's all"—he searched for the word—"*abstract.*" He found he'd used a Cathay word. He tried again. "Not real. Not here and now. Once his learning interested me. In Coldland, there's nobody like him. But we barely survived that journey from Cathay, and now this. What does it matter what this country will be like a thousand years from now? Somebody else might be trying to cross it then; it won't be us."

"True enough, my friend," said Himil.

Nelo asked, "Then why did you stay with my uncle?"

Avatak looked at the old man. "For what's inside him. Not his knowledge, all those numbers. Which is all he thinks there is to him."

"What then?"

"His sadness. At what he saw before anybody else saw it, before a single flake of snow had fallen. Sadness for the world, and all of us who must live in it. Even the generations to come. That's why I stay with him."

Nelo considered this. "You're a good man, my friend."

Avatak shrugged.

They followed the river upstream, traveling roughly northwest for some days, until they came to another large city, far inland. They left the boat here; it returned to the coast, taking the soldiers with it, and they were on their own.

This city was a mere shadow of what it must once have been. It had extensive walls, breached, burned and roughly repaired. Inside the walls whole suburbs looked abandoned, burned out. The country beyond seemed empty, with only a tracery of the walls of abandoned farms to be seen. Avatak wondered, in fact, how the city kept functioning at all.

"And no dogs," Himil said. "Have you noticed that? No barking. And no cats. Or cage birds singing."

"All long gone into the pot," Nelo said gloomily.

There may have been no dogs, but there were horses to be had, scrawny nags at a price that Himil the Carthaginian said was eye-watering. But Avatak knew their money did not matter; it would count for nothing once they got further north, and may as well be spent while there was something useful to buy.

Leaving the city behind, they worked their way northwest along the river valley, the companions taking turns to drive the carriage, ride the spare horses, or to walk alongside. After some days they came to another much reduced city straddling the river. From here they turned north, following a good Carthaginian road that crossed higher ground. Although this was early summer it felt markedly colder here than at the coast, and the land seemed even more barren, the towns and way stations burned out and abandoned. Avatak felt exposed without the guard, but there seemed to be no bandits on this empty tabletop of a country, and they made good progress.

They came to yet another city, another shrunken remnant. As they approached they came across a substantial procession forming up at the southern gates, men, women, children and old folk, most on foot, some dragging carts, evidently preparing to take the opportunity of the summer to head south. Avatak silently wished them luck.

At the gate Pyxeas' party was challenged by a different kind of authority. This, it seemed, was the boundary between the Carthaginian empire and the realm of the Franks, whose power base was further north. Guards at the gates asked for hefty tolls to allow this Carthaginian party to pass. They had some Frankish money, but the Franks preferred Northlander scrip, which made Pyxeas laugh. "Just pay the man, Avatak, pay the man."

North of the city they followed rougher tracks. The country was barren and bare, and grew steadily colder. In places, they threaded through broad mountain passes; the mountains were all white-capped, and streaked with the gray tongues of glaciers. When they stopped on scraps of higher ground they would sometimes glimpse structures in the distance, not on peaks but on high plateaus, lines and rings of stone. These did not impress Avatak much until the road took them close to one of them, and the Coldlander was able to appreciate the sheer size of the stones, the vastness of the layout, and the careful precision with which it seemed to have been designed. But even these great sky temples were disused now, and the tracks that crisscrossed the complexes were covered with blown dust.

On they journeyed, descending at last from the higher ground toward the coast. Ibera was a great peninsula, Pyxeas said, with its neck crossed by a tremendous mountain chain — and now, from higher ground, Avatak could glimpse those mountains marching into the distance. They skirted that mountain chain, passing west by the coast of the Western Ocean, and they entered Gaira.

There were cities on the coast here, substantial ports that now brooded within the remains of walls. The travelers avoided these places. Instead they stayed a few nights in smaller villages, where the local people survived by fishing. They were welcomed, if warily; few travelers came this way anymore, it seemed. Pyxeas said this was the pattern of the future in the coming longwinter, "when no man will venture more than a day or two's travel beyond his home village, the rest of the world forgotten."

In such places Avatak stared hungrily at the ocean. Somewhere beyond, far to the west, lay his own home. Though there was no sea ice, on clear days he saw splinters of white on the gray, surging water. Icebergs, drifting from the north.

On the travelers passed, moving inland. It was clear the country had changed greatly. This land had recently been forested, with tremendously tall and old oak trees. Now the remaining trunks stood barren. Though the spring was advancing they rarely saw a splash of green, a new leaf or a fresh shoot. And in places there was evidence of tremendous fires, whole landscapes reduced to ash and blackened stumps.

Pyxeas said the culprit was the climate, once again. "This is how forests die. Avatak, remember how we smelled the northern forests burning, all the way across Asia? And remember what we saw in Daidu? When you burn a tree it is like opening a tremendous bottle of fixed air, all at once! Imagine how much has been released in these vast conflagrations . . ."

They saw few people—fewer, if anything, than in Ibera—and those they did spot, always on the move, stayed well away from what must have looked like a well-armed party. They passed through clearings in the forest, cut into the woodland and connected by broad tracks, a little like Northland's communities. These settlements were abandoned, ransacked, burned out. In one place they found a gallows set up over the central hearth, with the remains of a human body suspended upside down over the ash. Nelo sketched the gruesome scene, and he cut down the corpse with a swipe of a sword, and buried the remains in the hearth.

Further north the country changed again, becoming more open. The air was much wetter now, colder, and rain was more frequent, even sleeting sometimes, though, as they kept reminding one another, this was summer. There was extensive flooding, much of what must have been farmland turning to marsh, the walls of long-abandoned farmhouses dissolving into the wet. There were none of the bright flowers Avatak remembered from similar seasons in Northland, but flocks of birds settled almost experimentally on the new wetlands. It grew steadily colder. Soon they found themselves pushing through flurries of fresh snow; the horses wheezed and dropped their heads as the wet stuff flecked their fur, and in the mornings they would wake to frost.

"We're walking into winter," Himil said, amazed.

They came at last to Parisa, the greatest city in Frankish Gaira, sprawling across its river. Avatak remembered it well. It was still a bustling place, still alive, as you could tell from the pall of smoke hung over it. But now snow rested on its rooftops and slim minarets, and there were ice floes on the river. And if you looked only a little further north you could see only white: not a scrap of earth brown or life's green anywhere. Avatak felt a strange thrill, of recognition, and of fear. How was it possible for such a great country to have changed so quickly?

Nelo slapped him on the back. "Ice! We're in your hands now, Coldlander."

They spent a few nights in Parisa. The city had lost most of its population, and was slowly consuming itself for firewood. Every day hunting parties went out into the country, on foot and on horseback, seeking the deer and oxen and aurochs that were colonizing the soggy, deep-frozen plains. Avatak was a brief sensation when he showed Nelo and Himil and a few local hunters the best way to trap a bird. You threw a net in the air to catch it in flight, and took it in your bare hands, then bent its wings back gently and pressed its chest over its heart, and it would die quietly.

But he spent most of those days in Parisa, preparing for the journey ahead. A journey over the ice.

74

On the seventh day out of Parisa they ran into a blizzard. The northerly wind was flat, hurling hard, heavy flakes into their faces. Avatak felt the ice build up on his beard, his eyebrows, his skin. He made Nelo and Himil watch each other's faces, the noses and the cheeks, for the pale white spots that were the first signs of ice blight. Pyxeas stayed tucked up in the tent on the back of the carriage.

A blizzard in summer!

They tried to keep moving. They had dogs now, a team assembled at Avatak's insistence, to draw them over the ice. At last he had dogs, and could show what he could do! But these were dogs of Parisa, dogs of the city and the forest, not the tough animals of Coldland. They were doing their best, but the wind polished the surface of the ice smooth, the dogs could get no traction, and unless he whipped them they would stop and huddle together for warmth, a squirming mass of fur.

There came a point where the dogs could do no more, and Avatak called a halt. It was not yet noon.

There was no way they could put up their shelters in the blizzard. The three of them, Avatak, Nelo and Himil, had to crowd into the little tent on the back of the carriage with Pyxeas, who had barely been awake for days, lying under a heap of wool and fur blankets. They soon got the fire started on its metal hearth. The tent, securely strapped to the back of the carriage, was stable enough, though the carriage itself, resting on its runners, creaked in the wind. The tent was too small for the four of them, though; Avatak could feel the wet mass of its fabric wall on his back as he tried to pull off his fur boots.

Something disturbed the dogs, and they howled.

Pyxeas stirred. "Avatak?"

"I am here, scholar." Avatak took the chance to sit him up gently, and let him sip at hot nettle tea.

"Umm . . . I have been asleep."

"Yes. You aren't well. We think you have had a fever."

"Ah. From those mother-forsaken marshes south of Parisa. I remember." He frowned, his bony fingers wrapped around his cup. "Can I hear dogs?"

"Yes, scholar. You remember, I bought them in Parisa."

Himil said, "And I said they were mangy curs that must have been weaned on liquid gold, they cost so much."

"We are on the ice," Pyxeas whispered.

"For some days now. You have been sleeping."

"I slip in and out of the world, it seems. But tell me, the carriage: did the mechanism work well, as the wheels were replaced by runners?"

"Perfectly," said Himil.

"I would have liked to have seen that. So here we are on the ice, in a sled, with dogs! This is why I brought you, you know, Avatak. Brought you all those years ago from your home across the sea. Because I knew the ice was coming. I wanted a man beside me who could handle a team of dogs, on the ice, for I knew that one day I would need it. And to teach you, boy, to shape your mind, of course, don't forget that ... Do you think we are in Northland yet?"

"It is impossible to say. It is some days since I have been able to sight the stars, or the sun," said Avatak.

"You have been keeping the journal, I trust."

"Of course. The weather holds us up."

" 'The weather holds us up.' I could not have summed up the longwinter better myself." He laughed, and burst into a fit of coughing.

Nelo crawled around the little tent and held his great-uncle, cradling his head on his own lap, and the old man settled. "Ah, thank you, boy, that is warming, that is kind."

Nelo blurted, "You never got your strength back after your trip to Cathay, and now this. I'm concerned."

"Concerned about what? Where's my trunk, Avatak?"

"In the carriage, master. It is safe."

Nelo said, "Forgive me, Uncle, but why don't you just tell us what it is you have learned? We can at least try to understand. And then, and then—"

"And then if you have to turf out my stiffening corpse into the snow before Etxelur the message has a chance of getting through? Is that what you think?" He sounded fretful.

Avatak said gently, "Perhaps they will understand a little of it. And it might make your mind easier."

Pyxeas sat up awkwardly and regarded him. "You are wise, Avatak, wiser than I ever was. Very well." He beckoned them closer, and began to whisper. "It is a great truth that I, Pyxeas, have discovered. But not a complex one. I will tell you the essence of it—you may check my facts and conclusions from the material in the trunk, the presentations I made in Carthage ...

"It is simply this: *fixed air*. That is the secret of the weather.

"I told you, Avatak, that the weather is controlled by the dance of the world around the sun, its nodding axis, its wobbling circuits. So it is—but not by that alone. There is a second factor—well, probably many more we have yet to discover. But the second most important factor, as the results of Bolghai clearly show, is the fraction of fixed air in the atmosphere that we breathe. For if the sun delivers heat to the world, fixed air, you see, traps that heat. The more of it there is, the more the heat is trapped.

"Bolghai proved too that the living things on the surface of the world affect how much fixed air is present. For a tree, as it grows, will absorb a great deal of fixed air—much more than the scrap of land it stands on, if that land is farmed. And conversely when a tree is burned, or rots away, the fixed air that it consumed in the growing is released again.

"And that, Avatak, is why the world's descent into longwinter has been such a puzzle to me. Not the fact that it is happening, but that it is happening now. We should have been in its grip already—and we are not, *because of human actions.* It is an astonishing thing to say, but it is true. It is clearly proven by an inspection of history, and the detailed records of the weather kept at Northland and elsewhere.

"Several thousand years ago the world began its slow descent into the next longwinter. But unlike all the previous longwinters before, now the farmers were at work, in Cathay as in the Continent, planting their crops. They worked their way across the Continent from the east, clearing a landscape that had been choked with forest. Do you see?"

"Ah," said Avatak. "And all that fixed air in the trees was released."

"Yes! And, warmed by all that fixed air, the world did not cool as it should have done. It *could* not.

"Now, some two thousand years ago there was a turning point. It came with the failed Trojan Invasion of Northland, which was the high-water mark of the farmers' expansion across the Continent. In the centuries that followed, our cultural influence expanded. In northern Gaira the farms were abandoned, slowly, and the forests regrew. From Albia, where the forests had never died and the old faiths survived, missionaries were sent out to preach the ancient ways of life, all across the north of the Continent."

Avatak nodded. "And again the forests grew. Devouring all the fixed air. And then—"

"And then the world resumed its descent into the cold—delayed by some centuries, but otherwise just as every longwinter in the past. There you have it—a simple model—the proof is detailed in the papers in the trunk and elsewhere—a simple truth, yet a staggering one: *people have held a longwinter at bay, all unknowing, for millennia.*"

Nelo seemed unable to believe this. "People did this? People shaped the world? We are not gods, Uncle, not ice giants or little mothers."

"No. But what each man and woman does, bit by bit, each small intervention, each tree cut down or field plowed, over enough time, adds up to the sweeping gesture of a god. Do you see?"

Avatak asked mildly, "Why did you not tell me this before?"

Pyxeas reached out a hand and grasped Avatak's wrist. "You said it yourself. I heard you, you know. You stopped listening. You came to see my intellectual abstraction as a kind of madness. And in a world like this, perhaps you're right!

"And I, I did not mean to disrespect you, dear boy. It is that I respected you too much. For I came to see that you know far more than I ever will about what is important in this world. You are loyal, constant, strong where I am weak. I became embarrassed about my own petty wisdom, my arrogant attempts to 'educate' you, to transform you into something else, something like me. What a fool I was! What a wise man you are. And your sort of wisdom will be increasingly relevant in the future, while mine will matter less and less. I hope you can forgive me—"

Again he succumbed to a fit of coughing. Nelo held him until he settled, and slipped into an uneasy sleep.

When he was asleep the three of them looked at one another.

Avatak shrugged. "See what I mean? Here we are stuck in a tent on the ice, with nobody within a day's travel of us, probably. What difference will any of that lot make?"

Nelo smiled. "None. Though if he really did see all this coming, no wonder he was sad. Anyone fancy a game of knuckle bones before we sleep?"

75

Crimm stood on the central mound of the Little Mothers' Door, looking down on the lone reindeer that padded between the great circular ramparts of the old earthwork. The animal was scrawny, rather bewildered-looking, young, with small, stubby antlers. Finding nothing to eat in these strange curving valleys, clearly lost, detached from its herd, it lowed occasionally, a mournful bellow that echoed from the pocked face of the Wall that loomed over the earthwork.

Crimm could see Ayto and Aranx and the others, fishermen by trade, reindeer hunters for the day, out of sight of the deer, around the bend of the walls. The hunters had their spears and nets ready, arrows nocked in their big hunting bows, their faces wreathed with breath-mist. Crimm waved and pointed, silently telling them which way the deer was coming. Equally silently they moved that way.

The day was clear, for once, the sky a deep empty blue. From up here Crimm could see, far to the south, the tremendous frozen plain that was Northland, and

behind him the face of the Wall was an icebound cliff
that ran from horizon to horizon. No people could be
seen in that long, battered face, but birds moved everywhere, and flapped overhead. Incredible to think that
this was midsummer. Somebody had said today was actually the solstice, but most people weren't counting.

And all around him was the Door, the great earthwork, said to be a survivor of the last longwinter, an age
buried deep in Northland lore.

Last year had been the best for the reindeer. Quite
unexpectedly they had come pouring down from the north
and east in tremendous herds, evidently as lost and confused as human beings were in the changing world. There
had been musk oxen too and other beasts, but it had been
the reindeer that had caught the imagination of the Wall's
would-be hunters. Their first hunts had been a shambles,
hunters who only a few years earlier had been innkeepers
or clerks, junior priests or government officials, sliding on
ice-crusted snow in leather boots and waving spears made
from bits of furniture and kitchen knives.

It had been Ayto, Crimm's companion from the *Sabet*,
who had come up with a better way. Fishermen had always
made their living from hunting, and knew how to think
like prey. Ayto watched where the herds had come from.
He had a series of bonfires set up along the route, big
heaps of rubbish from the Wall, piles of smashed-up furniture and wall panels, kindling made from screwed-up papers and parchments from the Archive. And Ayto had sent
out scouts to watch for the approach of the animals. The
next time a herd had approached Etxelur the fires had
been lit, the hunters had danced and shouted and waved
their spears—and the animals, alarmed, had veered in a
great mass, heading just the way Ayto had planned, into
the maze of frozen-over canals that was the Door. The
killing of the trapped, panicking animals had been great.

It had quickly been learned just how much you could
do with a dead reindeer. There was the meat, of course,
but the skin had endless uses, and you could make tools

and clothes-toggles from the bones, rope and fishing line from sinew. For one winter the people of Etxelur had become the reindeer people, and flensed skulls and antler racks adorned the caves on the Wall's seaward face where people lived now.

The Door had made a tremendously effective reindeer trap. Crimm wasn't given to thinking too deeply; in his experience it never paid off. But it had struck him that it was almost as if the Door had been *designed* for just that purpose, and maybe it had been, back in long-gone wintry days.

That had been last year. But this year was different, as the last had been different from the one before. There had been more snow, of course, masses of new stuff that fell and covered the old and, in the spring, once again stubbornly refused to melt. But this year, no more reindeer. Maybe they had gone further south still, in search of summer grass. And the Wall folk, eagerly waiting with their pyres and spears, had seen only a few beasts, including this one solitary specimen. Still, Crimm, from his mound, could see that the moment of the kill was coming, the animal approaching the humans, prey nearing predator, all in silence. Crimm felt his heart beat faster, imagined the splash of blood on the clean snow.

But then his eye was distracted by movement. A black speck crossing the ice, far to the south. For the last couple of years nothing good had come out of the south.

He yelled down to the hunters, "Ayto!"

His voice, echoing, startled the reindeer. It looked up, confused. Then it turned and began to run the other way, fleeing from the hunters. Ayto and the rest saw the deer's white rump as it bobbed away. Some of the men hurled their spears in frustration, even one-armed Aranx.

Ayto glared up at Crimm. "You famous idiot. What did you do that for?"

Crimm pointed south. "Somebody coming."

Ayto looked that way, but of course his view was obscured by the earthwork. "Who? How many?"

"Not many. Looks like one cart. A sled, I suppose."

Aranx, beside him, called up, "It's probably those bastards from the Manufactory."

"Maybe," Crimm said. But the Manufactory, with its ferocious, jealous hunters and their spears tipped with iron shapes torn from now-useless engines, was east of here, another District in the Wall, not south.

Ayto called, "You said a sled. Pulled by men?"

"I don't think so. Some kind of animal. Dogs, I think."

"Dogs? If it's dogs, it's probably not those bastards from the Manufactory."

"True enough."

"Different bastards, then."

"That makes sense."

"What do you think we should do?"

They were all looking up at Crimm. He sighed. He had no desire to be the leader of this little community of hunters. He didn't want to be king, the way the idiotic leader of those bastards from the Manufactory had declared himself King of his District, and Emperor of All the Wall. He had always thought Ayto was smarter than he was. It was Ayto who had found his way out through the Wall to the sea, in the first terrible season. Ayto who had figured out how to trap reindeer. Ayto who had grown into this new world of ice, as if drawing on memories from a very deep past. But just as when they had been nothing but fishermen, Ayto liked to stay in the background, leaving all the decisions, and the mistakes, to Crimm. Well, there was nothing for it.

"I think we should go greet them. They must have come a long way, after all."

"And maybe we can get their dogs," said Aranx.

Ayto called, "And if they're not friendly?"

Crimm shrugged. "Then it's the end of their journey."

"And we will *definitely* get their dogs," said Aranx.

———

The Wall had changed utterly since Avatak had last seen it, three years back, when he and Pyxeas had departed for Cathay. The great barrier, streaked with ice and heaped with snow, was not beautiful now, just an ugly growstone core pocked with holes. But it still blocked the horizon, and it was still, undeniably, the Wall, and perhaps the one human monument north of Parisa that would survive the longwinter itself.

Nelo, almost absently sketching the latest panorama, said, "There's somebody watching us. On the ice. See? Three, four, five of them. And they look armed."

Avatak reined in the team. The dogs, panting hard, jostled and growled, competing for their places in the pack.

Pyxeas pulled his thick fur coat around his skinny body. "To be expected," he muttered. "Diminishing resources, a collapse of population, an uncertain rediscovery of long-lost skills. The community will fragment into tribalism. Of course one must anticipate hostility to strangers."

Nelo said, "But you're hoping to find scholars here, Uncle."

"To be expected," Pyxeas muttered again. "Expected."

Avatak murmured, "Let's just not get ourselves speared so close to home."

The party from the Wall stopped perhaps twenty paces away, five men, anonymous in sealskin jackets and breeches, the clothing crudely cut, to Avatak's eye at least. Now one of them stepped forward. "Are you those bastards from the Manufactory?" He spoke in clear Northlander. "Because if you are you can clear off back there, and tell that clown Omim that if he thinks the hunters of Etxelur—"

"No." Nelo walked forward on the hard-packed snow. He pulled off his mittens to show his hands were empty. "We're not from the Manufactory. We're from—well, from here. Etxelur. We've come home. I'm Nelo."

The man stared. "Rina's boy?"

"Are you Crimm?"

The fisherman grinned. "Cousin. You've been a long time away. Things have changed."

"I can see that."

"And on that sled—is that you, Uncle Pyxeas? We thought you were long dead."

Pyxeas grunted. "Well, you were mistaken."

The hunters came closer now, lowering their weapons. One man stared at the dogs, wary, fascinated; one of them yapped at him. "We ate all our dogs. Any bitches?"

76

t was further than it looked to the Wall. Avatak realized that the hunters had spotted them from a distance and had come out to stop them. Once Etxelur had been the kernel of the oldest and greatest civilization in the world. Now, after a handful of cold summers, strangers were met with suspicion and raised spears. Pyxeas' dream of finding scholarship surviving here looked foolish indeed.

At last they came to the foot of the Wall. The wreckage of ruined superstructures stood in snow-covered heaps, reminding Avatak of the tide-cracked ice at the shore of a winter-frozen sea. A rope ladder led up to a shallow ledge in the exposed growstone face of the Wall, and then another ladder rose up past that, and then another, until you could make your way to the roof.

"It's ladders up and then ladders down the other side, I'm afraid," said Crimm. "Most of us live on the far side of the Wall now, facing the sea. We only come over this side to hunt."

Pyxeas asked, "What of the interior?"

Crimm shrugged. "Abandoned. Oh, there may be a

few souls left in there feeding off the old stores. We've blocked off a lot of the corridors and passageways."

Ayto said, "To stop raids from those bastards in the Manufactory. Among other bastards."

"Even *I* did not think it could be as bad as this," Pyxeas said mournfully.

Crimm eyed Pyxeas, the sled. "This is going to take some time. We'll have to get your goods over in relays. We can hide the sled somewhere—figure out what to do about your dogs."

Ayto said, "Need to be kept on this side, dogs, where they're useful. We ought to set up a base over here."

Crimm nodded. "For now, suppose you stay with the sled—Himil, was it? Aranx, you two others, stay with him and start preparing the stuff to haul over. And keep an eye out. In the meantime, the rest of you, come on over. Umm, Uncle Pyxeas, it's quite a climb—"

"And quite beyond me, I'm sure." He turned to Avatak.

With practiced ease, Avatak bent, took Pyxeas at the waist, and straightened up with the scholar limp over his shoulder. Nelo helped, throwing a blanket over Pyxeas.

Crimm grinned. "I can help you."

"I'll be fine," Avatak said. And so he would be; he and the old man in his charge had been through worse than this together.

Crimm went up first. He wore heavy mittens and carried a small axe that he used to knock ice off the ladder rungs. When it was his turn, Avatak took care to get a firm grip with hands and feet at each step. He worked his way up, breathing steadily, letting his muscles warm. He had ridden the sled too long, he hadn't had enough to eat for many days, and he was not in the best condition, but he could do this. Transferring from one ladder to the next was more tricky, trying to support himself on ice-coated, guano-stained ledges, holding the old man securely with one hand while reaching for the next ladder with the other. But he made no slips.

Pyxeas hung limp, passive, utterly trusting. Perhaps he was asleep.

They took a break on top of the Wall. Crimm had sacks of freshwater that he passed around. Pyxeas was set down on a blanket; he seemed more exhausted than Avatak.

The huge sculptures arrayed along the Wall roof, the old monoliths, the tremendous heads of long-dead Annids, the slim spires erected by more modern generations, had mostly survived, though their features were masked by snow. And from here a view of the Northern Ocean opened up. The level of the sea had evidently fallen, but it was still higher than the land, you could see at a glance; the Wall was still serving its most ancient and basic purpose of saving the land from the sea. On the sea itself, a strip of deep-blue water close to the Wall face gave way to thin ice floating in great patches. People were working on the ice, Avatak saw, looking down. One man sat by a mound on the ice that must be a seal's breathing hole. Further out there was a boat, silhouetted against the brilliance of the white ice behind. These were Northlanders learning to live like Coldlanders, he supposed. Further out still, icebergs, silent and stately as Cathay treasure ships, were trapped in thickening sea ice.

The familiar beauty of it all caught Avatak's breath. This might no longer feel like home to Pyxeas and Nelo, but it was home to him.

They followed Crimm's lead and began the climb down the seaward face. They quickly descended past odd cuttings in the growstone, heavily crusted with ice, that turned out to be docks cut into the face, now stranded in midair. This face of the Wall, once immersed in the sea, was rougher, just coarsely finished growstone with a heavy coating of now-dead barnacles, and you had to be careful not to scrape your hands as you worked your way down the ladder. Looking down, Avatak saw that at its base the Wall's vertical face bellied outward into the sea, making a rough shelf of growstone that extended under the shallow water. People were moving and working down there, on the growstone shore. There were fires built on hearths, racks of meat or fish, boats hauled up, blood splashed on the growstone ground. People looked up, wary. One little boy, a bundle in his furs, clung to his mother, one finger jammed up his left nostril.

Crimm jumped down the last few rungs and went forward into the little village on the growstone. "We have visitors! It is Pyxeas the scholar, you remember him, and Nelo, Rina's son, and their companion Avatak from Coldland." The mood of wary suspicion faded, Avatak thought. Or at least he could see no weapons. "They have come far to see us—and they have extraordinary tales to tell. And they have dogs! Think what we'll be able to do if we can breed dogs, Ferri, Yospex . . . Muka! Heat some soup and boil up some tea; we will take lunch, I think."

Avatak reached the base of the ladder and, with some help from Nelo, set Pyxeas down. Avatak saw now that there were caves in the growstone masses, either worn by the sea or deliberately hollowed out, with entrances covered by skin sheets. It was in these caves, evidently, that the people lived.

Crimm led them to one cave, where the covering sheet was drawn back to expose a deep interior, lit by small lamps of what smelled like seal blubber in bowls hacked from ancient growstone. This was Crimm's home, and the woman who smiled at them as she built up the fire in her hearth was Muka, the wife Crimm had taken since the group had come here to the ocean. But she looked ill to Avatak, her movements listless, her face pale, the signs of a nosebleed on her upper lip, and when she smiled she showed gaps in her teeth.

They set Pyxeas down in the mouth of the cave so he could see the village, the sea, and laid blankets over his shoulders. Soon he had a cup of nettle tea in his hands, and Avatak could smell a rich fish soup warming up. "So this is the new Etxelur," the scholar murmured. "If it wasn't for bad engineering in the past I suppose it couldn't exist at all."

"Bad engineering, scholar?"

He picked at the coarse growstone surface under the blanket. "Look at this stuff. We could never properly maintain the Wall's seaward face, you know. Oh, we would try, we would lower caissons to work at the face, but only for the shallowest sections. For the rest we would just dump growstone in great sacks down the face and let it harden. And in turn, of course, the sea steadily wore away at the face, exposing the interior. Strange to think this growstone might be a thousand years old—and hidden from the light until quite recently.

"But if not for that shoddy work, all that growstone thrown down the Wall's face, more in hope than judgment, this rough shore would not even exist. And these survivors would not be living on the ruins of the past. Ah! My dear." Muka brought him a bowl of hot fish soup. "A feast fit for the Great Khan himself. But, are you well? I think your nose is bleeding . . ."

Crimm tapped Avatak on the shoulder and beckoned. "Coldlander. Come. Walk with me, please. Come see how we live. Bring your soup."

He led Avatak down toward the sea. The growstone and the sea ice were bloodstained, and haunches of seal meat lay around, frosted with ice. Wooden frames stood in rows; fish were drying on the racks, and one big seal carcass. People stared as they went by, especially the children in their furs, who followed Avatak.

"Don't mind them," Crimm said. "We aren't used to strangers anymore. Odd to think that Etxelur was the navel of the world, just a few years ago. We held a Giving this year, of sorts, for old times' sake. Nobody came save a few of those bastards from the Manufactory, but we drove them off with stones."

In the blue sky the moon hung over the sea, almost full, startlingly bright. Avatak noticed that nobody was looking at the moon; they turned their heads, cupped hands over their eyes.

Crimm saw he observed this. "The moon is our goddess of death. She is bright in the sky, these days and nights."

"Pyxeas would say, because she shines in the reflected light of the ice lying on the earth."

Crimm shrugged. "Perhaps. She exults even so. Avatak, I remembered you were traveling with Uncle Pyxeas, and I always hoped you would return. All the Coldlanders who were here fled years ago, before we started starving. I'm sure *they're* prospering . . ."

Avatak had heard nothing of his people since leaving Coldland with Pyxeas, nothing of Uncle Suko and his sister Nona, and Uuna, his betrothed, who, he was sure, was still waiting for him. Yes, they would be prospering, even if they had had to abandon their old grounds and followed the edge of the spreading ice to the sea.

Crimm said now, "There is so much we can learn from you. We have done our best, to build a way of living in the unending winter—but you, you have your ancestors' knowledge, their old wisdom."

Avatak remembered Pyxeas predicting that it would be his wisdom of the ice and sea that would be in demand in the future, not the scholar's learning. He felt embarrassed. "I was pretty young when Pyxeas took me away from home, and I have been traveling since. I have probably forgotten much of what I know."

"I think you're too modest. Well, I hope you are. Take a look at this, for instance."

Crimm led him to a scaffold on which hung the flensed body of a seal, dripping blood onto the frozen ground. The eyeballs drooped, ugly and exposed. The black flippers, the only bit of skin left on the body, looked oddly like gloves. At the base of the scaffold was the evidence of a previous kill, a heap of purplish guts, tangled up.

Avatak asked, "Where do you get the wood for the scaffold?"

"Some driftwood, at first. A lot of it scorched from big fires burning somewhere, overseas. Not so much this year; I guess the gathering ice is seeing to that. But there's always the Wall, like a great mine, crammed with stuff. All you have to do is haul it out. We know how to salt fish; we've done that for generations. What do you think of how we've handled the seal?"

"You can use more of it." Avatak picked up a length of gut, and ran his fingers along the ropy stuff. "Squeeze out the blood like this, and boil it up. The liver is considered a treat, by the way, for the hunter who brings the animal in. There are ways to treat the hide so it's easy to wear—you dry it, rub it to keep it supple. I will show you. Oh, and the eyes . . ." He plucked an eye from its nerve stalk, popped it into his mouth, and chewed hard; it burst with a crackle, and cold fluid filled his mouth. "Mm," he said around the mouthful. "Delicious. A treat for the kids."

Crimm stared. "Ha! Well, I must try it myself. Look, Avatak—would you help with something else? We have sickness here."

"I saw your wife."

"We all suffer to some extent. But especially my wife's little niece. Please."

He led Avatak back up the beach to the cave, outside which Pyxeas sat, cradling an empty soup bowl, and Avatak was impressed that he had managed to finish a meal for once. Pyxeas had Muka help him up, and with the others followed Crimm into the dimly lit rear of the cave.

But Pyxeas paused by the fire where there was a heap of paper, evidently used as kindling. He riffled through this, appalled. "By the mothers' mercy—did this come from the Archive? I know this work—on the philosophy of the motion of the planets—centuries old! And it's been used to light a fire for a bunch of—"

"Not now, master," Avatak murmured firmly.

Pyxeas fell silent, visibly angry.

They walked deeper into the cave. At the back a little girl, not more than five years old, lay on a heap of skins. A woman, perhaps her mother, stood back as they approached, hope and fear obvious in her face. Avatak became aware that they were all watching him, all the Northlanders, and he felt a stab of self-doubt.

"Just do your best," murmured Pyxeas, leaning on Muka.

Tentatively, Avatak bent over the little girl. Listless, lethargic, she did not resist. He saw she had spots on her skin, on her face and arms and, he saw when he lifted a blanket, on her legs. She had evidently been suffering from nosebleeds, and when he gently opened her mouth he saw teeth missing from bleeding gums.

"She's been so down," said the mother. "So miserable for so long."

"Many of us have the same symptoms," Crimm said. "To one degree or another."

"And you know what she asks for, all the time? Cabbage! Who would have thought it? But you can't grow cabbage in all this snow and ice."

Pyxeas grunted. "I bet that's the answer. You people seem to have plenty of fish and meat to eat, but not a scrap of green."

Avatak felt faintly irritated, for Pyxeas was right. "We call it the bleeding fever. Yes, it comes about if you don't eat all you need."

"I need cabbage," whispered the little girl, and her mother stroked her head.

Pyxeas said, "So what's the answer, boy? Should we boil up some seaweed?"

"No. Not that. We call it *mattak*. You can chop it into small pieces and eat it raw, or you can fry it and boil it to make it easier for the children. That will stop this sickness."

Crimm frowned. "*Mattak*? What is that?"

"The skin of a whale."

There was a long silence.

Crimm said, "And to get hold of *that* . . ."

"First you have to catch a whale." Avatak grinned. "It's not hard. I will show you."

Crimm clapped him on the back. "You see? I knew you could help us! Why, with your help we'll be able to prosper—to do more than survive—we can live in this place as long as we want—"

"No," Pyxeas said. Suddenly he groaned, and leaned more heavily on Muka. Avatak rushed to his side, and helped lower him to the ground.

Crimm said, "No? What do you mean, Uncle?"

Pyxeas looked up. "Oh, you have done well—*despite* your barbaric consumption of books to light your fires. Yes, you are prospering. Yes, Avatak, if you can, show them how to catch whales, and all the other skills you have brought with you from the Coldland—skills you have used to keep me alive for so long.

"But, Crimm, Muka, the rest of you—you cannot stay here. *For the ice will not let you.* And before you leave here you have a great assignment."

Avatak said gently, "There is no scholarship here. You can see that."

"Yes. Yes, I see it. I was a fool to hope for more. Yet there is a duty to be fulfilled even so. Come, boy, help me back out into the light, may as well enjoy the daylight while we have it . . ."

77

hey sat on the growstone beach. Pyxeas was given a heap of blankets, and Avatak and Nelo sat with him, Nelo sketching intently. The folk of the little village, what was left of Etxelur, gathered around them: Crimm and his wife, the other adults, and the children, who stood and openly stared at the newcomers, with their exotic looks, their strange clothes. It was afternoon now, and the sun, hanging in a clear sky, cast a light of a strange quality, a rich golden yellow, on the face of the Wall behind them.

A small child, it might have been either a boy or girl in its bundle of furs, walked boldly forward, sat on Pyxeas' lap, and started to pull at his wispy beard. It struck Avatak suddenly that there were no old people in this village—none at all, save Pyxeas.

Crimm smiled at Pyxeas. "That's your great-grand-nephew. He's called Citeg. He's evidently a philosopher, like his uncle."

Pyxeas, cradling the child, seemed to gather what was left of his strength. "Indeed. What a tableau we must make—draw us, Nelo! Draw us for history. Myself the elder, who remembers the world before the coming of the longwinter. You adults who are living through this age of transition. And now this little one on my lap, one of a new generation rising already, who knows nothing of the days before the longwinter, and who will grow up thinking all this is normal—to live on a growstone beach, to trap seals to survive. Thus we humans forget the pain of the past. I sometimes think this is the little mothers' greatest gift, for otherwise each of us, even this little one, would carry inside his head the burden of ten thousand years.

"*But we must not forget.* We as a people. Ana, who founded the Wall itself, knew this long ago; we could not forget the great floods of the past, for if we had we would have been doomed to suffer them again. And we did not forget. We wrote down our memories, and organized ourselves, and remembered.

"Now we face the greatest calamity of all—this longwinter. A flood of cold that will last many thousands of years. Yet we understand why it has come about—I, Pyxeas, a handful of scholars in Carthage, and now these brave boys who brought me home. Knowing why it happens is a long way from being able to turn it back, from warming the world! Only the mothers can do that. But if we understand, if we anticipate, then we can *plan*. But we can only understand if we remember.

"I came here hoping to find scholarship surviving. Even I, Pyxeas, I admit, underestimated the damage done by the longwinter in its first few seasons. But what I have found here is you, Crimm, and your people, and your admirable determination to survive. And so I have modified my goals.

"I have written down my conclusions. I have already sent copies to scholars around the world, from Cathay to Egypt to Carthage. There will be a New Etxelur, built on the Carthaginian shore. That too has copies. But we know the world is in flux, and who knows what will survive of that?

"But here we are, at the Wall, at Etxelur. And I want you to help me now. I have copies of my findings, stored in my trunk, my conclusions set out. I want more copies made, more sets compiled—more trunks filled. I know you can write, Crimm, you others—you haven't forgotten yet. And I want these copies distributed in safe places the length of the Wall, as far as you can reach."

Crimm nodded. Though he must have known what a burden this would be for a folk already on the edge of starvation, Avatak thought he seemed enthused. "We will do this, Uncle. We are Northlanders; this is Etxelur. This is what we are for. And then our children, and our children's children, will stand guard on the Wall until the day the warmth returns to the world."

Pyxeas sighed. "Brave words, Crimm. But it's impossible, I'm afraid. I told you—the ice will see to it."

And he spoke to them of what was to come.

"The snow will continue to fall, and none of it will melt. It will gather deeper and deeper, the lower layers compressing to hard ice. At last, around centers to the north of Albia, in Scand, in Asia, in the Land of the Sky Wolf, huge sheets will accumulate. How do I know this? Because this is how it was before. I have seen the marks of it. And this ocean, this ancient land, even the Wall itself, *will be entirely covered over*, with a great thickness of ice—as thick as a day's walk! And so you must leave here. Go south, to the edge of the ice. Find a new place to live. For this land is doomed.

"*But the Wall will survive.* The growstone core is tough enough for that. Riding out the years, resisting the ice as it has already resisted the ocean for millennia. And in its growstone carcass, to be discovered anew by the children of a distant future, will be the secrets of the world. Those children will *begin* knowing as much as we know now. Who knows what they will go on to learn? And you will leave them your drawings too, Nelo. Let them look upon the faces of their ancestors."

This was met by silence, save from the gurgle of a baby somewhere.

Crimm waved a hand at the growstone village, the sea. "You speak of generations yet unborn. *We* have survived. We are proud of what we have built here. Must we lose it all?"

"It is already lost," Pyxeas said gently. "The land is only ever loaned from the ice; now the ice takes it back. But next time, next time . . ."

"Crimm! Aranx!"

The call came from the west, along the growstone shore. People stood, peered into the sun, hands over their eyes. Crimm waved. "I'm here! Ayto, is that you?"

"We found an animal," Ayto called, his cry distant, small. "A big one. A bear! White, or yellow."

Crimm was baffled. "A *white bear*!"

Avatak was already on his feet. "*Nanok.* I knew he would come."

Crimm grinned, took a spear from a pile, threw it to Avatak. "After you."

A party of hunters quickly formed up. Wielding their spears, tightening their skin jackets around their bodies, they jogged across the growstone shore toward the west, where the bear padded cautiously over a bit of sea ice, silhouetted by the lowering sun.

78

*The Fourth Year of the Longwinter:
Autumn Equinox*

At last word came that ships had been seen, on the eastern horizon.

The three women stood in the shade of Xipuhl's house, here at the heart of the city called the Altar of the Jaguar. Xipuhl took Sabela's hand, and Walks In Mist's, and the three of them stood together as they had that night in the growstone bar in the Wall, three summers ago. Three women, two of them widows now, for Walks In Mist had lost her husband in the flood that had driven her and her children out of the River City, and Xipuhl's husband had succumbed to the plague last year—and Sabela might as well have been a widow, for Deraj had been dead to her since his betrayal of her with the nestspill girl.

Sabela, a guest here, had already called the twins and packed her bags. And when Walks In Mist arrived she'd had only one question. "Are they Northlander ships?"

"We don't know yet," Xipuhl said gently. "They are too far away. And they are very late, if it's them—midsummer has long gone—"

"They have come," Sabela said firmly. "I knew they would, late or not. Come, let's go to the shore."

Walks In Mist glanced at Xipuhl, and they shrugged, and made ready.

Sabela would not be sorry to see the last of the Altar of the Jaguar, thankful though she had been for Xipuhl's hospitality when she had fled north from Tiwanaku with the twins.

The city was set on a high plateau, dominating a river basin. The heart of it was a raised platform on which sat temples, courtyards, the houses of the very rich—and monuments, gigantic stone thrones and carved heads as tall as she was, their ancient faces eroded and pitted. The big faces made the twins cry. The city had its own deep history; it had been the capital of an empire that, according to its own legend, had been the first civilization west of the great ocean, and would also have been the first to have fallen long ago if not for links with Northland across the sea. Well, in the years since, the Empire of the Jaguar had waxed and waned. This age had seen a fragmentation of states under the pressure of drought and heat, and there had been endless petty, wearing wars. The Altar was much reduced from its eerie pomp. But you wouldn't know it from the way the rulers and the rich paraded around the city in their finely woven skirts, and their upper bodies adorned with bangles, necklaces, pendants, and big mirrors of polished stone. And they were *deformed*, their heads misshapen from their skulls being bound up when they were infants, and grooves worn into their teeth. Xipuhl said this was part of a revival of ancient customs; facing an uncertain future, the people of the Altar were reaching back to a more secure past.

Now, in any event, Sabela was seeing her last of it.

The three women, with their children and baggage, were loaded onto a couple of carts driven by Xipuhl's servants. As they rolled out of the city toward the coast, they were not alone; Sabela saw a steady trickle of vehicles, and foot traffic too, heading out to greet the first ships to be seen from across the ocean all year.

Xipuhl had sent servants ahead to rent a small property on the edge of the coastal town, and there they spent a restless night. Sabela's twins had trouble sleeping this close to the sea; they had been born into the clear, dry, thin air of the mountains, and sometimes they found the clinging humidity of the lowlands unbearable. In the early morning they gathered by the harbor, watching the dawn gathering over the ocean, waiting for their first glimpse of the ships. The children quickly got bored. Walks In Mist had brought her Northland chess set, and Sabela's twins settled down to a game.

And then the ships emerged from a bank of mist, tall shadows on the horizon. There was a ripple of applause from the waiting people.

"Here they come," murmured Walks In Mist. "But why now? Too late for the midsummer. I suppose they could have been delayed—difficulties with the journey, with ice on the sea . . ."

Sabela was not listening. "I knew they would come. Before the winter we will be drinking again in that funny little tavern in the Wall, and our troubles will be behind us."

But Xipuhl said now, "We know nothing of conditions in Northland. Or anywhere across the ocean. What if *they* are fleeing *here*?"

And Walks In Mist said, "There seem to be rather a lot of ships."

Now Sabela could see there were many vessels—she counted seven, eight, nine, and more emerging from the mist behind the leaders—a tremendous fleet, soon too many to count. The Giving transport usually numbered only three or four vessels. She felt a stab of doubt.

Walks In Mist raised her hands to her eyes. "They have tubes sticking out of their sides. I see it clearly.

Tubes of iron. And the sails. There is a design on the sails."

"A design?"

"A man. Painted huge. His hand upraised. And crossed palm leaves across his chest . . ."

The crowd on the quay were falling silent, as they gazed into the eyes of Jesus Sharruma, and watched the Hatti armada approach.

79

Millennia had passed since the last retreat of the ice. Human lives were brief; in human minds, occupied with love and war, the ice had been remembered only in myth.

But the ice remembered.

And now the long retreat was over.

Once more the ice covered continents. The silence of the world was profound.

Afterword

This book opens in the year AD 1315, according to
our calendar, at the beginning of the so-called "Little Ice Age," centuries of cooler and more turbulent climatic patterns in Europe (see *The Little Ice Age*,
Brian Fagan, Basic Books, 2000). It is a useful starting
point for the fictional but much more severe glacial epoch depicted here.

The Holocene, the period of warm climate since the
last Ice Age—the long summer that gave civilization its
chance—is in fact the longest stable interglacial warm
period in four hundred millennia. And if not for farming, the ice might already have returned. American cli-
matologist William Ruddiman (see *Ploughs, Plagues
and Petroleum*, Princeton, 2007) argues that the main
forcing factor in the Earth's long-term climate changes,
changes in the planet's orbit and axial tilt, should have
driven the world to the brink of a new glacial period by
now, but this has been offset by humanity's injection of
greenhouse gases, not just since the Industrial Revolution but since the beginnings of agriculture in 6000 BC.
As with much of the current debate about humanity's
impact on our climate future and past, Ruddiman's argument is hotly contested (see "The Climate Changers,"
New Scientist, 6 September 2008).

In this novel the world collapses into Ice Age conditions in just a few years. This has some basis in reality.

Beginning about 12,800 years ago, the period known as the Younger Dryas (named after an Arctic flower) was a relapse back into glacial conditions, triggered when a glacial lake in Canada burst its banks and reached the sea, chilling and diluting the North Atlantic, and forcing a shutdown of the Gulf Stream. Much the same mechanism is postulated here. Recently (see *New Scientist*, 14 November 2009) scientists from the University of Saskatchewan used a finely grained mud core from a lake in Ireland to prove that during the Younger Dryas temperatures collapsed within mere months, or a year at most.

Bolghai in Daidu (Beijing) precociously studies the properties of carbon dioxide ("fixed air"), some centuries ahead of similar studies in the West in our timeline, by scholars like Jan Baptist van Helmont, Joseph Black, John Tyndall and Svante Arrhenius.

The names I have used here are primarily chosen for clarity and familiarity.

"German" is a name used by Greek and Roman writers, not by the people the term was meant to describe. I have followed the Pinyin system for Romanization of Cathay names, erring always on the side of clarity. Pyxeas' journey to the East very roughly mirrors that of Marco Polo in our own timeline, and I have used names from that source (for a recent study see Laurence Bergreen's *Marco Polo*, Quercus, 2008). Daidu is on the site of modern Beijing; Quinsai is Hangzhou. I also drew on the memoir of Ibn Battuta, a great Muslim traveler of the period (see Ross Dunn's *The Adventures of Ibn Battuta*, University of California Press, 1986). My Northlanders use ancient Cathay terms relating to the manufacture of gunpowder, which they call the "fire drug" (see Clive Ponting's *Gunpowder*, Chatto & Windus, 2006). Saltpetre was known as "solve stone."

I have loosely used modern terms for military rankings like "sergeant," "general." Ancient equivalents are often unknown.

In our history, Carthage did not survive as an independent power after its famous destruction by the Romans in 146 BC (see Richard Miles' *Carthage Must Be Destroyed*, Allen Lane, 2010). I have referred to Carthage by its modernized name throughout, which derives from a Latinized version of the Phoenician "Qart-Hadasht," "new city" (Miles, p. 62).

I have used the name "Anatolia" for modern mainland Turkey. The "people of the Land of Hatti" are the great Bronze Age kingdom we know as the Hittites (see Trevor Bryce's *The Kingdom of the Hittites*, Oxford University Press, 2005, and his *Life and Society in the Hittite World*, Oxford University Press, 2002). In our timeline, by 1159 BC, the setting for my Book Two, the central Hittite empire had already collapsed. Its Anatolian heartland later became the center of the Byzantine empire, and my fictional history reflects something of the Byzantine reality (see Judith Herrin's *Byzantium*, Allen Lane, 2007). The Hittites' "Constantinople" is a rebuilt Troy—an option considered by Constantine I when he moved the capital of his empire from Rome (Herrin, Chapter 1). "Greater Greece" is Italy. "Hantilios" is on the site of Venice. In the Hittites' pantheon, many gods were "syncretized," that is, identified as aspects of one another. Sharruma was the offspring of the Hurrian gods Teshub and Hepat, later syncretized with Hittite gods. The potato blight, which causes famine in my Hittite empire here, caused the similar and similarly terrible nineteenth-century "Great Hunger" in Ireland (see Christine Kinealy's *A Death-Dealing Famine: The Great Hunger in Ireland*, Pluto Press, 1997).

My "River City" is the city now called Cahokia, on the flood plain of the Mississippi (the "Trunk"). Tiwanaku was near Lake Titicaca in the Andes highland. The "Altar of the Jaguar" is the Olmec city known as San Lorenzo. A provocative recent survey of the pre-

6993.

Columbian Americas is Charles Mann's *1491* (Alfred A. Knopf, 2005).

A recent study of the life of the great sixth-century sage Pythagoras and his heritage is Kitty Ferguson's *Pythagoras*, Icon Books, 2010. Pyxeas' "world position oracle" is loosely based on the Antikythera mechanism. This remarkable gadget (see *Decoding the Heavens* by Jo Marchant, Windmill Books, 2009, and Lucio Russo's *The Forgotten Revolution*, Springer, 2004) is evidence of an advanced mechanical capability among the ancient Greeks—which, in the universe of this novel, led to a precocious development of steam engine technology. The Northlanders' Atlantic fishing craft depicted here are based very loosely on the sturdy British design known as "doggers," which in our timeline appeared a little later in the historical record, during the seventeenth century (see *The Oxford Companion to Ships and the Sea*, ed. I. C. B. Dear, Oxford University Press, 2005).

This is a novel, not meant to be taken as a reliable history. Any errors or inaccuracies are of course my sole responsibility.

Stephen Baxter
Northumberland
Winter Solstice,
2011